The
Railway Girls
in Love

Maisie Thomas was born and brought up in Manchester, which provides the location for her Railway Girls novels. She loves writing stories with strong female characters, set in times when women needed determination and vision to make their mark. The Railway Girls series is inspired by her great-aunt Jessie, who worked as a railway clerk during the First World War.

Maisie now lives on the beautiful North Wales coast with her railway enthusiast husband, Kevin, and their two rescue cats. They often enjoy holidays chugging up and down the UK's heritage steam railways.

Also by Maisie Thomas

The Railway Girls
Secrets of the Railway Girls

The Railway Girls in Love

MAISIE THOMAS

arrow books

1 3 5 7 9 10 8 6 4 2

Arrow Books
20 Vauxhall Bridge Road
London SW1V 2SA

Arrow Books is part of the Penguin Random House group
of companies whose addresses can be found at
global.penguinrandomhouse.com.

Penguin
Random House
UK

First published in Great Britain by Arrow Books in 2021

www.penguin.co.uk

A CIP catalogue record for this book is available from
the British Library

ISBN 9781787463981

Typeset in 10.75/13.5 pt Palatino
by Integra Software Services Pvt. Ltd, Pondicherry

Printed and bound in Great Britain by Clays Ltd, Elcograf S.p.A.

The authorised representative in the EEA is Penguin Random House
Ireland, Morrison Chambers, 32 Nassau Street, Dublin D02 YH68

To the memory of Dennis Bourke (1921–2001) and Frank Grant (1924–2014), who served in the RAF during the war.

And to Roger and Michael

Acknowledgements

I am grateful to two unknown people who each took a snap of a wartime wedding. These two photographs provided the inspiration for the wedding in this story.

Love and thanks to Jen Gilroy and Christina Banach; Kathy Evans and Gayle Biggins; Catherine Boardman for organising the wonderful prize draws; and Lou Capper, Julie Barham, Karen Mace, Shaz Goodwin and Vikkie Wakeham for their support.

Special thanks to Kevin for finding the perfect job for Gil; and a big hug for Beverley Hopper. She knows why.

Chapter One

With her gloved hands thrust into the big patch pockets of her rust-coloured wool coat, and her scarf wound snugly around her neck and tucked in beneath the wide lapels, Mabel Bradshaw tramped along, lifting her feet clear of the thick snow so as not to let it spill over the tops of her calf-high galoshes. The benefit of wearing two pairs of thick socks over her stockings wouldn't last long if they got wet.

Beside her, Althea, her best friend, matched her pace.

'Your cheeks are glowing,' said Mabel.

'Which is a polite way of saying they're bright red,' said Althea, 'and so's my nose.'

'Mine too.'

'What would your mother say?' teased Althea.

Mabel laughed. Mumsy lived and breathed etiquette. 'But just think how pale and interesting I'll look when I've thawed out.' She snuggled her hands deeper inside her pockets; only up here on the tops could she get away with such slovenly behaviour.

The two of them crunched through the snow to the edge of the steep hill above Mabel's home and looked down into the long valley below. Behind them stretched the Lancashire moors. Usually the breeze here was so full of brisk smells that Mabel could practically taste them as a rich, earthy, green concoction, but not today. Today, as for the past month, the moors had been coated in snow and the air was as fresh as peppermint.

Below lay the town of Annerby. It was still called a market town, but it had its share of factories too, as well as a railway station. Mabel's gaze was drawn to the building that housed Bradshaw's Ball Bearings and Other Small Components, the factory that represented her father's life's work. The son of a railway worker, he had made good – and more than good. He had prospered to the extent of purchasing – note, purchasing, not renting – Kirkland House, one of the town's poshest properties, high up on the side of the hill. It was here that Mabel had grown up.

Now she looked down at Bradshaw's Ball Bearings. Would their factory still be producing small components this time next year? Pops said that when the war came – when, not if, and Mabel had trembled inwardly – factories up and down the country would be called upon to turn over production to whatever they were told to make to help win the war. Mabel had longed to ask a dozen questions, but couldn't, because Pops hadn't been talking to her. It was something she had overheard.

'Here comes a train,' said Althea.

Mabel felt a burst of pleasure. She liked trains. They made her think of Grandad. He might be gone, but he definitely wasn't forgotten, especially not by her. His son might have risen in the world, but Grandad had stayed put in his cottage near the railway tracks and had never for a single moment considered leaving his job as a wheeltapper, using a long-handled hammer to tap train wheels, the quality of the ring that was produced telling his experienced ear whether or not the wheel was in good order.

Down on the valley floor, white clouds puffed out of the funnel on top of the front end of the locomotive, which pulled a line not of coaches, but of goods wagons. Some

2

had names painted on the sides because they belonged to companies that used the railways all the time. At the rear came several unbranded wagons, their contents covered by tarpaulins.

'D'you suppose the train is bringing us our air-raid shelters?' asked Mabel. 'Distribution is starting this month.'

'We won't get ours for ages yet,' said Althea. 'It'll be the cities that get them first, and ports and places like that.'

She almost made it sound as if Annerby would have no need of them. Mabel thought of Bradshaw's Ball Bearings and Other Small Components being turned over to war work, but kept it to herself. Would Jerry know where the factories were? If rural Annerby wasn't near the top of the list for Anderson shelters and the war suddenly started, was her beloved hometown in danger of taking a clobbering, with no protection for its citizens? A shudder ran through her.

'Cold?' asked Althea. 'Daft question. It's freezing up here. We should start walking again before our feet turn into blocks of ice.'

She dug her hand into the crook of Mabel's elbow and moved in close, their arms pressed up against one another. Mabel squeezed her elbow against her side, creating a warm nest for Althea's hand as they set off.

They were more than friends. They were as good as sisters, something they had never tired of telling people when they were growing up. As a child, Mabel had wished she had smooth buttermilk-blonde hair so that they could look like sisters too, but her own hair was dark brown and she reckoned she kept the hairpin industry in business, since, left to their own devices, her long waves liked nothing better than to fluff up all over the show.

'I wish your family was coming to London for the Season,' Mabel sighed.

Her brief hope that Their Majesties' state visit to Canada and America in May would mean there would be no London Season this year had been well and truly dashed by the news that the Season was going to commence several weeks early, in March.

'Why don't I ask Mumsy if you can come with us?' she suggested.

'No, you mustn't. My parents don't have the same aspirations as yours.'

That was true. Althea's folks were minor gentry and content to remain so. There had never been any question of Althea's being spirited off for a London Season. It was the girls' lifelong friendship that had created the connection between the two families, and if Althea's parents entertained any reservations about the nouveau-riche Bradshaws, all Mabel could say was that the girls had never been made aware of it.

Sometimes the thought of the forthcoming Season made her feel as if she had a weight lodged inside her chest, but Pops was determined, so there was no getting out of it. Heaven alone knew how he had brought it about, but he was now in touch with a dowager viscountess who made a considerable income each year by presenting debutantes at court if they didn't have a mother or aunt who was allowed to present them. A quick flick through Mumsy's etiquette book had shown that there were more reasons than you could shake a stick at as to why a lady wouldn't be deemed eligible to do the presenting. Well, that was a comfort of sorts. If the viscountess made a living in this manner, it meant that Mabel wouldn't be alone in not being presented by her mother.

'I just wish you were having your dresses made up here,' said Althea, 'so I could come with you to the fittings and see them all.'

But no, Mabel's wardrobe was to be the product of the most high-class London dress salons. Was it ungrateful not to look forward to that? Possibly. But honestly, what place was there in the London Season for the granddaughter of a wheeltapper, even if she had been privately educated and her father had money to burn? Knowing that the Bradshaws wouldn't be the only new money on the circuit was no help. Mabel just wanted to stay at home. Simple as that.

With no Althea to back her up, Mabel coped alone with dress fittings and curtseying lessons.

> *Yes, curtseying lessons!* she wrote to Althea. *Who would have imagined such a thing existed? I am able to sink to the floor with perfect steadiness, but how I'm supposed to rise again without wobbling beats me. I've taken a tumble more than once, I don't mind telling you. The thought of making my curtsey in the presence of royalty is terrifying.*

She shared her coming-out ball with a girl whose family was of limited means but impeccable social standing, which meant they could invite all the right people, who were then obliged to acknowledge the Bradshaws. Mabel had cringed at the idea of this until she realised it would have been a whole lot worse to have had her own dance and run the risk of not being able to fill the ballroom of the splendid house Pops had rented.

What made it worse was that Althea was having a whale of a time without her.

> *The Thornleys had a dance at their house. There were lots of young men, as Bobby has three chums visiting. It so happens I'd already met them when I was out riding. Bobby introduced them as Will, Ollie and Gil, so I assumed they*

were William, Oliver and Gilbert, but at the dance it turned out they are Wilson, Ollerton and Gilchrist, but I still think of them as Will, Ollie and Gil and everyone calls them that.

It became clear that she seemed to be doing a lot of thinking about Gil in particular. His first name was Iain, with an 'i' in it twice because of Scottish ancestry. Althea didn't call him Iain because of not wanting to sound forward, though it was perfectly acceptable to call him Gil, that being his nickname. Gil and the others – and it didn't escape Mabel's notice that the others were soon lumped together without individual names – had been chums at Oxford. Gil had been taken into his family's law firm, but if war broke out he intended to join up.

Gil had hazel eyes and a lean face that was serious in repose, though when he smiled ... Mabel grinned as she read the rest. *If you're ever in need of extra money, you could always write romantic novels,* she wrote back. Gil could write and shoot and he was very good with children (underlined twice) and had played lions and tigers with Caroline Walsh's young twins for simply ages. And last night he had played the piano all evening so everyone else could dance, which was utterly spiffing of him, of course, but oh how Althea had longed for someone to offer to take over from him so she could drag him onto the floor.

Are you practising your new signature? Mabel replied.

She imagined Althea canoodling in the orchard. She wouldn't mind a spot of canoodling herself if the right man came along. Pops was hoping for what Mumsy called a socially advantageous marriage, which was a delicate way of saying that they hoped Mabel would bag herself a young gentleman with an impeccable pedigree and preferably a title. Would said gentleman be permitted by his family to show an interest in the granddaughter of a railwayman? He might well be, if the family was all pedigree and no cash. From wheeltapper to Honourable in three generations, with the highly successful Bradshaw's Ball Bearings and Other Small Components in between. Was that what lay in store for Mabel?

Did all the old families look down on the Bradshaws because they were new money or were some of the old families eyeing them up for the very same reason? It was impossible to tell, because everyone was faultlessly civil. That was a sign of good breeding, wasn't it? Courtesy to all, regardless of circumstances. But you didn't know what they murmured in private, did you?

With her pulse fluttering in unhappy self-consciousness much of the time, Mabel lapped up Althea's letters, which featured Gil more and more. With the threat of war in the offing, the young Thornleys seemed to be racketing around having a high old time, and the more friends they could persuade to join in the better. By day, there were rambles across the moors and drives to beauty spots, while the evenings were filled with music and merrymaking.

Meanwhile, Mabel lived more or less in terror of the dances in London. Was she the only girl here whose throat ached in dread at the mere sight of a dance card? First, there was the desperation to have her card filled with the names of partners, but instead of making her feel better, a full card then engendered a fresh anxiety. Was it a 'pity' dance? Worse, might it be a 'fishing' dance, where a chap requested the pleasure because he had heard about the Bradshaw fortune?

While Mabel endured all this, the young set in and around Annerby were having all kinds of fun.

We played hide-and-seek last night, Althea wrote. *Can you believe it?*

A faint shiver travelled across the skin on Mabel's arms. It happened sometimes. Mostly she was wryly amused by Mumsy's obsession with the rules of etiquette ('Smile prettily as you enter the room, Mabel ... Don't *shake* hands, Mabel. Apply gentle pressure ... Oh, heavens, I can never remember whether these tongs are for sandwiches or asparagus ... '), but occasionally she experienced a frisson of what she thought of as nouveau-riche nerves – the feeling that, while proper gentry could stretch the rules to snapping point and get away with it, folk from new money had better watch their p's and q's.

In the game of hide-and-seek, which had taken place on the ground floor of the Thornleys' house, there had evidently been a great deal of scuffling and muffled laughter as chaps opened a cupboard or slid behind a potted palm in search of a hiding place, only to discover the place was already taken, obliging them to scuttle off and try somewhere else before time ran out.

There I was, in an alcove in the rear of the entrance hall, and who should choose the same place but Gil! What wonderful luck! The moment he saw me, he started to withdraw, but just then Ollie shouted, 'Coming, ready or not!' so I pulled him back and there we were together in that tiny space. My heart was hammering fit to burst. I wanted to snuggle up to him – purely for the purpose of the two of us squeezing into a single hiding place, of course!! – but Sarah Walsh burst in, seeking a hidey-hole, and instead of Gil and myself enjoying a secret moment, we had to put up with Sarah playing gooseberry. I wonder if she realised. Honestly, I could have crowned her.

Mabel eagerly awaited the next letter, certain that, having been thwarted in the alcove, Gil would get Althea on

8

her own by some other means – but apparently not. Mabel's pen flew across the page in response as she tried to make Althea look on the bright side.

Don't be down-hearted. It shows he's a gentleman. You don't want a chap who's NST.

Althea's next letter ended with *PS NST?*

Not Safe in Taxis, wrote Mabel. *This London Season might be hell on earth, but at least I've brushed up on my slang.*

Althea's next letter was a heartbroken scrawl. Gil had gone home – he'd had to return to the office. She couldn't wait for them to be together again: *... but of course we can write. I admit to being the most frightful hussy – I wrote first! Imagine what the etiquette book would have to say about that!*

Lucky Althea, having a man to love, even if they were obliged to be apart for the time being. Althea might be down in the dumps, but to Mabel she was the luckiest girl in the world.

When the Bradshaws returned to Annerby, minus the heirloom engagement ring that Pops had hoped for, Mabel was relieved to leave London behind. She was eager to talk over the dire experience in minute detail with Althea, but Althea's thoughts were elsewhere.

Mabel slipped her arm around her friend's shoulders. 'Chin up. I know how much you miss him, but think of all the love letters.'

Althea's face crumpled, her body curling over in distress as she began to cry. As well as being concerned, Mabel was astonished. What had she said wrong?

'I heard from Gil's sister this morning,' Althea managed to say.

'Well, that's good, surely? More or less a welcome to the family.'

'If only.' Althea groaned. 'I can't believe how stupid I've been.' She released a huff of breath and shut her eyes for a moment. When she opened them, she shook her head. 'My letters to you weren't as honest as they might have been. That is, everything I said was true. Everything happened just as I said. It's just that … ' Althea's words caught on a sob and she cupped her hand over her mouth while Mabel sat close with an arm about her shoulders. 'My letters were wishful thinking. I can see that now. I wanted so much to believe that Gil felt the same way I did.'

'Do you mean … ?' Mabel couldn't bring herself to finish the question, just in case she had got hold of the wrong end of the stick. She couldn't believe what she was hearing.

'He didn't feel the same – he doesn't feel the same. I've made the most dreadful ass of myself. I threw myself at him. Not just once either, but time and again. I just wanted it so much. I must have embarrassed the heck out of everybody.'

'Oh, sweetheart.' Mabel leaned in close, stroking Althea's back. 'Why has his sister written?'

Althea's whole body shuddered. 'Because I'm an idiot, that's why. Gil and I never exchanged addresses – oh, I know I let you think it, but we didn't. At some point during his visit, he admired the jumpers Caroline's twins were wearing. You know how she dresses them alike. He said something along the lines of it being the sort of pattern his sister would like for her own children. He was just being polite, I suppose. Anyway, after he'd gone, I got the pattern off the Walshes' nanny and wangled Gil's address out of Ginny Thornley on the pretext of sending the pattern to him for his sister. I made it sound as if he'd told his sister to expect it.'

'So you used it simply as a reason to write to him.'

'Deep down, I knew I was making the most frightful howler, but I couldn't help myself. Give it one more chance, I kept thinking, just one more chance. I was desperate for him to write back. I – I so very much wanted something to cling to.'

'And instead his sister wrote,' Mabel said gently.

'Oh, it was the loveliest letter you can imagine. What a gorgeous pattern, and how kind of me to think of her. She even spent a few lines telling me about her flower beds.' Althea rubbed her temple as if she had a headache coming on.

'It sounds like a kind letter,' Mabel ventured.

'Oh yes, most kind. Beautifully worded. And not from Gil.'

'Perhaps you'll hear from him tomorrow.'

'Don't.' Althea pressed her fingertips to Mabel's lips. 'Don't make me hope, not now that I've faced up to it. I can see now what an unutterable clot I've made of myself.' Her voice dropped to a whisper. 'I chased him. I was so desperate for him to feel the same way that I saw only what I wanted to see.' There was such pain in her eyes that Mabel's breath caught. 'D'you remember when I wrote to you about the game of hide-and-seek? How I hid in the alcove and then Gil came along?'

'And you ended up hiding together.'

'That's the polite way of putting it. When he saw me, he was about to withdraw. I thought he was obeying the rules of the game. I thought I was doing us both a favour by grabbing hold of him.' Althea laughed bitterly. 'Really, he was about to run for his life, but he couldn't without hurling me aside. When Sarah darted in with us, she must have been the answer to his prayers.'

Mabel stroked Althea's arm. 'He's a fool if he can't see what a lovely girl you are.'

'I don't think he had a chance to see me in all my loveliness. He was too busy seeing me as the lustful girl in hot pursuit – and he was right. I was crazy about him. I couldn't think about anything else. I barely slept because I was so busy fantasising about him.' Althea closed her eyes. 'God, what an idiot I've been.'

'Don't be so hard on yourself.'

Althea's slim shoulders had been slumped. Now they sprang to attention. 'There was one evening when the boys rolled back the carpet and we had a Charleston competition, with Gil belting out the music on the piano. I spent the entire evening willing someone to offer to take over so he could dance. Then Jonty Blower offered, but Gil said he was perfectly happy playing. I was beside myself with disappointment – but now I wonder if he felt safe behind the piano. Safe from me.' Her shoulders slumped again and she groaned.

'Are you still … ?' Mabel began, then changed it to: 'Do you still feel the same about him?'

'You'd think that knowing I'm a sap of the first water would put an end to those feelings, wouldn't you? But if he were to walk through that door now … '

Mabel struggled over what to say next. It had never occurred to her that love could be so messy. Poor Althea. What could she do to help, to make her feel better?

The most useful thing seemed to be to keep Althea away from their usual set as much as possible, so that she wasn't obliged to keep up a brave face.

'Besides,' said Althea, 'I can't bear to think what they're saying about me.'

'Nobody has said anything to me,' said Mabel, 'other than to ask if you're feeling up to the mark, seeing as you've dropped off the scene. There have certainly been no catty or curious remarks about you-know-what.'

'That's something to be grateful for.'

'Maybe you weren't as obvious as you thought you were,' Mabel suggested.

'Try telling that to Iain Gilchrist!'

There wasn't even a trace of humour in her words. Poor Althea was as wretched as ever. Mabel was anxious to support her through her heartbreak. The hardest part was the way Althea now despised herself, and nothing Mabel said could lift this.

She tried to comfort herself with the thought that, however bad this time was for Althea, she would eventually feel better.

One morning, Mabel and Mumsy bumped into Mrs Thornley in town. Mrs Thornley was inclined to look down on the Bradshaws because they were new money, but she couldn't snub them because they were accepted by everyone else, especially Althea's family, who had been minor gentry since Georgian times. Mabel's heart was sent plummeting into her shoes when Mrs Thornley said that Will, Ollie and Gil had been invited back for a spell in the summer.

How would she tell Althea?

It was a funny summer that year. With hostilities in the offing, lots of folk were determined to have their usual holidays in case war was suddenly declared, while plenty of others decided not to go away for the same reason. The Thornleys, by staying put and filling their home with guests, seemed intent on a bit of both. Althea, however, was to be spared the colossal embarrassment of seeing Gil. Her parents had arranged a tour of the West Country and Althea, who could always get round her father, had prevailed upon them to extend it.

'It can't be long enough, as far as I'm concerned,' Althea declared. 'Gil would have to outstay his welcome with bells on to be still here when we get back.'

Mabel said all the right things, but the truth was she was dying to meet the man who had captured her friend's heart. To start with, wanting to stay loyal to Althea, she deliberately kept out of Gil's way, excusing herself from invitations, but she couldn't do that indefinitely and, if she was honest, she didn't want to. She wanted a social life, especially if war was on the horizon.

She met Gil one evening at the Thornleys'. It had been another scorcher of a day and what in a cooler summer might have been an indoor party, on this occasion involved trees draped with coloured lanterns. The windows and French doors had been left wide open so that the music could drift outside.

'Are those Bobby's friends?' she asked Ginny Thornley, nodding across the garden to where three strangers were engaged in a team game of quoits amid much laughter. Mabel turned to Ginny as she asked, 'The famous Will, Ollie and Gil?'

'The very same,' said Ginny. 'Or, to be precise, from left to right, Ollie, Gil and Will.'

Mabel looked at them again. As she did so, Ollie turned and looked at her. Their glances caught and held. Self-awareness poured through Mabel. She liked him. She *liked* him. She had to turn away, trying to bring her heart back under control, and when she next looked, he had abandoned the game and was heading for her.

Ginny did the honours. 'Mabel, allow me to introduce my brother's friend, Mr Iain Gilchrist.'

Mabel's heartbeat changed from a happy flutter to a thump of dread.

'But – I thought you were Ollie.'

'No,' he said, smiling. 'I'm definitely Gil.'

In the time between Ginny doing her left-to-right identification and Mabel looking around again, they had changed places.

Not Ollie, but Gil.

Althea's Gil.

They mustn't be attracted to one another. They mustn't fall in love.

Too late.

In the following days, Mabel tried to avoid Gil, but how could she? She couldn't help herself. She remembered Althea saying 'I couldn't help myself' and boggled at finding herself in the same position – except she wasn't in the same position, was she? Althea's wretched love had been one-sided, but Mabel's feelings were returned.

Iain Gilchrist was the man for her, the one and only man with whom she had ever felt completely right and natural. He felt the same about her. It was as simple – and as complicated – as that. When she was with him, it was as if they were the only two people in the world. It was a summer of snatched kisses and darting glances, of making sure they accepted the same invitations. If it hadn't been for Althea's previous disappointment, they would have got engaged. As it was, Mabel was determined to keep this wonderful new love a secret from the world. She owed it to Althea to tell her first – oh, and didn't that sound like the easiest thing in the world? But easy was the very last thing it was going to be.

'I'm truly sorry Althea got hurt,' said Gil, 'but I swear I didn't lead her up the garden path.'

'I know you didn't. She knows it too. She knows it was all on her side.'

Gil's respect and concern for the lifelong friendship she shared with Althea made Mabel love him even more. Her skin tingled all over in those private moments when she could brush her fingertips against his cheek. He had a serious face – Althea had been right about that. But when he looked at her and smiled, his lean features took on a soft cast that made her thoughts scatter all over the place. Was it dreadfully wrong of her, as much as she yearned for their relationship to be out in the open, to find the secrecy rather thrilling?

Yes, it was wrong, because the secrecy was all to do with how distraught Althea was going to be when she found out.

'It's so hard writing letters to her about picnics and dances,' Mabel whispered to Gil, 'and knowing what I'm keeping back.'

'It must be.' Gil touched her hair, gently winding an errant curl around his finger. 'Maybe you should tell her in your next letter.'

It was as if a bucket of cold water had been poured over her head. She drew back.

'I couldn't – not in a letter. It would be cowardly. She deserves better than that, from me of all people.'

Gil's visit was drawing to a close. Mabel couldn't bear to think of saying goodbye.

'I've been thinking,' Gil murmured.

They were sitting on the grass, watching the others play doubles. Jonty was throwing himself around the court as if the sweltering heat was nothing to him. Ginny had left Gil and Mabel and had gone indoors to ask for cold drinks. Mabel had offered to go with her, knowing that Ginny would tell her not to bother.

'Thinking?' she asked Gil. 'What about?' Something private, presumably, since he had waited for Ginny to make herself scarce. She felt a thrill of anticipation.

'Maybe I should leave tomorrow instead of Thursday.'

A tingle ran all over Mabel's skin. 'No! Why?' She stared at him.

'To take the scenic route back to Wiltshire.' Gil kept his gaze on the game. 'Via the West Country, I mean.'

'To tell Althea.' It wasn't a question.

'It would save you doing it.' Gil turned his head to look at her with such love in his eyes that it was all she could do to restrain herself from touching him.

'You mustn't,' she told him. 'It has to come from me.'

Besides, she couldn't bear it if he left tomorrow. It was hard enough to contemplate his going on Thursday, which would mean seeing him for the final time on Wednesday.

Wednesday came. There was no official goodbye, such as would be accorded to an acknowledged couple. Mabel felt as if her insides were quivering, but she had to maintain a sunny smile for the sake of appearances. Telling herself the smile would give Gil one final, happy memory to take with him gave her courage.

On the day Althea's family returned, they had the Bradshaws and two other families over to dine. How Mabel managed to hold her head up all through the evening, she didn't know. And what would Althea think of her when she looked back afterwards?

'Let's go for a drive tomorrow,' said Mabel when the ladies were being helped into their wraps at the end of the evening. 'I'll call for you.'

'Perfect,' said Althea. 'We can have a proper talk.'

Oh, they were going to have that all right.

Wearing a blue and cream dress with a flared skirt, teamed with a natty blue straw hat, and carrying a linen jacket over her arm, Althea ran down the front steps between the two bay windows at the front of her parents' house. She slid into the two-seater Mabel's father had bought her for her birthday last year. Normally, Mabel adored rattling around in it, especially on a day like this with the top rolled down, but today dread knotted in her stomach as she turned the key and pulled the starter knob. Her fingers fumbled on the handbrake and she flexed them before exerting a firm grip. Gravel spat and crunched beneath the tyres and they were on their way. She had planned this, had built up to it, so why did she feel so hopelessly unprepared?

Braking gently at the gates, she leaned forwards to look both ways before she turned the MG onto the road and headed up towards the moors. It was another fine morning and no doubt the afternoon would be another roaster. As they coasted along the road that meandered across the tops, with rough grassland and drystone walls to either side, the breeze skimmed the top of the windscreen and Althea laughingly raised a hand to her hat.

Drawing over to the edge of the road, Mabel pulled on the brake.

'Why have we stopped?' asked Althea.

Mabel swivelled in her seat to face her. 'There's something I have to tell you.'

'What is it?' Althea's expression was interested – questioning, not alarmed. Not frightened.

Mabel swallowed. 'It's about Gil.'

Althea's expression froze. 'What about him?'

'He came for another visit.'

'I know. That's why I was so keen to get away.'

Dragging this out was making it harder. Time to dive in. 'We met and – and I liked him.'

'You liked him? Well, yes, he's a perfectly likeable chap, I suppose. Wait – oh, Mabel, d'you mean you liked him in the same way I did?' Althea laid a hand on Mabel's arm, giving it a sympathetic squeeze. 'Was this man sent here to ruin our lives?'

The misunderstanding made it even worse. 'No. I mean … I mean he liked me too.'

Althea went utterly still. She turned her face away, then swung back again to stare at her. 'It was mutual? You and – him?'

If only she had never become entangled with Gil – but the attraction between them had been instant and so strong.

'It's more than liking,' said Mabel.

Althea uttered a choked cry and clasped her hand, the hand that had rested lovingly on Mabel's arm, to her mouth. Mabel made a move towards her, but dropped back when Althea didn't respond.

'I'm so sorry,' said Mabel. 'You know the last thing in the world I want is to hurt you.'

'How could you? The one man in the whole world that – that ... How *could* you?'

'I tried not to let it happen.'

'You can't have tried very hard.'

'I'm so sorry. You know how much you mean to me.'

'I thought I did. "The sister of my heart" is what you've always called me, and that's what you are to me too. But you've been carrying on with the man who broke my heart.'

'Be fair,' Mabel begged. 'It's not as though he did it on purpose. It's not as if he strung you along.'

'That's all right, then,' Althea retorted. 'As long as it's just me that's been a prize chump.'

'Oh, Althea.'

'Don't "Oh, Althea" me when you've done the dirty on me—'

'I haven't!'

'—in the most despicable way possible.'

'I never wanted it to happen. In fact, when I first laid eyes on him, I thought he was Ollie. I thought I was attracted to Ollie,' said Mabel, her voice pleading for understanding. 'It happened so quickly. We – we love one another.'

Althea flinched. 'It's love now, is it? It was liking a minute ago.' She dashed away tears. 'So that's it, is it? Him or me – and you've made your choice.'

'No! Never. You're my dearest friend.'

'Am I really? You know, you *know* how much I love him. I bared my soul to you. Or don't my feelings count, since he never loved me back? Did you have a good laugh about me? Poor, silly Althea, making a twerp of herself. "What a lark – should we ask her to be bridesmaid?"' Althea's eyes widened and her mouth dropped open. She moved her lips as if to say more, but nothing came out.

Bridesmaids. When they were still in pigtails, they had vowed to attend one another up the aisle. One of their favourite childhood games had been to dress up and play at weddings, taking turns to be the bride.

'Are you … ' Althea's mouth twisted as if she had eaten something sour. 'Are you going to marry him?'

'We're not engaged, if that's what you're asking.'

Althea's eyes hardened in a way Mabel had never seen before. 'No, that isn't what I'm asking, because I'm sure you aren't engaged. I expect you've told yourself that by not getting engaged you're doing the decent thing, sparing my feelings. I expect you're feeling pretty damn pleased with yourself for being high-minded. I repeat: are you going to marry him?' She curled her lips in distaste. Her eyes were cold and flat. 'You haven't got the guts to answer. That's an answer in itself.'

'I'm sorry,' Mabel whispered.

'And you waited all this time to tell me. You might at least have written, so I could start to … to … but oh no, you had to wait and tell me the news in person, didn't you?'

'I wanted to tell you in person. I needed to—'

'What about what *I* needed?' Althea demanded. 'Other than to have my nose rubbed in it. I can't believe this is happening. I just can't believe it.'

Suddenly, Althea was scrambling out of the motor. Mabel reached across and yanked her back.

'I'll take you home.'

'I don't want to go anywhere with you.'

'It's miles.'

'I don't care. I hate you. I'll never forgive you and I never want to see you again.'

Mabel touched her throat. For a moment, she couldn't breathe. 'You don't mean that.'

'Don't I?'

With a heavy feeling in the pit of her stomach, Mabel turned the key in the ignition and pulled the starter. The MG jolted forwards and they bounced in their seats. She swung the vehicle round in a great arc to head back the way they had come. They went over a bump and her teeth snapped together. Then something dragged the steering wheel away from her. Was it because of that bump? No, the pull was something more, something greater, and it was still happening. They were sliding across the road. She tugged hard on the wheel, but all that happened was that the skid altered course. They headed straight for a boulder beside the road.

She caught a flash of blue from the corner of her eye as Althea's hat flew off. They didn't seem to be moving at all. Rather, it was the boulder rushing towards them. A gigantic thud flung Mabel forward over the steering wheel, the breath whooshing out of her. Her ribs seemed to be hooked onto the wheel. Then she was wrenched free from the steering wheel and hurled backwards in her seat, as if she might disappear inside the upholstery. A sharp twang in her neck threaded hotly up into her ears and out across her shoulders. All the air was knocked from her body and she couldn't move, couldn't breathe. A gasp set her breathing again with an agonising jolt. Her eyes stung; she realised they were stretched wide open. She blinked.

Althea – she turned to her friend.

Althea was slumped back, head lolling, nose oddly twisted. Her face was cut, her temple reduced to a deep gash, inside which white bone was visible.

On the windscreen – oh my, on the windscreen was the faint imprint of Althea's face, her mouth gaping in mid-scream, her eyes enormous with disbelief and fear. A chill ran through Mabel and lodged deep in her heart.

It was like looking at Althea through a sheet of ice. That image on the windscreen had caught Althea's final moment of life. She had died in terror. And she had died hating Mabel for betraying her.

Chapter Two

April 1941

Joan kept glancing into the wicker basket on the front of her bicycle as she pedalled along Barlow Moor Road, keeping one eye on the jug of water that she had wedged into the basket along with a bunch of yellow tulips. Yellow was a good colour for cemetery flowers – eye-catching. Now that spring was in the air and the weather was kinder, the nights weren't so cold, so flowers placed on graves were much less likely to be blasted by the chill and would keep better. Bringing flowers to Letitia was all she could do for her now.

She cycled past the long stone wall, which was only a couple of feet tall, having relied for the rest of its height upon metal railings that had been removed to be melted down for the war effort. Slowing as she approached the ornate stone gateposts, Joan turned off the road, stepping off her bicycle as she entered the grounds of Southern Cemetery, the old trees creating a sense of peace as she pushed her bike along the paths among the headstones.

As she approached Letitia's resting place, she came to an uncomfortable standstill. Gran was there. Should she turn around and creep away? No – why should she? They had both loved Letitia and they both missed her. Besides, she wanted to tell Gran she had sorted out her personal life and that she was now back together with Bob. The episode when she had become romantically entangled with her late sister's boyfriend, Steven, had been a mistake brought about by grief – at least, it had on her side. She dearly hoped it was the same for Steven, but he hadn't seemed to think so when she had told him that Bob was the man for her.

She used the side of her foot to flick down the stand and left her bicycle beside a bench on the path, then removed the jug and the tulips from the basket. As she drew closer to the graveside, Gran glanced round and gave her a look, though she said nothing. Wouldn't she ever unbend? Losing Letitia should make the remaining family all the more important to one another, shouldn't it? Would Gran have preferred it if Joan had been the one to lose her life in an air raid? It wasn't the first time she had wondered.

'Hello, Gran.' Joan propped her bicycle against a bench and walked nearer. 'How are you?'

'I'm well, thank you.'

Gran had brought up Joan and Letitia to say, 'Very well, thank you' with a polite smile. To be merely well, instead of very well, was a snub of sorts and Joan felt it as such. Had she made a mistake in approaching Letitia's grave while Gran was there? It was too late to back away now. Gran was her only relative. They ought to be on speaking terms, even if the words weren't loving.

Joan looked at the ground. 'Someone's removed my flowers.'

'Oh, you brought those, did you? I should have known.'

'What's that supposed to mean?' She felt nettled and her natural good manners deserted her.

'I come to see Letitia every other day,' said Gran. 'I've been watching them die. I threw them in the bin yesterday.'

Shame engulfed Joan. 'I couldn't come before today. I've been at work every day and on first-aid duty every night. Today is my first chance to be here since last week.'

'You shouldn't leave flowers if you aren't going to be here to attend to them.'

Gran eyed the flowers in Joan's hand. It took all Joan's willpower to crouch down, tip away what remained of the old water and put in fresh before arranging the tulips.

'Letitia always did love tulips,' she remarked.

'That's true,' Gran conceded. 'As a little girl, she had a dress with a pattern of tulips around the skirt. She adored that.'

'I don't remember.' But how she wished she did. How she wished she could share the memory and edge a little closer to Gran.

'You wouldn't,' said Gran. 'You were too young. You wore it after she grew out of it, but it didn't suit you as well, not with your colouring.'

She should have realised it was too good to be true. She should have known that Gran's apparent softening would end with a barb directed at her, the second-best granddaughter. Some younger sisters might have been jealous of the beautiful, clever favourite, but not Joan. She had loved Letitia and been proud of her. Nevertheless, it had always been hard knowing that Gran loved Letitia more.

Gran blew out a breath and pulled back her shoulders, making ready to depart. She was dressed in her biscuit-brown coat with her reddish-brown felt hat. She always wore brown or black. She said it befitted her age, but since she had been saying this for as long as Joan could remember, she must have perceived herself as being old when she was still in her fifties.

'Gran.' Joan reached out, stopping short of touching her. Even so, Gran raised her eyebrows at Joan's hand. 'Before you go, can I tell you something important?' The words got stuck in her throat. This mattered dreadfully and she wanted – needed – Gran to care about it. 'I – I want you to know that I shan't be seeing Steven again.'

'Am I supposed to raise three hearty cheers? It's just like you to expect congratulations for stopping doing something you should never have started in the first place.'

A mixture of humiliation and hurt made her heartbeat turn sluggish, but she had to stand her ground. 'I know it was a mistake to become involved with Steven, but it was all tied up with the grief of losing Letitia. Grief can make people do mad things.'

'Can it really? Does that mean I didn't really grieve for her because I didn't run off with the coalman?'

'You know I don't mean that.'

'I go by what I saw, namely you and your sister's boyfriend canoodling in my front parlour. You might as well have danced the fandango on her grave.'

'Gran!'

'Don't "Gran" me, as if you're as innocent as the blossom in May. You're your mother all over again, that's what you are. Estelle was a tart and you're following in her footsteps.'

Not that again. It had hurt Joan deeply when Gran had first levelled this accusation at her, but it didn't hurt so much any longer; or rather, knowing Gran wanted to injure her was distressing in itself, but being told Estelle was a tart – well, these days it was more likely to make Joan wonder if she should be on her mother's side. Joan of all people knew what it was to be torn between two men. Was that what had happened to Estelle? Had she agonised between her marriage and her new-found love?

Not that that made what Estelle had done acceptable. She had abandoned Daddy years ago when Joan was a baby and Letitia just a year older, running away with her lover and leaving Daddy to pine away and die of a broken heart. Gran, Daddy's mother, had brought up the girls to know what a wicked thing Estelle had done – so wicked and shameful, in fact, that no one outside the family could ever be told about it. Gran had even left their old home down south and moved the girls up here to Manchester so they could have a fresh start in a place where everybody believed Letitia and Joan to be orphans.

Joan had never told anybody the truth – not her friends at school, nor the girls she had met at Ingleby's, where she used to work as a sewing machinist before the war; not even her friends on the railway, to whom, in the heightened emotional atmosphere of wartime, she had quickly grown closer than she had been to any friends in her former life. Neither had she told Bob about Estelle, nor his family, the Hubbles, no matter how much she loved them and appreciated the way they had welcomed her into their ranks.

With Bob, his parents and his three sisters, Maureen, Petal and Glad, she had experienced home life of a sort that had been nothing short of a revelation. She hadn't known that jokes could fly so freely or that children could tease their parents. She hadn't known that a father might be ragged by his children, such as had happened after Mr Hubble, on fire-watching duty one night, had reported seeing the light of an enemy aircraft, only for it to turn out to be the North Star.

The very idea that the father of the family could be spoken to in such a way had astounded Joan. Her own father had died many years ago, way before her earliest memories began, but he had always been spoken about with the deepest respect at home. His photograph enjoyed pride of place in the parlour. How handsome he was, as swoon-worthy as any film star. Dead he might be, but in the Foster household he had always been an important figure, in some ways the most important member of their household.

'Would Daddy be proud of you for that?' Gran would ask and, oh, the shame and disappointment should the answer be no.

Living up to Daddy's high standards had been a central part of their everyday lives. It was something that characterised the Foster family. A frown tugged at Joan's brow and she couldn't help shaking her head as uncertainty flooded her, as it had so often recently, ever since she had discovered that the Fosters weren't the Fosters after all.

The day after a bomb had landed near their house in Torbay Road, Joan had seen Gran's marriage certificate. Foster wasn't Gran's married name. Her married name was Henshaw – which meant Daddy had been Donald Henshaw and Joan and Letitia were Joan and Letitia Henshaw. Joan now had her birth certificate in her possession as confirmation of this. She wasn't Joan Foster and never had been. She was Joan Henshaw.

No, she mustn't be all dramatic about it. Cordelia, one of her railway friends, was married to a solicitor and according to him, since she had been known as Joan Foster virtually all her life, she was entitled to continue using the name. There would be additional paperwork should she marry, though this would be a mere formality, just a written confirmation of why she had two surnames.

Anyway – or anyroad, as another dear friend, the blunt, big-hearted Dot, would say – there was simply no call to be dramatic about it. It was dramatic enough without any help from her.

Gran had several times refused point-blank to say why she had altered the family name and nothing Joan said could make her explain.

'For all the good it'll do you,' Gran had said when she had reluctantly handed over Joan's birth certificate.

Did she really think that Joan could bear to leave matters like that?

Joan spent much of her time at work meeting trains and assisting passengers with their luggage. She enjoyed working with the public, something she hadn't had the chance to do when she worked at Ingleby's. Most people were polite and appreciative. Some even tipped her a thrupenny bit or a tanner for her help. That had been embarrassing to start with, but 'Just smile and say thank you' had been Dot's advice, which she now happily followed, later popping the coins into the Red Cross collection box.

She had spent a couple of hours this morning trundling heavy sacks to a goods wagon, where she had to negotiate a wooden ramp that vibrated with every step she took. After her midday meal of vegetable pasty followed by a carrot scone, she was due to spend the rest of her shift inside the station. She was proud to wear her uniform of jacket, skirt and peaked cap. Some girls wore trousers, something Gran would never have tolerated, but now that she didn't live with Gran any longer, maybe . . .

She met train after train, stacking her sack trolley with suitcases and carpet bags. Some passengers knew precisely where to go and she simply followed in their confident wake. Others relied on her to lead them to Victoria Station's entrance, the waiting room, Left Luggage or to another platform. She had been a station porter since last autumn and the pleasure of efficiently escorting people had not worn off. She often thought of dear little Lizzie, who had had this job before her and who had tragically lost her life in a brutal air raid. Lizzie had loved the job too.

After ferrying luggage to the taxi rank for a thin, elderly gentleman who carried himself with military bearing in spite of his advanced years, Joan was hailed next by a middle-aged couple descending from a taxi across the road.

She swung their suitcases onto her trolley. They were real leather cases, not the cardboard ones most folk had, and they were adorned with several pasted-on labels of holiday destinations, including a photograph of *The Grand Hotel, Bristol* with a bright blue edge all around it.

'Which platform, sir?' It was the done thing to ask the man, but Joan made a point of smiling at the lady to show she was paying attention to her too.

'Southport, please. We already have our tickets.'

'You'll have a bit of a wait, I'm afraid,' said Joan. 'The Southport line has been disrupted today.'

'Giving way to troop trains or munitions, I imagine,' said the man.

'I couldn't say, sir.'

Even had she known, she wouldn't have said. *Be like Dad – keep Mum!* and *'Ware spies! Keep it under your hat* said the posters.

The couple knew where to go, so Joan tagged along behind with their luggage. She always liked going onto the Southport platform because there was a chance of seeing Dot, of whom she was enormously fond, as well as admiring her for the courage she had shown recently. Some people might find it odd that she, a twenty-year-old, considered a grandmother in her forties to be her friend, but she did. She felt lucky to be part of a close-knit group, who had all, apart from Persephone, started work at Victoria Station on the same day in March last year. They had been welcomed to their new place of work by Miss Emery, the assistant welfare supervisor for women and girls, who had given them a piece of advice that wasn't included in the rule book: 'Be friends with one another – regardless of age or background or anything else that would normally come between you. If you can turn to one another for support, it will help you all.'

And this was what they had done. It wouldn't have been possible without the consent of the two older ladies in the group, Cordelia and Dot. Before the war, the idea of two such women becoming friends would have been unthinkable. Cordelia was the elegant wife of a well-to-do solicitor, Dot a working-class housewife. But they had followed Miss Emery's advice and later, when Joan had been harassed by a slimy middle-aged colleague, the two of them had banded together to send him packing. Quite how they had achieved this, Joan didn't know, but Dot and Cordelia had been firm friends ever since.

Following the couple, Joan made her way along the busy concourse, with its long, handsome ticket office all decked out in highly polished wood panelling and its large noticeboards between the sets of platform gates. Walking onto one of the long platforms, she pushed her trolley alongside the line of dark red coaches, which were filling with passengers. In one window, a man with an eyepatch and a livid, creased scar down one side of his face leaned forward to light a cigarette for a young woman wearing a pillbox hat. At the next window, two middle-aged women were deep in conversation, and at the next, a pretty girl pushed up the eye veil on her hat to check her appearance in the mirror of her compact before deftly applying some powder. How Gran would sneer at doing that in a public place, but Joan found such behaviour appealing. There was something modern and dashing about it.

The couple chose a carriage and Joan was about to lift their suitcases on board, but the gentleman beat her to it.

'We can't have a slip of a girl like you heaving suitcases about.'

Joan forbore pointing out out that heaving suitcases was what she was paid to do. Even now, after all these months of having female porters – or porteresses and porterettes, as some people still insisted upon calling them – there were still some men who felt it shouldn't be the done thing to let girls tackle this job.

Pushing her empty trolley, Joan went to the guard's van, where the big double doors were fastened open. Peering inside, she saw the long wire cage in which trunks, boxes and parcels were stored in various stacks according to where along the line they needed to be put off the train.

'Mrs Green,' Joan called. Although her friends used each other's first names in private, they were scrupulous about using everyone's proper titles in public. 'Are you in there?'

'Boo!' said a voice behind her and Joan turned round, laughing, to come face to face with Dot, who wore a similar uniform to her own.

'How's today going?' Joan asked.

'The usual fun and games. One of my so-called parcels this morning was a pig. You know how I love being in charge of livestock.' Dot briefly cast her eyes heavenwards. 'Then, with the train packed solid, a group of young navy lads thought what a lark it would be to climb up into the net luggage racks and stretch out for the journey, which meant, of course, that everyone's luggage was left all over the floor.'

'Did you make them come down?'

'Yes, though first I had to climb over all the luggage to get close enough.' Dot smiled. 'Just another day in the life of the railway.'

'You wouldn't have it any different,' said Joan, 'except maybe for the pig.'

'Give him his due, Mr Hill helped with the pig.'

'Mr Hill?' Then Joan remembered. 'He's the guard standing in while Mr Bonner recuperates, isn't he?'

'He has a better opinion of women working on the railway than Mr Bonner does, and that counts for a lot.'

'After what you did to save the train, not to mention his life, I should hope Mr Bonner's views will be different when he returns to work.'

'We'll see,' said Dot.

'I know the trains are running late today. Shall you manage to meet us in the buffet this evening?'

'I've been put on duty in the parcels office for the rest of my shift, so, yes, definitely.'

'Lovely. You can tell us about the adventure of the pig.'

'I'm pleased to report there was no adventure this time.'

'Not like when you had those goats to look after,' grinned Joan.

Dot groaned. 'Don't remind me.'

They parted company. Joan had barely set off with her trolley again when she was hailed by the man in the newspaper stall halfway along the platform. He reached across the display of newspapers and books to hand her a gas-mask case.

'This was left behind on that bench over there this morning. Will you take it to Lost Property? It belongs to a lady, but I didn't see her.'

Joan took it from him. 'There's no label on it. How do you know it belongs to a lady?'

'I opened it up, of course. No mask inside, just a lipstick.'

Joan slung the strap over her shoulder and headed for Lost Property, where she was surprised to find Alison behind the counter. Alison was wearing a pink dress with a V-neck beneath a uniform jacket, her brown hair hanging in waves from under a peaked cap.

'What are you doing in here?' Joan asked.

'Filling in. Hence the horrid jacket over my dress.'

Joan didn't respond to that. Personally, she loved her uniform.

'Remember the raid when your gran's road was hit?' said Alison.

Remember it? That was what had led to her finding out about the Henshaw name.

'Salford had casualties as well that night,' said Alison. 'A member of staff from Lost Property has been in hospital ever since. He passed away, unfortunately, though I gather it wasn't a surprise, and his funeral is today. He was a widower and both his sons are fighting overseas, so all the staff wanted to attend the funeral and give him a good send-off. That's why I'm here.'

'Holding the fort.'

Alison nodded at the gas-mask box. 'Lost?'

''Fraid so.' Joan handed it over.

'Along with about a million other gas-mask boxes. If you ever get the chance to have a look around in here, it's fascinating – well, for the first half-hour, anyway. You wouldn't believe some of the items people have left behind. I kid you not – there's a wooden leg back there. How can you lose a wooden leg? But mostly it seems to be gas-mask boxes.'

'Are you coming to the buffet later?'

'Yes. I'll see you there.'

Joan returned to her duties and was given the task of ferrying boxes of Mansion Polish and Brasso to the cleaning store and a milk churn to the buffet, where Mrs Jessop greeted her with a smile. Joan and her friends were among Mrs Jessop's regulars and she allowed them to keep a notebook under the counter in which they wrote each other messages to arrange when to meet up.

When the time came for Joan to clock off, she rolled her shoulders, which were aching, but it was the pleasant ache of a job well done. She went to the Ladies. There still weren't any lavatory facilities specifically for the female railway workers. To compensate, they had hung an Out of Order sign on one of the doors, so that there was always a cubicle at their disposal. Unknown to the powers that be, they also used a bent nail to open the door, which was supposed to open only when a penny was put in the slot.

Joan removed the snood she wore for work and tidied her hair, which she wore in gentle waves to just above her shoulders and scooped away from her forehead. These days, she wore her snood only for work and when she was on first-aid duty, unlike when she had lived under Gran's roof. Then, the only times she and Letitia had been permitted to set foot outdoors without their hair in a snood had been when they went to church or out dancing.

A pang of sorrow cut through Joan. Letitia had loved dancing. She had been killed in the Christmas Blitz. Now it was April, nearly Easter, and life was continuing without her. Sometimes the thought of a world without her beloved sister seemed to tear Joan's heart in two.

She sniffed softly and blinked. This wasn't the time to let emotion well up. She fastened her coat over her uniform. They weren't allowed to sit in the buffet with their uniforms on show in case the public thought they were slacking. Her coat, with its large collar, padded shoulders and flap pockets, had once been Letitia's; Joan had made it for her. She put her porter's cap in her bag and put on her blue felt hat with its upswept brim and a petersham bow at the front. Again, the hat had been Letitia's – hence its colour and the jaunty brim that had shown off Letitia's beautiful face. Joan's own clothes had vanished in the bomb blast that had destroyed Mrs Cooper's house, where Joan had gone to live after Gran threw her out. Now, she had some of Letitia's clothes, which she had hidden away to prevent Gran from donating them to bombed-out families, and she was going to start making some garments too, using all the skills she had learned at Ingleby's.

She went to the buffet, which stood in a group of small buildings on the concourse, each one with tiles of soft yellow on the exterior wall and, above the entrance, its name written against a deep blue background – GRILL ROOM, BOOKSTALL, BUFFET, RESTAURANT. Inside the buffet was a curved wooden counter with shelves of crockery lining the wall behind it.

Mrs Jessop caught Joan's eye and nodded across to where her friends were crammed around a table. Cordelia, with her perfectly coiffed ash-blonde hair showing below her grey felt hat, wore her wine-coloured coat with the topstitched collar that was the height of elegance compared to the old faithful habitually worn by Dot. Dot was always in a hurry to get somewhere and get a job done, but when she sat and listened to you, she gave you her full attention. Mabel was a friend to whom Joan was growing closer now that the two of them bunked together. They had both recently sorted out their tangled love lives and Mabel was now happy with Harry Knatchbull, her cheeky blighter, at the same time as Joan felt settled with her Bob. Next to Mabel was Alison, whose engagement to her long-time boyfriend Paul they had all been anticipating for ages, and beside her was Persephone, beautiful Persephone, whom it was as easy to picture bathing muddy dogs as it was to picture her waltzing beneath sparkling chandeliers.

The only one missing was Colette, but that was nothing new. Colette seldom came to their get-togethers, because her attentive husband met her from work and spirited her off home. But now that Joan lived in Wilton Close with Mrs Cooper, she had hopes of getting to know Colette better as after Lizzie had died last year, Colette had started calling on Mrs Cooper once a week.

'We're talking about hairdressers,' said Mabel, patting the empty chair beside her. 'When I lodged with Mrs Grayson, I arranged for a hairdresser to visit her house and do her hair into a modern style instead of that awful old bun she wears, but then we had to move out in a hurry and it never happened. Now that we live in Chorlton, I was just asking Cordelia if she knows of a good hairdresser.'

'I can certainly give you the name of mine,' said Cordelia, 'though whether she'll visit the house is another matter. It's an unusual request.'

'A smart hairstyle might build Mrs Grayson's confidence,' said Dot, 'and help her start going out. I know there's a lot more to it than just having a new hairdo, but it might help.'

There were murmurs of agreement. Joan pictured Mrs Grayson. Might a new look assist her in taking those important but oh-so-difficult steps through the front door? She had lived indoors for years because unhappiness had got on top of her. What a strange half-life that must have been. But now she was in Wilton Close with Mrs Cooper, Mabel and Joan, and she had a new group of acquaintances in the other railway girls, Joan hoped the dear lady's new life would start to open up, a wish that she knew was shared by her friends.

Persephone looked at her. 'Now that you've had time for a breather after getting back together with Bob, have you given any more thought to what to do about your surname?'

'There's nothing she can do if Mrs Foster won't say anything,' said Mabel.

'That isn't strictly true,' said Cordelia, 'though there's something to be said for leaving well alone. You need to consider the matter carefully, Joan.'

'Don't feel pushed into doing something,' Alison added, with a glance in Persephone's direction.

'I wasn't pushing,' Persephone said at once. 'I'm sorry if I said the wrong thing. Maybe it's my journalistic ambition coming to the fore. Pay no heed to me, Joan. I didn't mean to pry.'

'You didn't pry,' Joan assured her. 'I know you have my best interests at heart and it's natural to be curious. Goodness knows, I've certainly learned the meaning of curiosity since this blew up.'

Persephone's lovely features relaxed and she gave Joan a grateful smile. Joan warmed to her. Persephone might be out of the top drawer, and an Honourable no less, but she was a kind and generous person with no airs and graces. Moreover, her question hadn't been intrusive and Joan wished Alison hadn't made out that it was.

It was time to make her announcement. Joan took a breath, surprised to feel her heart thumping, making her realise the importance of what she was about to say.

'As a matter of fact,' she began, looking around at her friends, who were the only people with whom she had shared the mystery of her family name, 'I've decided what to do. I'm going to take some leave so I can go down south and see what I can find out about my family.'

Chapter Three

Dot had a jumpy feeling under her skin, as if her nerve ends were jangling. It was all she could do to concentrate on loading up her flatbed trolley with boxes and parcels. She had arrived in the parcels office expecting to work on the Southport train as usual, only to be informed that she would be on the Leeds train today. That was all. No explanation, just an instruction. Had Mr Hill complained about her? She knew from experience what happened when a complaint was made against a member of staff. A shiver went through her. That hadn't been her finest hour. Anyroad, Mr Hill had no call to complain – had he? They seemed to get on well. She pulled herself together. She had been assigned to a different route today, that was all. She shouldn't read too much into it.

Anyroad, if she was on the Leeds train for the day, she might be teamed with that nice Mr Emmet who had been so friendly and helpful last year when she had travelled with him. That, however, turned out to be wishful thinking. The train guard, who had been brought out of retirement for the duration, was Mr Andrews, whose gaunt face made him look rather forbidding, though he turned out to be perfectly pleasant and certainly didn't behave as if she had been foisted on him.

He helped her to load up all the parcels for Leeds and all stations along the way into the wire cage inside the guard's van, showing her the best place to put each pile. It made Dot realise how accustomed she had become to performing

39

this task on the Southport train, putting everything into exactly the right place. She did it almost without thinking.

When it was nearly time for the train to leave, Mr Andrews closed the van's double doors and secured them, then descended onto the platform from one of the ordinary doors. Dot went to another door, pulled it shut and thrust the window down so she could look out as Mr Andrews paced alongside the dark red coaches, slamming doors that were still open and checking those that had already been closed. When he started walking back to the guard's van, Dot turned to look along the platform to catch a glimpse of blue sky where the canopy finished. The horizontal bar on the signal was raised, which meant the train had permission to leave the station. Arriving beside the door he had climbed down from, Mr Andrews lifted his whistle to his lips and blew it, receiving a blast from the train whistle in reply before he stepped up into the train, pulling his door shut behind him. Just as he leaned out of the window to wave his green flag, a man came racing onto the platform, clutching his trilby to his head and flinging himself aboard at the last moment, just as the sound of hissing came from the front of the train, followed by a huge burst of steam from the funnel. The much-loved *puh ... puh ...* started up, slowly to begin with. Then came the sound of creaking from the couplings that linked the coaches to one another and the train pulled away.

Dot enjoyed the journey. It was good to have different scenery to look at, though the unfamiliar route kept her on her toes. Mr Andrews explained to her which carriage she had to ferry parcels to so as to be in the right place for them to be taken off at the next station.

When they arrived in Leeds, the final stop, she trundled the remaining parcels on a flatbed trolley to the parcels office and was surprised to be told that she didn't need to load up.

'We've got another porter doing the return journey. It's his first day. He'll have been shown round and kitted out with his uniform by this time. Now it's up to me to show him the ropes.'

'I wish him well,' Dot said sincerely. 'It's a wonderful job and I love it. But how will I get back to Manchester?'

'Never fear. We've arranged for you to hitch a lift on a goods train.'

'You're kidding me.'

Dot got herself a cup of tea and visited the Ladies, then reported back to the parcels office, where a porter was given the job of taking her where she needed to go. To her surprise, they walked right along a platform and down the ramp at the far end, then across the boarding that was laid for railway workers to cross the tracks. Finally, with a strong sense that her leg was being pulled, Dot followed her guide into the sidings, wondering what on earth was happening.

Then she saw. Behind the locomotive and coal tender of a goods train was a series of four long flatbeds, each bearing an army tank complete with gun turret and caterpillar treads. Dot's mouth fell open.

'The guard's van is at the rear,' said the porter who was escorting her. When they got there he stood beside the open double doors and leaned his head inside. 'Permission for your visitor to come aboard?'

The guard appeared. 'In you come, love. There's a box there you can stand on to get in.'

Dot climbed aboard and introduced herself. The guard was Mr Grant, who sported a walrus moustache and bushy side whiskers such as she hadn't seen since she was a lass.

'Tanks,' said Dot. 'I've never seen the like.'

'Convincing, aren't they?' said Mr Grant.

'I should jolly well hope so, if they're going to be defending us from the Hun.'

'They are defending us, in a manner of speaking. They're dummies.'

'You what?' Dot asked.

'Dummy tanks. Models. Pretend. We ferry 'em about on the railways so that if Jerry comes looking, he goes home thinking we've got tanks and heavy artillery coming out of our ears. Clever, eh? We run ghost trains as well.'

'What's one of them when it's at home?'

'It's when we move trains around the country just for the sake of it. It keeps Jerry guessing.'

'Just wait until I tell my grandson.'

'You can't say a word, not to anyone.'

'Of course I can't. Sorry. I wasn't thinking.'

'Aye, well, think on.' Was he about to make a disparaging remark about women who couldn't stop gassing? But his eyes twinkled instead. 'You'll have quite a tale to tell him after the war, though, won't you?'

Dot sat in the buffet with Persephone and Cordelia. She would have loved to tell them about the pretend tanks, but she mustn't. She smiled to herself. It would be good practice for not telling Jimmy.

The door opened and a pair of women in WVS uniform came in.

'I always feel a twinge of guilt when I see WVS ladies,' Dot admitted, 'or when I see girls in their ARP tin hats heading off for a night on duty.'

'Why would you feel guilty?' Persephone asked.

'Should I be doing war work?'

'You're already doing war work,' said Persephone. 'Full-time war work with compulsory overtime thrown in.'

'Even so,' said Dot, 'I often see women going out of an evening to do their bit in the rest centres and the mobile cup-of-tea stations and what have you, and it makes me wonder if I'm right to stop at home, though, honest to God, I need my time there. There's the house to look after, and Reg, and queuing up at the shops, and as for the cleaning – I don't think I've ever cleaned so much in my whole life as I have since this dratted war started. That's summat they don't warn you about in all them government information leaflets. They tell you all about gas masks and what to do before you leave the house in an air raid, but they don't tell you how each bomb that's dropped raises every single speck of dust for miles.'

Persephone laughed, but she leaned forward, looking interested. 'That's a wonderful idea for an article. It's the kind of thing they might like at *Vera's Voice*, if I could strike the right tone.'

'Aye, love,' Dot said drily, 'you write a witty article about cleaning up after an air raid. Meanwhile, I'll carry on with my housework.'

'I know I can't say anything to stop you feeling guilty about not doing more for the war effort,' said Cordelia, 'but don't forget you've also got your two daughters-in-law looking to you for guidance—'

'Which is a polite way of saying they land at my kitchen table when they want a spot of help,' put in Dot.

'—and you often look after your grandchildren, especially Jimmy,' Cordelia added. 'He stays the night regularly, doesn't he?'

'And that makes it all the more important for you to be at home,' said Persephone, 'with Mr Green out on ARP duty.'

Cordelia's grave features softened. 'Our railway jobs may be vital, but there's nothing more important than caring for children.'

'That's summat else I feel guilty about,' said Dot. 'We evacuated our Jimmy and Jenny at the start of the war, like we were supposed to, but then we had the phoney war and no bombs were dropped, so we brought them home again. Now, with all the raids we've had, I ask myself if we did the right thing. Then I remember listening to that broadcast on Christmas Day, when they had evacuated children sending Christmas messages to their parents, and I know I couldn't bear to let our two go away again.'

'How is Emily?' Persephone asked Cordelia.

'Her exams are coming up. She's a good letter writer, but it's not the same as having her at home.' Cordelia looked at Dot. 'I don't blame you and your daughters-in-law for wanting to keep the children close to you.'

It was her and Pammy rather than Sheila, but Dot kept that to herself. Dot rather suspected that Sheila wouldn't have minded losing their Jimmy for the duration. Well, he was a handful, but even so. Pammy was the opposite. A besotted mother, she poured her energy into creating a beautifully behaved daughter with perfect manners. Eh, it was one extreme to the other with Pammy and Sheila. It was all the P's with Posh Pammy – pristine, picky and perfect pronunciation – while Sheila the Slattern was a sloppy housewife and a slapdash mother.

Cordelia and Persephone looked at their wristwatches. Dot did too, then looked over her shoulder at the clock on the wall above the fireplace on the other side of the buffet.

'My old watch has been losing time recently,' she remarked.

'Maybe the insides need a clean,' Persephone suggested.

'They'll have to go on needing it,' said Dot. 'I've got better things to do with my money. Anyroad, if there's one good thing about working at a station, it's that there are plenty of clocks.'

'What about when you are on board the train and passengers ask you for the correct time?' asked Cordelia.

'Oh heck,' said Dot, 'I'd better get it seen to.'

Standing up and gathering their things, they tucked their chairs under the table and left the buffet. Cordelia and Persephone went to buy magazines before going home. Dot said goodbye and set off to catch her bus. As she rounded the corner near the long line of ticket-office windows, she saw her friend Mr Thirkle standing quietly in front of Victoria Station's handsome war memorial, dedicated to the memory of the brave railwaymen of the Lancashire and Yorkshire Railway, as it then was, who had answered the call and gone off to serve King and country in the Great War.

The war to end all wars – and look at us now.

Mr Thirkle sometimes stopped here, beneath the huge tiled map showing the layout of the railway lines across England, from Southport, Liverpool, Blackpool and Fleetwood on the west coast to Hull, York and Goole in the east. He had worked here since he left school at the age of thirteen and he had known some of the many men whose names were inscribed on bronze plaques beneath the giant map. Dot's heart softened to see him there in an attitude of private reflection, oblivious to the passengers hurrying past him. He was a good man, considerate and caring.

Did he care for her? As in, not just care about her, like you would care about your friend, but did he care *for* her? That moment just over a week ago, when Dot had been attacked and he had rushed to her rescue and then she had clobbered the attacker round the ears with a railway lamp and they had stood very close together afterwards – in that moment, she had realised the warm fondness she felt for him was … somewhat warmer than that. Had friendship really tipped over the edge into love? Did she, a married woman, have feelings for another man?

And the revelation that had happened to her in that moment – had it happened to Mr Thirkle an' all? Did he return her feelings? And if he did – what then?

Chapter Four

It was jolly hard work, but Mabel loved her job as a length-man out on the permanent way, packing the ballast under the railway tracks. Whenever a train went past on one of the other lines, even though it was some distance from Mabel's gang, it almost took her breath with it as it rushed on its way, puffing white clouds from its funnel. Mumsy and Pops would far rather she had been given a clerical post in, say, the ticket office, but Mabel was happy doing what she did, not least because she felt Grandad would have approved.

She worked as one of a gang of four, led by Bernice Hubble, who was mum to Joan's boyfriend, Bob. Bernice was a sensible, good-humoured woman, but she took no nonsense and Mabel respected her as a boss and valued her as a friend. Then there was Bette, who was in her thirties and had been a barmaid before the war. The last member of their group was Louise, who still bore the remains of the bruises her rotter of a brother had inflicted on her at the beginning of the month before he took to his heels and vanished off the face of the earth. What Lou and her family didn't know was that Dot had uncovered a conspiracy to steal food from a secret food store and Rob Wadden had been involved. Dot had confided in her friends and together they had tackled the thieves, though it was Dot who had been the true heroine. It felt odd, knowing what Rob Wadden had done and knowing that she couldn't tell his sister.

The group of friends had been warned to keep quiet about the thefts because of morale.

Bette stopped work for a moment to roll her shoulders. Looking at Mabel, she gave a hoot of laughter. 'If your Harry could see you now!'

Mabel looked down at herself. 'No one ever said packing ballast was glamorous.'

She wore slacks with a baggy jumper beneath a shapeless jacket. Her dark brown wavy hair was tied back and she wore a beret perched on her head. Her hands were deep inside thick gloves, which were essential when you spent your day handling shovels and pickaxes. But it was her face Bette was looking at.

'Grime?' she asked.

'Covered in it,' Bette replied cheerfully. 'Give me your hanky. Spit.'

Obediently, Mabel spat onto her hanky and let Bette wipe her face for her. 'Thanks, Mum,' she teased.

'Less of that, if you don't mind. I'm not nearly old enough.'

It was time to stop for a tea break. As the four of them tramped across the tracks towards the scrubby cutting for a sit-down, Mabel's mind filled with thoughts of Harry Knatchbull, her handsome, charming boyfriend. It had taken quite some time for her to let herself enter into a relationship with him because she had been tormented for months by grief and guilt over the death of her beloved friend, Althea. She had felt that she didn't deserve to have anything good happen to her, but Dot, Cordelia and her other friends had encouraged her to embrace happiness. Mind you, they didn't know what she had done. She had told them that she was the one driving the motor at the time of the accident in which Althea had lost her life, but that was all she had told them. She was too ashamed to admit to the full circumstances of Althea's death. Sometimes she thought she could; sometimes she played with the hope that her new friends would support her if they knew the truth – but she could never bring herself to open up.

Instead, she had concentrated on her relationship with Harry and given how in love she was, this had been the easiest thing in the world to do. Everything had gone swimmingly with Harry until she had learned that his original interest in her had been due to her father's money rather than her own charms. Even the memory of that night made coldness strike right at the core of her being. But Harry's heartfelt contrition, together with her own certainty that whatever the reason he had pursued her in the first place had been replaced with true love, had convinced her that it was right for them to be together. Only Joan and Persephone knew the truth about Harry and that was the way Mabel wanted it to stay. It wasn't that she didn't trust her other friends, but the fewer people who knew about Harry's fortune-hunting ambitions, the better. She wanted everyone to think well of him and she couldn't bear to have anyone questioning his motives.

She was going to see him tonight. He was based at RAF Burtonwood, so they couldn't see one another as often as they would have wished, but that made their time together all the more precious. Tonight they were to go to a dance, which was a fund-raiser for a Spitfire.

At the end of the day, Mabel gave herself a lick and a promise in the Ladies before she headed for home. The house in Wilton Close in Chorlton-cum-Hardy was her third home since she had come to Manchester in the spring of last year. Pops had sent her to Darley Court, courtesy of Cousin Harriet, who was the housekeeper there. It hadn't suited Mabel, and Cousin Harriet had found her a billet with her old friend Mrs Grayson. Now, the two of them and Joan all lodged with Mrs Cooper, Lizzie's mum, who was taking care of the house for its elderly owners, who had relocated to North Wales for the duration.

As she opened the front door, the rich, sweet aroma of baking greeted her. She found Mrs Grayson in the kitchen.

'What has the magic mixing bowl produced today?' asked Mabel.

'You and your magic mixing bowl.'

'No, Mrs Grayson, *you* and the magic mixing bowl. It smells divine.'

'It's shortbread – or should I say, wartime shortbread. I can't answer for what colour it will be, not with the flour we're given nowadays. I'm making it for Easter. Hitler might have ruined Christmas for us, but he jolly well isn't going to spoil Easter.'

'I'll tell you one good thing that came out of the Christmas Blitz,' said Mabel. 'You and I becoming friends.'

Mrs Grayson couldn't hide the pleasure on her face, but her tone was dry when she said, 'You mean, you stopped thinking I was doolally.'

'Something like that.' Mabel dipped her finger in the pan on a low heat on the stove and sucked it. 'It was your cooking that won me over.'

Mrs Grayson rapped her knuckles with the wooden spoon. 'Get your fingers out of my carrot curry. Shoo. Tea will be on the table in twenty minutes.'

Mabel went upstairs to freshen up. She was changing into a jumper and skirt when Joan walked into their bedroom.

'Thanks for doing my first-aid duty tonight,' said Mabel.

'Pleasure. Let's hope it's a quiet night. What are you going to wear to go out?'

Mabel had brought two evening dresses back with her the last time she went home to Annerby. When she had forgiven Harry and told him she wanted them to stay together, she had been wearing the pearl-grey silk-crêpe dress, so tonight she was going to wear the jade-green dress. It had a ruched bodice and attached to the shoulder straps were long pieces in the same pale green chiffon that fell to the floor behind her and wafted gracefully as she moved.

Taking it from the wardrobe, she held it up for Joan to see.

'That's lovely. It'll look beautiful with your hair.'

'Feel free to borrow it. Your hair is brown like mine, so it'll suit you too.'

Joan laughed. 'My hair is brown, but it's nothing like yours. Yours is dark and rich. Mine is an ordinary old brown – but that won't stop me borrowing the dress.'

'Were you able to take some holiday so you can go and investigate your family?'

'I'm going in the middle of May. I'll travel down on the Friday and come back on the Sunday afternoon.'

'That won't give you much time there. Won't you need longer?'

'There's no knowing until I get there. I could have got more time off, but only if I'd waited a few more weeks for it. I'd prefer to go sooner rather than later.'

'Are you sure it's not worth asking your grandmother again?' Mabel asked. 'If she knows you're prepared to go to these lengths ... '

Joan shook her head. 'She's refused to say a word on the subject and I shan't ask her again. This is something I have to do. It's important.'

'Have you told Bob you're going away?'

'Not yet, but I will. He deserves to know the reason why. I have to solve the mystery of my family name.'

Mabel gave a snort of laughter. 'That sounds like the title of an Agatha Christie novel.'

'It sounds more like Enid Blyton to me,' said Joan. 'On the subject of books – you, my girl, will be stepping into your very own Ursula Bloom novel this evening, and you know what those books are like. They always have happy endings.'

There was only one thing better than being all dressed up and walking into a brightly lit ballroom and that was being on the arm of a handsome man in uniform as you did so. Mabel pretended not to notice the heads that turned Harry's way, but really she was thrilled, so thrilled that it wouldn't bother her – well, not much – if any of his old chums were there. It had been from overhearing a conversation between some girls that she had learned the devastating news that Harry had originally been set on marrying her for her money. But so what if any of those old friends were present? She and Harry had sorted out their problem and that was the only thing that mattered. Mabel's spine stiffened defiantly. If she ever had the chance to set those girls straight – yes, and Algy as well, the fellow who was the real owner of the Austin Ten Harry had passed off as his own – she would do so with her head held high.

Harry found them a table and bought drinks, but it wasn't long before they were on the dance floor, quickstepping and waltzing with one another, neither of them having any wish to change partners. As a foxtrot came to an end and the dancers applauded the band, the evening's master of ceremonies entered the stage, standing behind the microphone to welcome everyone and tell them how much money had already been raised for the Spitfire through ticket sales.

'As well as the usual ballroom dances,' he went on, 'we'll be inviting you to take part in old favourites such as the Gay Gordons and the heel-and-toe polka.'

'Oh, good,' Mabel murmured. Grandad had taught her these dances and she could still hear his voice in her head, reminding her of the steps, every time she danced the military two-step or the Dashing White Sergeant.

'And a word of warning for the gentlemen,' continued the MC. 'If, when a tango is announced, you decide to leave the floor, you'll be asked to pay a sixpenny forfeit.'

This was greeted with laughter and cheers from the girls, as everybody knew that plenty of men generally made a dash for their drinks the moment the band struck up a tango. Mabel laughed too, but she caught hold of Harry's arm and gave it a squeeze. He was good at the tango.

It was a wonderful evening. Mabel and Harry joined the other couples on the crowded floor, then sat out a few dances while they caught their breath and sipped their drinks.

'Take your partners for the St Bernard's Waltz!' The master of ceremonies invited everyone, and there was a good-humoured rush to find places in the large circle that formed around the dance floor.

'Not the St Bernard's Waltz,' groaned Harry, feigning reluctance. 'It's so old-fashioned.'

Laughing, Mabel pulled him to his feet, smiling an appeal at two couples, who made space between them for her and Harry. Stepping into a ballroom hold with Harry sent a shiver through her. No matter how many times she danced with him, that moment when she slipped into his arms always sent fireworks fizzing through her.

Harry glanced round. 'Just making sure I'm facing the correct way.'

All the gentlemen had their backs towards the centre of the circle. The band struck up the introduction and the dancers began on the same beat. This was another one

Grandad had taught her and Mabel heard his voice in her head. 'Side, together, side, stamp-stamp. Back, together, in, two, out, two. Twirl and waltz ... and pass the girl on.'

Harry loosened his hold and Mabel moved to the next man in the circle to start again. It was an easy dance, the sort that at a family gathering would see children dancing with their grandparents, just as she had done, and the room filled with good humour and happy memories.

Half a dozen times, Mabel was passed to her new partner and then – and then—

Seeing her next partner, she stopped. Stopped dead. Right there on the dance floor. The sequence started again with its side, together, side, stamp-stamp, and the couple behind Mabel dodged around her.

Gil. *Gil*, in army uniform. That lean face, those keen eyes. Exactly as she remembered from what felt like a million years ago; as familiar as if she had seen him yesterday.

'Hello, Mabel,' said the man she had once believed was the love of her life.

Chapter Five

Drat. Jimmy had left his PT kit at home. Dot clicked her tongue. Did it really matter? PT these days wasn't what it used to be. Sometimes the kids were taken down the allotments to dig for victory. Other times, they might do first aid, which, if their Jimmy was to be believed, provided splendid opportunities for trussing up classmates you weren't keen on. Jimmy was a lad who needed his PT – races, rounders, anything to use up his energy.

Which brought Dot back to the problem at hand. Jimmy was stopping the night with her and Reg and would be going to school from here in the morning. Should she dash round to Sheila's and fetch his PT kit? Trust him to have forgotten it – aye, and trust Sheila an' all. All said and done, it was her responsibility. She was his mother.

Dot padded quietly upstairs and pushed open the door to the bedroom that had once been Archie and Harry's when they were boys. Now Harry's little lad was asleep in there. He stayed with her and Reg a couple of nights every week to give his mum a break, though why any mother would want or need a break from her child was beyond Dot's understanding. As she looked down at Jimmy, her heart turned to mush. He looked like an angel when he was asleep. Dot loved having him to stay overnight – adored it, in fact. You sometimes heard grandparents joke about handing 'em back to their parents when they'd had enough, but Dot had never felt like that, not once. Jimmy and Jenny meant the world to her.

She sighed. Yes, of course she would go and fetch Jimmy's PT kit. There would be no time to sort it out in the morning as she was on an early shift and would be crawling out of bed at half past stupid, leaving Reg to see Jimmy off to school. Reg was out tonight on ARP duty, which meant she would have to leave Jimmy alone in the house while she nipped out, but it wouldn't be for long. It was five minutes each way, less than that if she hurried. She would knock next door and ask them to look after Jimmy if necessary, which meant if the siren went. Eh, it came to summat when you had to make arrangements for your grandson to be looked after in a life-or-death situation just for the sake of a PT kit.

A few minutes later, she was on her way through the pitch-dark streets, her torch with its tissue-dimmed light providing what guidance it could. DST was due to start next month – double summer time. What would that be like? Lighter evenings stretching on for ages were difficult to imagine.

At Sheila's, Dot opened the letter-box flap and slid her fingers inside, feeling for the string. She pulled the key through and let herself in, shutting the door softly behind her. It was just as dark inside as it was outside. There was no sound. Sheila was either tucked up fast asleep after a twelve-hour shift at the munitions or else out with her friend Rosa. Dot wasn't keen on Rosa. Her mother had had a reputation for being free with her favours and Dot remembered Rosa earning a bit of a reputation herself after she left school. Marriage seemed to have settled her down, but now that her husband was away, she wasn't exactly stopping home every night with her knitting.

Dot didn't switch on the light. It was best not to cause any disturbance, just in case Sheila was asleep. She used the dim light from her torch to guide her to the kitchen, where she played the beam around the room and pursed her lips at what lay before her. Did that make her an evil mother-in-law? What if Sheila caught her checking the kitchen in the dead of night! But Dot couldn't help herself. It was second nature to her to give other women's kitchens the once-over and it was second, third and fourth nature to do it to Sheila's.

Through the open scullery door, the washing-up sat upside down on the wooden draining board. Why couldn't Sheila use a tea towel instead of leaving the crocks out to dry? In the kitchen, the bread board was still out – well, that was asking for mice, that was. One side of the kitchen table was covered by a sheet of newspaper on which sat a pair of shoes and a tin of Cherry Blossom with its lid half off and altogether too close for comfort – for Dot's comfort, anyroad – to the sugar bowl, inside which a spoon lay discarded, encrusted with sugar. Not only had Sheila dunked a wet spoon in the bowl, it wasn't even the right spoon. It was a teaspoon and Dot knew full well that a boxed set of a sugar bowl and sugar spoon had been Archie and Pammy's wedding present to Harry and Sheila. The softened beam of torchlight caught a trail of sugar crystals scattered across the table. A small mirror was propped up against the milk bottle, beside a saucer full of cigarette ash. Honest to God, if Dot hadn't already privately christened her Sheila the Slattern, she would be tempted to think of her as Fag Ash Lil.

It wasn't just fag ash either, but fire ashes an' all. When had that ash pan last been emptied? A knitted jumper of Jimmy's had been slung over the back of one of the kitchen chairs and even in the torchlight, Dot could see the gaping hole in the elbow. Those threads needed catching and darning in or a bigger hole would grow and, before you knew it, there would be hardly any jumper left. Over another chair lay Sheila's swing coat. Aye, and she had fixed that loose button, which was more than could be said for her son's holey jumper. A single green-and-white leather peep-toe slingback sat on the floor – aye, and that floor hadn't been swept for a day or two, neither.

Judgement boiled up inside Dot and she had to remind herself that she wasn't meant to be here. Where was Jimmy's PT bag? Oh yes – beside the bread bin. A home-made drawstring bag with his initials embroidered on it in blue for Manchester City, not made by his mum, mark you, not made by the woman whose job it was and who should be proud to do it, but made by his ever-loving nan, that's who.

Dot swiped it, gave it a shake in case of crumbs and returned to the hall way. As she was shutting the kitchen door, she heard a sound from upstairs. She was about to call, 'Don't fret, love. It's only me,' when she heard – no, it couldn't be … yes, it was – a man's voice.

Harry! Dot's heart went wild with excitement for all of half a second before her insides turned to ice.

It couldn't be Harry. He was in North Africa.

Oh, dear God.

Part of her wanted to storm up the stairs and play merry ruddy heck, but her body had gone weak. She would be lucky if her legs could carry her home.

Somehow, she made it down the hallway without staggering, opened the front door and, with shaking hands, closed it silently behind her.

Oh, dear heaven. Oh, Harry … Oh, Harry …

Had Sheila the Slattern turned into Sheila the Slut?

It wasn't until Gil said, 'Shall we sit down and talk?' that Mabel realised she was still standing there, staring. Gil extended a hand to guide her off the floor. Her hand reached out of its own volition, but before her hungry fingers could brush his, Harry's arm snaked around her waist.

'Who's this? Aren't you going to introduce us?'

She fought a mad urge to pull free. What was it to her if Gil saw her with another man? They had been over and done with long since, blasted apart by guilt. She had barely been able to look at him after what she ... they ... she had done to Althea. Will, Ollie and Gil had all attended the funeral, and afterwards Gil had sought her out and told her he intended to join up, but what had anything mattered beyond her terrible loss?

'Go, then,' she had said.

And he had.

She had never expected to see him again, had never wanted to, not when grief and guilt had distorted her world into a cold, desperate landscape. But her vicious self-loathing had eventually subsided into a gentler focus and she had moved on with her life.

With Harry.

Harry had let her down badly, but she had taken him back. She knew that people weren't perfect. She, of all people, knew they weren't perfect.

She hadn't responded to Harry's demand for an introduction quickly enough. He introduced himself to Gil, who responded likewise. Harry threw back his shoulders. Was he squaring up to Gil? Gil's gaze was locked on Mabel. It was that moment in the lantern-bedecked garden all over again. Mabel's heart thumped.

'You'd best find your girlfriend, Gilchrist, if you want the next dance.' Harry held Mabel more tightly. 'Lucky for me, I've already got mine.'

'Very lucky,' said Gil.

She wanted to say – she didn't know what she wanted to say, and anyway, the chance was lost, because Harry whirled her into the middle of the floor the instant the band struck up the opening bars of a waltz.

'Who was that?' Harry asked.

'He told you. Iain Gilchrist.'

'You know what I mean.'

'Someone I used to know.' She resisted the urge to look round to see Gil's partner.

'Used to know well, I'd say. You were dumbstruck.'

'I haven't seen him in a long time. Not since before the war.' Before the war, when she was a hundred years younger and deeply in love, when she had believed with all her heart that she had met the man she was going to marry. But that was before Althea died and guilt had consumed her. Cutting all ties with Gil had been the only thing to do.

Harry made an effort to laugh. 'It's not exactly flattering to a chap when his girl goes all gooey at the sight of another bloke, especially one she used to know.'

'I didn't go all gooey.'

'I should hope not, unless it's over me.' After a moment, he added, 'Do you remember when I asked if you'd had a serious boyfriend before?'

'Goodness, that was ages ago. Fancy remembering that.' But she did remember it. She remembered dodging the question.

'You never gave me an answer. Is Gilchrist the reason why?'

'You're being ridiculous, but, yes, Gil was my first love. It was a long time ago and it all went completely wrong.'

'Well, you've got me now.' Harry nuzzled her hair, his voice a low rumble. 'And things are completely right.'

Gil appeared beside them. 'May I cut in?'

'No.' Harry changed direction.

Mabel looked back, trying to see Gil, but Harry steered her into the throng.

'That was rude,' she said.

'You can't blame me for wanting to keep you to myself, especially given how much I have to make up to you. You know how badly I want to make it up to you, don't you?'

She couldn't help melting. 'Yes, I do.'

Harry's hold tightened. 'I love those words. "I do." And I love hearing them from you.'

The waltz was followed by a quickstep, after which the MC announced a gentlemen's excuse-me dance.

'I'm not sharing you.' Harry led her to their table and sat her down. 'It's my job to protect you from all the Romeos out there.'

'Excuse me.'

Mabel looked up to see Gil smiling at her. She glanced at his hand, hating herself for looking. No ring.

'We're sitting this one out.' Harry made it sound matey, but there was an edge to his voice. 'Go and excuse someone on the dance floor.'

Gil didn't budge. 'May I have the pleasure?'

Mabel stood up. 'It's only an excuse-me,' she told Harry.

She moved into Gil's arms. The dance steps were the same and the dance hold was the same, yet dancing with Gil was different to dancing with Harry. Gil was clean-limbed, lacking Harry's bulkier muscle, and he held her lightly. She had forgotten how it felt to dance in his arms – or had she? Had her senses been waiting for this all along?

'I never thought I'd see you again,' said Gil. 'You're just as beautiful. Your hair suits you like that. It's how I remember you, with your hair swept back from your face and left to hang loose.'

'It's good to see you.'

'Is that chap your boyfriend?'

'Yes.'

61

'I don't want to cause trouble for you, but when I saw you in the St Bernard's Waltz, I couldn't leave it like that. I had to speak to you. We never talked after Althea died and we should have.'

'I couldn't – not at the time. I couldn't bear it.'

'I know. I couldn't have discussed it back then either. But I've never been able to lay her to rest. However hard that is for me, it must be a hundred times worse for you. You were best friends all your lives.'

'I spent a long time hating myself for what I did to her,' said Mabel.

'What *we* did to her.'

'Thank you for saying that. I carried the burden alone for a long time, but I've moved on now.'

'With the help of your boyfriend.'

'I was going to say, with the help of the good friends I met through work.'

'What do you do?'

'I have a job on the railways.' She described her work as a lengthman.

Gil's serious face relaxed into a smile. 'I'm not surprised. The Mabel Bradshaw I knew had lots of spirit. Trust you to follow in your grandfather's footsteps.'

'You remember him being a wheeltapper?'

'Of course. I remember everything you told me.'

Of course. Why was she surprised? They had talked endlessly in the brief time they'd had and Gil had always been an attentive listener.

Leaving his right hand on her back, firm yet gentle, he released her hand, making a quick dive into his pocket. When he took her hand again, there was a small, torn-off piece of card between their palms.

'I hope you'll get in touch,' said Gil.

Her insides trembled. 'I don't know—'

'What I said about not wanting to cause trouble for you … I find I very much want to cause trouble, if it takes you away from your boyfriend and brings you back to me. I've never stopped loving you.'

Harry materialised and tapped Gil on the shoulder.

'Excuse me,' he said and whirled Mabel away in his arms.

Chapter Six

There had been at least one raid every night from Monday to Friday. Would the Luftwaffe leave them alone over Easter? Joan met up with Bob and his sisters at the big house in Chorlton that belonged to the Conservative Association, where the WVS was going to hold an afternoon of fun and games for local children. Walking through the gateway with a tin of Mrs Grayson's fairy cakes under her arm and her gas mask slung over her shoulder, Joan's breath caught at the sight of the Hubbles. She loved them all dearly, but goodness, sometimes it was hard to see them all together, their family intact, when she had lost her one and only sister. She plastered a smile on her face and went over to them.

Maureen had on her WVS hat, its ribbon adorned with her badge, and she wore the green uniform jacket over a cream-and-amber striped dress. She hadn't bought the rest of the uniform, as it was too costly for her means. Her chestnut-brown hair fell in abundance over her shoulders in a mass of large bouncy curls that made Joan wonder how she managed to get any sleep with her rollers in. Beside Maureen, Petal wore a pretty headscarf tied at the nape of her neck beneath her fair hair. Both of them were lookers and Joan had always felt an affinity with Glad, the youngest, who, while perfectly nice-looking, wasn't a stunner. Joan, too, had had a ravishingly beautiful sister, without being a dazzler herself.

As she approached them, Joan's heart gave a happy little flip at the sight of Bob. Gratitude washed through her that

Bob still loved her after the madness of her wanting Steven. He had pushed his flat cap to the back of his head, emphasising his boyish good looks, and stood with his hands in his pockets, taking them out when he saw her, a smile warming his face as he came towards her and greeted her with a kiss on the cheek that might look like no more than a peck to any onlooker, but the loving expression in his eyes was for her alone and her skin tingled.

'This is a trip down memory lane for you two, isn't it?' said Petal.

'Don't listen,' said Bob. 'They've been making cooing noises about it all the way here.'

'This is where our dear brother made such an impression on you, isn't it?' said Glad.

'Never mind me,' said Joan. 'Get him to tell you about the impression he made on Mrs Parker.'

She made light of it, but actually it was rather special to be back here with Bob in the place where they had first met almost a year ago, when they had taken part in a first-aid event to assess their suitability to become members of the first-aid teams that assisted during the air raids. Their 'casualty' that afternoon had been Mrs Parker, who had entered into the spirit of the event with great gusto and had flirted outrageously with Bob.

'Shall we go inside?' asked Petal. 'The children will be arriving in half an hour.'

Soon they all had jobs to do. Glad and Petal were put on sandwich-making duty and Bob helped the other chaps set out tables and chairs. Joan was given a box of old beakers. She half filled each one with water and set them out along the tables, following two girls who were setting out paints and brushes. As she passed Maureen, who was cutting a roll of lining paper into large pieces, she stopped.

'For making Easter bonnets,' Maureen said before she could ask.

It turned out to be a jolly afternoon. The children painted their bonnets with varying degrees of skill, after which they were given ping-pong balls to decorate in lieu of hard-boiled eggs. In the absence of a hill to roll them down – the WVS lady in charge refused to let them use the road's natural slope – Bob and a group of the oldest boys constructed ramps, using upside-down trestle tables, which resulted in high-speed egg-rolling that had the children whooping with excitement.

'I hope the siren doesn't go off,' one of the WVS women said drily, 'because I'm not sure we'd hear it.'

After the Easter-bonnet parade, the children sat down to a simple tea of paste sandwiches and squash, after which it was time for them to go home. When the clearing away was finished, Maureen filled the urn and made tea for everyone. With a small jerk of his head, Bob indicated to Joan that they should slip away for a few minutes. He led her round the side of the building to the fire escape.

'Remember this?'

She laughed. 'We had to clatter up here because the staircase was supposed to be impassable in our pretend emergency.'

They sat side by side on the metal steps, arms brushing.

'I'm glad we have a few minutes alone,' said Bob.

'So am I,' Joan replied. 'I've got something to tell you.'

'Something good, I hope.'

'I'm not sure yet if it's good, but it's certainly interesting. It's something I've found out about my family. When Gran was taken into hospital, I saw her marriage certificate. She isn't Mrs Foster. She's Mrs Henshaw.'

Bob turned to her, his handsome face clouded by a frown. 'Say that again.'

'Gran's real name is Henshaw and so is mine.'

'Are you sure? It doesn't automatically make you a Henshaw. Your gran might have been Mrs Foster when she had your dad and then she married Mr Henshaw later on. But when your parents died and she knew she was going to bring you up, maybe she decided to be Mrs Foster so she'd have the same name as you and Letitia.'

Joan shook her head. 'Do you imagine I didn't think of that myself?' A sigh found its way up from deep inside her. 'She gave me my birth certificate. My father was a Henshaw and I'm a Henshaw.'

'But why ... ?'

'I've no idea. Gran won't talk about it. Believe me, I've tried to get her to tell me, but she refuses.'

'Well, that's ... Actually, I'm not sure what to call it. Strange. Mystifying.'

'Frustrating,' said Joan. 'But not for much longer, I hope. You see, now that I've got my birth certificate, I know the exact address where my parents were living when I was born. I've arranged to take some time off work and I want to go down there and see what I can find out.'

Bob put down his mug on the step beside his feet and took her hand. 'Sweetheart, it was twenty years ago and your parents are both long gone. What do you hope to find?'

'I don't know. Maybe I won't uncover anything, but I have to have a go. My birth certificate also has my mother's maiden name – Hopkins. With that information as well as the address and the Henshaw name, there must be something I can find out. You aren't going to try to talk me out of it, are you?' She would be bitterly disappointed if he did.

'Wouldn't dream of it. Thank you for telling me. It can't be easy, finding out something like that.'

'It was rather a shock.' Joan's heartbeat was getting louder. 'There's something else I have to tell you and it isn't something I've only just found out. I've always known it and – and I'm worried you'll be ashamed of me.'

'Because of keeping quiet about it?'

'Just because of ... what it is. I say "just". There's no "just" about it. It's horrible. It's shameful.' Her insides crumpled and she had to stop.

Bob's arm came around her, snuggling her close. He pressed his temple to hers. 'Tell me,' he said softly.

'I have to ask you to keep this secret. I know it's rotten to ask you not to tell your family when you're all so close, but I have to ask. You'll understand why when I tell you. It's my parents – well, my mother. She isn't dead. That's a story Gran made up years ago. Letitia and I were supposed to be orphans, because that was respectable. The truth is ... ' Once she had uttered these words, there would be no taking them back. 'The truth is, my mother left us. She ran away. She had a – there was another man. She ran off with him and left us. Poor Daddy died of a broken heart. So now you know.'

Bob was quiet for a few moments. 'I've been wondering about the best time and place to do something and now feels like the natural occasion.'

'The time and place for what?'

He removed his arm from around her. Rising, he took her mug and set it on a step, taking her hand in his to lead her down the iron stairs to the ground.

'Where are we going?' Joan asked as Bob took her round to the front of the old house, past the shrubbery and across the lawn to the drive.

In the middle of the driveway, he stopped and turned her to him.

'You have entrusted me with your family secret. I swear not to breathe a word about it to anybody. You're going to try to find out why your grandmother changed your surname. There's no way of knowing what you might find out about your family. I can see how much this matters to you and I hope you find what you're looking for, whatever it is.'

'I've no idea what I'm looking for. Just … answers.'

'That's what I mean. Who knows what those answers will be? Whatever happens, I'll be here – always. I can't pretend not to be shocked at what your mother did, but I'm not shocked in a way that would make me turn away from you. Mostly what I feel is concern for the way you and Letitia must have felt while you were growing up. When you set off to find the answers about your family, I won't care what those answers are. It doesn't matter to me what you find out – I'm expressing this badly. What I mean is, of course it matters. I don't want you to be hurt or let down. All I want is your happiness. But whatever happens, it won't make any difference to me or to the way I feel about you. You have my complete support in this – and my complete love.'

'Bob … '

'You're the best girl I've ever met and you're my girl. I can't believe how lucky I am. I want to take care of you and part of taking care of you is accepting that you don't come from the perfect family. Do you remember when we stood here before? It was the day we met and I asked you to come out dancing with me and you said no.'

The change of tack sent surprise fluttering through her. 'As soon as I said it, I knew I'd made a mistake.'

'I'm going to ask you another question, here, in this place. You might not have the perfect family, but I do and I want you to be part of it. The best way I can express my love and support for you … '

As Bob sank down on to one knee, Joan caught her breath.

'... is to take your hand in mine and ask you, Joan Foster, if you will do me the honour of agreeing to be my wife?'

Joan was aware of a ripple in the air and realised they had an audience a short distance away, but she didn't care. Her thoughts and senses scattered all over the place, then suddenly rushed back into position, giving her a clarity of feeling and a certainty that she had never known before.

A breath burst out of her, accompanied by tears. She couldn't speak – but she could nod vigorously and smile and nod again. As Bob stood up and took her in his arms to kiss her, Joan was vaguely aware of applause before she melted into his embrace.

Joan couldn't stop smiling on Sunday afternoon as she made her way to Bob's house for tea. She didn't think she had stopped smiling since yesterday afternoon. From the Con Club, she and Bob had gone straight to Millington's the jeweller's to buy a ring, which, joy of joys, was precisely the right size, so she hadn't had to leave it in the shop to be altered. Then they had gone to Wilton Close, where their news was greeted with all the happiness Joan could have hoped for. Now she was going to Bob's house, not as his girlfriend but as his fiancée – his fiancée! Elation bubbled up inside her. It wasn't just Bob she loved. She loved his whole family. They had made her welcome right from the start.

She was wearing the dress she had made for Letitia to go dancing in. The lilac had been chosen to suit Letitia's fair colouring, but it looked nice on Joan too, and the style looked very good on her. She had always liked elbow-length sleeves and the rounded neck had no collar, giving a carefree look to the dress.

She had barely reached Edge Lane, which would take her to Stretford, when she saw Bob coming to meet her en route. There was nothing unusual in that, but today his sisters had joined him, all in pretty dresses and short-sleeved cardigans. The girls came flying towards her, hanging on to their hats, and she was enveloped in hugs, perfume and squeals.

'Let's see the ring,' Petal demanded. 'Bob said he took you straight to the jeweller's the moment you said yes. Oh, it's perfect. Which one of you chose it?'

'I wanted us to choose together,' said Joan, 'but the moment I saw this, I knew.' Never mind her future sisters-in-law gazing at it, she could hardly tear her own eyes away from the dainty sapphire flanked on either side by a small diamond.

Maureen laughed. 'Starting as you mean to go on? Let him think he's choosing when really all the decisions are yours.'

Bob joined them. He was wearing his tweed jacket with the elbow patches and his flat cap. His dark eyes, always warm and kind, now had a new glow in them. Joan wanted to hug the whole wide world. It wasn't just Bob's presence that made her happy. It was because, with Maureen and Glad each linking arms with her, she felt accepted. The Hubbles had always made her feel wanted.

'I suppose you want us to give you your fiancée back,' Glad said to her brother.

Bob grinned. 'If you're sure you've quite finished with her.'

The girls let go of Joan. Taking her hands, Bob kissed her cheek to a sisterly chorus of 'Ahh'. Joan laughed, feeling herself blush. She wasn't used to being the centre of attention. At Gran's house, Letitia had been the important one.

'We've knocked your hat about with all that hugging,' said Petal, straightening it for her.

'We must get home to help Mum,' said Maureen. 'We'll go on ahead and leave you lovebirds to follow.'

'Good show,' said Bob, deadpan. 'Off you trot. We'll time our arrival for when all the work's done.'

The three girls hurried away, chattering.

'It was kind of them to come with you to meet me,' said Joan.

'Couldn't stop them. They're thrilled to bits. The whole family is.'

'What did Maureen mean about helping your mum?'

'The girls aren't the only ones who are thrilled. Mum and Dad are too and Mum's got the whole family coming round.'

'The whole family?' All Joan had ever had was Letitia and Gran.

'As much of it as she could muster. You'll like them. She's got two sisters and Dad's got a brother.'

'It's going to be a bit of a squeeze.'

'You'll have to sit on my knee then, won't you?'

'We'll see,' she teased.

'Please do. If you don't, Auntie Florrie might want to.'

Joan felt a little flutter. It was one thing to be the centre of attention with Bob's immediate family. She would have relished that in these wonderful circumstances. But the thought of these extra relations made her feel a bit shy.

However, the moment she set foot in the Hubbles' two-up two-down and was drawn into Mrs Hubble's arms, she knew the big family occasion was exactly the right thing. Bob's relatives were delighted to meet her and it was obvious how highly they thought of Bob, which filled Joan with pride.

'You're one of my lasses now,' Mrs Hubble said softly into her ear, 'and about time an' all.'

'My turn,' said Mr Hubble. 'Let me give my new daughter a hug.'

A lump stuck in Joan's throat. She was going to have a father. For the first time since she could remember, she was going to have a dad. After growing up gazing longingly at the studio portrait of Daddy that had pride of place in their parlour, she was going to have a father in real life.

'Where are my sisters?' Mrs Hubble looked round. 'I especially want you to meet Florrie.'

'Oh aye? Am I not important enough for you?' demanded a middle-aged woman in a pale green twinset, her hair piled up in curls.

Bob appeared behind the woman, placing his hands on her shoulders as he told Joan, 'This is Auntie Marie.'

'And I'm Auntie Florrie.' Another woman appeared. She had a double chin and wore her fringe curled round like a sausage. 'And I can tell you now that you'll think me a lot more special than our Marie, because I'm the one what's going to offer you and Bob a roof over your heads when you get wed.'

Joan caught her breath. A home? Her first married home!

'I'm a widder,' said Auntie Florrie, 'and my four have all joined up, which leaves me rattling about like a pea in a drum, so you're more than welcome.'

Never mind that Gran had brought her up to keep her hands to herself. Joan flung her arms around Auntie Florrie.

'Eh, pet,' said Auntie Florrie, hugging her in return and giving her a smacking kiss on her cheek. 'There's nowt to stop you setting the date now, is there?'

Chapter Seven

It was a shame when the siren sounded on Easter Monday morning, shortly before Dot was due to set off for her early shift, because, other than that, the Easter weekend had been clear of air raids. The same couldn't be said for her mind. Clear was the last thing it was. She couldn't rid herself of the memory of that man's voice in Sheila's house. Afterwards, she had cursed herself for not taking decisive action on the spot, for not yelling up the stairs and making her presence, not to mention her outrage, well and truly felt. Having not acted instantly, she now felt herself to be at a disadvantage. She might have had good reason to let herself into Sheila's house in the dead of night, but if she tackled Sheila now, it might rebound on her. Sheila had a sharp mind and could easily turn the tables and accuse her of snooping. Anyroad, she couldn't afford to fall out with Sheila. She couldn't risk pushing Sheila into doing something barmy, like taking up permanently with another bloke. She had to sort this out in such a way that Harry would have a wife to come home to and no one, except herself, would be any the wiser.

She tried not to think about it at work, but it was never far from her mind. She had decided what to do and could only hope her plan would be a success. When she clocked off, she walked briskly out of the station, feeling very much the woman with a mission – well, two missions, actually. It wasn't just Sheila who needed sorting out. She wanted to speak to Alison an' all.

Alison first. She knew Alison was down to do overtime in Hunts Bank, the admin building, and should be clocking off shortly. Dot hung about on the opposite side of the road, keeping an eye on a couple of doorways, waiting for Alison to appear. Ah, there she was, with her brown hair neatly curled under and sitting on her shoulders. That smart hat with the topstitching and the upturned brim suited her, showing off her face.

Dot crossed the road, calling to her.

'Have you been working today too?' sighed Alison. 'I can't wait to get home.'

'Me an' all,' said Dot, 'but I wanted a quick word first.'

'Is something wrong?'

'No. Summat lovely has happened and I want to have a word with you about it. Are you walking to Piccadilly for your bus? I can get one from there an' all.'

As they walked along Market Street, past all the shops with their windows criss-crossed with anti-blast tape, the sound of the siren lifted into the air, sending shivers all over Dot's skin.

'Trust this to happen on a bank holiday,' said Alison, 'when we can't shelter in a shop basement.'

'We'll have to make a run for it to the shelters in Piccadilly,' said Dot. 'You go on ahead. Don't wait for me.'

'Don't be daft. We'll stick together.'

Alison grasped Dot's arm and they ran down the road, clutching their hats, their handbags and gas masks swinging and bumping. Seeing a young mother struggling with a pushchair at the same time as hanging on to her son of about five, Dot pulled free of Alison.

'Here, love, you come along with us. You carry the little lad and I'll take the pushchair.'

'Give me your gas mask,' Alison said to the young mum. 'We're nearly there.'

The entrance to the shelter was flanked by a pile of sandbags.

'Take the kiddie out,' a man told Dot, 'and I'll carry the pushchair in for you.'

They made their way down the steps and found places on the long wooden benches that grew more fiendishly uncomfortable the longer you sat on them. With shy thanks, the young mother strapped her sleeping infant back in the pushchair and sat the older child on her knee. She fished a piece of string out of her pocket and started doing cat's cradle, which the boy seemed to find fascinating.

'What did you want to talk about?' Alison asked.

Dot turned to look her full in the face. 'Joan and Bob are engaged.'

Alison's eyes flickered. 'When did that happen?'

'Saturday. I only know because I called round to see Mrs Cooper.' Dot waited.

'That's wonderful news,' said Alison.

'Yes, it is,' Dot agreed. 'I don't want to stick my nose in, but will you listen to a word of advice?'

Alison smiled, but Dot wasn't fooled. The girl's eyes had narrowed, making her look wary.

'When you see Joan, give her a big hug. Say "You beat me to it" or some such, as if you're making a joke.'

'But—'

'But you don't feel like joking? I know, chick. You're fed up because your Paul hasn't asked you yet and now Bob's got there first. If you're feeling put out, keep it to yourself. This is Joan's happy time and goodness knows, she deserves it. You might not have a ring on your finger, but you've got both your parents and your sister.'

Alison nodded.

'Good girl,' said Dot.

Good girl? Poor girl, more like, thought Dot. A few months ago, Alison had confided in her how anxious she was for Paul to pop the question. The trouble was that with both their mothers and all their friends watching him like hawks, Alison feared he might never find the right moment.

The all-clear sounded after half an hour and Dot and Alison helped the young mother get her children and the pushchair out of the shelter. Saying goodbye, Dot headed for her bus stop. She had another job to do before she went home. She had given Alison a nudge and now she had to sort out Sheila.

In Withington, she headed for the rest centre in the Sunday-school building in Burton Road. The biggest room contained makeshift sleeping quarters, with sleeping bags on top of mats, and lines of rickety-looking put-you-up beds. Another room had racks of donated clothes and boxes of linen and household bits and pieces. There was a row of tables for people to sit at while they were interviewed about their circumstances and given help and information, and a few rows of chairs for folk to sit on while they waited.

Dot took a seat, feeling uncomfortable. What if she was seen? She didn't want the neighbours tittle-tattling. If necessary, she would say she was holding the place in the queue for a friend.

She was doing this for Harry. It was horrible to think of Sheila being unfaithful, but more than that, she couldn't bear the idea of her darling boy being hurt. Life was hard enough for him at present without that. Dot owed it to him to keep his family together – and she had to do it without getting into a slanging match with Sheila. She was doing it for Jimmy an' all, and never mind that her instincts were boiling over with the need to grab all his worldly goods from Sheila's house and move him in with her and Reg permanently. Harry, Sheila and Jimmy were a family, and that was the way they would stay.

When it was her turn, Dot sat at the table with her handbag on her lap. A WVS lady in full uniform gave her a bright smile, but her eyes were tired.

'How do I add a house to the list for billeting?' Dot asked.

'You need to see the billeting officer ... ' the woman began.

'If I give you the details, could you pass them on? I work full-time, you see, and it'd be such a help to me if you could.'

The woman reached for a pen. 'Your address, please?'

'It's not my house. It's my daughter-in-law's. She's not got a big house, but it has three bedrooms. There's only her and my grandson.'

'Really it's your daughter-in-law who should be here saying this.'

'I know, but ... ' Dot leaned forward, dropping her voice as if confiding. 'Between you, me and the gatepost, she's not best keen, but it's what my son wants.' God forgive her for lying. 'He's away fighting.'

'I'll see what I can do.'

'Before I give you the details, could I ask one thing? Could you keep it secret who put our Sheila's house forward? I'm doing this for my son, but she'll think—'

'That you're the interfering mother-in-law.' The woman nodded. 'Believe me, I understand completely. My daughter-in-law is exactly the same. What's the address, please?'

Satisfaction sent warmth through Dot's body. Having someone, or perhaps even a couple, billeted on her would cramp Sheila's style.

*

For once, there wasn't a queue in the buffet and Mabel went straight to the counter, where Mrs Jessop started pouring without having to ask. A piece of string caught Mabel's eye. One end was tied to a block of wood and a teaspoon was tied to the other end.

Mrs Jessop saw her looking. 'Cutlery is starting to be in short supply, so I've decided to provide one teaspoon that no one can walk off with.'

'Good idea.' Mabel handed over three pennies and picked up her cup and saucer, weaving her way between the tables to get to where Cordelia, Dot, Alison and Persephone were sitting.

'Is this all of us?' asked Persephone. 'Or are we expecting Joan?'

Mabel laughed. 'She'll come dancing in with the spotlight on her. She's so happy and she's got a ring to flaunt as well.'

Mabel was delighted that Joan was finally engaged, especially after the Steven business. Mabel, Mrs Cooper and Mrs Grayson had been the first to see the ring, which Mabel felt was an honour, but she had experienced a pang of sadness too. In normal family circumstances, Mrs Foster would have been the first to see it, but she and Joan were on difficult terms these days. Mabel felt a comfortable warmth inside her chest at the thought of the love she received from Mumsy and Pops. How fortunate she was to be so secure in her parents' love.

It wasn't long before Joan appeared. Ignoring the short queue that had grown at the counter, she headed for their table. A chair scraped as Alison got up and went to meet her, giving her a hug and then seizing her hand.

'Let's see it,' said Dot.

Joan extended her hand to show off her pretty sapphire and diamonds. Everyone cooed over it and made a fuss of her. Joan's face was radiant. After the strain her expression had shown since Letitia's death, it was good to see.

'I'll fetch a cup of tea,' said Joan when everyone had finished admiring her ring.

'I'll get it,' said Persephone. 'You sit down.'

'Thanks, but I want to show Mrs Jessop.'

'You want to show the whole queue,' teased Mabel.

'I heard you got no work done today,' Alison added, 'because you were busy showing all the passengers.'

'Pay them no mind, chick.' Dot gave Joan a little push. 'Off you go and show Mrs Jessop. She'll be chuffed.'

As Joan headed for the end of the queue, they all looked at one another and laughed, a loving sound filled with the warmth they all felt towards her.

When she returned, Cordelia asked, 'Have you told your grandmother?'

'Not yet. Bob and I are going to see her together.'

'I hope it breaks down the barrier,' said Cordelia.

Joan looked uncertain, then she smiled. 'Bob's folks are delighted. His mum said "About time an' all," and his sisters all wanted to try on the ring.'

'What did his father say?' asked Persephone.

Joan's blue eyes were suddenly bright with tears. 'He called me his "new daughter". I felt so wanted.'

'Eh, chick,' said Dot, 'it's grand to think of you being welcomed into your new family.'

'Bob's mum is thrilled to bits,' said Mabel. 'It's all she can talk about on the permanent way.'

Joan looked around the table. 'Thank you all for making a fuss, but that's enough about me. What were you talking about before I arrived?'

Dot laughed. 'Actually, we were talking about you and your ring.'

Mabel sat up straighter. 'If no one minds, there's something I'd like to ask you about.' She looked at her friends, struck anew by how dear they were to her, but she couldn't help feeling anxious. Their staunch support had made such a difference when she had been struggling with her guilt over Althea – but they hadn't been aware of the whole story then. Might that staunchness be about to falter? 'I need advice, but before you can understand the situation I'm in, I need to tell you the truth about something. It's to do with Althea.'

'Your friend who died?' said Alison. 'You told us about her.'

Pinpricks of shame touched Mabel's cheeks. 'I didn't tell you everything. I didn't dare.'

'That sounds serious,' said Joan.

'You're going to think badly of me.'

'Kindly refrain from telling me what I'm going to think before I have the chance to think it,' said Cordelia.

'Listen, love,' said Dot. 'Not so long ago, I sat at this table practically shaking in my shoes with nerves because I had to tell everyone about Edie Thirkle-as-was making a holy show of me in public, and I thought what you're thinking right now. You're asking yourself, what if they take against me? But no one took against me – including you. Have more faith in your friends.'

Mabel's shoulders relaxed as confidence raised its head. With her heart beating in a steady thump, she opened up for the very first time and revealed the whole truth about Althea, about her love for Gil that had turned out to be wholly one-sided, and about how Mabel and Gil had met and fallen deeply in love ... and the tragedy that had unfolded when Mabel had told Althea.

'She died hating and despising me and that has been so hard for me to live with.'

'Eh, chick,' Dot commiserated.

'What a dreadful thing to happen,' Persephone said in a quiet voice.

'But it's not as though you did anything wrong,' said Alison. 'You didn't steal Gil from her.'

'It isn't a question of right and wrong or who is to blame,' said Mabel. 'It's to do with Althea and me being as good as sisters. It's to do with us being best friends ever since we were children. I'm the last person, the very last, who should have hurt her. You've no idea how bad that final meeting was. She said – she said she'd never forgive me, and a few minutes later she was dead.'

There was a charged silence, then Cordelia spoke.

'And now you'll never know whether, in time, you might have settled your differences.'

'That's the trouble with death,' said Persephone. 'It doesn't happen at a time that's convenient for all concerned, with everything neatly wrapped up. It happens right in the middle of things.'

'It was brave of you to tell us,' said Dot. 'Has it helped to talk about it?'

'It's helped that you haven't denounced me for betraying my best friend,' said Mabel. 'But you see, this isn't what I really wanted to tell you. But I needed you all to understand about Althea before I could explain the rest.' Anxiety tightened inside the pit of her stomach. 'It's – it's Gil. He's come back.'

Everyone sat up straighter, though Mabel felt like sliding down in her seat as she felt their attention locked on her even more keenly. Quietly, she related what had taken place at the Spitfire dance.

'I'm afraid I didn't behave awfully well. I was so shocked. I hardly knew what to think, and Harry – well, let's say he wasn't exactly thrilled.'

'You mean he's jealous?' asked Dot.

'I think so.' Was that mealy-mouthed? She more than thought so. She knew so.

'Is there anything he should be jealous of?' Cordelia asked bluntly.

Heat rose in Mabel's face. 'Of course not.'

'Then what's the problem?' said Cordelia.

'Gil wants to see me again. We never saw one another properly after Althea died. He was at the funeral, but I was still in a state of shock, I think, and my parents stuck to me like glue. Everyone felt sorry for me because I'd been in the same accident. I couldn't look anyone in the eye in case they saw the truth on my face.'

'Do you mean you never spoke to Gil again?' said Alison.

'He told me he was joining up and I said, "Go, then," and he did, and that was that.'

'Until the other night,' said Dot.

'He said he'd never been able to lay Althea to rest and that struck a chord deep inside me.' Mabel's voice had sunk to little more than a whisper. She swallowed and blinked away a tear she didn't deserve to shed. 'That's how I feel too.'

Cordelia said gently, 'It sounds as if you and Gil have a lot to talk about. It'll be painful, but it might, to use his words, enable you to lay Althea to rest.'

Mabel drew a breath that was almost painful. 'Is that what the rest of you think?'

'Never mind us, love,' said Dot. 'It's what you think that matters. We'll stand by you, whatever.'

'I need to talk to Gil, I really do. Meeting him has stirred up things that I've tried so hard not to think about. I need to talk about what happened and Gil's the only person I can share it with in a – a meaningful way.'

'Then that's decided,' said Persephone, 'and Harry's job will be to take care of you and make you feel better afterwards.'

'Ah,' said Mabel.

'"Ah"?' Alison repeated. 'What's that supposed to mean?'

'In my experience,' said Dot drily, 'it usually means a complication.'

'Gil is serious about wanting to talk about Althea, he truly is. It was one of the first things he said to me. But the last thing he said, just before Harry practically wrenched me out of his arms on the dance floor, was that he's never stopped loving me. He wants us to get back together.'

Walking hand in hand, Joan and Bob turned the corner into Torbay Road. Joan's heart thumped. Gran would consider it flighty to hold hands in public, but she didn't let go. Instead, she held on tighter. Bob lifted her hand to his lips and kissed it.

Down the street stretched the long line of red-brick houses with bay windows, chimney stacks and black-tiled roofs. In front of each house was a small garden with a brick wall, but the flower beds that in happier times would have been bright with hyacinths and primulas were now given over to the frothy greenery of carrots and bursts of large leaves with creamy-white cauliflowers in the centre. Some folk had window boxes as well, with radishes and lettuces, and a few gardens had glass cloches to protect their tenderest plants.

At Gran's gate, Joan and Bob stopped.

'Ready?' Bob's voice was kind and there was understanding in his eyes.

'As ready as I'll ever be.'

Oh, it wasn't right! It shouldn't be like this when you were going to tell your closest relation that you were engaged. You should be anticipating exclamations and excitement, hugs and congratulations. That was the response they had received on Saturday afternoon in Wilton Close and again on Sunday at Bob's house.

With Gran, there was the possibility she might rake up the Steven business again. Or would she? She had always approved of Bob. Would she simply be grateful that Joan had seen sense? They wanted to tell her about the engagement so they could ask her permission for them to get married, and soon. Would Gran agree?

When she answered the door, Gran's glance went instantly to the linked hands and her faded eyebrows lifted as she turned her gaze on Joan.

Joan started to say hello, but Bob said in his usual cheerful voice, 'Good evening, Mrs Foster. May we come in? We've got some news for you.'

Gran pursed her lips for a moment, then stood back and let them enter. How different this house was to the one in Wilton Close – and Joan wasn't thinking about the extra space in her new home. It was the atmosphere. Under Mrs Cooper's genial eye, the Wilton Close house had a snug feel about it. In spite of her devastating bereavement, she ran a happy home. Gran's house was summed up by the net curtains in the parlour, which were thicker than nets normally were and made the room gloomy even on the brightest day, as if the Fosters lived in a sepia-coloured world ... which they always had, hadn't they? Gran, Letitia and Joan had lived in the shadow of the past, with the need to make Daddy proud, and under the clinging shame of what Estelle had done. The past was everywhere in this house – even more so now that Letitia was no longer with them.

Gran sat in the chair where she always sat, next to the hearth. Joan and Bob sat on the sofa.

'Well?' Gran demanded. 'What have you got to say?'

Joan felt a flare of annoyance. Why did Gran have to be so brusque? But she smiled and held out her hand, displaying the engagement ring that had captured her heart the moment she'd set eyes on it.

'We're engaged. Do you like the ring?'

Gran leaned forward. 'Very pretty.' Still that brusque voice. She wouldn't have been brusque if it had been Letitia and Steven sitting here. 'I hope things go well for you.'

'Thank you, Mrs Foster,' said Bob. 'My family is very happy about it and it means a lot to have your blessing as well. We aren't here just to make our announcement. We also want to ask for permission to get married this summer.'

'This summer?' Gran looked at Joan. 'You're not old enough.'

'That's why we need your permission,' said Joan.

Gran's voice sank into a hoarse whisper. 'How can you think of a wedding, with Letitia so recently gone?'

'That makes it all the more important,' said Joan. Her voice was steady. She had prepared this. 'I used to think that people should wait and look forward to special things, but not any more, not after what happened to Letitia. This is my chance for happiness and I want to seize it with both hands. So does Bob.'

'I've got a job for life,' said Bob. 'I won't ever be rich, but once the war is over and new houses are built, I'll be able to rent a decent little place. I'll always do my best for Joan, I promise.'

'You've always struck me as the reliable sort,' said Gran.

Joan held her breath. Was she about to say yes?

'But I won't change my mind,' said Gran. 'It's up to me whether you can marry before Joan is twenty-one and I refuse to give my permission.'

'That's a great shame,' said Bob, and Joan blessed him for sounding dignified when she was inwardly reeling. 'Obviously we're disappointed. Perhaps you'll think it over.'

'There's no need,' said Gran. 'My mind is made up. The law does not require me to explain myself, but since you seem determined to discuss it, I'll tell you my reasons. It's hardly five minutes since Joan was off gallivanting with Steven and now she's hurled herself at you again, Bob. You can get married next January when she turns twenty-one – *if* the engagement lasts that long; if it isn't – what did you say that day in the cemetery, Joan? – doing something mad out of grief.'

'This is nothing like what happened with Steven.' Joan felt a sharp stab inside her chest. Gran was never going to let her forget her terrible mistake. 'What Bob and I have is real and it's what I want.'

'Then you won't mind waiting, will you? It'll show that you mean it. And if you're going to be flighty and change your mind, it'll allow you time for that too.'

The breath caught harshly in Joan's throat. *Flighty … change your mind …* Was Gran comparing her to Estelle? She was. That look in her eyes dared Joan to answer back. It was all Joan could do not to slump.

'You should be grateful that I'm still prepared to put your best interests first,' said Gran, an edge of triumph in her tone. 'You'll thank me one day.'

Chapter Eight

'Look, there's a gap near that policeman. Let's stand there. Stay together.'

With one hand on Jimmy's shoulder, Dot propelled the lad towards the kerb while keeping an eye on Jenny. Thank goodness for a fine day. Not that she would have cared if it was bucketing down. She would have turned out, come rain or shine. It wasn't every day you got the chance to see your prime minister in the flesh. There was that saying, wasn't there, about special occasions? 'It's summat to tell your grandchildren about.' Well, she was going one better than that. She had brought her grandchildren with her, and in the years to come, they could tell their own grandchildren about the day their nan took them to see Mr Churchill.

It was the last Saturday in April. Dot looked round the crowd lining Oxford Road. Eh, it was good to see such a mixture – men in suits, others with a jacket over their work apron, the bowler-hatted, the flat-capped, young lads of apprentice age, old boys who had seen it all before in the last war. There were plenty of women an' all, poor ones in shawls, the better-off in coats or jackets, many of which bore the marks of having been given a new lease of life with pretty binding along the pocket flaps or a frilly jabot. Dot quite liked the idea of a jabot. Not one with lots of frills, but a few discreet folds falling from the front of her collar would tart up her Sunday best no end.

Jimmy was a fidget, but Jenny was happy to help keep him in check, which was good in one way, but disheartening in another. Not that Dot wanted the little lass to be a terror, but why had Pammy brought her up to be so darned perfect?

The sound of voices increased and everyone stepped forward. Dot held on to her two and craned her neck. Here came a handsome black motor with an open top and – oh, how perfect – Mr Churchill wasn't sitting down with the other men in the vehicle. He was on his feet, acknowledging the crowd. He wore a dark overcoat and homburg and he had a cigar sticking out of his mouth. The men politely raised their hats as he went by and Jimmy held up a hand to give the famous V-sign. Dot grabbed Jimmy's cap off his head, whereupon he snatched it from her and waved it madly.

'There,' said Dot. 'Wasn't that special? Mr Churchill has come here to inspect the damage that was done in the Christmas Blitz and meet some of the men who did the rescue work.'

'I wish he was meeting Grandpa,' said Jenny. 'Then Grandpa could tell him about how he helped dig Jimmy out from beneath that house.'

The crowds started to break apart. The atmosphere was one of satisfaction mingled with excitement. Dot breathed it in. Manchester had taken a heck of a battering before Christmas and it felt good to know Mr Churchill had come here to acknowledge it. It was a moment to be proud of.

'Come along,' she said to the children. 'Let's go to a café for a little treat.'

'Oh good,' said Jimmy. 'Can I look for shrapnel on the way?'

'Only if you're happy to miss out on a bun,' said Dot.

'Are we going to the buffet at Victoria Station?' asked Jenny as they walked past what used to be the Free Trade Hall. In its ruins, a temporary centre had been set up where folk who had lost their ration books in air raids could get new ones.

'No, we aren't,' said Dot, 'though I do love to have a cup of tea there sometimes.'

'Mum says you should spend less time in that buffet and more time at home,' Jimmy piped up.

'I expect she was kidding you,' Dot lied. 'We're going to a café called the Worker Bee. Mind your step as you go around this corner. There are deep holes in the pavement from the Blitz.'

'There might be shrapnel,' Jimmy said hopefully. Who cared about cigarette cards now that shrapnel was available?

'There might be broken ankles if you don't watch where you're going,' said Dot.

The Worker Bee was busy, but a couple of tables were free. Dot left the children guarding one in the window and went to the counter to order tea, squash and buns, then took the tray to the table and set everything out.

'Elbows off the table, Jimmy,' said Jenny, sounding just like her mother, though in fairness Dot had been about to say the same thing herself. Poor Jimmy! He must think he'd been put on this earth for the specific purpose of being nagged by his female relatives.

Dot relished the time spent with her grandchildren. She would write letters to their dads telling them about seeing Mr Churchill and taking the children for a bun afterwards. She would tell Archie what a little angel his Jenny was and she would joke with Harry about Jimmy wanting to search for shrapnel. Writing to her sons was important to Dot. She filled her letters with all the latest family news and local matters she could think of. Her boys must think her a right old gossip, but all she wanted was to make them feel they were home again, sitting at her kitchen table and hearing all the latest. She wanted them – well, if it didn't sound plain barmy – she wanted them to get lost in her letters. She ached to provide them with a short reprieve from the war.

When they left the Worker Bee, Jimmy held the door open for her and Jenny without any prompting and they set off for the bus stop.

'Mrs Green.'

The familiar voice brought Dot up short. Warmth rushed through her, accompanied by a frisson of delight at the idea of Mr Thirkle meeting her grandchildren – delight mingled with something not far off fear. Were the two parts of her life about to join up? Work and home. Be honest. It was more than that. Mr Thirkle didn't just represent work. He meant a lot more than that.

She turned round, a smile already on her face. It froze in position as she saw who was with Mr Thirkle.

Crikey. It was his daughter, Edie Thirkle-as-was. Mr Thirkle thought the world of her, which was only right and proper, but she was very far from being Dot's favourite person and the feeling was entirely mutual. Not long ago, before Dot had involved her railway friends in tracking down the food thief, she had confided in dear Mr Thirkle and they had met up a couple of times in the Worker Bee, where one of Edie's neighbours had been most interested to see Edie's father with an unknown woman. Edie had tackled her dad about it and he had gladly told her about his new friend, Mrs Green. Next news, Edie had come piking along to Victoria Station and given Dot a dressing-down in front of the world and his wife. Mr Thirkle had promised that after the thief was caught he would set Edie straight about why he had been with Dot, but then he wasn't able to because the police had sworn those involved to secrecy for reasons of public morale.

'Are these the grandchildren I've heard so much about?' asked Mr Thirkle, smiling at the two children. He had such a kind face. He wasn't what you'd call good-looking. His nose was beaky and he hadn't got much of a chin, but oh my, those brown eyes were so warm and kind. As far as Dot was concerned, they more than made up for what he lacked in the good-looks department.

'Aye, this is Jenny and this scallywag is Jimmy,' she said. 'Children, this is Mr Thirkle, who is a ticket collector at Victoria Station. He sometimes opens the gates for me to get onto the platform when I have a heavy trolley. And this lady is his daughter.' She didn't know Edie's surname.

'Mrs Chisholm,' said Mr Thirkle.

Dot gave her a tight smile. 'How do, Mrs Chisholm.'

Edie nodded her head, a sharp gesture. 'Mrs Green. And these are your grandchildren. You must be older than you look.'

'We're on our way to the Worker Bee,' said Mr Thirkle.

'We've just come from there,' said Dot.

'Have they got nice buns there today?' Mr Thirkle asked the children.

'Nan made me choose between having a bun and looking for shrapnel,' said Jimmy.

'And you opted for the bun,' said Mr Thirkle. 'Very wise. Did you come into town to see Mr Churchill?'

'We were right at the front,' said Jenny.

'We mustn't keep you,' said Dot. 'I must get the kids home.'

'Busy weekend?' asked Mr Thirkle.

'We're very busy,' said Edie before Dot could answer. 'We wanted to see Mr Churchill, of course, but other than that, we're moving Dad in with me. My husband's away fighting, so I'm on my own. Dad's on his own an' all, so it makes sense for us to live together in my house. That way, Dad can let a deserving family move into his place for the duration.'

Dot smiled at Mr Thirkle. 'I hope you'll be happy in your new home.'

'I'm sure I will be.' He looked lovingly at his daughter.

Edie caught Dot's eye. 'I'll be able to look after him properly from now on.' She dropped her voice and said softly, 'So you needn't think you're going to get your feet under his table.'

Edie didn't actually fold her arms and purse her lips, but she might as well have done. Dot's breath caught as sharply as if she had just swallowed a fly. Had Edie just said what Dot thought she'd said? Flaming cheek!

Did Edie Thirkle-as-was still view her the same way that Dot now viewed Sheila?

Dot had arranged to spend Sunday afternoon at Mrs Cooper's. That good lady had kindly hosted a tea party that the railway girls had held to celebrate Dot, and Mrs Grayson had provided the delicious tea. Dot didn't want them thinking she had no use for them now that her special occasion was over and done with. Besides, she had a lot of time for Mrs Cooper and hoped their friendship would last a lifetime. As for Mrs Grayson, Dot, in common with everyone else, had thought her pretty barmy to start with, but now she understood the deep unhappiness that had lain for years beneath Mrs Grayson's inability to set foot outside her own front door. With her new friends around her, there was hope that she could gradually be helped to return to a normal life.

With seven adults in it, the front room was pleasantly full. Dot's parlour couldn't have taken that many without at least one of them swinging from the ceiling light. As well as the four residents and Dot, Colette was here, which Dot was very pleased about. Colette wasn't often able to attend their get-togethers in the station buffet, so seeing her was a treat. Persephone was here too. She had walked over from Darley Court, where she was billeted, and soon she and Mabel would walk back there for Sunday tea. Mabel's father's cousin was the housekeeper there. Joan was going out to tea an' all and would be setting off for the Hubbles' soon.

They talked about Mrs Foster's refusal to give permission for Joan and Bob to wed. Eh, the more Dot heard about that woman, the more of an old bag she thought her. Not that she would ever say so to Joan.

'She says we have to wait until I'm twenty-one,' said Joan.

'It's not so long to wait,' said Dot, knowing full well that to a young couple in love, it seemed like for ever. If she didn't already know it, the look in Joan's eyes would have left her in no doubt.

'It's like I told Gran,' said Joan. 'I used to believe in waiting and looking forward to things, but I've changed. I made some dubious decisions after Letitia died, but I won't do that again. I know what I want.' She looked at Mrs Cooper. 'How old were you when you married?'

'If you're asking if I was younger than you,' said Mrs Cooper, 'then yes, I was.'

Dot laughed. 'I were not only wed by your age, I had two little lads an' all.'

'Did you really?' asked Persephone.

'Aye. I married at sixteen. Mind you, I had to get married, if you know what I mean. Make sure you don't find yourself in that position, young Joan.'

'Mrs Green!' Mrs Cooper sounded shocked. 'Really!'

Dot shrugged. 'It needed saying. Plenty of morals go flying out of the window in wartime.' She looked at Joan. 'Just make sure yours aren't amongst them. That really would give your grandmother summat to complain about. Eh, lass, there's no call to blush.' Reaching across, she covered Joan's slender hand with her own. 'I'm not setting out to upset you. I'm just reminding you to be a good girl, that's all. Look at me, wed at sixteen and a mother five months later.'

'On that happy note,' said Mabel, 'look at the time.'

Joan stood up. 'I'd better go.'

Dot caught her hand as she passed and made her stop. 'I hope you're not offended by what I said about morals. I didn't mean folk become immoral as such. I just meant that in wartime, folk get carried away, and understandably so. I never meant to hurt you, chick, but you haven't got a mam to say these things to you.'

Joan bent and kissed her cheek. 'The only thing that hurts is not being allowed to get married when it's what I want more than anything.'

After Joan left the house, those remaining exchanged glances with one another, sharing the sympathy they all felt for her. Then Mrs Grayson asked, 'Has anyone got something cheerful to say?'

Persephone stirred. 'As a matter of fact, yes.' She looked at Dot. 'Do you recall that article you gave me the idea for, about cleaning up after an air raid?'

'Don't tell me housework is your idea of cheerful conversation,' said Mrs Grayson.

'Maybe not the housework, but writing articles is,' Persephone replied, smiling. 'I wrote a piece and submitted it to *Vera's Voice*.'

'Ooh, I get that sometimes,' said Mrs Cooper.

'They liked it,' said Persephone, 'but said it ought to include some hints on how to tackle the cleaning.'

Dot laughed. 'Sorry, I can't help it. It's the mystified look on your face.'

'Of course she's mystified,' said Mrs Cooper. 'What does Miss Persephone know of such things? She's a Lady with a capital L.'

'Actually,' said Persephone, giving her a warm smile, 'I'm an Honourable with a capital H, but thank you for promoting me.'

'*Vera's Voice* sometimes prints articles that are written in what you might call a homely way,' said Mrs Grayson.

'Give us a for instance,' said Mabel.

Mrs Grayson addressed Persephone. 'You might try writing your article as if you're a newly-wed who's shocked at the amount of clearing up that can be required after an air raid. You could write about your landlady telling you the difference between wet dusting and dry dusting.'

'Or you could pretend to be the landlady,' suggested Dot, getting into the swing of it, 'sharing the advice you gave your young lodger. We can give you a few tips to include.'

'That would be wizard of you,' said Persephone.

Dot looked at Mrs Cooper. 'You used to be a cleaner, didn't you, when you lived in your old house? You wouldn't mind passing on a few tricks of the trade, would you?'

To Dot's surprise, instead of looking pleased, Mrs Cooper pressed her lips together and her brow crinkled into a frown.

'Are you all right, Mrs Cooper?' Colette asked.

'I wish I still had my cleaning jobs. I had a couple of shops and an office that I did every morning before opening time and some houses I did twice a week. Some of the places where I worked were bombed the same time as my house was, and as for the rest, when I said I were moving to Chorlton, they wanted a local cleaner.'

'You've got this house to look after now,' said Mabel, 'and the shopping to do, not to mention running around after Joan and me.'

'Bless you, you're no trouble,' said Mrs Cooper. 'I love being here, but I still have to look for a job. To be honest, I need the money. I'll need it even more when the war ends and I have to start again. I won't live here in Wilton Close for ever.'

'Don't you get paid to be the housekeeper?' Dot asked. It wasn't something she had thought of before.

'Only a small amount. It's not a proper wage, but Mr Masters said Mr Morgan ought to pay me summat so as to be able to prove he's my employer, and I have to pay back a little bit of what he gives me as rent.'

'That hardly seems fair,' said Persephone.

'It's only a peppercorn amount,' said Mrs Cooper. 'I think the idea is that because there are wages and rent, it proves I have no right to stop here after the war.'

'That's ridiculous,' Dot exclaimed. 'As if you're going to dig your heels in and refuse to move out!'

She felt indignant that Cordelia's husband would treat Mrs Cooper in such a way, but, to be fair, he was a solicitor and he was only tying things up legally. Not that she altogether wanted to be fair to Mr Kenneth Masters, not after the way he had hauled her over the coals when he was supposed to be on her side in the aftermath of the trouble Edie Thirkle-as-was had caused her a few weeks back.

'The truth is that being here in this lovely house has spoilt me,' said Mrs Cooper. 'So far I've just revelled in living here, but I do need to find work. All I know is cleaning, but I'd really like not to return to the rigid hours I've always had.' She smiled ruefully. 'There, I told you I was getting spoilt.'

'I have it!' Persephone exclaimed and they all looked at her. 'We've just been talking about it. A special cleaning service for the aftermath of air raids.'

Mabel sat up straight. 'We can put postcards in shop windows for you.'

'And ask Cordelia to recommend you to her friends,' added Persephone.

Their excitement infected Dot. 'A special service deserves a fancy name.'

'Don't be daft,' said Mrs Cooper, but she was obviously pleased. 'It's just me.'

'I've got it,' Mabel exclaimed. Her skin glowed and her brown eyes were warm. 'We've already got Mrs Grayson and her magic mixing bowl. Your service can be called Magic Mop.'

'Magic Mop?' cried Mrs Cooper. 'I never heard owt so daft in all my life.'

'I think it's perfect,' said Persephone, rising to her feet with natural grace, 'and I hope you'll give it some thought. Now, if you'll excuse us, Mabel and I should be on our way.'

As the two girls left the room, Dot smiled to herself. She knew Mrs Cooper would seriously consider Magic Mop now. She thought highly of the upper-class girl whom she always insisted on calling 'Miss' or 'Miss Persephone'.

'I do enjoy having these young girls coming and going,' said Mrs Grayson. 'I know I shouldn't say it, but my life has livened up because of the Blitz.'

'And it's good to have you here this afternoon an' all,' Dot said to Colette. 'We don't see anything like enough of you at work.'

'I wish I could stay longer,' said Colette, 'but Tony will be here to collect me shortly.'

'Invite him in to have a cup of tea with us,' said Mrs Cooper.

'I will,' said Colette. 'As a matter of fact, he wants me to ask you something. He says that since I'm coming to see you every week, what about if he comes too and does a spot of gardening for you or helps out around the house if you need any small repairs done?'

'That's a generous offer,' said Mrs Cooper, 'but he really doesn't have to do any work. He's welcome to come with you without that.'

'Really, I think he'd prefer it,' said Colette.

'You can't expect a man to sit supping tea and gossiping with a load of women,' said Dot. 'If you don't want him helping out here, he can come round to mine any time. I can always find jobs to do.' She made light of it, wanting to make it easier for Mrs Cooper to say yes.

Mrs Cooper laughed. 'If he's sure, Colette, then of course the answer's yes.'

After Tony Naylor rang the doorbell, he came in, holding his trilby, and said how do, which in itself was a bit of a turn-up for the books. Usually he waited on the step for Colette to put on her coat and hat but this time he sat down.

'Did you ask?' he said to Colette.

'Mrs Cooper says yes,' she answered.

'Mrs Cooper says yes please and thank you very much,' chimed in Mrs Cooper. 'Joan and Mabel are very good about doing their share in the garden, but another pair of hands would be most welcome.'

Tony nodded. He was a good-looking young man, his narrow face ending with a clearly defined, rather pointed chin. Brylcreem made his slicked-back hair look a deeper shade than it likely was, dark brown rather than mid-brown, and also had the effect of making his hazel eyes look a bit on the light side. His build was slim and athletic and he smelled faintly of tobacco. He sat leaning forwards slightly, turning his trilby round and round in his fingers. It made him appear shy. Was that why he had kept his distance from his wife's friends until now?

'It'd be a pleasure,' he said to Mrs Cooper. 'It helps to have a man about the place. I'll come every week and get some work done while Colette chats with you.' He glanced at Colette, a look of pure love. 'We ought to make a move.'

'Thank you for this afternoon,' said Colette, standing up.

Mrs Cooper went with her into the hall to fetch her things. They came back a minute later. She had a lovely trim figure, did Colette, and the coat, with its softly nipped-in waist and the gentle flare of its skirt, suited her to a T.

'You have a lovely wife,' Dot said to Tony.

'Yes, I do.'

He stood up to say his goodbyes and there was a dash of charm in the way he refused to be thanked for his kind offer to lend a hand every week.

Mrs Cooper saw the Naylors on their way, then returned to the front room.

'Such a lovely young couple,' she said.

'She's lucky to have an attentive fellow like that,' said Mrs Grayson. Was she thinking of her own husband, who was now shacked up in their old matrimonial home with Floozy?

'Aye, that's what we want for all our young friends, isn't it?' said Dot. 'A loving husband and a happy home life.'

'It certainly is,' Mrs Cooper agreed. 'I wish Mrs Foster had given Joan and Bob her consent. Bob is going to be every bit as good a husband as Tony Naylor.'

'I wonder if it might be worthwhile us having a word with Mrs Foster,' Dot mused.

'What, you and me?' asked Mrs Cooper.

A plan was forming in Dot's head.

'Nay, love. She wouldn't give me and thee the time of day – but I know who she will listen to.'

Chapter Nine

It was the first day of May and Mabel couldn't help thinking back to last May, when the nation had pulled together as the boys of the British Expeditionary Force had been rescued from the beaches of Dunkirk. Her own contribution to the effort had been to work on a hospital train, an experience that had exhausted her physically and emotionally, but which she had never for one moment regretted. Of course, Dunkirk had happened at the end of the month, not the beginning, but she was willing to bet that merely turning over the page on the calendar and seeing the word 'May' was enough to bring memories rolling back into the minds of every single person.

It wasn't memories of Dunkirk that were making her feel edgy this evening, though. It was because she was going out with Gil – not going out with as in going out with a fellow you were interested in, just going out with because certain things needed to be talked about in private. Why was she telling herself that? Was it because she had gone to such lengths to explain it in her letters to Harry?

'I want to reassure him that he has nothing to worry about,' she explained to Joan.

They were upstairs in the bedroom they shared. Joan was dressed ready for a night on first-aid duty and Mabel was supposed to be preparing to go out with Gil, but instead she was sitting on her bed, needing to talk.

'The trouble is,' she went on, 'the best reassurance would be for me not to see Gil at all, but I simply can't do that.

Meeting him again has brought so many memories to the surface. I lost Althea in the most appalling circumstances, without ever having the chance to say goodbye. I never said goodbye to Gil either. Maybe I need to do that. It's been so hard living with what I did. Gil was the only person who truly understood. Maybe talking with him will … I don't know … somehow make it possible to accept it.'

'It holds you and Gil together,' said Joan. 'It's like when Steven and I got involved. It happened because we were both heartbroken over Letitia.'

Mabel looked at her. 'I hope you're not suggesting I might have a fling with Gil.'

'Of course not, silly,' said Joan. 'I'm just saying that I can appreciate the importance of a shared experience. You definitely won't do anything mad with Gil, because you've got my horrible example to warn you off. I might have lost Bob for ever through what I did.'

'You could never lose Bob,' said Mabel. 'He adores you. Anyone can see that.'

Joan's expression melted into one of radiant happiness. She deserved her happy ending. It was a rotten shame her grandmother refused to give permission for the marriage to take place though.

'If you want to reassure Harry,' suggested Joan, 'why not telephone the base once or twice a week as well as writing? Letters are important, but if you can telephone him too, he'll see even more clearly how much he means to you.'

'That's a good idea. I haven't telephoned before because I felt I mustn't tie up a line to the base, but if we can agree on the best times to call, it's worth doing.'

'It'll make you both feel better,' said Joan.

Mabel didn't say that one of the reasons it would make her feel better was that she had made this evening's arrangements with Gil by telephone. If she started telephoning

Harry, no one would ever be able to say she had given Gil preferential treatment.

'That's settled,' said Joan. 'Now, what are you wearing for Gil?'

Indignation rose. 'I'm not wearing anything for Gil – crikey, that came out wrong,' she added as Joan burst out laughing. 'I mean, I'm wearing this because I like it.'

Getting up from the bed, she removed a dress from the wardrobe. It was light green silk and fastened all down the front with silk-covered buttons. The skirt featured inverted box pleats that would swing nicely without looking flirty.

She couldn't blame Harry for getting his feathers ruffled after the dazed way she had behaved when she had seen Gil at the Spitfire dance. No chap could possibly be pleased to see his girl apparently stunned at the sight of another man. But it had been pure shock that had hit her that night. She was over it now and there was no reason to mention to Harry that Gil had said he hoped to rekindle things with her.

She had already given herself a wash using her Elizabeth Arden scented soap and applied Number Seven hand lotion before putting on her make-up. Now she swept her dark hair back from her face and secured it with tortoiseshell combs, allowing it to hang in full waves down her back. Or should she wear it differently? This was how Gil liked it, but it was also her own favourite style. It would be daft to change it now.

Slipping on her high heels with almond-shaped toes, she opened her handbag to check she had her identity card, then took her hat from the top shelf of the wardrobe and her gloves from a drawer and threw her jacket over her arm. Downstairs, she put her outdoor things on the hallstand, placing her gas-mask box alongside them. Not so many people were carrying their gas masks now, but Mrs Cooper wouldn't let 'her' girls leave the house without theirs. Besides, as a trained first-aider and part of the rescue services, Mabel was required to keep hers with her at all times.

She and Joan went into the front room, where Mrs Grayson and Mrs Cooper admired Mabel's appearance.

'It's like having two mums,' said Mabel. 'And while we're discussing appearances, isn't it time, Mrs G, that you let me sort out a hairdresser for you? Cordelia gave me the name of hers and I've spoken to the lady and she's prepared to come here to the house. Shall we put a date in the diary?'

Mrs Grayson put a hand up to the back of her head. She wore her hair in a bun, which was a style Mumsy swore would put years on a woman; looking at Mrs Grayson, she had a point, though Mabel would never have dreamed of saying so. Mrs Grayson insisted on putting the front of her hair in curlers every night to try to give it more volume, but the curlers would have a much easier job if she had a proper style.

'Do say yes,' Mabel encouraged her. 'Get rid of some of the length and have some layers put in. Then you could have pin curls on top, with the rest scooped away from your face, falling into a plump roll at your shoulders.'

'I don't want to look like mutton dressed as lamb.'

'Well, let the hairdresser advise you,' Mabel urged her. 'Once you've got a good cut, a regular shampoo and set is only two and six. At least let me arrange for her to come round.'

'Yes,' said Mrs Cooper. 'Sort it out, Mabel dear. Who knows, Mrs Grayson, once you've got a new hairstyle, you might feel more like going out, and that would be a good thing, wouldn't it?'

After the years Mrs Grayson had spent trapped inside her old house by the cumulative effects of tragedy and long-term unhappiness, going outside was something that was still new to her. Mabel had started it when she was Mrs Grayson's lodger and, during the Christmas Blitz, had insisted that her landlady mustn't take shelter in the cupboard under the stairs any more, but must go to next door's Andy. It had been one of those things that was far easier said than done, but with the help of Mabel and their old next-door neighbour, this had been achieved. Later, when she had ended up living with Mrs Cooper in Whalley Range, Mrs Grayson had had to get used to walking as far as the public shelter – and it was a jolly good thing she had, or she wouldn't be there now to tell the tale, because Mrs Cooper's house, along with others in her road, had been bombed.

Now that they were all in Wilton Close, Mabel, Joan and Mrs Cooper accompanied her on short – very short – walks, arms firmly linked, and Mrs Grayson was finding it easier to go out, though the only way for her to do so without panicking was to follow exactly the same route each time. In this way, she had been able to attend church for the first time since … 'since before my son died,' she had whispered, overcome with emotion after her first church visit.

Mabel slid an arm around her former landlady, who she had started off thinking was completely crackers but for whom she now held warm affection. 'I don't want to push you into anything, but Mrs Cooper's right. It might give you a boost. We all feel better when we know we look good. And you know what they say these days – beauty is a duty!'

'*You're* certainly doing your duty,' said Mrs Grayson. 'Your friend will feel very lucky to have you on his arm tonight.'

Gil arrived right on time. He wasn't in his army uniform but wore a navy suit with a double-breasted jacket, a silk tie showing at his neck. He took off his trilby as he entered the house. He had been a solicitor before the war. Something inside Mabel was pleased he wasn't in uniform. Harry always wore his uniform when he took her out and she was so proud to be seen in his company. She didn't want to feel that sort of pride at being with Gil.

She showed him into the front room to introduce him. He shook hands with Mrs Cooper, Mrs Grayson and Joan, smiling and saying, 'Pleased to meet you.' He wasn't handsome the way Harry was. Harry had been blessed with the sort of looks that made you catch your breath the first time you saw him. Gil was good-looking in what Mabel thought of as an intelligent sort of way. Harry had a broad forehead and a square jawline, while Gil's face was lean, his build slimmer, and his hazel eyes paid attention. Mabel knew what she had seen in him when they first met, but her life and her heart had moved on since then.

'So you're Mabel's old friend,' said Mrs Grayson.

'Where are you taking her?' asked Mrs Cooper.

'I came from London Road Station on the local train to Chorlton and saw a little place when I arrived where I thought we could have dinner or a light supper, whichever Mabel fancies. I booked a table.' Gil looked at Mabel. 'I hope that's all right with you.'

'Don't let us keep you,' said Mrs Cooper. 'You must have a lot of catching up to do.'

They set off. The day's gentle warmth had eased into a pleasantly cool evening, edged with the crisp aroma of privet hedges.

Gil offered his arm. 'I promise not to read anything into it if you take it.'

Mabel hesitated, but it would be churlish not to link up. Unfriendly. They would look like strangers. Besides, she trusted Gil. He wouldn't take advantage.

'There was a large bombed-out building diagonally opposite Chorlton Station,' said Gil.

'The main post office,' she told him. 'There's a temporary one opposite the library.'

'It might be there temporarily for some years. It's going to take a long time to rebuild when this is over.'

'I told you about my job on the railways,' said Mabel, 'but I don't know what you do, other than that you're in the army. What brings you to Manchester?'

Please don't let him be stationed here. She didn't want that complication.

'I'm doing some work for the Red Cross,' said Gil, 'finding items for them to put in parcels to send to our boys in the POW camps.'

Mabel hid her surprise. 'What sort of things?'

'Greatcoats, jigsaws, writing paper. Just ordinary things, you know, but it's the sort of stuff that will make their lives that bit more comfortable.'

She had to hide not only her surprise but also a certain scorn. Gil's work didn't sound exactly heroic, especially compared to that of her Harry, who was a bomb aimer, which was widely known to be one of the most dangerous jobs in the whole war. A great surge of love for Harry swept through her. Pride, too. Imagine being Gil's girlfriend and having to be proud of him for collecting greatcoats and jigsaws! She almost laughed.

The thought relaxed her – which made her realise she had felt tense before. Had she been worried about the effect Gil might have on her? Well, not any more.

At the restaurant, they were shown to a corner table and the waiter presented them with menus. Gil chose the jugged rabbit, Mabel the vegetable goulash. She told Gil about Mrs Grayson and her magic mixing bowl, then about Mrs Cooper's plan to set herself up as Magic Mop.

'I'm sorry,' she finished. 'I'm gabbling on. Now we're here, I'm feeling nervous at the idea of talking about ... you know.'

Gil smiled, but there was sadness in his eyes. 'So much for wearing civvies instead of my uniform. I thought putting on a suit would make tonight feel more like old times. I thought it might make it easier for us to talk.' He shook his head. 'Sounds crazy, put like that, doesn't it?' He paused. 'I've never stopped thinking about it,' he said quietly. 'I'll never forget when I opened the letter from Bobby Thornley with news of the accident. It felt like cold water pouring through me.'

Tears sprang into Mabel's eyes. 'It was such a frightful thing to happen.'

'Did she – I mean, had you told her before ... ?'

Memories came flooding back, not images or words, just a wave of emotion: the distress of having to tell Althea, the shame, the wild drumming of her heart. She had to put down her glass. She nodded.

'And a few minutes later ... '

Gil shut his eyes for a moment. When he opened them, the hazel had deepened to a warm toffee colour. 'I'm so sorry.'

'I wasted tons of energy wishing that if the accident had had to happen, it could have happened before I told her, so at least she'd have died as my friend. It took a long time to realise that it wouldn't have helped, because then I'd have felt guilty about her believing that I was the same person she had always thought I was – that I was worthy of being her friend.'

'I was told she died instantly,' said Gil.

'Yes. She did.' The image of Althea's face imprinted on the MG's windscreen. That weird feeling that she was looking at her friend through a sheet of ice. 'That's the one good thing. It was merciful.'

Mabel looked down. Her hand was on top of his, which meant she had been the one to make the move. She withdrew her fingers and settled them in her lap. Gil left his hand where it was on the tablecloth. Mabel interlaced her fingers. She mustn't touch him again.

'I tried to write to you,' Gil said. 'I started that letter I don't know how many times. Then I thought I'd better wait until I saw you at the funeral instead.'

'I knew you were there,' said Mabel, 'but I couldn't speak to you. I couldn't speak to anyone. It was a struggle not to break down. The truth was a massive weight I had to carry in secret, but I knew I had to pull myself together because however hard it was for me, it was a hundred times worse for Althea's parents. I – I never went to see them after she died. I knew I should. I knew it was cowardly not to, but I couldn't face them.'

'I wrote to them,' said Gil. 'I said I hadn't known Althea well, but that she was good company, a caring person. I put in the letter everything I remembered about her. I wrote about the events we'd both attended, the way she joined in, how she threw back her head when she laughed. I filled it with all the little details I could remember.'

'It sounds like a lovely letter,' said Mabel. 'I'm sure it must have helped them.'

'It's important to put memories in a condolence letter. My mother taught me that.'

In a different life in which Althea hadn't been killed, Gil's mother would have been Mabel's mother-in-law. Mabel would have been Mrs Iain Gilchrist. She had even practised her signature.

Are you practising your new signature? she had written to Althea.

'You haven't asked what I wanted to say in the letter I tried to write to you,' said Gil.

'I'm not sure I want to know.'

'We came here to talk about what happened.'

Mabel inclined her head.

'I felt wretched, not just because Althea was dead, but because you'd lost your dearest friend. I never saw the two of you together, but I felt as if I had, because it was so obvious how much you meant to one another. She told me all about you.'

Emotion welled up. 'Don't.'

'You and she said the same thing about one another. Did you know that? That you were like sisters. You both said it.'

Mabel went hot and cold. She hadn't been aware of tears overflowing, but she now felt little drops resting on her cheeks, making her skin feel tight. Excusing herself, she went to the Ladies to check her make-up.

She returned just as their meals arrived. It didn't seem right to continue the conversation while they ate, so by unspoken consent they talked of other things. Gil was excellent company. Had she forgotten that? Not exactly, but, as with so many memories, it had been pushed far beneath the surface.

The food had been cooked well, but Mabel was too unsettled to enjoy it properly, though she made a point of telling the waiter how good it was.

They left the restaurant, slipping outside into the darkness. It was colder now and the scent of rain was in the air.

'This way,' said Mabel, taking the arm Gil offered. 'If we go down Cavendish Road and Holland Road, we can cut a corner.' Did that sound as if she was keen to get home and say goodnight? That hadn't been her intention.

'We've talked about what happened to Althea and about her funeral,' said Gil, 'but there's one subject we haven't touched on: us.'

Us. Mabel's heart gave a heavy thud. Did she want to talk about *us*? Could she bear to?

The familiar moan of the siren rose in the air.

Gil stopped. He let go of her arm and took her hand. 'Where's the nearest public shelter? Should we return to the restaurant and use their cellar?'

'My friend's grandmother lives in Torbay Road. We can get to her house in two minutes. She has an Anderson in the back garden.'

She pulled Gil in the direction of Cavendish Road. Already the drone of aircraft engines filled the night and beams of light cut through the darkness, searching for the enemy. One found a plane and two more streams of light immediately latched on as well, the three of them shifting with the plane as the anti-aircraft guns let loose.

Mabel's ears were filled with the whistling sound of bombs falling to earth. As they rounded the corner into Cavendish Road, she was wrenched away from Gil as a great wall of air crashed into her and picked her up. The breath was ripped from her lungs and her mind turned to wool, all except for a tiny pinprick of memory. Albert Square – Harry – the blast of a bomb. She was with Harry in Albert Square and it was before Christmas. Were she and Harry destined to die together?

She landed in something – not so much landed as was hurled into it. It yielded to receive her, but there was nothing soft or comforting about it. Even though she was numb, she knew she was being torn and scratched. She ought to fight her way free, but her lungs hadn't caught up with what was happening and she wasn't sure which way was up.

A pair of hands took hold of her arms and half lifted, half pulled her. She moved but her hair didn't.

Gil's face appeared in front of hers. His lips moved, but her hearing hadn't come back yet. Gil fiddled with her hair. You heard of girls in factories who suffered terrible injuries when their hair got tangled in a machine. Would her hair have to be cut off? Gil now had one arm behind her back and the other beneath her knees. Lifting her, he set her on her feet, holding on to her when her legs nearly gave way. She clung to him. She had pins and needles all over. Gently, Gil let go and Mabel discovered that her body could hold itself upright.

She turned to see what had broken her fall. A holly bush. There was something strangely appropriate about that. Before Christmas, on the first night of the Manchester Blitz, it had been a wall that had stopped her flight through the air. She now realised how that had been entirely appropriate, since she had been in the presence of an RAF hero. With Gil, whose job was to find greatcoats and jigsaws for POWs, it was a holly bush. There was nothing heroic about a holly bush.

What were these mad thoughts? She was a trained first-aider. She wasn't supposed to drift off to fairyland in an emergency.

Her hearing was returning. It was like listening underwater, all far away and distorted.

'Come along,' said Gil. 'We must help.'

The air was pungent with the smell of smoke and cordite and it tasted of dust. Mabel's hand was in Gil's as they hurried along Cavendish Road. Her legs kept her upright and moving, though goodness only knew how. Two ARP men in boiler suits and tin hats ran past, which made Mabel pick up her pace. She might not have full control of her legs, but she knew her duty.

The two pairs of semi-detached houses that marked the corner of Cavendish Road and Chatsworth Road were gone. Destroyed. Mabel and Gil joined a human chain to remove rubble. The night air was packed with the sound of engines and gunfire, but the rescuers carried on. Then came the cessation of work that indicated a person had been found. It was one of the strange things about being part of a rescue. The human chain seemed to know, without being told, when to pause.

Gil strode forward. 'My friend is a first-aider.'

Mabel followed him, preparing herself to administer treatment without the benefit of the proper kit, but Gil turned to her, shaking his head.

Dead, then. It shouldn't have come as a surprise, not after seeing the remains of the houses, but it was, just the same. As the rescue effort continued, it turned out they were all dead, all of them. Not rescue then, just retrieval. Two men and five women. Gone. All of them. Just like that. Mabel watched, unable to remove her gaze as the bodies were lifted onto stretchers and covered with blankets, ready to be taken along the road to the wartime mortuary. Had they ever joked, these dead people, about how if they were blasted to kingdom come it would be very handy being just along the road from the mortuary? Possibly. There was a lot of grim humour around these days.

If she and Gil had run a bit faster in their need to get to Mrs Foster's house, if they had got fully round the corner and into Cavendish Road, it would probably have been them too. She might now be lying dead in the road.

Mabel waited for the shock and distress to flatten her, consciously waited for it to happen. Instead, the blood surged through her veins and she felt marvellously, nerve-tinglingly alive.

Chapter Ten

Joan was tired, but wasn't everyone? Thanks to Hitler, it wasn't so much a question of gathering nuts in May, as per the old song, but here we go dodging bombs in May. Each night of air raids was followed by another. She still felt shaken at the thought of the damage that had occurred so close to Gran's house – the second time that had happened to Gran. Word had it that the bombs had been meant for Chorlton Station, or possibly for the electricity substation on St Werburgh's Road, but there was no way of knowing for certain. She and Gran might not be on the best of terms, but the idea of something bad befalling her made a cold hard lump form in the pit of Joan's stomach. When she heard, she had wanted to dash to Torbay Road and envelop Gran in a huge hug, but even when Letitia was alive, Gran had never been a hugger.

Besides, she had other reasons for preferring to keep her distance from Gran for the time being. As hurtful as they were, she could swallow Gran's sniping remarks about her fling with Steven because she deserved them, but now that Gran had refused to give permission for her to marry Bob, it was best for Joan to keep away. Others might think she was in a sulk with Gran; Gran undoubtedly thought so. But actually the reason for keeping away was—

'Wake up, Dolly Daydream. We've got to give the goods porters a hand before we clock off.'

Joan was jolted from her reverie. Pushing her sack trolley, she followed Mrs Golden, a senior porter whose daughter and granddaughter also worked on the railways as a hammer girl and a painter.

The station porters and the goods porters did two separate jobs and there wasn't meant to be any crossover, but you could guarantee that if there was – and needs must in wartime – then it was always one-way. A station porter could help ferry goods, but a goods porter couldn't work on the station with the general public because they wore dungarees instead of a smart uniform.

'Thanks for your assistance, ladies,' said a mustachioed goods porter who was standing in the centre of several stacks of crates, clipboard in hand. 'Those four need to go to the engine shed.'

Joan manoeuvred her sack trolley into position. 'What's in them?'

'Broom heads.'

Broom heads? Joan knew better than to question it. She had heard of too many joke errands where the unwary were sent to ask for tartan paint or a left-handed screwdriver. She wasn't about to make a twit of herself by rising to the bait.

But when she and Mrs Golden set off, she did ask.

'Not any old broom heads. These attach to hosepipes, so that the outsides of the carriages can have a good wash. The water comes out among the bristles.'

In the engine shed, they passed a colossal locomotive that was being cleaned. There was no sign of any adapted broom heads in use. Women in slacks or dungarees, many of them with their hair tucked inside turbans, were busy cleaning and polishing with rags, which must have been oily, judging by the sharp tang in the air. Joan and Mrs Golden delivered their first two crates, then, on the way back, paused to watch.

'I used to do that job in the last lot,' said Mrs Golden. 'There was some feeling against it to start with, against

115

letting women do it, I mean, because traditionally cleaning the engine was seen as the first step towards one day being an engine driver, but in the end they had to let us.'

'What's that girl up there doing?'

The circular door at the front of the engine was open and a girl was up there, leaning forwards and pushing something with a long handle inside.

'She's cleaning the tubes,' said Mrs Golden. 'That thing she's using is like a giant bottlebrush. Inside the smokebox are tubes that stretch all the way along as far as the firebox, where the coal goes. The tubes need to be kept clean because otherwise the loco doesn't steam so well and it uses more coal. Anyroad, we mustn't stand here gawping. We'd best get back and fetch them other crates.'

'Coming.'

As Joan started to turn away, the girl cleaning the tubes brought herself upright, raising one arm to rub her forehead with the back of her hand. From below, someone called up to her and she looked around and down, affording a glimpse of her profile. Didn't Joan know her from somewhere?

Pushing her trolley, she hurried after Mrs Golden. 'Do you know who the girl is who's cleaning the tubes?'

'Haven't the foggiest.'

'I'm sure I know her from somewhere.'

'It'll come to you at two o'clock in the morning,' said Mrs Golden. 'That's what always happens when you're trying to remember summat. Mind you, I'd sooner wake up for that reason than because of the siren going off yet again.'

Having delivered the next pair of crates, Joan started to follow Mrs Golden from the engine shed. Mrs Golden was a short distance ahead when Joan paused as a group of women came around a corner and crossed her path, calling thank you to her for giving way. She glanced round the corner to see if more women were coming – and there was the girl again, only this time she knew exactly who she was.

Joan lifted herself on her toes, about to call to her, but the girl took one look and dived through a doorway.

'Come along, Miss Foster,' came Mrs Golden's voice, 'or I really will change your name to Dolly Daydream.'

Joan set off again. That girl was Margaret Darrell. They had been colleagues at Ingleby's, where Joan had worked before she became a railway girl. They hadn't actually worked together, because Joan had been a sewing machinist and Margaret had worked on the shop floor – in the haberdashery department, if memory served – but they had sometimes shared fire-watching duty on the roof. Later, in her capacity as a first-aider, Joan had helped Margaret in her hour of direst need.

Why on earth would Margaret Darrell choose to avoid her?

Rescue party returned to St Cuthbert's depot, back from Rudheath Ave. Fit for further service.

Joan read the words upside down as Mr Varney recorded them in the log. She had glimpsed those words so many times before. Goodness alone knew how many times they had been written, or words very like them, in logbooks and reports all over the country. With luck, only the name of the bombed place would differ and the rescue party would always be fit for further service.

Rudheath Avenue in Withington had been a good rescue, which was a way of saying there had been no fatalities. Right now, Mrs Brown and her daughters from number 20 and Mr Wilson from further up the road were on their way to Withington Hospital.

'Come on,' said Mabel. 'We need to re-equip. How many bandages have you got left?'

They had to have six each every time they went out, as well as a water bottle, six dressings, four splints and six labels, which were used to write an initial on – F for fracture and so on – to make things a little speedier when a casualty reached hospital.

There was no time for a sit-down, let alone for a cuppa. Their first-aid party was sent out again at once, this time to Whitchurch Road, where they split up to attend at three damaged houses. Joan was allocated to number 68, where half the roof, complete with chimney stack, had slid down onto the road, knocking a lamp post skew-whiff. Grimy-faced men in boiler suits, each tin hat marked with an R for Rescue, worked ceaselessly to free the residents, while a female warden stood by with her arms full of blankets.

Presently, a woman was brought out, just about able to walk, with assistance, over the rubble of her home, her face white with shock. The female warden wrapped a blanket around her shoulders. When Joan stepped forward and attempted to examine her, the woman wafted her arm, trying to bat her away, at the same time turning her head to cast an anguished look behind her at the ruins of her house.

Joan took her arm. 'Let's find you somewhere to sit down. Can you tell me who was in the house with you? The rescuers need to know.'

The air-raid victim stuttered through her reply, then the woman with the blankets took charge of her and a WVS lady appeared with an offer of tea. Joan returned to the rescuers to tell them there were two more people under the rubble.

'Stay put,' she was ordered. 'We may need you.'

Fortunately, when the other two – a man and a woman – were dug free, there were no serious injuries. Joan quickly patched them up, then handed them over to the ambulance men.

One of the rescue team stood swigging a mug of tea. 'They were lucky.' His eyes, bright in his filthy face, gazed at the remains of what had once been a family home.

Was that what it came down to – luck? Even though the homes of these folk tonight had been hit, the people had escaped with their lives, whereas the people inside the houses where Mabel had helped out a few nights ago had all copped it. *Luck.*

How long would her own luck last? Mabel's luck might so easily have run out the night she went out with Gil. Imagine if that conversation in their bedroom had been the last time she and Mabel had ever talked to one another. Joan's mind, her instincts, everything inside her rejected the idea. It was impossible to contemplate it. Yet that was how it had been with Lizzie. Joan had dashed out of the park-keeper's house, leaving Lizzie manning the telephone under the stairs, and when she had returned, there had been no house to return to, just a whopping great crater.

Oh, this bloody war.

All she wanted was to be with Bob. He was her anchor, her hope for the future. It honestly astonished her that she could ever have developed feelings for Steven. All she longed for now was to be Bob's wife.

Coming off duty at six in the morning, she and Mabel cycled home, refreshed themselves with a quick wash, then got changed, ready to go to work – but not before they'd had breakfast. Mrs Cooper and Mrs Grayson insisted on that.

Finishing the final mouthful, Joan pushed back her chair. 'Excuse my dashing off early.'

'You don't need to set off yet,' said Mrs Cooper.

'Yes, she does.' Mabel smiled. 'She's meeting up with Bob, aren't you, Joan?'

'He's been on nights and if I go now, we can grab half an hour together before my shift starts.'

'Best get your skates on, then,' said Mrs Grayson.

Full of happiness, Joan scurried off to get ready and then ran for the bus. Glancing around at her fellow passengers, she saw that plenty had bags under their eyes that spoke of sleepless nights in air-raid shelters or on duty with the ARP or the Auxiliary Fire Service or staffing a WVS mobile canteen. Working all day, then slogging away all night, was just how it was while Manchester was enduring one of its all too frequent phases of constant air raids.

At Victoria Station, Bob was waiting for her outside the mess. She ran into his arms, but when he opened the door, she tugged him away.

'Not in there. I want to talk privately.'

'In a busy mainline station?'

'There's a place Dot – Mrs Green – sometimes sits with a friend.'

They went onto the concourse. Mr Thirkle was on duty at the ticket barrier Joan was heading for, which felt appropriate. He was the friend of Dot's she had referred to, though she hadn't mentioned him by name. It wasn't that she didn't trust Bob – far from it – but Dot had already been in enough hot water from having her name linked with Mr Thirkle's.

Joan smiled at the ticket collector as he waved them through the barrier. He had been an enormous help when the railway girls had set out to catch that thief.

At this end of the platform, sufficiently far away from the train not to be of much use for waiting passengers, was a bench. Joan led Bob to it and they sat down close to one another, holding hands.

'This is cosy,' said Bob. 'It gets my vote over the mess any day.'

'I brought you here because I need to tell you something important.'

'Mrs Foster hasn't changed her mind about the permission, has she?' Bob asked at once.

'No, but it is a family matter. It – it's to do with my mother.' Emotion swelled inside her and her voice froze.

Bob waited before saying gently, 'Take your time.'

But time was the one thing she didn't have, because her shift started soon. That galvanised her.

'When I go down south, I don't know what I'll be able to find out about my family, if anything, but I've been thinking about my mother. If by any chance I can discover where she went when she left us and I can track her down ... ' Her throat closed over, as if the words were too significant to be uttered aloud.

'Yes?' Bob prompted.

Joan looked deep into his dark eyes.

'She could give us permission to marry.'

Her feet might be aching after her long railway shift plus overtime, but Dot walked in triumph up Heathside Lane. By, it had been an interesting day. She felt tired, but it was a good kind of tired. Satisfying. Aye, that was the right word. She had been entrusted with her first lot of homing pigeons and Mr Hill had shown her how to release them on Southport Station. She had also been responsible for three dozen boxes of eggs – not a crate with three dozen boxes inside it, mind, all nicely protected with straw, but three dozen separate boxes each holding a dozen eggs – and there hadn't been a single crack, let alone a breakage, when she had handed them over at their destination. Looking after eggs might not sound like much, but little things like that mattered – they certainly mattered to the recipients. That was one of the things Dot loved about the railways. You could tie a label on a punnet of fresh fruit and send it on its way, knowing it would arrive safe and sound.

To add to the day's achievements, she had been able to buy liver on her way home without having to queue up. Using the key that hung inside the letter box, she let herself in, calling, 'I'm home.'

Reg was at the kitchen table, with the newspaper and an ashtray in front of him. 'Oh, it's you. Our Sheila's here. She were about to put the kettle on.'

Sheila promptly pulled out a chair and sat down, taking a packet of Craven 'A' from her handbag, as if she couldn't possibly make so bold as to brew a pot of tea in Dot's kitchen now Dot was home. Dot struck a match and the gas ring emitted a *pop* as the blue flame sprang to life. Shaking the kettle to see if it was full enough, she plonked it on the gas, then delved into her shopping bag.

'What have you got there?' Sheila asked.

'Liver.'

'Liver?' Reg sounded considerably more interested in that than he had been in her homecoming.

'Where's our Jimmy?' Dot asked.

'Playing out,' said Sheila.

'We haven't had him to stay for a few days,' said Reg.

Damn right they hadn't. Dot had fobbed Sheila off with excuses – yes, all right, lies – about late shifts, so Sheila had been obliged to keep Jimmy at home with her. Dot wasn't going to do any child-minding just so Sheila could drop her knickers for that bloke, whoever he was. Not that Sheila would have had much opportunity recently, what with all the raids. Or maybe she would. You heard of folk who found danger to have aphrodisiacal qualities.

'Have you got a pen, Dot?' Reg looked at a piece of paper lying on top of his *Manchester Evening News*.

It was tempting to pat herself down as if searching, but all she said was, 'Not on me, no. What's that?' Dot nodded at the sheet of paper.

'Pa's got to sign it for me,' said Sheila. 'I've lost my ration book.'

'Oh, Sheila, you never,' said Dot. Honestly, the girl was hopeless. It was probably down the back of the sideboard.

'And I need a respectable witness to say I'm telling the truth.'

'It'll cost a bob an' all,' said Reg.

'Reg!' Dot exclaimed.

'I don't mean I want paying for signing, you daft bat. That's what they charge you for a new ration book. A shilling.'

The kettle started to sing. The tea caddy was nearly empty. Dot opened a fresh packet to pour in. Times were when she would have upended the packet and tipped out its contents, casually tapping the packet on the rim of the caddy. Had she really been so cavalier with tea? It was a precious commodity these days. After emptying and tapping the packet, she slit it open to be sure of getting out the final dusty bits at the bottom.

She warmed the pot, swilling the hot water around in it before emptying it down the drain outside the back door. Then it was one per person and none for the pot, just like Lord Woolton said. Dot had a lot of time for Lord Woolton. Rationing was tough, but it meant fair shares for all, and she put that down to him. She liked hearing him on the wireless an' all. He wasn't one of them know-it-all types. He sounded civil and sensible, as if he understood the difficulties housewives faced and appreciated the way they coped. Eh, it had come to summat when you felt more appreciated by a disembodied voice than by your own husband.

Dot poured boiling water on the tea leaves and left the pot to stand while she fetched the cups and saucers, taking a moment to light the gas in the oven, ready for the shepherd's pie she had thrown together at the same time as making the breakfast this morning.

She was still on her feet and had just poured the tea when the door opened and Pammy arrived with both children.

'I found this one pinching empty bottles from the crates behind the grocer's,' said Pammy, 'so he could take them into the shop and get the deposit.'

'Jimmy!' Dot's voice chimed in with Reg's and Sheila's.

Jimmy squirmed. Sheila clipped him around the back of his head, sending his cap flying.

'There was no call for that, Sheila,' Dot said in a mild voice. You didn't tell off an adult in front of children.

Sheila shrugged. 'He shouldn't be wearing his cap indoors anyroad.'

'Jenny, love, get a beaker of milk each for you and Jimmy,' said Dot, 'and go in the parlour.'

'Does Jimmy deserve one?' asked Pammy, earning herself a narrow-eyed look from Sheila.

'Have you got a pen, Pammy?' asked Reg.

Pammy held her cream leather handbag tighter. She opened a drawer. 'Mother's pen is in here, isn't it, Mother?' Out came Dot's pen and her half-finished letters. 'In the middle of writing to the boys?'

Give her her due, Pammy didn't look at the half-written letters. Sheila would have. Pammy handed Reg the pen and popped the letters back into the drawer.

'Aye,' said Dot, fetching another cup and saucer as Pammy sat down. 'I write the letters side by side and try to make them as different as I can.'

Sheila blew out a stream of smoke. 'I'm no good at writing letters. Neither's Harry.'

'It doesn't matter if Harry's not much good at it,' said Dot. 'You must still write to him regular. It means a lot.'

'I never know what to say,' said Sheila. 'I'm not supposed to write about the munitions because it's unpatriotic to tell servicemen owt that might worry them about what's happening here. Besides, work is deadly dull.'

At long last, Dot took the weight off her feet. 'I tell the boys all about my railway job.'

'Aye, but I bet it's all the funny bits, isn't it?'

'You make it sound like it's a laugh a minute,' said Dot.

Mind you, Sheila wasn't far wrong. Dot didn't want Archie and Harry worrying about her. She wanted to bring smiles to their faces. She wanted them to be filled with the feelings they associated with home. So she never mentioned the absence of the pretty flower beds that had graced the platforms of local stations before the war, or how the pre-war smartness of station buildings was fading away. Instead, she wrote about the soldiers who had removed their boots for comfort before going to sleep and had almost stunk out the whole carriage. She joked about hapless passengers who got off at the wrong stations in the blackout, and she rejoiced in describing the occasion when the train was stuck between stations for over an hour and it turned out there was a choir on board and they had eased everyone's travel-weariness with four-part harmonies.

The oven would be hot by now. Dot got up to put the shepherd's pie in.

'What are you having?' asked Pammy.

'Liver,' said Reg.

'That's for tomorrow,' said Dot. 'Shepherd's pie.'

'The fishmonger had the most splendid cod you've ever seen,' said Pammy. 'I queued for nearly an hour. Then it turned out that the woman in front of me runs a billet for men brought here to work on Blitz repairs, and she took twelve portions. Twelve! All I could get was the tail.'

'Talking of billets,' said Sheila, and Dot's ears pricked up, 'I had the billeting officer round yesterday. He wanted to put someone in our spare room.'

'Oh aye?' Dot's heartbeat quickened.

'But I wasn't having that.' Sheila threw back her head and aimed a stream of smoke at the ceiling. 'I told him I'll ask my friend Rosa to move in.'

Chapter Eleven

With trails of tobacco smoke drifting up all around her, Mabel sat watching Rosemary Lane on the cinema screen. She had seen *Always a Bride* before, though she hadn't told Harry that. Actually, it was probably just as well that she had already seen it, since she wasn't exactly concentrating. They had held hands to start with, then he had let go for a moment to shift slightly in his seat, after which, instead of taking her hand again, he had placed his hand on her knee, sending a flame of desire shooting through her. In the back rows, couples were no doubt kissing and canoodling, but they couldn't be feeling any more eager or excited than Mabel. It was a good job she shared a bedroom with Joan or she might be tempted to sneak Harry upstairs. It was all very well being brought up to have standards and morals and to scorn girls who had a reputation, but honestly, no one warned you what it was like to feel this way.

At the end of the film, they stood for the national anthem before joining the crowd making its way up the aisles and downstairs to the doors. Outside, Mabel and Harry moved away from the front steps. Small, dim glows appeared as people switched on their torches. An exclamation of 'Blast!' followed by a gurgle of laughter showed that someone had walked into something. It happened all the time in the blackout. The other thing you often heard was a voice saying, 'I beg your pardon,' followed by laughter because they had just apologised to a pillar box or a telegraph pole.

'I don't think I'll ever get used to this darkness,' said Mabel.

'They say it's easier if you shut your eyes for a minute,' said Harry.

'That's barmy.'

'Try it.'

Mabel shut her eyes and Harry kissed her.

'Cheeky,' said Mabel, but she couldn't help smiling.

'That's me, your very own cheeky blighter.'

And not just her cheeky blighter, but her handsome and irresistible blighter, only she mustn't tell him that or goodness knew where it might lead.

'Let's try it again,' said Harry.

Mabel moved willingly into his arms, lifting her face, her eyelids fluttering closed as his mouth found hers. Then someone walked into them and they broke apart.

'I say!' exclaimed the stranger. 'I'm so sorry to, um, interrupt.'

The young woman on his arm giggled.

Mabel coughed, embarrassed and exhilarated at the same time. Seizing Harry's arm, she started walking away.

'Did you like the film?' Harry asked.

I liked having your hand on my knee. 'Yes, I did. Thanks for taking me.'

'Where did your friend Gilchrist take you?'

Something inside her went very still. 'For supper.'

'Where?'

'Does it matter? Somewhere local. We walked there from Wilton Close.'

'He collected you from Wilton Close?'

Mabel experienced an unexpected twinge of vexation. She didn't appreciate being subjected to the third degree. 'Would you have preferred me to meet up with him somewhere? I deliberately got him to pick me up from home so he met everyone and it was all above board. I wouldn't have done that if there was anything untoward going on.'

'I never suggested there was anything untoward.'

'I told you how important it was for me to talk to him.'

'Did it help?' If only Harry could have said the words solicitously instead of with that note of challenge.

'I think so.'

'Good. Then you won't be seeing him again.'

She suppressed a sigh. Squeezing Harry's arm, she said lightly, 'It's very flattering that you're so protective, but you have nothing to worry about regarding Gil and me. It was over long ago. I've got you now and you're all I want.'

Harry stopped and turned her to face him. Holding her shoulders, he rested his forehead on hers.

'I know and I'm sorry. I can't help worrying. I didn't do right by you to start with and I don't want you remembering what a fine chap this Gilchrist is.'

'Oh, Harry.' Standing on tiptoes, she kissed him softly on the mouth. 'What you did is all forgotten.'

His hands left her shoulders and moved to her collarbones, her throat, the sides of her face, as his mouth descended on hers. Mabel longed to throw her arms around his neck but made them stay by her sides. Harry had once said, 'Hand over the control to me,' and that was how this felt. It was unbearably exciting. When the kiss ended and Harry removed his hands, it was all she could do to remain upright. Every nerve end tingled with desire. She pressed her lips together, savouring the lingering taste of him.

'I'll give you one good reason why I could never prefer Gil over you,' she said as they started walking again.

'What's that?'

'You'll never believe what he does in the army. His job is to put together comfort parcels for POWs. I know how important it is for our boys in the prison camps to receive parcels, of course, but I suppose I imagined putting them together was women's work. I never thought it would be the job of an army officer. Talk about having a cushy war. Compared to what you do, his job is trivial.'

She expected Harry to laugh, to agree. She had intended her words to provide the necessary boost to obliterate his jealousy for ever. But Harry didn't respond and all at once she felt mean. How could she have done Gil down like that? But she knew she wouldn't have felt mean if Harry had laughed along with her – and that made her feel meaner still.

'I've decided to go up to Annerby for a day or so,' she said, 'if I can arrange it.'

'Excellent. Am I invited?' Harry's tone declared he was confident of a yes. 'I'll let you know when would be best for me.'

Her heart dipped. 'I didn't mean the pair of us. I meant just me.'

'You know how much I want to see your parents, not as a friend like last time, but as your boyfriend. I want to ask for your father's permission to court you.'

'I know, but I'm going for a different reason.'

'Don't tell me. It's something to do with Gilchrist, isn't it?'

Was that a stab in the dark or had he sensed it?

'Yes and no. It's something I should have done a long time ago. Talking to Gil made me realise I ought to do it now.'

'Perfect,' Harry muttered. 'Just what I wanted to hear.'

Something tightened inside her chest, but this was deeply important. She hadn't written to Althea's parents or been to see them after Althea's death. She should have done both, but her involvement in the accident had let her off the hook. Everybody had understood she was too shocked, too heartbroken, and then she had left home and come here.

Now she was going to do the decent thing. And about time too.

'So the two of you will be going away at the same time next weekend,' said Mrs Cooper as they got ready for church on Sunday. 'The house is going to be very quiet without you.'

'Don't let the billeting officer fill our bedroom while we're away,' Mabel teased.

Joan put on her linen jacket and felt hat. She was feeling bleary-eyed after the air raid last night, but she would soon shake off that feeling, she knew. You had to. You'd walk around in a daze most of the time if you didn't. There had been a raid every night in May so far, apart from two.

Mrs Grayson put on her coat, self-consciously lifting her hair out of the collar. She had had her hair done by Cordelia's hairdresser yesterday. Gone was the old uncompromising style, with everything pulled back into a bun. Now her hair was gently layered at the sides and curled away from her face. She had a fringe as well, which curled under, and the hairdresser had left most of the length at the back and showed her how to arrange a softer bun at the nape of her neck.

Now, Mrs Grayson stood in front of the hall mirror, about to put on her old cloche hat.

'No, you don't.' Mabel twitched it out of her fingers. 'You don't want to wear this old thing.'

'It's the only hat I've got,' Mrs Grayson protested. 'It's not as though I've needed hats all these years.'

'Don't move.' Mabel dashed up the stairs, returning a few moments later with her own felt hat, stylishly trimmed with a petersham ribbon that was fashioned into a cluster of curls to make a rosette on one side. 'Stand still.' Looking over Mrs Grayson's shoulder into the mirror, she positioned the hat. 'There – very swish.'

'I can't borrow this—' Mrs Grayson began.

'Yes, you can. There's no point in having a smart new hairstyle if you don't have a good hat to show it off. It suits you.'

'She's right,' said Mrs Cooper. 'You look very smart and that hairdo takes years off you.'

They set off for church, with Mrs Grayson firmly linked between Mabel and Mrs Cooper. Joan was happy to walk behind, enjoying the sunshine and birdsong as well as the sight of Mrs Grayson in Mabel's hat. What a love Mabel was to think of it.

After church, they went home for their Sunday roast, which today meant herby oatmeal sausages, followed by sultana pudding. Mrs Grayson was very big on what she called patriotic puddings, which she made without using sugar, eggs or milk. When Joan had first lived with Mrs Cooper and Mrs Grayson, the two ladies had shared the housework and the cooking, but these days Mrs Grayson seemed to be doing most if not all of the cooking and baking.

'Don't you mind?' Joan had quietly asked Mrs Cooper. 'After all, if you're out doing Magic Mop and then you have to start all over again when you come home ... '

'Bless you, I don't mind that, chuck,' Mrs Cooper had replied. 'Me, I was born to clean.'

Joan was going to have tea at Bob's, as she often did on a Sunday, but she could stay at home for a while yet, which was good because it meant seeing Colette and Tony when they came round. Cordelia arrived at almost the same time.

'I hope it's in order for me to turn up unannounced,' said Cordelia.

'You're always welcome,' said Mrs Cooper. 'I like having visitors, though I hope you don't mind that it's a bit of a squash in here.'

'I'll disappear outside and make a start on the garden,' said Tony.

'I didn't mean to make you leave,' said Mrs Cooper. 'Stay and talk for a bit.'

'Have you had your hair restyled, Mrs Grayson?' asked Colette. 'It suits you.'

Mrs Grayson put a hand to her head. 'Mrs Masters kindly recommended her hairdresser to me.'

'She's done a very good job,' observed Cordelia, 'but I'm sure Tony doesn't want to listen to us talking about hair, or we really will have him running for the garden shed. I've come here with a date for your diaries. I'm on the organising committee for a dance later in July in aid of the local War Weapons Week.'

'Harry and I would love to come,' Mabel said at once, 'assuming he can get a pass.'

'So would Bob and I,' Joan added, 'if we aren't on the night shift.'

Cordelia looked at Tony and Colette. 'What about you?'

Colette looked at Tony. 'We'd love to, wouldn't we?'

'Of course we would.'

'I'm delighted to hear it,' said Cordelia. 'If you don't mind my saying so, I'm very pleased that we're seeing more of Colette in the buffet after work these days, as well as her coming here every weekend.' She wagged her finger at Tony in a humorous way. 'You kept her too much to yourself.'

'I'm a protective husband, I don't mind admitting,' Tony replied good-naturedly. 'Maybe I'm overprotective, but wouldn't you be, if you had a lovely young lady like this to care for and keep safe?'

'That's what I like to see,' said Mrs Cooper, 'a happy couple. Joan and Mabel are in happy couples an' all.'

'And Alison,' said Mabel. 'Don't forget Alison. We'll have to sort Persephone out.'

'Talking of happy couples,' said Joan, rising to her feet, 'I'd better make a move or my other half will think I've abandoned him.'

She ran upstairs to get ready, taking the clips out of her hair, giving it a good brush to make it shine, then putting them back again. Back downstairs, she said goodbye, which Tony appeared to use as a natural break in the conversation to get up and head outside to do some work in the garden.

As Joan set off, she thought ahead to this time next week. She was travelling down to Buckinghamshire on Friday and by this time on Sunday she would be on her way home again ... having found out about her family. That was going to happen, wasn't it? Of course it was. It was bound to. She had the address of the house where her family had lived at the time of her birth and that was an excellent starting point.

This time next week, she could well have a clue as to where to find Estelle.

Together, Joan and Mabel examined the railway timetables, sorting out their respective routes. 'Delays permitting,' said Joan with a rueful smile. Passenger trains played second fiddle to trains carrying servicemen, armaments, food and fuel – even rubble, in some cases. Bob had told her that rubble from the London Blitz had been carried by rail to East Anglia to build runways. Was rubble from their own Christmas Blitz also being put to good use?

Before she went away, there was something Joan was determined to get to the bottom of. What had made Margaret

Darrell snub her the other day? Hadn't she recognised her? But Joan knew that she had.

The day before her journey down south, her shift finished mid-afternoon, but instead of rushing home to pack, she headed for the engine sheds. She stopped a woman in dungarees and a turban, who was carrying two full buckets of water.

'I'm looking for Margaret Darrell.'

'Ask the boss.' The woman nodded, glancing over Joan's shoulder, and went on her way.

Looking round, Joan headed towards a man with smears of dirt on his cheeks and posed her question.

He screwed up his eyes thoughtfully. 'Late shift. She'll be here presently.'

That put paid to Joan's hopes, but as she retraced her steps, a cheery-looking blonde spoke to her. She wore a boiler suit and was carrying a huge wrench. Her hair was a mass of bubbly curls and she wore a full face of make-up.

'Margaret Darrell? Try the mess. Between you and me, I don't think the nosh in her billet is up to much. She eats here more than she does at home.'

Joan made her way to the mess, where station staff could get meals and drinks and have a sit-down. She stood in the doorway, peering round, then stepped aside with an apology as someone behind her wanted to get in. She couldn't see Margaret anywhere. Maybe she wasn't eating here today.

Disappointed, she was about to leave when once again she had to give way, this time to a pair of women ticket collectors who were coming in. The act of stepping backwards enabled her to see beyond a tall cupboard to where a girl sat alone at a table, her back to the room. Margaret Darrell? Her build was slimmer than Joan remembered, but maybe that was down to the physical nature of her job. Her hair, hidden inside a turban, was invisible.

Joan went across. 'Excuse me.'

The girl looked up. A couple of brown curls showed on her forehead. The curiosity in her hazel eyes immediately turned to a mixture of shock and dismay.

'It *is* you,' Joan exclaimed. 'I knew it was. Don't you remember me, Miss Darrell? Joan Foster. We did fire-watching together at Ingleby's.'

Margaret's face flooded with colour and she looked away. What was the matter with her?

'I'm sorry to have bothered you,' Joan said stiffly.

Margaret caught her hand before she could walk away. 'No – I'm the one who's sorry.'

Joan slid into the seat opposite her. 'I don't understand. You saw me a few days ago in the engine shed, but you looked right through me. Why?'

Margaret's glance shifted sideways. She pursed her lips together so tightly they nearly turned inside out. When she settled her gaze on Joan, there was a sheen of tears in her eyes.

'What is it?' Joan pressed. 'Please tell me.'

'I came here for a fresh start.' The words were uttered in a fierce undertone. 'The last thing I need is someone who knew me before.'

'At Ingleby's? Why not?'

'Not at Ingleby's.' Margaret looked around, checking how close other people were; Joan couldn't help following suit. Leaning forwards, Margaret whispered, 'That night in the air raid.'

Heat bloomed in Joan's chest and surged up her neck into her cheeks. In her memory, that night lived for ever as the night Lizzie had died, but something else had happened too. She and Mabel had attended first-aid incidents and Joan had seen to Margaret, who, trapped in the cellar beneath her badly damaged home, had suffered a miscarriage. Joan had tried to be professional, but she had been utterly terrified of the responsibility, not to mention profoundly shocked that a girl she knew, however slightly, had got herself into trouble.

'I can understand that you want to put it behind you,' she said in a neutral voice.

'You make it sound so simple. Do you know what happened to me after that? When I came home from hospital, everyone knew, *everyone*, all the neighbours. I couldn't hold my head up.'

'They didn't hear it from me.'

'It was worse than if you'd blabbed. When I was carried from the cellar on a stretcher, my father walked beside me all the way to the ambulance, berating me and leaving nobody in any doubt as to what had happened. My own father!'

Joan didn't say so, but she had witnessed that. Her stomach twisted at the memory of poor Margaret strapped on to the stretcher, her arms pinned down by her sides, so she couldn't even cover her face as her father yelled about her being in the pudding club.

'Our house was destroyed and the one next door was as good as. While I was in hospital, the billeting officer found places for Dad and me and the neighbours with people up the road. Dad and I were given to the same lady, Mrs Riley. She kicked up a stink about not wanting the likes of me, but the billeting officer said she had to. That was the attitude that met me when I came out of hospital.'

'That must have been difficult,' said Joan.

'It was wretched. I spent every evening sitting in a cold bedroom. Dad wouldn't let me go out because I couldn't be trusted and Mrs Riley wouldn't let me in her parlour because I was a harlot. In the end, I had to get away. All I could afford was the grottiest bedsitter you can imagine – and Dad let me go.' Margaret bit down on her bottom lip for a moment. 'That hurt. Even after everything else, it hurt that he didn't try to stop me.'

'What about your boyfriend?' Joan asked. 'Didn't he stand by you?'

'Him! He was after one thing and once he'd got it, I didn't see him for dust.' Margaret hung her head. When she looked up again, she said quietly, 'I'm not that sort of girl. It was only once and I thought he loved me. I really believed it.'

'I'm so sorry.'

'Not half as sorry as I am.'

'When did you leave Ingleby's? When the Registration for Employment Order came in? You look like you're the right sort of age to be covered by that.'

'When was that issued? March? April? About the time that treacle and preserves were rationed, anyway. I'd already left Ingleby's by then. I knew I had to hand in my notice the first time I caught sight of a woman from our road in the shop. Would you believe it, I actually told the floorwalker I needed to be excused and I sloped off and hid in the Ladies. What if the neighbour had seen me and complained to the management? I'd have died of mortification.'

'Surely she already knew that was where you worked.'

'I'd left Dad's billet by then, driven out by shame. The neighbours very likely thought I'd left my job too.'

'So you applied to the railways,' said Joan.

'I remembered you joining and being so proud and excited. I was too upset to think of anything else and it seemed a better option than going to the labour exchange and being shunted into the Land Army. That poster of the girl in her sparkling-clean clothes and perfect make-up, bottle-feeding a lamb, is very misleading, you know.'

'And here you are.'

'When I passed the tests and the medical, I wrote and asked if I could possibly have a job behind the scenes. I knew it was a frightful cheek, but I had to ask. I couldn't bear the thought of being a ticket collector and coming face to face with someone I knew. I wondered about asking to be sent to another place altogether, but I wasn't brave enough to leave here. That's pathetic, isn't it? Ashamed to stay, but frightened to go.'

Joan's heart gave a bump of shock. 'You can't live your life trying to avoid people.'

'There speaks someone who has never been publicly shamed.' Margaret shook her head. 'I don't mean to sound sorry for myself. You must think me an awful drip as well as not being a nice girl any more. Don't bother denying it. I remember the look on your face that night in the cellar when you saw I didn't have so much as an engagement ring.'

Joan remembered too. She had judged Margaret severely – just as Gran had done later when she heard about it; just as Margaret's father had, and their neighbours. But since then Joan had experienced her own fall from grace when she'd had her fling with Steven. In spite of how strictly Gran had brought her up, she had turned out to be considerably less than perfect. Thank goodness Bob was so understanding.

'I'm sorry for pouring all this out on you, Miss Foster.' Margaret sat up straight, signalling the end of their conversation. 'I suppose it comes of having nobody to confide in for such a long time.'

That was something else where Joan was fortunate. She had been able to share her turmoil with her friends, who, instead of condemning her, had provided support. What a difference that had made. Without that, might Joan now feel lonely and ashamed, like Margaret?

She could see that, having opened her heart, Margaret was now closing up. What a hard time she must have endured, coping alone. And how rotten of her father to have turned against her like that. His shame was understandable, but even so.

'Would Daddy be proud of you for that?' Gran's voice asked inside Joan's head. Daddy would have been appalled at her for going off with Steven, the more so because Estelle had run away with another man. Would Daddy have despised and hated her for straying with Steven? But if Bob didn't hate her, no one else had the right to.

'I'll leave you to finish your meal.' Joan pushed back her chair. She felt certain that what remained of Margaret's pasty would be slipped inside her bag for later. 'It's good to see you again.'

Margaret glanced away, but not before Joan had caught a glimmer of disbelief in her eyes.

'I'm going away tomorrow for the weekend,' said Joan, 'but when I return, I hope we can meet up. And if we do, I hope it won't be as Miss Darrell and Miss Foster, but as Margaret and Joan. What d'you say?'

'How are you, Mrs Green? I haven't seen you in a few days – well, not to speak to.'

About to pass through the gate from the platform onto the concourse, Dot halted her flatbed trolley of parcels to have a quick word with Mr Thirkle. Such a casual thing to do, but there was nothing casual in the way her heart thumped and her skin tingled. They hadn't spoken since the day of Mr Churchill's visit at the end of April. Dot had been keeping well away.

Their easy friendship and comfortable conversations had blossomed into love while she wasn't looking, or so it felt. That night, back at the beginning of April, when they'd caught the food-dump thief, everything had changed. Rob Wadden, who was a nasty piece of work, had attacked Dot, whereupon Mr Thirkle, in spite of being old enough to be Wadden's father, had launched himself at the would-be thief. Dot had clobbered Wadden round the head a couple of times with a railway lamp and he had scarpered. Breathless and bruised, Dot had dropped to her knees beside her friend to make sure he was all right. As they helped one another to their feet, she had found herself standing just inches from Mr Thirkle. Call it the emotion of the moment if you must, call it the result of all that adrenaline, but that was the moment when she had realised that this dear man was more than a friend, so much more. She loved him. Not with the breathless, drop-your-knickers passion she had felt, aged fifteen, for Reg, but with a steady, enduring flame that would stay with her for the rest of her life.

Did Mr Thirkle feel the same? In that moment of closeness in the depths of the night at the railway shed, she had thought he did. No, it was more than that. She had known he did. But he had given no indication since, so maybe she was wrong. But then, what indication could he possibly give? He was above all a decent man, one of nature's gentlemen, and he would never make advances towards a married woman. Did she want him to? Oh yes. She yearned for him. Her spirit, her very soul reached out to him.

Her soul had never reached out to Reg. Reg had been the dashing young blade who had got her up the spout and then done the decent thing by putting a ring on her finger.

Mr Thirkle was the other half of her.

Dot hoisted a smile into place. 'You know what it's like. Busy, busy, busy.'

'Will it be time for your break once you've seen to that lot?' Mr Thirkle glanced at the loaded trolley.

Should she say no? Disappear into the crowd on the concourse and not return? Edie Thirkle-as-was had made it clear that Dot had no place in her father's life – and she was right. Dot didn't – shouldn't.

But surely, just as a friend …

'Aye, it will,' she told Mr Thirkle, her heart turning somersaults as he smiled at her.

'Good. It'll be my break then an' all. I'd enjoy one of our chats if you feel so inclined.'

'You can tell me all about moving into your Edie's house.'

That would make it respectable, wouldn't it? Talking about Edie?

Who was she trying to kid?

Chapter Twelve

Joan's first railway journey since the war began was an eye-opening experience, to say the least. She had heard numerous stories of wartime travel from Dot, but none of them had prepared her for the real thing. It made her appreciate Dot's good humour even more. A different sort of person would have taken the opportunity to indulge in a good old moan on a regular basis, but Dot never did, and Joan, sitting squashed against a window in a train painted in austerity black, vowed she wouldn't either. For a start, she was jolly lucky to have a seat. The carriages were packed, yet, as impossible as it seemed, more passengers climbed aboard at every station. The journey lasted much longer than the timetable said. The train had to stop twice at every station because it was pulling so many carriages. At one point, it stopped dead for nearly an hour and when it got going again, it went backwards for a worrying number of miles.

But in spite of the discomfort, there were bright moments. It was impossible not to feel cheered by the kindness of adults passing a couple of young children over their heads all the way down the carriage towards the lavatory; and when folk started to bring out the food they had brought with them, there was a certain amount of sharing and swapping, so that instead of having only her sandwiches, Joan ended up with an apple, a stick of barley sugar and a potato scone. Having something to eat gave people a bit of a boost and the atmosphere became quite jolly, even when the train made yet another stop in between stations.

There was a public house on the road that ran alongside the permanent way, its swinging sign depicting a cloaked man on a rearing horse. He wore a bicorne hat and brandished a sword. Joan, along with her fellow passengers, might well have not paid attention, except that the name of the pub was The Victor of.

'The Victor of what?' asked a few people, which led to a general discussion about who the man could have been.

'Waterloo!' exclaimed a rotund gentleman in a dog collar. 'Must be. Why else would they paint it out? Can't have Jerry thinking this is anywhere near Waterloo Station.'

'I don't see why not,' said someone else. 'I thought the whole point of painting out place names was to confuse the enemy. Letting them think Waterloo Station is nearby would be pretty confusing, I'd have thought.'

At last the train pulled in at Cheddington Station – assuming it was Cheddington. A couple of passengers assured Joan it was and she had to take their word for it. It certainly added a sense of adventure to alighting from the train. At least she had arrived in daylight. You heard of all sorts of mix-ups happening in the dark.

With her handbag and gas-mask box on her shoulder, threatening to slide down her arm, and her suitcase grasped firmly in her hand, she stepped down onto the platform.

'Is this Cheddington?' she asked the people waiting to climb aboard.

'Yes, miss.'

She moved out of their way and waited for the guard to walk along the platform, slamming shut the open doors before returning to his van to blow his whistle and wave his green flag as the signal for the train to pull out. Only then did she approach the stationmaster to ask about the local train to Aylesbury. Would he notice the badge on her lapel? The LMS emblem of the English rose and the

Scottish thistle beneath a wing bearing the cross of St George showed her to be a railway worker, just as he was.

Armed with the information she needed, she sat on a bench with a couple of other passengers, her suitcase by her feet. The sun was still shining but the late afternoon was turning distinctly cool. She drew her jacket snugly around her. Actually, it was Mabel's jacket, which she had lent her so that she could look smart on her travels.

'I insist,' Mabel had said. 'Yours is linen and will crease like mad.'

'But what shall you wear on your journey to Annerby?' Joan asked.

'It won't matter if I arrive all rumpled,' said Mabel. 'I'll have a full wardrobe to plunder when I get there.'

From her handbag, Joan retrieved a postcard. She had intended to save it for when she finally arrived in Wendover, but she had time to kill and a few suitable sentences in her head, so now seemed like a good opportunity.

Dear Mrs C and Mrs G
Nearly there! Feel as if I've lived through every story
Dot Green has ever related. Packed trains, confusion
over place names, children asleep in the net luggage
racks. All I need is a couple of goats and I'll have
the full set!

She squeezed *Much love, Joan xx* at the bottom, then thrust the card into her handbag as the train came chuffing into view.

There were no empty seats, so she upended her suitcase and used it as a stool in the corridor, glad to have the room to do this. On the previous train, the passengers had been crammed in so tightly there was standing room only. In fact, thought Joan, if someone had fainted, no one would have known because the press of bodies would have held them upright. Tiredness seized her, but even this wasn't the last leg of her long journey. The train pulled into Aylesbury High Street. From here, she had to get to the main station to catch the Marylebone train, which would stop at Wendover. According to the timetable, Wendover was the second stop along the way and double summer time meant that there was still plenty of light for her to be sure of getting off at the right place, even if there was an unscheduled stop between here and there.

Just before the train pulled out of Aylesbury, a couple of old dears carrying wicker baskets climbed aboard and sat opposite her, nodding a greeting and starting to chat.

'Going far, are you?'

'Wendover,' said Joan.

Both women sat up a little straighter.

'We live there.'

'Is the Red Lion easy to find?' asked Joan. 'That's where I'm staying.'

'Don't worry,' said one woman. 'We'll point you in the right direction.'

'Meeting your young man, are you?' asked the other.

Her friend gave her a hefty nudge. 'Dolly Clement! What a thing to say!'

'I'm only asking,' said Mrs Clement. 'She's a lucky girl if she's got a chap who'll put her up at the Red Lion.'

'Honestly, I can't take you anywhere.'

Mrs Clement's bright blue eyes regarded Joan. 'No offence intended.'

'None taken,' said Joan. It was true. Gran would have been massively offended, but Joan was no longer under her sway. 'My fiancé wouldn't be very pleased if I came down here for an assignation.'

'In the forces, is he?'

'Reserved occupation. Railway signalman.'

'So, if you've not got yourself a handsome young officer at RAF Halton,' said Mrs Clement, 'what brings you here?'

There could be no harm in answering. 'My family is from here originally, though I'm too young to remember.'

'From Wendover? What name?'

'Foster,' she replied automatically.

Mrs Clement looked at her friend. 'I don't recall any Fosters. Do you, Mrs Piggott?'

Mrs Piggott shook her head, her lips crinkling into a disappointed line. Before Joan could correct her error, the train arrived at Stoke Mandeville. When it set off again, Joan's new friends wanted to hear about her signalman fiancé and how they had met, topics that Joan was more than happy to discuss.

As they got off together at Wendover, Joan was glad to have been taken under the two women's collective wing. They took her to the high street and she looked down the gentle slope towards a spired clock tower at the bottom, where the road curved around a corner.

Mrs Clement and Mrs Piggott stopped.

'The Red Lion is down there on the right,' said Mrs Piggott. 'You can't miss the archway. Go under it and you'll find the way in.'

'Thank you. You've been very kind.'

In spite of her fatigue, Joan walked briskly as she headed down the pretty road. She had arrived and tomorrow she was going to find out about her family.

Dot got off the bus at the Chorlton terminus to find Cordelia waiting for her.

'It's less than five minutes from here,' said Cordelia, linking arms as they set off.

Normally, when Dot alighted from the bus at the terminus she went down Beech Road, on her way to Wilton Close. But today Cordelia took her in the other direction, turning off the main road at a church and taking the second or third on the left. Dot looked at the sign: Torbay Road. A long line of red-brick semis stretched away along the street. Further down were the houses that had been hit in one of the March raids. Dot suppressed a shiver. It could so easily have been Mrs Foster's house that had taken the brunt of the blast.

'This is it,' said Cordelia.

She opened the gate and let Dot go in first, which didn't feel right to Dot. Cordelia ought to be the one going first. She was a lady and Dot was working class. Cordelia rang the bell and they waited.

Mrs Foster opened the door. She was dressed in a brown cardigan and skirt with a white blouse. A brooch might have been a nice touch, but she wore no adornment. Her iron-grey hair was drawn back into the bun she always wore. Her blue eyes narrowed at the sight of them.

'Good evening, Mrs Foster,' said Cordelia. 'I hope we haven't called at an inconvenient time.'

'We work with your Joan,' said Dot. 'We were introduced at young Lizzie's funeral.'

'I remember you,' said Mrs Foster. 'Mrs Green and Mrs Masters. You attended Letitia's funeral as well. What brings you here? Has something happened to Joan?' The words weren't spoken with a gasp and a hand clutched suddenly to her heart, but at least they were uttered.

'No,' said Cordelia, 'but we have come here to talk about her, if you don't mind.'

'I do mind, as it happens, Mrs Masters. I mind very much. I won't have others poking their nose in my family's business.'

'If it helps,' said Cordelia, unruffled, 'Joan has no notion we're doing this.'

'But we are here about her,' Dot added. 'We understand that you and her have got your problems and we don't want to interfere, but—'

'But you have come to interfere,' Mrs Foster put in. She moved her hand as if about to shut the door.

'Please let us in,' said Cordelia. 'We have something important to discuss and if you decline to discuss it with us, you may find yourself discussing it with a magistrate instead.'

Mrs Foster's face hardened. Was she about to refuse? 'You can't come here and push your way into my house.'

'We aren't pushing in,' said Cordelia. 'We have Joan's best interests at heart, as I'm sure you do as well, and we'd like to talk something over, if you'd be so kind.'

It was amazing the way she could bulldoze her way through obstacles while sounding as if she was politely asking whether you took sugar, Dot thought. A similar thought was possibly going through Mrs Foster's head because, after a moment or two, she took a step backwards.

'You'd best come in, then.'

Mrs Foster's parlour was rigidly clean and tidy, with solid old furniture. In pride of place was a studio portrait of a handsome man, who Dot was sure must be Joan's father. In other circumstances, she might have admired the picture, but it didn't seem appropriate today. It would feel too much like buttering up. In spite of the smell of polish, there was something dingy about the room. It took Dot a moment to realise what it was. Ah, yes – those nets. Crikey, they were thick.

'Have a seat,' said Mrs Foster.

Dot and Cordelia politely waited to see where Mrs Foster sat and then they sat next to one another on the sofa.

149

'Well, what's this about?' demanded Mrs Foster. 'Not that I need to ask. I assume you're here because I refused to give Joan permission to get married.'

'That's right,' said Cordelia.

'You're wasting your time if you think you can change my mind,' said Mrs Foster. 'I'm Joan's guardian and what I say goes.'

'But are you her guardian?' asked Cordelia.

Mrs Foster bristled. 'Of course I am. I brought her up, her and her sister, as you know perfectly well.'

'Of course you did, but haven't you since abdicated your position of authority? You obliged Joan to pack her bags and quit your house. I believe you even required her to return her front-door key. Then, when she moved into a house that was subsequently bombed, did you invite her home? No, you left her to tag along with Mrs Cooper to Wilton Close, where, fortunately, there was room for her. So are you still her guardian? I wonder what my husband would make of it.'

'What the hallelujah has it to do with your husband?'

'Mr Masters is a solicitor,' said Dot, feeling it was high time she said something instead of sitting there like a lemon.

'If I sought his professional opinion,' said Cordelia, 'he could well feel obliged to look into the matter and who can say what the outcome might be? You might still be Joan's guardian – or you might not. If you aren't, and Joan wishes to marry into a decent, hard-working family such as the Hubbles, a magistrate might take the view that this is the best thing for her.'

'Especially with her being under twenty-one and in need of a guiding hand,' said Dot.

'Are you threatening me?' asked Mrs Foster, almost through clenched teeth.

'I'm merely stating the facts as I see them,' Cordelia answered lightly. 'I'm very fond of your granddaughter, as is Mrs Green. And it wouldn't be the first time my husband had assisted a friend of mine in a legal matter.'

Aye, that was true. It was also true that Mr Kenneth Masters had been insufferably rude to Dot afterwards in private, making it clear she must never again ask Cordelia for help. Not that she had asked for it in the first place, but after the way Mr Masters had spoken to her, Dot would chew off her own arm sooner than submit to being helped by him ever again.

'Doesn't it occur to you that I have perfectly good reasons for refusing my permission?' said Mrs Foster. 'Not that those reasons are any of your business.'

'Indeed they aren't,' Cordelia agreed. 'But there are also good reasons why being allowed to marry soon would be the right thing for Joan. She's been through so much and she needs love and stability.'

'Are you saying she never had that from me?'

'Please don't put words into my mouth, Mrs Foster. Whatever you provided in the past is beside the point, since apparently you're not providing anything now. The simple fact that you made Joan move out is evidence of that.'

This was going to get nasty in a minute. Cordelia and Mrs Foster were both strong women. Dot stepped in, trying to inject a lighter note.

'Look, Mrs Foster, me and Mrs Masters have known your Joan since her first day on the railways and we care about her. I'm not saying you don't care, but you must admit you've turned your back on her. Now, I don't know owt about magistrates and the law, but I do know that Joan is a good girl who deserves the chance of a happy marriage without waiting until next year. You can give her that chance. What d'you say?'

Chapter Thirteen

Armed with a pretty posy, Joan walked into the spacious, grassy churchyard. The parish church was a handsome building, situated not in the middle of Wendover, but on its edge. In the May sunshine, a vase of yellow blooms stood in front of a gravestone that had tilted over the years. Beyond it, a man was digging a fresh grave. The old grave and the new provided a sense of continuity that added to the feeling of tranquillity.

Rather than seek help, Joan wanted to walk around the churchyard and read the headstones and find Daddy's grave herself. The scent of the grass lifted softly in the air as she walked, taking her time. She did find a stone with HENSHAW at the top – two, actually – and her heart bumped hard inside her chest, but they were old stones. The most recent name recorded was a Juliet in 1917. Somehow, she had missed Daddy's grave. She walked around once more, reading the names at the top of every stone, even though she was aware that she had looked properly the first time – except that she couldn't have looked properly, could she, or she would have found Daddy.

At the end of her second circuit, her heart accepted what her head had known the first time. She approached the gravedigger.

'Excuse me. I'm looking for a particular grave, but I can't find it. I can see you're busy, but if you could point me in the right direction ... '

'Sorry, miss, no can do. I've not lived here long. I ended up here after I was invalided out of the army. Well, the bits of me that are left ended up here, anyway.' He tapped his leg with the edge of his spade. There was a tinny sound. 'You could ask the vicar, but he's getting ready for a wedding and probably won't have time.'

Her heart dipped in disappointment and it must have shown on her face, because the gravedigger clambered out of the hole, pulling off his thick gloves. He stabbed his spade into the heap of soil and chucked his gloves on top.

'He's probably in the vestry. Let's go and see, shall we?'

He removed his cap as they entered the church. It was cool inside. Joan had a sweeping impression of loftiness, graceful arches and stained glass as she hurried to keep up with her companion, who, in spite of his loping gait, moved at quite a lick. As they neared the top of the aisle, the vicar appeared.

He eyed the gravedigger. 'I hope you aren't going to tell me we haven't got an organist today.'

'Don't know anything about that, Vicar. This young lady is trying to find a grave.'

'I'm afraid I haven't much time at present. A wedding, you know.' The vicar's voice was kind. 'Can you come back this afternoon? Say, between four and five. I could see you then.'

'That would be difficult. I'm only here today and tomorrow morning. I'm trying to find out about my family and this is my starting point.'

'Do you know the name and the date you're looking for?'

'The name and the year.'

'That'll do. Come with me and I'll let you go through the parish books. We record baptisms, marriages and burials. When you find the one you're looking for, make a note of the burial-plot number and Mr Jackson here will show you.'

The vicar nodded to Mr Jackson, who withdrew, then, with a wave of his hand, he invited Joan to follow him into the vestry.

'Which year?'

'Nineteen twenty-one.'

'Here we are.' The vicar took a large volume from a shelf and placed it on a table. 'Please take care turning the pages and don't leave any marks.'

'Thank you.'

'Not at all. Now, I must press on. Close the book when you've finished.'

He left her. There were no chairs, so Joan stood leaning over the table, her heart beating steadily as she opened the book with its long lists in neat writing. The year was stated at the top of each page. She found 1921 and started going down the page. She trembled inside, but her hand was steady as her fingertip ran down the first list. Each entry began with a surname, so it was going to be easy to find Daddy.

A chill rushed through her body, sending tingles in all directions. Not Daddy, but herself. Her baptism record. HENSHAW, Joan Angela. Her heartbeat, which had started off steady and sure, was now jumping about all over the place and wouldn't be calmed. She scanned the rest of the year, but couldn't find Daddy's burial. She went back to the beginning and tried again. Still no Daddy.

Maybe he hadn't died in '21. She was born that January. Daddy had died and Gran had moved to Manchester with her and Letitia when Joan was not yet one. So maybe Daddy had been buried at the very beginning of 1922.

But he wasn't there either. She went back through 1921, but hers was the only Henshaw name in that year. She trailed her finger lightly all the way through 1922 in case Gran had got muddled about the year. She didn't stop until she had reached the end of 1924.

There was no record of HENSHAW, Donald Robert.

Mabel stood at a distance from Althea's grave. How could something feel as if it had happened a hundred years ago and like it had happened yesterday, both at the same time? She had attended two funerals since Althea's. She didn't remember much about Lizzie's because although she hadn't realised it, she had been dreadfully ill at the time, collapsing in the middle of the service, and Cordelia and Persephone had carted her off to hospital. The other funeral had been one of the two mass burials held after the Christmas Blitz. She had gone to the one that had been held in Southern Cemetery, not because she knew any of the dead personally, but because, after working flat out as a first-aider during those two terrible nights, being present at the mass burial had been the right thing to do. The only person she knew who had been killed in the Christmas Blitz was Letitia, but Mabel hadn't been able to get time off to attend her funeral. If they had granted time off to attend funerals after the Christmas Blitz to everybody who had needed it, no one would have been at work.

An urgent need stole into Mabel's heart to cross the grass and wind her way between the headstones so that she could stand beside Althea's grave and possibly even rest her fingers along the top of the stone. She had been in such turmoil at Althea's funeral, floundering in the depths of guilt and grief. She badly needed some quiet thinking time now beside Althea's grave.

But not quite yet. She had to earn it. She had to call on Althea's parents.

Turning, she walked out of the churchyard, which was in the oldest part of town, on the valley floor. She made her way to Hill Climb, though Steep Hill Climb would have been a better name for it. Before she left Annerby to become a railway girl, the climb had been easier thanks to a series of posts at regular intervals with strong rope slung between them so you could haul yourself up if you needed to, but the metal posts, donated to the town fifteen years ago by Pops, had vanished now, taken away to be melted down.

She would have preferred to drive over to Althea's house. It would have been a more formal way to arrive, but she couldn't justify using petrol for a house call, which left her a choice between going by bicycle or on horseback, neither of which felt appropriate. But riding a horse seemed altogether too healthy, so a bicycle it was.

She had chosen her dress with care. The short sleeves and boat neck would be cool for cycling, while the navy colour added a serious touch in keeping with the purpose of her visit. Her beret was a snug fit and wouldn't blow off. Instead of wearing her hair loose, she pulled it back and secured it with a large clip at the base of her neck. To complete her ensemble, she wore the amethyst and crystal beads with matching earrings that Althea's parents had given her for her twenty-first birthday.

She cycled through the clear morning air, breathing deeply and enjoying the moorland scents in spite of her mission. Along the way, she picked out various places where she might take cover should an enemy plane appear – tucked against the drystone wall, or over there in that shepherd's hut. Did everyone take such eventualities into account these days or was it just her?

Cycling up the drive, she left her bicycle at the foot of the stone steps up to the Wilmores' front door. Had she really not been back here since that final time she had called for

Althea? All her life, she had run up and down these steps, in and out of the front door, as if this was her own home – which it was, in a way, just as Kirkland House had been Althea's home, well, as good as.

But not any more. Today, she felt like a stranger. She felt as unsure of her welcome as a stranger would, too.

Her pulse quickened as she was shown into Mrs Wilmore's morning room. It hadn't changed a bit, with its Regency stripes and the large wicker basket of logs on the hearth. In a few weeks, the roses would be nodding at the windows.

Before she could utter a word, both Althea's parents stood up. Mrs Wilmore hurried across to draw her in, holding her hand and saying, 'Look, Roger, look who it is,' as if she had magicked Mabel up. Mr Wilmore kissed her cheek, murmuring, 'My dear girl.'

How could she have ever been unsure of her welcome from this darling couple?

And *how* could she have abandoned them?

'Let me look at you.' Still clasping her hands, Mrs Wilmore stood back and took her in from head to toe. 'Come and sit down – no, not there, here, next to me. I saw your mother at the Anstruthers' bridge evening and she said you'd be coming up for a day or two, but I never thought – it's been so long—'

Pain tightened Mabel's throat as guilt washed through her. 'I'm sorry.'

'It's been dashed hard.' Mr Wilmore's voice was gruff. 'For all of us.'

'But you're here now,' said Mrs Wilmore. 'You've come to see us and we aren't going to frighten you off with recriminations – are we, Roger?'

'No, old girl.' Mr Wilmore patted Mabel's shoulder in rather the same way he might have patted the dog. 'We're pleased you've come.'

How generous they were. But hadn't they always been? Hadn't they accepted her presence under their roof as if they had two daughters, not one – just as Mumsy and Pops had accepted Althea? Fresh grief stormed through Mabel and she went hot and cold, as if Althea had died yesterday instead of before the war.

'Now then,' said Mrs Wilmore. 'No tears or you'll set me off.'

'I'm sorry I didn't come to see you after Althea died. I'm sorry I never wrote.'

'We understood,' said Mrs Wilmore. 'We tried to, anyway.'

'Then you went away,' said her husband, 'and that was a slap in the face, going away without a goodbye.'

'I know,' said Mabel. 'It was cowardly. I've come today to say all the things I should have said at the time, all the things I should have written in a condolence letter. She meant the world to me.'

'Oh, my darling girl.' Mrs Wilmore squeezed her hand.

'I'm just so sorry I never came before. And you were so kind about visiting me last year when I was recuperating from that dashed blood poisoning. That made it even worse that I hadn't done the right thing by you.'

'Now then, now then,' said Mr Wilmore.

'My dear Mabel,' said his wife, 'of course we came to see you. You mean a lot to us – and not just because Althea loved you. We care for you for your own sake. We always have and we always will.'

'I say,' said Mr Wilmore, 'd'you remember the day you and Allie built that den in the orchard?'

And they were off, the three of them, romping through memories, laughing, sharing, wiping away tears, clinging to what they had left of their beloved Althea; hurt by the memories, but bolstered by them too, in an urgent mixture of poignancy and solace.

Mabel made no mention of Gil; no mention of that terrible fight before the accident. She hadn't come here to cleanse her soul. She had come to give these dear people what comfort she could.

It was the one final thing she could do for Althea, the sister of her heart.

Chapter Fourteen

Joan stood outside her family's old cottage. Quoting the address on her birth certificate, she had asked a couple of locals for directions and now here she was. The cottage was one of the two middle ones in a terrace of four, each with a poky window beside the door and another above the ground-floor window, though there was no second upstairs window over the door. Each of the doors was divided across the middle halfway up, suggesting that the top part could be opened on its own, like a stable door. Joan absorbed the moment as she plundered her memory for some sort of recognition. It was daft, but she couldn't help it. She had been a baby when she left here; she couldn't possibly remember.

There had been no picture of the cottage in Gran's box of photographs. She had never realised that before. After Letitia's death, she had trawled through all the photos, desperate to see her sister's smiling face, appalled that she would never again see her in the flesh. She had gone through the whole box, so fixed upon finding snaps of Letitia that it hadn't occurred to her that certain pictures weren't there. Well, she had known there wouldn't be any of Estelle, of course. Gran had probably torn those to shreds before dropping the pieces into the heart of the fire. But it seemed odd that there had been no picture of this cottage – or was it? Did people take pictures of their homes?

It was time to knock on the door. Would the lady of the house think her quite mad or would she smile and say, 'I

remember the Henshaws. They lived here before we did'?
Joan needed to hear that. After failing to find Daddy's
grave, she badly needed to hear it. Not finding Daddy's
burial in the parish register had left her with the feeling
that something was slipping away from her.

There was the tiniest of front gardens. It was hardly
three steps to the door. She knocked.

'She's out.'

Startled, Joan turned to find a sour-faced woman on the
other side of the low, ivy-bestrewn wall. She was old enough
to be Joan's mother. In fact, old enough for Joan to have been
the youngest of six. Her face, beneath her turban, was pudgy.
She wrapped her arms across her chest in a manner calcu-
lated to appear forbidding, but Joan wasn't going to be put off.

'Do you know when she'll be back?' she asked.

'Who wants to know?'

'I was hoping to speak to her. I've come a long way.'

'You have, have you? What's her name, then?'

'I beg your pardon?' Joan thought of Mrs Clement and
Mrs Piggott, with their twinkling eyes and ready smiles.
She could do with some of that now.

'This lady you've come miles to see. You must know her
name.'

'I'm afraid not. It's not that simple.'

'I'll tell you what would be the simplest thing: for me to
send for the police.'

'There's really no need. I used to live here, but we left
years ago.'

'What name?'

'I'm Joan Foster now, but my name used to be Henshaw.'

'Henshaw?' The neighbour's eyes widened. 'Henshaw,'
she said again.

Joan took a step closer. 'Did you live here back then? Do
you remember my family?'

The neighbour's expression was unreadable. Her fleshy face ought to be soft and expressive, but it was set like stone. 'What brings you back?'

The Foster-Henshaw mystery was too complicated and Joan was reluctant to confide in this unyielding woman. 'I'd like to trace my mother.'

'Your mother?' There was disbelief in the words. 'Mrs Henshaw?'

'Estelle. Yes. Estelle Henshaw.' It was the first time she had applied the new surname to her mother.

'You want to trace her? You mean – find her?'

'I'd like to meet her.' Joan lifted her chin. Was Estelle's disgrace remembered with disgust all these years later? 'I have a particular reason.'

'I don't know what to say – and that's not something that often happens to me.'

Joan could imagine that. 'I'm also interested in finding out about my family in general.'

The woman stared at her. 'You're Joan.'

'Yes. I am. Do you remember me?'

The arms that had folded uncompromisingly across the neighbour's ample bosom dropped to her sides. 'I'm busy. I can't talk now.' She turned to go indoors.

Joan reached across the wall and caught her arm. 'You *do* remember. I can see you do. Please talk to me, Mrs …?' She held her breath. Would the neighbour introduce herself?

The woman stared down at her hand until Joan let go.

'Reed. Mrs Reed. But I told you. I'm busy. I've the stairs to finish and the brass to do.'

'Please don't go,' begged Joan. 'If you do, I'll knock on your door until you answer.'

'You try that and I really will send for the police.'

Joan's mind raced. Why wouldn't Mrs Reed help her?

162

'I can understand if you have nothing to say about my mother. It must have caused a dreadful scandal when she ran away. But I would so appreciate it if you would tell me anything you can recall about my father. It would be a great kindness if you would.' She held her breath.

'When she ran away?' Mrs Reed repeated. 'Is that what they told you?'

'My grandmother never kept it secret from us – from my sister and me, I mean – though, of course, all three of us kept it a secret from everybody else. That was why my grandmother took us away from here, so we could start again.'

'Bloody hell.' Mrs Reed didn't utter the words loudly or angrily. Her voice was shocked, yes, but it was quiet. 'You say your mother ran away.'

'Yes.' Why did Mrs Reed keep repeating her?

'And there was a scandal? Why?'

'Because – because – you know why.'

'Tell me.'

'You must know if you lived here at that time.'

'I do know, but I want to know what you know.'

'My mother abandoned her family and ran away with another man.' There. She had said it.

'And you've come here to see if you can trace her.'

'Yes.'

'So that you can meet her.'

'Yes.'

'And find out about your family – about your father.'

'Yes.'

Mrs Reed stood stock-still. Only her eyes moved. Her gaze left Joan's face and she stared at the ground.

'Please,' said Joan. 'Will you help me?'

Mrs Reed came back to life. She heaved a deep sigh. 'I suppose I have to, but it's going to come as a shock.' She looked straight at Joan and her eyes narrowed. 'Are you sure you want to know?'

'*For all the good it'll do you.*' That was what Gran had said.

'If you've come looking for your mother, you're twenty years too late. She's dead.'

'Auntie Rosa saw a ghost,' Jimmy said through a mouthful of vegetable rissole.

'Don't speak with your mouth full – Auntie Rosa?' Dot bridled. 'She's Mrs Walters to you. Auntie Pammy's your auntie.'

'Mum said to call her Auntie Rosa.'

'Don't answer back,' said Dot.

'She did,' muttered Jimmy.

Dot looked at Reg. A bit of support wouldn't go amiss, but Reg was concentrating on his plate.

'Finish your dinner and no more talking,' said Dot, but she already knew she was going to ask Jimmy questions afterwards. Auntie Rosa, indeed! So much for her plan to get somebody respectable billeted on Sheila. Dot didn't like the feeling that she'd been got the better of, even if Sheila had no idea about her billeting scheme.

At the end of the meal, she cleared the table and put the kettle on to make tea for her and Reg.

'Please may I leave the table?' asked Jimmy.

Normally, she would have sent him out to play, but today she said, 'You can hang on and help me wash up.'

'Oh, *Nan.*'

'You can't have him washing up,' said Reg. 'That's women's work.'

'I'll wash and dry. Our Jimmy can put the plates away. I want a word with him.'

'I'm not in trouble, am I, Nan?'

'Nay, love.'

'Good, cos I usually am.'

'I just want a chat,' said Dot. 'We haven't had you round to stop with us for a while.'

'I like it here,' said Jimmy. 'There isn't as much lipstick.'

A while later, Dot washed up and Jimmy stood beside her on one leg, leaning against the wooden draining board, describing his newest piece of shrapnel.

'You'll have enough bits and pieces to build your own Spitfire at this rate,' said Dot.

Jimmy's eyes shone. 'Cor, really?'

'No.' Best nip that in the bud or heaven knew where it might lead. 'What's this about Mrs Walters seeing a ghost?'

'Mum saw it an' all, only it wasn't a real ghost. It was a baker.'

Dot stopped in the middle of drying a plate. 'What are you on about?'

Jimmy's glance suggested he couldn't make it any plainer. He sighed. 'They were on their way home in the blackout and this ghost came towards them. They screamed, then it turned out it weren't a ghost after all. It was a baker on his way home from the late shift. Covered in flour, see?'

Dot resumed drying the plate, her mind working furiously. What time would a baker's late shift finish?

'Is that plate dry now, Nan?'

'Oh aye. Don't drop it,' Dot said automatically.

Jimmy talked on his way to the cupboard. 'There was white on Auntie Rosa's – Mrs Walters' coat this morning. I asked where it came from and she told me about the ghost. Her and Mum couldn't stop laughing.'

'I bet they couldn't,' said Dot in a jovial voice. Flour – on Rosa's coat? 'Whereabouts on her coat? On the arm?'

Beside her once more, Jimmy shrugged. 'All over, I think.'

'All over?' It nearly killed her to do it, but she kept her tone light and chatty.

'It were on the back, because I saw it when I went in the kitchen. Her coat was over the back of a chair. I touched it and they both yelled at me not to because of smearing it into the wee.'

'Into the what?'

'Summat like that.'

'The weave. Then what?'

Another shrug. 'Nowt. There was flour on the front of her coat an' all. She hung it over the washing line and got me to bash it with the carpet-beater.'

In a light-hearted voice – and God forgive her for making use of an innocent child – Dot asked, 'Was there flour on your mum's coat an' all?'

'Dunno. Is that plate ready?'

'Here you are.'

Dot finished the drying. Her mind was still working overtime. What *had* those girls been up to? And what had the baker been up to that involved getting flour all over Rosa's coat?

'Last one.' She handed Jimmy the plate. 'Where were you when this was going on? If the baker was coming home off his shift, it must have been during the night. They never left you on your own, did they?'

'Don't fret, Nan. I was round at Nanny Donna's.'

It was a good job Dot wasn't holding a plate or it might have slipped through her fingers. Either that or she would have hurled it against the wall.

'Nanny Donna?'

'She's Auntie – Mrs Walters' mum.'

'I know who she is, thank you.'

Oh aye. Donna Woods, Donna Bardsley-as-was. Donna no-better-than-she-flaming-should-be. Heaven knew, Dot was no saint. She'd had a bun in the oven when she walked up the aisle, but at least she'd known who the father was, which was more than Donna Woods could say about her eldest.

And Sheila had let Jimmy stop the night with Donna Woods. Nanny Donna, indeed! It was all Dot could do not to grind her teeth.

'I'd rather stay here,' said Jimmy, 'but Mum says you've got fed up of me and you don't want me stopping the night no more.'

In spite of the sunshine, the inside of the cottage was dark. The windows were small and the building faced the wrong way to catch the sun at this time of day. Joan was hazily aware of being hauled over the threshold into a low-ceilinged room with a vast fireplace on one side and a bed tucked against the opposite wall.

Mrs Reed practically frogmarched her across the room towards the corner as if about to make her stand there like the class dunce. With her mind still reeling from the shock of what the woman had said outside, Joan just had time to glimpse the rush-seated chair before she was thrust onto it. Her brain had gone fuzzy. She could barely think.

'Here.' A beaker of water was placed in her hand. 'You're not going to drop it, are you?'

'No,' she whispered. 'I can manage.'

She clutched the beaker in both hands. When she raised it to her lips, it tapped against her teeth because her fingers were trembling.

Mrs Reed snatched it from her. 'I'm not having you spilling it. I told you it'd come as a shock. Lord, I wish I hadn't said anything now.'

The clip of vexation in her tone brought Joan struggling to the surface of her distress. She had to pull herself together. She couldn't risk losing the neighbour's goodwill, such as it was.

167

'No – I'm glad you did.' Glad? Glad to be told her mother was dead? How could Estelle be dead?

'Who's this, then?'

A new voice, thin with age. The bed was occupied by an elderly lady in an old-fashioned nightcap tied beneath her chin.

'No one for you to bother about, Mother,' said Mrs Reed. 'She'll be gone soon enough.'

'It looked like you were kidnapping her, the way you dragged her inside.'

'Leave it be, Mother.' To Joan, Mrs Reed said, 'If you're feeling better, you'd best be on your way. I can't help you.'

Panic streaked through Joan. 'You said you would. You said you'd tell me.'

'That was before you had a funny turn on me.'

'Tell her what?' demanded the old lady.

'Nothing, Mother.'

Was Mrs Reed going to throw her out? Addressing the old woman, Joan said, 'I'm sorry to have barged in on you. I'm Joan – Henshaw. Joan Henshaw. My family used to live next door.'

'Henshaw ... ' The old lady digested this, then sat bolt upright. 'Henshaw?' There was a slight slur in her voice.

Mrs Reed went to her mother and pressed her shoulders, trying to ease her back against the pillows. She resisted.

'You mustn't get upset, Mother,' said Mrs Reed.

The old lady batted her away. 'Glory be, *that* family?' She might not enunciate her words with complete clarity, but there could be no doubting her excitement. 'I remember it like it was yesterday.'

'Nonsense, Mother. You lived in Lee Common.'

'I've got ears, haven't I? The reverend read it out loud from the newspapers in the pulpit. He said he'd never seen the church so full.'

'For all the good it'll do you.' Joan felt a tightening in her chest and an ache at the back of her throat. Whatever had happened?

'Are we talking about the same people?' she asked. 'My parents were Donald and Estelle Henshaw. Their daughters were Letitia and Joan. We were tiny when ... ' When what?

'Do you mean to say she doesn't know?' demanded the old lady.

Her daughter sighed. 'She's come here to find out. She thought her mother was still alive.'

'She never.' The old lady all but wriggled in excitement. 'If you don't want to tell her, I will.' She looked at Joan. 'Come and sit next to me. Where are my teeth?'

'Never mind your teeth,' said Mrs Reed. 'I'll do the talking.' Another sigh – a sharp sound, not a sympathetic one. 'I've lived in this cottage nigh on thirty-five years.'

'So you remember my family,' breathed Joan.

'There was your father and mother and they had two little girls, very close in age.'

'A year apart, almost to the day.'

'I helped deliver whichever one of you was oldest.'

A tiny chill passed across Joan's skin as something shifted inside her head. Not just in her head, but in her heart. A sense of wonderment. This wasn't just old memories being revisited. It wasn't just whatever had gripped the congregation in Lee Common. This was real and personal, not just to her, but also to the brusque Mrs Reed.

'Letitia,' said Joan. 'Letitia came first.' Leaning forwards, she asked quietly, 'Won't you please tell me what happened? I need to know. I've spent my whole life believing my mother ran off with her fancy man, but you say she died.' Why would Gran lie about that?

'Oh, there was a fancy man all right,' Mrs Reed's mother burst out, her words clearer now but accompanied by a clicking sound that suggested her dentures didn't fit as well as they might.

'Stop it, Mother,' said Mrs Reed. Another of those sighs. 'There were problems between your parents. Raised voices. Don't ask for details. I'm not the sort to pin my ear to the wall, unlike some. Yes, there was a fellow. That all came out at the trial.'

'The trial?' Joan exclaimed.

Mrs Reed shook her head. 'You've already had one hope blighted, hearing about your mother. Why not leave it there? There's nothing to be gained by digging over old ground.'

Shock had left Joan's skin clammy. She felt shaky, but she had to appear composed or Mrs Reed might refuse to say more. 'I'd prefer to be told, if you don't mind.' Her pulse was jumping about. Please don't let it show in her voice. 'Whatever it is, it can't be worse than hearing that my mother is dead.'

'Don't be so sure,' said Mrs Reed with a return to sharpness. 'You heard me say there was a trial, didn't you?'

'You said it came out that there was another man. My gran always said they ran away together. Did my mother die before they could? Was she in an accident?'

'For pity's sake, stop dragging this out,' said the old woman from her bed. 'Just tell her.'

Mrs Reed looked at Joan and for the first time, there was real sympathy in her eyes. 'Were your mother and this fellow planning to run away together? Who can say? They never got the chance. I'm sorry to say it, but your mother was killed.'

'Killed?'

'Murdered.'

The world slowed down. *'Murdered?'* Joan's heartbeat was heavy and slow. 'By this man?'

'No, not by him. No one ever knew who he was.' Mrs Reed blew out a breath. 'It was your father. He killed your mother in a jealous rage.'

Chapter Fifteen

It was an effort to cycle home to Kirkland House. It wasn't just Mabel's heart that had taken a battering that morning. It seemed that talking endlessly about Althea with her parents had sapped the strength from every muscle she possessed. But it was a good sort of exhaustion. Could exhaustion be exhilarating? She might well carry to the end of her days her guilt over the way things had ended between her and Althea, but here, today, she had given Althea's mother and father some comfort and that mattered far more to her than her own feelings.

She had pictured herself visiting the Wilmores and then going to the churchyard, finally able to take her place beside Althea's grave, but it turned out there was one more thing she needed to do first.

Arriving home, she just had time to tidy herself before lunch. Mumsy linked arms with her as they went through to the dining room with its oil paintings and wood panelling. It was at the rear of the house, its windows overlooking the lawn and shrubbery beyond. Half of the garden was now given over to growing vegetables. Incongruously, in the centre of the vegetable beds was a stone statue of a girl in a Grecian-style robe, seated, her head bent over a book. The cat was curled up asleep on her sunwarmed lap.

Lunch was potato-and-bacon omelette followed by nut-and-apple slices. Cook had promised to send Mabel home with a hamper to boost Mrs Grayson's cupboards. Mabel made a mental note to beg Cook for the recipe for the baked chocolate pudding they'd had for dessert at dinner yesterday.

Her heart thumped at the thought of what she was going to tell her parents, but it wasn't right to make table conversation of it. It needed to be discussed afterwards, but the moment luncheon was over, Pops stood up.

'You'll have to excuse me. I need to get back to the factory.'

'Pops is there until all hours these days,' sighed Mumsy. 'I hardly see him.'

'Don't go yet, Pops,' said Mabel. 'I need to talk to you. It's important. Please,' she added.

'Very well, but make it snappy.' Pops looked at her expectantly.

'Could we go into the drawing room?' Mabel felt a twinge of unease. She had felt so certain about this earlier, but now it was as if she was being rushed into it.

'What's this about?' Mumsy asked as they rose to leave the room. 'Should we be worried?'

'No,' Mabel hastened to assure her. 'At least, not in the way you mean.'

'But there is something to worry about?'

'Esme,' said Pops, opening the drawing-room door for them, 'let's wait for Mabs to tell us.' When they were seated, he said, 'Well, Mabs, whether you intended it or not, you've succeeded in worrying us, so let's have it, please, and no shilly-shallying.'

'It isn't a matter for worry, in that it happened quite some time ago. But – but it might make you think less of me.'

Mumsy uttered a small exclamation. Pops looked at Mabel intently.

'It's to do with Althea,' said Mabel. She explained about Althea falling hook, line and sinker for Gil.

173

'Gil?' Mumsy frowned. 'I don't recall anyone called Gilbert.'

'Iain Gilchrist.'

'That rings a bell. Wasn't he one of Bobby Thornley's friends? I remember a gaggle of them coming to stay.'

'Yes, but I never met them until their second visit, in the summer.' Mabel pressed her lips together. 'I'm getting ahead of myself.'

'Let her tell it in her own way, Esme,' said Pops. 'Go on, Mabs.'

Mabel described how Althea had finally been forced to face up to the distressing truth that the man she adored had no romantic feelings whatsoever for her.

'The poor child,' said Mumsy.

'That was why she persuaded her parents to extend their tour of the West Country that summer – so there'd be no chance of her bumping into him again.'

'How frightful for her,' said Mumsy. 'Good heavens. This wasn't why you went to see the Wilmores this morning, was it? To tell them?'

'Absolutely not. They don't have an inkling and you must never breathe a word about it, because – because there's more.'

Quietly, looking down at her clasped hands more than at her parents, Mabel told of her own relationship with Gil.

'You – and Iain Gilchrist?' Pops exclaimed. 'Why didn't we know anything about this?'

'Because she had to tell Althea first – didn't you, darling?'

The understanding in Mumsy's voice pierced Mabel's heart. She nodded, unable for a moment to speak. Then came the hardest part of all: telling the truth about that final drive.

Pops surged to his feet and stomped across the room as if about to grab a decanter, but instead he turned to face her. 'Why choose now to tell us?'

'Because I've felt so horribly guilty all this time. I finally found the courage to see the Wilmores and I've done the decent thing by them, and now I want you to know what happened. It's been hard keeping such an important secret from you.'

Pops said nothing, but Mumsy's mind was apparently working overtime.

'So this Iain Gilchrist – are you and he … ? Only Pops and I were certain that – I mean, your letters are full of Harry.'

A wave of love for Mumsy gushed through her. The possibility of a wedding hat was never far from her mother's thoughts.

'Yes, my letters are full of Harry and for a very good reason. As for Gil, I admit he did pop up recently, completely out of the blue, and it brought all those memories to the surface. That's why I'm here now. It was talking with Gil that made me realise I had to see the Wilmores.'

'Talking with Gil?' said Mumsy. 'So you've been seeing him?'

'No. Well – yes. That is, we bumped into one another at a dance and we saw one another once after that, purely for the purpose of talking over everything that happened with Althea.'

Mumsy nodded. 'And what does Harry think of that?'

'He's not keen, but there's nothing for him to worry about, honestly.'

'I'm pleased to hear it.'

'You said Gilchrist turned up out of the blue,' said Pops. 'Are you sure about that? I don't like to think he came looking for you.'

'Oh, Pops! It was nothing like that. He's stationed in Manchester at the moment, working with the Red Cross.'

'He's a Red Cross man? Doctor, is he?'

'No, he's in the army, but he works alongside the Red Cross.'

'Doing what?'

Mabel laughed. 'It's not a very impressive job, I'm afraid. He spends his days choosing things to go into Red Cross parcels for our boys in POW camps. You know, jigsaws, greatcoats, what have you.'

'Oh aye?' Suddenly Pops was all business. 'I'm glad you told us the truth. Honesty is the best policy and all that. I must get back to the factory now, so I'll leave you to cry all over Mumsy if you feel the need.' He kissed them both and went to the door, then turned round to add, 'And Mabs, could we have a private word when I get back?'

Lord, what could that be about? Some sort of wigging, she supposed, rather like when she had failed her School Cert so miserably the first time round. Whatever he said, she would take it on the chin. It couldn't be easy for a doting father to think of his darling daughter having awkward entanglements with men.

When Pops had gone, she turned to Mumsy.

'I thought I'd visit Althea's grave this afternoon. I could never face going before, but now it feels like the right time. Will you excuse me?'

'Of course, if that's what you want, but would you like me to come with you? I don't mean to suggest you aren't up to doing it on your own. I'm just offering my dear girl a hand to hold if she needs it.'

'That would be perfect,' said Mabel.

It was a great treat to dress for dinner. Sifting through her wardrobe, Mabel selected a green silk-taffeta dress with a

176

flared skirt, which she wore with a chiffon wrap around her shoulders. The garnets she took from her jewellery box might have a Victorian setting that suggested a beloved family heirloom, but the jewellery had been in her possession for all of three years. Perhaps the set had been another's girl's heirloom before her family fell on hard times.

She went downstairs, trailing her hand along the smooth, polished wood of the bannister rail. There was something special about walking downstairs dressed for the evening. She was in good time. There was still twenty minutes to go before the dinner gong. She smiled. Mumsy would have liked to have a dressing gong as well because it was in her precious etiquette book, only Pops had put his foot down.

'I don't need a blessed gong to tell me it's best-bib-and-tucker time.'

Darling Pops. Mabel was so proud of him. There he was, in the hall, shrugging off his coat and hat and holding out his hands to her as she reached the foot of the stairs.

He kissed her cheek. 'I shan't hug you in case you get rumpled. Goodness, you look beautiful.' He turned to the maid, who was hanging up his things. 'Doesn't she look beautiful, Doris?'

'She does that, sir.'

'Now, Mabs, let's have our little talk, shall we?'

'Is there time?' she asked as he led her across the hall towards what Mumsy referred to as his study and what he, since he was obliged to call it something, called his den.

'It won't take me two minutes to fling on a bit of evening dress.'

'If Mumsy could hear you now,' she teased, preceding him into the room.

'Well, maybe a little more than two minutes, but what I have to say won't take long. Have a seat, Mabs.'

Mabel sat in one of the leather wing chairs with a deeply buttoned back. She had always liked the den and its paintings of railways that Pops had bought as a tribute to Grandad.

'Should I be worried?' She smiled as she deliberately echoed her parents' words from earlier on, expecting Pops to smile back.

But he looked serious. 'No, but I think perhaps you should be ashamed.'

'Ashamed?' Crikey, he really was going to haul her over the coals for having a secret relationship with Gil.

'I'm afraid so. It's what you said earlier about this Iain Gilchrist.'

'Pops, I never intended to fall in love. It's not something you can help. And we had to keep it under our hats for Althea's sake.'

Pops held up his hand. 'I don't mean all that. I'm referring to what you said about his war work – about it not being impressive.'

'I'm sorry if that offended you. Of course I'm glad to think of our boys in prison camps receiving comforts from home.'

'Mabs, will you kindly put a sock in it and let me speak.' Pops sat in the armchair opposite hers, but instead of sinking into it as the old, butter-soft leather invited, he sat forwards, hands on knees, his keen gaze on her face. 'I've spent the afternoon wondering whether to tell you this and I've made up my mind that I shall. But what I'm about to say stays in this room and you're not to repeat it to anyone. I refuse to have you thinking ill of Iain Gilchrist and all the other boffin chappies. That doesn't sit right with me, the more so because of Bradshaw's Ball Bearings being involved.'

Boffin chappies? What was this about? Mabel sat forward, her attention riveted on her father.

'Shall I tell you some of the things we've been making at the factory, as well as all the things that everyone knows about? I have a small group of workers who've been sworn to secrecy. They work in a separate part of the building to everyone else and they make certain special items. You mentioned greatcoats earlier, didn't you? We provide the buttons.'

That broke her concentration. Buttons? She didn't know what she had expected Pops to say, but she had thought it would be something vital.

'Aye, buttons. It doesn't seem like much, does it? But on every greatcoat, one button has a compass inside it. Now d'you get the idea? The POWs are sent sewing kits and amongst the pins will be one that's been magnetised so it points to magnetic north. We're involved in the production of jigsaws as well – jigsaws that contain information hidden in the pictures. We make other things too, but I hope there's no need to tell you anything else.'

'I had no idea,' Mabel whispered.

'Your Iain Gilchrist and other clever types spend their days dreaming up ways of supplying POWs with articles and information that'll help them if they manage to escape. They even find ways of supplying German money. They had a go at hiding it underneath the labels in the centre of gramophone records, but I think Jerry got wise to that. But the point is, this work is not something to be made light of.'

No, it wasn't. Mabel's ideas about Gil shifted rapidly. How could she have underestimated him so badly?

Joan sat bolt upright on the carpet, her back leaning against the bed, knees drawn up, arms wrapped tightly around them. She had been sitting here for – for hours, she supposed. Since way before darkness fell, at any rate. She hadn't moved even to draw the curtains. With no light in her room, there was no need, surely, and anyway, she couldn't bear the thought of being enclosed by the blackout. Her life was black enough without that.

Her heart was still beating. It was a good thing it beat of its own accord, because if she'd had to tell it to do so, she would have forgotten. Her life seemed a long way away.

She had fought hard not to believe Mrs Reed. Deep down, she had known the woman must be speaking the truth. Why would she lie? Even so, she had fought not to believe.

But in the end, there had been no room for doubt. Prompted by Mrs Reed, who was probably glad to see the back of her, Joan had spent all afternoon in the bowels of the building that housed the *Bucks Herald*, her skin growing cold as she found and digested the various reports. They hadn't been difficult to find. It had been the most prominent story for weeks.

Donald Henshaw had murdered his wife.

Daddy – *Daddy* – had murdered Estelle. The man Joan and Letitia had been brought up to revere had been hanged for murder.

'*Would Daddy be proud of you for this?*' That was what Gran had asked them time and again. She had claimed it was a way of making Daddy live on in their hearts, but it had also been a jolly effective way of exercising control over them.

No wonder Gran had taken her two little granddaughters to live nearly two hundred miles away. It wasn't Estelle who had run away. It was Gran.

All those lies. All those years of lies, of adoring Daddy, poor darling Daddy who had died of a broken heart.

A broken neck, more like.

Joan's muscles were clenched so tight they burned, warning her that they needed to move, to relax, to stretch, but she didn't care. She couldn't have moved even if she'd wanted to. Horror locked her in position. All that moved were the thoughts, the new knowledge, the fog of emotion that writhed around in her head beneath the dense layer of shock.

She continued to sit there, desperate for oblivion, but too scared to sleep. Frightened of the images sleep might bring.

It took for ever to get to the village of Cuddington and travelling on a Sunday didn't help. Joan caught the train into Aylesbury and then found a bus that trundled through the green countryside.

'This is your stop,' the clippie told her.

She climbed off the bus and looked around for someone to ask for directions, then realised she didn't need to. The bus had slowed as it passed a pub with a thatched roof before pulling in just beyond a wide lane, down which, clearly visible before it snaked around a corner, was the church. Joan's throat was dry and she had a strange, hollow feeling inside as she walked past the village shop and headed for the church.

This was it. The culmination of her visit down south.

She had hoped she would be able to track down her mother and ask for permission to marry – demand permission to marry. The mother who had abandoned her children wasn't in any position to refuse. The mother who had run off with her lover should be grateful, frankly, that her daughter had gone to the trouble of finding her.

Except, that wasn't what had happened. Estelle Henshaw had been killed by her husband. More than killed – *murdered*. Use the right word. Donald Henshaw had murdered his wife, the mother of his daughters.

A tweedy couple with a black labrador gave her curious looks as they went by, the man touching his hat to her. Joan gave a nod of greeting, barely making eye contact. These people had no place in what was happening. Neither did the young children kneeling on a cottage doorstep playing a game involving lots of twigs; nor did the folk chatting outside the village hall. Beyond the hall was the school, obviously built in Victorian times, and between it and the village hall was a house in a large garden, presumably the dwelling that went with the headteacher's post. Lucky headteacher. Maybe, in a small place like this, the head-teacher was the only teacher.

Opposite the school stood the church. The lane had nar-rowed. Joan stopped. If she passed under the lychgate, she would find her mother's grave. That was what she had come for, wasn't it? No, it wasn't. Yes, it was, in the here, now, today sense; in the context of what she had discovered yesterday. But in the wider sense, it wasn't. She had trav-elled down from Manchester expecting to find Daddy's grave and hoping to uncover a clue as to Estelle's whereabouts.

She had spent her whole life believing Daddy had wasted away from a broken heart, thinking of Estelle as the faith-less wife who had abandoned her children. That was what Gran had said. That was the shocking family secret Joan and Letitia had been trained never to breathe a word about.

But it wasn't that way at all. Instead of finding Daddy's grave, she was now moments from standing beside her mother's. Estelle had been a Cuddington girl and, after the tragedy of her murder, she had been brought home to be buried. It had said that in the newspaper.

The day had assumed a dreamlike quality. Joan stepped onto the path that led to the church porch. Headstones were dotted about in the grass. To the right, the ground was a little higher than the path and here she saw the war memorial. A stone Celtic cross stood tall above a stepped base. Approaching it, she read the names. The Frosts and the Vines had lost more than one chap. Brothers, cousins? Was there a Hopkins? Estelle's brother, perhaps? Her own uncle. Good heavens, this place, this village, was a part of herself.

She remained beside the memorial, head bowed, trying to pay her respects, but really she could barely think. She still hadn't taken in what she had learned yesterday. The horror of her father's actions – the scale of Gran's deception – it was too much. She felt a deep, urgent need for Letitia's company and support, but that was denied to her for ever.

People emerged from the church's wide doorway, dressed in their Sunday best, couples, families. There must be a number of farms around here. That was a reserved occupation. Three young women set off up the path. Land girls?

Not wanting to draw attention, Joan slipped away across the grass. She didn't want to speak to anybody, to be asked questions. Then she stopped and looked back. She might be related to one of these people.

It didn't matter if she was. Not today. Today was for herself and Estelle. If she had a few more days ... but she didn't. She had to set off for home this afternoon. Her suitcase was in the Left Luggage at Aylesbury Station. She had hours of travelling ahead of her. One day, she might return and find Estelle's family, if any remained, but that was for the future. She couldn't begin to contemplate it now.

Quietly, respectfully, she walked from stone to stone until she found the name HOPKINS. The grave was old and had received its final remains towards the end of the last century. Was this to be a repeat of yesterday morning, when she had trailed around St Mary's in Wendover?

No, it wasn't. She came upon it a minute later, an age-darkened stone in the peaceful shade of some trees. She almost missed it, because the name at the top wasn't Hopkins but Matthews. Eric Matthews had been born in 1840. With him in the grave was his wife Abigail, their daughter Caroline and her husband, Ivor Hopkins. At the foot of the stone, it said, *And their daughter Estelle, aged 25.*

No mention of Henshaw. Nothing to suggest she had ever been married.

And their daughter Estelle, aged 25.

Chapter Sixteen

Dot clocked off and fetched her hat and coat. It was too warm for a coat, especially on top of her uniform jacket, but she had no option if she wanted to go in the buffet. She walked through the station, her pulse speeding up. Oh, she was mad to feel this way at the prospect of catching sight of Mr Thirkle, but she couldn't help herself. She was fifteen years old all over again, longing for a glimpse of Reg. No, wait, actually it wasn't at all like that. Well, the thumping heart and the eager self-awareness were the same, but with Reg it had been the heat of attraction, pure and simple – only, not so pure when you considered how quickly she had whipped her knickers off. But the point was that with Reg, the attraction had come first and the getting-to-know-you bit hadn't happened until two babies later.

With her and Mr Thirkle, it had started out as friendship and it really had been pure and simple. Aye, pure. Like minds. Kindness. Understanding. An easy way of making conversation. Kindred spirits, that's what they were. Summat inside each of them recognised and responded to summat similar inside the other and it had made them into true friends.

Aye, friendship had come first and the love that had followed was all the deeper and steadier for it. This was what she had never had with Reg. Depth, steadiness. A meeting of minds that had blossomed into an entwining of hearts. Was Reg as disenchanted with her as she was with him?

Dot's breath caught, almost tying a knot in her throat. Mr Thirkle was at his ticket barrier and it looked like he was handing over duty to a fellow ticket collector. Any moment now he would turn around. Would he see her? What if he did? It wasn't as though she could push her way through the crowd and run into his arms.

Would he want her to? That was summat she didn't know, not for certain. Were her feelings returned? That night when they had caught the thief, she would have sworn that, yes, the moment of revelation had happened to him at exactly the same time as it happened to her. But since then, nothing had been said or indicated between them. Was he holding back, just as she was?

The temptation to go to his side was so strong that her feet had turned in his direction before she knew it. Crikey, she shouldn't do this, she really shouldn't, but, oh, how could she not?

An arm slid through hers and she turned, startled, to find herself linked with Cordelia. Blimey, did Cordelia know? Was she saving Dot from making a holy show of herself?

Of course not. Cordelia was simply accompanying her to the buffet – and a jolly good thing an' all. Imagine if she had headed for Mr Thirkle in such a public way. Was she mad?

She squeezed Cordelia's arm. 'What must folk think when they see us two, eh? You in your fine clothes and pearls and me in my ancient coat and stout shoes.'

'I hope they look at us and think what good friends we must be.'

Dot laughed. 'Maybe. More likely they wonder what the likes of you is doing with the likes of me.'

'In which case, more fool them. Don't do yourself down, Dot. You're the most important friend I've had in a long time.'

Delight spread through Dot. Cordelia unlinked herself as she stepped forward to open the buffet door and they went inside. For a wonder, there was no queue. The moment she saw them, Mrs Jessop put two cups and saucers on the counter.

'Here we are again, Mrs Jessop,' said Cordelia.

'Like bad pennies, you lot.' Mrs Jessop poured the tea.

'Let's bag that corner table,' said Dot. Corner tables always felt more private.

'I wonder how Joan got on in her family's old home,' said Cordelia as they sat down. 'I hope she was able to contact them, especially after the tragedy of losing Letitia. Mrs Foster isn't someone I'd pick to be my only living relative.'

'Joan will be a Hubble soon enough,' said Dot, 'and by all accounts, you'd have to go a long way to find a better family.'

'I wish Joan and Bob all the best,' said Cordelia. 'Of all our girls, she's the one in the greatest need of happiness.'

'I like the sound of that. "Our girls". When I joined the railways, I didn't want to end up being a substitute mum to my younger colleagues. I do enough running around after others at home. But it hasn't been like that. I don't feel like a mum to the youngsters, but I do want to watch over them.'

Cordelia nodded. 'You're protective of them and so am I.' She smiled, her grave beauty softening. 'That's why I so dearly want Joan to marry Bob and be part of his family. Mabel, Alison and Persephone all come from solid family backgrounds, and Colette has her husband, but whom does Joan have, other than her grandmother? I hope she's been able to find a Henshaw relative or two on her travels. Family is so important.'

'Aye, it is. It won't be long before your Emily comes home from school for good.'

'My husband is talking about making arrangements for her to stay away.'

'Not come home after all, you mean?'

'He says her safety matters more than anything – and he's correct, of course.' But Cordelia's eyelashes fluttered over her grey eyes and she didn't meet Dot's concerned gaze.

'Eh, love, I understand that, but it'd be hard on you. I lie awake sometimes, fretting about the right place for our Jenny and Jimmy to be – here or evacuated. Every time we have a few nights clear of air raids, I thank the Lord I've got them close by. Then the bombs start dropping again and I feel like I'm a monster of selfishness.'

'It's a complicated business.' Cordelia's momentary distress had vanished behind her customary composure. 'There's no escaping it. Family is the most important thing. Have you heard from your boys recently?'

'Not for a while. You know what it's like. You don't hear and you don't hear and you worry yourself silly, then two or three letters arrive all in one go.'

'Or, from their point of view, waiting for letters from home; they wait and wait and then they get a whole sack-load from you, Dot. I know how often you write to them.'

With the feeling she was dipping her toes into what could turn out to be painfully hot water, Dot said, 'Our Sheila, my daughter-in-law, says she's no good at writing letters.' The remark might sound offhand but she was being dreadfully careful.

'I should think that relating Jimmy's antics would give her plenty to write about.'

'Ah, but she doesn't view Jimmy's shenanigans as funny,' said Dot. 'She sees them as a dratted nuisance.'

'But I expect you turn them into funny stories for Harry, don't you?'

'Aye, I do.' This wasn't going the way Dot wanted it to. Bugger how hot the water was. She was going to jump in with both feet. She leaned forward. 'Cordelia, can I tell you summat, private like?'

'Of course. Is there a problem?'

Dot huffed out a breath. 'I think so, though I don't know absolutely for certain.' Was she about to bad-mouth Sheila when there was an innocent explanation? Oh aye, and what kind of innocent explanation could possibly involve a man's voice upstairs in the dead of night when the husband was away fighting for his country? 'It's our Sheila.'

Quietly, Dot described the night when she had nipped round to fetch Jimmy's PT bag. Instead of feeling anger or resentment towards Sheila, she felt her cheeks tingle with shame. It was a measure of the trust she had in Cordelia that she was able to share her anxiety.

'... so I know I never saw nowt, but I do know what I heard and I'm that worried.'

'I'm very sorry to hear it.'

'I'd never have thought it of her, but if she's being unfaithful to Harry—'

'Alison, how nice to see you,' Cordelia interrupted her, looking over Dot's shoulder. 'Where are you going to sit?'

Dot rearranged her thoughts, giving Alison a welcoming smile. 'Look, there's Colette in the queue – and Persephone.'

Soon, Colette and Persephone joined them, putting down their cups and saucers and pulling out chairs.

'No Joan yet?' said Persephone. 'I can't wait to hear what happened on her travels.'

'I was round at Mrs Cooper's yesterday afternoon,' said Colette and everyone's attention homed in on her.

'Had Joan got back?' asked Alison.

'No, they weren't expecting her until late evening at the earliest. Tony came with me to do some gardening. He offered to meet her off the train, but Mrs Cooper said not to, because there was no knowing what time she'd arrive. You simply never know whether a train will be on time these days.'

'How are the ladies in Wilton Close?' asked Dot.

'They're fine,' said Colette. 'Mrs Cooper is excited about starting her Magic Mop business.' She delved in her handbag and produced some plain postcards, which had been written on in capitals on one side. She offered them to Cordelia. 'Mrs Cooper wondered if you would kindly pass these on to your friends.'

Cordelia took the cards and looked at them. 'My friends already have daily helps, but yes, if there's a mess after an air raid, they may well want additional cleaning. The only thing is ... ' she addressed Dot '... these cards would look so much better if they were typewritten. Do you think Mrs Cooper would mind if I got some cards typed for her? I could ask my husband to get his secretary to do it.'

Dot's heart gave a thump as it all came flooding back – the way Mr Masters had wiped the floor with her for, as he saw it, prevailing on Cordelia's good nature to get herself some free legal representation, though it hadn't been like that at all.

'You mustn't put Mr Masters to any trouble,' said Dot.

Cordelia laughed. 'It would be no trouble to Kenneth. It would be Miss Douglas doing the work, such as it is. Frankly, when I think of the wedding present she is going to receive from us in a few weeks' time, typing a few cards is the very least she can do.' She slipped the cards into her handbag. 'I'll sort it out. Good, here's Mabel. I'll ask her to tell Mrs Cooper what I'm doing.'

Dot swallowed. With luck, Mr Masters would never have cause to meet Mrs Cooper. The thought of that lovely woman being carpeted the way he had carpeted her was too much.

'May I give you a message for Mrs Cooper?' Cordelia asked Mabel as she sat down.

'Of course, if it's not urgent. We're off to the flicks straight from here.' Mabel indicated Alison and Persephone.

'It isn't urgent,' said Cordelia, 'but on second thoughts, I'll go home a different way and drop in on Mrs Cooper.'

'There's still no sign of Joan.' Persephone glanced towards the door. 'We want to hear about her weekend.'

'She sends apologies,' said Mabel, 'but she's not coming. Don't worry. She's all right, just exhausted, poor thing. Her journey yesterday was pretty frightful. She didn't arrive home until the early hours and then she had to drag herself out of bed for work this morning.'

'Did she mention how she got on?' asked Alison.

'That's for Joan to tell, not Mabel,' said Cordelia.

'She said to tell you all that she didn't discover anything,' said Mabel. 'She came across an old family grave, but that's all. She didn't meet any Henshaws.'

'So she still doesn't know why her grandmother changed the family name,' said Colette.

'What rotten luck,' said Persephone. 'It's a pity she wasn't there longer or she might have done some serious digging.'

'Perhaps she'll go back another time,' said Alison. 'After the war.'

Mabel tilted her head from side to side, as if weighing up the matter. 'She said she wants to put it behind her and concentrate on the future.'

'So we mustn't harp on about it when we see her,' said Dot.

'It's a shame for her,' mused Cordelia, 'but perhaps it's for the best.'

'How so?' asked Colette.

'For Mrs Foster to have moved such a long way and changed their surname suggests a big bust-up in the past.'

'You mean Joan's better off not knowing?' Persephone asked.

'I know it wouldn't suit you, with your reporter's instincts,' said Cordelia, 'but put yourself in her shoes. Think what she's been through already. What does she stand to gain? More questions? More heartache?'

'She's had quite enough of that already,' said Colette. 'Dot's right. We shouldn't keep on at her about it.'

'Agreed?' Cordelia looked around the table, collecting nods and murmurs.

'Good,' said Dot. 'Our Joan has got a lot to look forward to and it's our job to help her concentrate on that.'

Cordelia picked up her handbag. 'If you'll excuse me, I'll go and have a word with Mrs Cooper about Magic Mop. If Joan's there,' she added with a glance at Dot, 'I'll have a word with her too.'

It took Dot a moment to twig what she meant. Of course – Mrs Foster's agreement to the under-age marriage. That would give Joan a boost after the weekend's disappointment.

Dot got to her feet. 'I'll love you and leave you an' all. I must fetch our Jimmy. He's stopping the night with us.'

'That's nice,' said Colette.

'It's been a while since you mentioned having him to stay,' said Alison.

A fierce feeling surged through Dot, though she couldn't have said whether it was Sheila or herself she was vexed with. Her master plan to prevent Sheila from entertaining her gentleman friend by no longer having Jimmy overnight until such time as Dot could get someone billeted on her had backfired twice over. Not only had Sheila got Rosa to move in, but Jimmy now thought Nan and Grandpa didn't want him any more. Well, Dot wasn't having that.

'Our Jimmy's welcome at my house any time,' she announced. 'As far as I'm concerned, he can move in, if he wants. I'd have him like a shot.'

She would an' all. Might it come to that? Would she have to prise Jimmy off Sheila? But she couldn't do that without Harry's say-so. Sheila was right about one thing. Unless it was unavoidable, you couldn't send bad news to men serving overseas, because what were they supposed to do about it?

The problem nagged away at Dot all the way to Sheila's. Sheila would be out doing her stint at the munitions, but Rosa would be there, looking after Jimmy. Dot shook her head at the thought of Rosa Walters taking care of their Jimmy, at the thought of having to say thank you to Rosa, as if Rosa was someone she liked and respected.

In spite of everything, she couldn't help feeling a tug of pride as she turned the corner into Sheila's road. The houses here had three bedrooms. All right, the third bedroom was the size of a shoebox, but even so. Harry had grown up in a two-up two-down and now he had three bedrooms. You always wanted your children to have more than you had yourself.

She opened the gate, noting it needed a lick of paint. She must get Reg to see to that.

'Mrs Green,' called a voice from behind her.

Dot turned. The woman from over the road was coming towards her. Dot's thoughts scrambled around, trying to come up with her name, but, very inconveniently, all she could remember was that Sheila referred to her as Mrs Nosy.

'Have you come for your Jimmy?'

'Aye.' Dot made to walk through the gate.

'He's not in there.'

'You what?' What was that monkey up to now?

'He's over at mine. He was playing out with the other kiddies, but when they were called in for their tea, he was left sitting on yon wall.'

'But Rosa – Mrs Walters—'

'Oh aye, Mrs Walters. She went her own sweet way an hour or more since.'

'She's meant to be looking after our Jimmy until I fetch him.' Dot pulled at her collar as guilt consumed her. Why hadn't she come straight here instead of going to the buffet?

Mrs Nosy laughed. Dot nearly died of shame. She knew that laugh. She had uttered it herself a thousand times. It meant scorn. That she should have lived to hear that laugh applied to her own family was unbearable.

'Done up to the nines, she was,' said Mrs Nosy. 'Any looking after she was thinking of doing, it wasn't your Jimmy she had in mind. A flaming disgrace, she is. I'm surprised you let your daughter-in-law take in the likes of her. I could name a dozen women up and down our road who aren't pleased. Lowers the tone, she does, that Rosa Walters.'

Dot couldn't agree more, but she didn't say so. She settled for a stiff 'Thank you for taking our Jimmy in.'

'I've given him a slice of bread and dripping to tide him over.'

'Thank you,' Dot said again.

'Aye, well, somebody needs to do the right thing by him.'

A flash of cold fury held Dot rigid. There were two things she had never done in her life. Unlike some backstreet women, she had never screeched like a fishwife and she had never lashed out at another woman, no matter what the provocation. But she was riled up enough to do either of those things right now. 'Somebody needs to do the right thing by him' indeed! Dot's whole life was devoted to doing the right thing by her sons and her grandchildren.

'You're Mrs Green's mother-in-law, aren't you?' said a new voice. Another neighbour appeared, removing her wrap-around pinny to signal the day's housework was over. 'I hope you don't mind me saying so, love, but us neighbours aren't best pleased to have the likes of Donna Woods's lass moving into our street. I'm surprised you let your girl take her in.'

A couple more women appeared.

'Don't be so polite about it, Nettie Higgins,' said one. 'Say it like it is.'

'She lowers the tone, that Rosa Walters,' declared another. 'You know what they say. Like mother, like daughter.'

There was a chorus of 'Aye' and 'I reckon'. A small crowd was gathering. Crikey. Dot wasn't scared. She could hold her own in any situation. But what was she to say to these women? She agreed with them wholeheartedly, but if she said so, it would get back to Sheila, who would dig her heels in. She had an obstinate streak, did Sheila. But neither could Dot pretend to take Sheila's side. She would sooner cut out her tongue than demean herself in that way.

That left one option.

She inhaled deeply through her nose, saying nowt, just looking calm. They would talk about her behind her back for what she was about to say, she knew, but it couldn't be helped. There was a saying, wasn't there, about living to fight another day?

'Thank you all for your concern, but I mustn't keep you.' She looked Mrs Nosy in the eye. 'Shall I call our Jimmy or will you? Oh, here he comes now.' She cuffed him affectionately. 'Let's get you sorted out with some tea, eh? Come along. Evening, ladies.'

The group took a collective step backwards as, with her hand on Jimmy's shoulder, Dot threaded her way through them. She kept her chin up and her shoulders back, but once she was clear of the group of women, tears of fury and humiliation filled her eyes. She blinked them away before Jimmy could catch on. It would bother him to see his nan upset.

Eh, walking away might be the sensible thing, but it was ruddy hard an' all. She could crown Sheila for this, she really could, but that wasn't the answer.

The trouble was that since her clever billeting scheme had failed, she didn't know what the answer was. Should she confront Sheila? But she had no proof. Hearing wasn't the same as seeing. It wasn't the same as throwing open the bedroom door and catching a couple in the throes of hanky-panky. As it was, Sheila could make up some cock-and-bull story and brazen it out – and she could write to Harry and complain about his nasty-minded mother an' all.

'Are you all right, Nan?'

Dot smiled down at her beloved grandson. 'Course I am, chick. How d'you fancy sardines on toast?'

That was one of the first things you learned when you became a mum. You had to be on good form all the time if you wanted your children to feel happy, confident and safe. They got their feeling of security from you and that meant you had to put on a brave face, no matter what.

No matter flaming what.

Chapter Seventeen

By now, Mabel would have told their friends that Joan hadn't found out anything about her Henshaw family. Joan tried to feel relieved, but she was too churned up. She had lied through her teeth since arriving home last night – well, in the early hours of this morning. Mrs Cooper, bless her, had waited up, never imagining how bad her kindness made Joan feel as she dashed off a few lies. Apparently, Tony Naylor had offered to meet her off the train. Thank goodness he hadn't or that would have meant more lies.

At last, Joan had fallen into bed, only to tell more lies to Mabel while they were getting up, and she had trotted out yet more for Mrs Grayson's benefit over the breakfast table. Lies, lies, lies. She felt a complete heel, because at heart she was an honest person.

Except that she wasn't, was she? Hadn't she grown up telling lies? Telling anyone who asked that she was an orphan.

'Nobody must *ever* know the truth,' Gran had instilled in her and Letitia. 'What your mother did was shocking and disgraceful. It's better that everyone thinks she's dead. Otherwise we could lose our respectability.'

The extraordinary thing was that in saying Estelle was dead, Joan and Letitia had actually been telling the truth.

It turned out that the biggest liar of all was Gran.

Joan was exhausted after the weekend's emotional strain, plus all the travelling on top of it. She hadn't minded the long journey on the way there because she had been looking forward to what was to come, but the journey back, when she was weighed down by the terrible truth about her father, had been arduous. Today at work had had an odd quality about it. How could her life be carrying on as normal? She was the daughter of a murderer. Everything should be different.

She had been brought up believing she was the daughter of a trollop and instead she was the child of a murderer.

But even the children of murderers had to do their bit for the war effort. Even the daughters of wife-killers had to smile at passengers, load their sack trolleys with luggage and head for the taxi rank. Would these kind passengers tip her a thrupenny bit or a tanner if they knew what her father had done?

Her father. Not Daddy. Not the Daddy she had been brought up to love and revere. As a little girl, she had day-dreamed that his death was a big mistake and he would come back and swing his darling daughters up in the air and they would all live happily ever after. It was a fantasy that had fed a need deep inside her – and not just a childish fantasy either. She had still indulged in her daydream when she was sixteen or seventeen.

She sucked in a breath that burned her lungs. How could Gran have done this to her and Letitia? How *could* she?

Now she had to tell Bob. She would never afterwards utter a word to another living soul, but she had to tell Bob. He was entitled to know he was engaged to a murderer's daughter. Would he stand by her? Of course he would. He was staunch and strong and she didn't doubt him for one moment, but even so, it was a lot to ask of him.

She was seeing him this evening. Before she went away, they had agreed that, weather permitting, they would meet at the top of Limits Lane, which marked the boundary between Stretford and Chorlton. It was a short lane with a row of ramshackle Victorian cottages, each in its own little garden. At the end of the road, which was no more than a wide cinder path, was a bumpy slope down to the meadows that ran for miles alongside the Mersey. There was an ack-ack gun emplacement in this part of the meadows, but as long as they kept their distance, it would be all right.

When they had made their arrangement, Joan had pictured a warm May evening, whispered confidences and hopes for the future. Heaven help her, she had imagined being a step closer to seeking Estelle's permission to marry.

Fighting back a wave of emotion, she took one of Letitia's dresses from the wardrobe. Was it time to stop thinking of them as Letitia's dresses? She didn't want to. She wanted to cling to every last piece of her sister, now more than ever. The dress was one that Joan had made, with inverted box pleats in the skirt and tiny puffs in the short sleeves. She wore her hair brushed back from her forehead, falling in soft waves about her face.

'You have a young face,' Letitia had once told her.

A young face? It was difficult to tell when you looked at yourself. She wasn't young on the inside any more. She felt as if she carried the weight of a hundred lifetimes.

Fixing a smile in position, she ran downstairs to say cheerful goodbyes, catching the warm glance that passed between Mrs Cooper and Mrs Grayson that told her they wanted her to enjoy the evening with Bob to make up for not finding out about her Henshaw family.

As she was about to open the front door, the bell rang. She swung the door open and found Cordelia outside.

Cordelia laughed. 'That was quick.'

'I'm on my way out. Mrs Cooper's in the front room.'

'As a matter of fact, I'm here to see you as well. Could you spare a minute?'

Crumbs, it wasn't going to be sympathy over her supposed lack of success down south, was it? 'I really have to go. I'm meeting Bob.'

'This will take a minute, two at the most. I'm happy to tell you that your grandmother has changed her mind.'

Joan blinked. She couldn't think what Cordelia meant.

'About giving permission for you to marry,' explained Cordelia. 'She's reconsidered and decided that it is, after all, the best thing for you.'

Joan's mind had been crammed so full of the weekend's revelations that Gran's refusal seemed to have happened years ago.

'I knew you'd be surprised,' said Cordelia, 'but you look positively shocked.'

Joan pulled herself together. 'It's wonderful news, but how do you know?'

'I bumped into Mrs Foster. Now, I mustn't keep you. I need to pop in and see Mrs Cooper about her Magic Mop enterprise.'

Joan stepped out of the house so that Cordelia could walk in. On top of everything else, here was a fresh shock – was shock too strong a word? She ought to be jumping up and down for joy, but how could she after everything else that had happened?

As she walked to Limits Lane, the sight of pink and white blossom in the gardens of the smart houses along Edge Lane pierced her heart with their beauty. Was it just her or did other people think of brides when they saw blossom? Bob would stand by her, wouldn't he? Of course he would.

He was already at the corner. As soon as he saw her, he came towards her and he looked so handsome and so downright lovable that she broke into a run. He caught her in his arms. Not long ago, she would have shrunk from such a public display, but not any more. Life was too short.

'How did you get on down south?' Bob asked.

'Let's sit down and I'll tell you everything.'

Hand in hand, they walked down the lane and onto the meadows. Joan shut her eyes to the sight of the gun emplacement, concentrating on the rich yellow of the buttercups and the rosy pink of the ragged robins.

The ground was dry, but Bob removed his jacket and laid it down for her to sit on. Joan's heart melted. He was so considerate. She couldn't imagine anything better than being looked after by Bob for the rest of her life. She would take the best possible care of him too.

Slowly, with her pulse rushing in her ears, she revealed all that had happened, all she had learned. Bob asked a question here and there, but mostly he let her talk. That was good, because it meant she didn't miss anything out. Or was it horror that held him silent?

'So that's everything,' she finished. 'I'm trusting you with this because I know that whatever you decide, you'll keep this to yourself.'

'What do you mean, whatever I decide? Joan Foster, are you suggesting that I might want to break up with you?'

'I wouldn't blame you.'

'You're right about that. You won't blame me because it very definitely isn't going to happen.' Bob caught her hand and held it lightly, as if giving her the chance to pull away. 'Can't you see? This makes me want to cherish you all the more. Yes, I'm shocked. I'm appalled, in fact. If you want the truth, it's going to take time for it all to sink in. But it won't make me change my mind about you. Nothing could do that.'

Joan's hands trembled as relief poured through her. 'You've no idea how glad I am to hear you say that.'

'Did you really think I'd leave you?'

'No, not deep down, but on the surface I knew you'd have every right to.'

Bob nodded slowly, his normally cheerful face taking on a sombre cast. 'It's a serious matter. You say you haven't told anyone.'

'Only you.'

'That's how it has to stay. We can never tell anybody. Other folk might make judgements. They might not want to know the couple with a murder in their background.'

'Thank you for saying "the couple" and not "the girl".'

'Of course I said "the couple". Anything that affects you affects me.'

'I'm sorry we have to build our lives on a lie.'

Bob leaned over and tenderly kissed her mouth, then rested his forehead against hers. Joan felt the brush of fabric as his cap and her hat both slid back.

'Our life together will be built on love, trust and hope,' said Bob. 'More than anything, it's going to be built on the fact that we're two decent people who know what's right.'

Joan sighed softly. The words couldn't have touched her more deeply had they been Bob's wedding vows.

'So that's settled, Joan Foster, or Joan Henshaw or whatever you want to call yourself. Actually, all I want to call you is Joan Hubble.'

Joan realised her cheeks were damp, but after the strain of the weekend, these were tears of happiness. She laughed.

'It so happens your wish can be granted.'

All through Tuesday, Joan felt as if she was being pulled in different directions. Her discovery that she was the daughter of a murderer was still sinking in, but Bob had taken part of the knowledge, the shame, the secret, and had hoisted it onto his own shoulders. Knowing she would never have to bear the burden alone made her heart overflow. Bob was the best man in the world and she was the luckiest girl. Whoever would have thought that such a tragic secret would bring them closer? But it had – and it was Bob's warm heart and steadfast character that had enabled it to happen. Plenty of men would have run a mile, but not Bob Hubble. She loved him even more, if that was possible.

'Then let's set a date,' he had said yesterday when she had shared Gran's unexpected change of heart. 'Let's get married as soon as we can.'

And she wanted to, oh, how she wanted to. Marrying Bob would make everything slot into place and give her the life, the future she wanted. She knew it in her bones.

But she couldn't dwell on that, couldn't look forward to it, until she had confronted Gran. Yes, confronted. It wasn't a word Joan would ever have expected to apply to herself, especially not where Gran was concerned. She had spent a lifetime obeying and conforming, doing as she was told, trying to please but never quite succeeding.

Vexation made her skin feel hot and sensitive as she thought of all the questions she needed to ask, all the lies Gran had told. She was going to go round to Gran's tonight. All day long, questions stormed across her mind.

At last, the working day ended. She clocked off and fetched her things, ready to dash home, the sooner to go out again and see Gran. *Confront* Gran.

'Joan! I'm glad I've caught you.' Alison came hurrying up to her, her dark hair bouncing on her shoulders. 'Have you got a minute?'

'I have to go home. I've got something important to do.'

'This won't take long – and it's important too. Please, Joan.'

'Well ... ' It wasn't in Joan's nature to turn away a friend.

'It's about Mabel,' said Alison, her brown eyes full of concern.

'Has there been an accident?' Joan pictured the gangs of lengthmen with their crowbars and pickaxes—

'She's fine. It's nothing like that, but I do need to speak to you.'

'I'm listening,' said Joan.

'Not here. I know you haven't time for a cuppa, but if the buffet isn't full, we can nab a table for a few minutes. I'm sure Mrs Jessop won't mind.'

Joan allowed herself to be led into the buffet, where there was an empty table in the corner.

'What's this about?' she asked as soon as they sat down.

Alison drew a breath. 'Mabel's being unfaithful to Harry.'

'What? Don't be ridiculous.'

'I know. I can't believe it either. But I heard Dot and Cordelia discussing it.'

'You must have misheard.' Sheer disbelief made Joan laugh. 'She adores him.'

'I distinctly heard Dot say, "I'd never have thought it of her, but if she's being unfaithful to Harry—" and then Cordelia saw me and started talking about something else.'

'Didn't you ask them about it?'

'I told you, Cordelia changed the subject. They clearly hoped I hadn't heard.' Colour stained Alison's cheeks and she dipped her head for a moment. When she looked up, she leaned forward, lowering her voice and speaking urgently. 'Look, I'm not trying to spread gossip. I care about Mabel. I've been wondering whether to talk to her, but I think it'd be better coming from you.'

'From me?' The words came out almost as a squeak.

'If she's having problems in her personal life, I might not be the best person to approach her, not with Paul and me

204

being such an established couple. But you've had problems of your own.'

'You mean Steven.'

'She might listen to you. She'd feel that you understand what she's going through.'

Joan didn't know what to make of it. Mabel, unfaithful to Harry? Impossible. Then she recalled the way Harry had originally wormed his way into Mabel's good books when he was in search of a wealthy wife, something about which Alison knew nothing. Mabel had sworn she'd forgiven him, but had the crack in their relationship not been mended after all?

'I'll talk to her.' Joan pushed back her chair and stood up. 'Now, I must rush.'

Alison rose as well. 'You don't think I'm a gossip, do you? I'm honestly just trying to help.'

'I know.' Joan was about to dash away, but she stayed put and said it again, this time more warmly. 'I know. Now I really do have to go.'

Hurrying out of the buffet, she wove her way through the passengers crowding the concourse. It was always busy at this time of day. Passengers queued at the ticket-office windows; others consulted the departure board. Men smoked or read newspapers to pass the time as they waited. A group of young women in pretty dresses, their hair newly curled, laughed as they made a dash for their platform, holding on to their hats as they did so.

'Miss Foster – or Joan, if I may ... ?' It was Margaret Darrell. 'Have you finished for the day? Me too. Perhaps—'

'It's good to see you, it really is, but I'm in a tearing hurry. I'm sorry. I'll see you another time, I promise.'

At last she was on her way. She had asked Mrs Grayson this morning if she might have her tea as soon as she arrived home instead of waiting for everyone else. When she walked through the front door, Mrs Grayson appeared.

'I've made a vegetable and macaroni casserole. It'll be ready when you are.'

Joan ran upstairs for a quick wash and changed into a simple skirt and blouse. She would have preferred to wear a dress. It would have looked smarter and more grown-up. But after Mrs Cooper's previous home had been destroyed, the clothes Joan had ended up with were Letitia's and a dress would have looked more obviously Letitia's than the skirt and blouse did. Today of all days, she didn't want to look like a second-rate Letitia. She wanted to look like Joan. It was Joan who had suffered the emotional battering over the weekend and Joan whom she wanted Gran to see.

Over the blouse she wore a pretty, lightweight cardigan that Mrs Grayson had knitted for her, incorporating lacy leaf stitches down the front. She removed the snood she wore for work. On previous occasions when she had visited Gran she had worn her snood because Gran approved of it. She had worn it to keep the peace and show respect for Gran. Now she left it off out of respect for herself. Let Gran make of that what she would.

To Joan's surprise, Mrs Cooper and Mrs Grayson ate with her.

'I thought you'd eat at the normal time with Mabel,' she said.

'Mabel is going out with that nice Lieutenant Gilchrist,' said Mrs Grayson.

'Is she?' Good grief, could Alison be right? Surely not.

Mabel arrived home as Joan was getting ready to leave. Joan didn't want to hang about. She needed to speak to Gran, but she also needed not to be bothered with other matters when she did so. She cast her gaze upwards, annoyed at Alison for lumbering her with this unpleasant business, then shook off the feeling. What sort of friend was she? She cared about Mabel and this needed saying before Mabel went out with Gil again. Joan still couldn't bring herself to believe in Alison's suspicions, but nor could she dismiss Dot and Cordelia's words.

By the time she had followed Mabel up the stairs, Mabel had already disappeared into the bathroom and Joan had to wait until she walked into their bedroom. Mabel loosened her hair and tilted her head to one side to start brushing.

'You're seeing Gil this evening,' said Joan.

'I promised I would. He knows I went to see Althea's parents at the weekend. He'll want to know how I got on.'

Mabel tilted her head the other way and brushed the other side of her dark brown waves. She had such beautiful hair. Joan would have grown her own to that length if there had been even half a chance of its looking as voluminous as that.

Mabel turned to face her. 'Is something the matter? You're frowning.'

'I need to ask you something and it's rather difficult because I don't want to overstep the mark. I want you to know the question comes out of friendship.'

'Fair enough,' Mabel said slowly. She sat on her bed. 'Fire away.'

Joan winced inwardly and hoped it didn't show. Why had she agreed to do this? Mabel thought the world of Harry. The fact that she had taken him back after finding out about his original intentions was evidence of that. But why would Cordelia and Dot think such a thing without good cause?

'The reason I'm asking is that I know what it's like to be torn between two men.'

Mabel sat bolt upright. 'I don't like the sound of this. I think you'd better spit it out.'

'Are you and Gil … ?' It must be Gil, mustn't it? 'What I mean is, there's talk that you're being unfaithful to Harry.'

'That I'm … ' Mabel's face flooded with colour and her mouth dropped open. 'What sort of talk? Who's talking?'

'I'm sorry. I'm doing this very badly.'

'You mean there'd be a good way of doing it? Come on, Joan. I'm entitled to know who's talking about me.'

So much for Mabel collapsing into her arms and pouring out her troubles. Joan could see that only frankness would do.

'Alison overheard Dot and Cordelia saying something about it.'

'Are you serious? Dot and Cordelia? What would give them an idea like that?'

'I don't know, but Alison swears she heard Dot say, "I'd never have thought it of her, but if she's being unfaithful to Harry … "'

'Well, it's balderdash. Utter tripe, as my grandad would have said. Wait a minute. "*She's* being unfaithful", not "Mabel's being unfaithful"?'

'I think so.'

'Didn't it occur to Alison that one of Dot's sons is called Harry?'

'Oh.' It hadn't occurred to Joan either. 'I can't apologise enough. I wish I'd thought of that before.'

Mabel gave a crisp nod of satisfaction, but then her face softened. 'Poor Dot. She'd be mortified if she knew word had spread.'

'I'll make sure Alison knows she got it completely wrong.'

'No, I'll tell Alison,' said Mabel, 'and I shan't mention Harry Green. I'll just make out she's made a frightful mistake.'

'But that would be so awkward and embarrassing for her.'

'Exactly. With luck, it'll make her want to put it well and truly behind her. If you tell her, she'll want to discuss it and then she might end up realising about Harry Green.'

'Poor Alison,' said Joan.

'Poor Dot,' Mabel answered immediately. 'She's the one we want to protect.'

It occurred to Joan that for the second time this evening, she had let a friend make the rules. First, Alison had prevailed upon her to tackle Mabel and now Mabel had decreed how the resulting situation should be handled. Did that make her a pushover? She hoped not. She had agreed with Alison that she was the right person to speak to Mabel and now she'd agreed with Mabel that Dot's secret must be respected. That wasn't weakness, was it?

Really, the question was: was she strong enough for the confrontation with Gran?

Chapter Eighteen

Following Gran into the parlour, Joan felt the room close in on her. Growing up here, she had never questioned the gloom created by the dense net curtains, but now she felt stifled.

'I assume you've come crawling back for permission to marry,' said Gran, taking her customary chair.

Joan was so full of all the things she wanted to say that this caught her unawares.

'I've decided to grant permission – against my better judgement, I might add.'

'I know. Mrs Masters told me.'

'Did she?' Gran's eyes narrowed. 'What did she tell you, precisely?'

Joan tried to recall. She really wasn't interested in talking about this. After she had challenged Gran, that would be the time to think about getting married.

'Only that she'd bumped into you and you'd told her.'

Come to think of it, that was odd – or was it? Cordelia lived in a posh house on Edge Lane and Gran lived near the bus terminus. Perhaps they had been out shopping at the time. Even so, why would Gran confide in a relative stranger? Gran was the last person to share her private business. Or maybe Cordelia's position as the wife of a solicitor had been reason enough to prompt Gran to do so.

Joan tore her thoughts away. Who cared? That wasn't why she was here.

'In that case,' said Gran, 'I assume you're here to thank me.'

This was ridiculous. It was time to get on with it.

'I'm here because – because I went down to Wendover at the weekend.'

Gran froze. 'You did what?'

'I went to Wendover.'

'You had no business doing that. You had no right. You should have told me what you intended.'

'Told you? And then what? I suppose you'd have said I'm under twenty-one and not allowed to go. Not that it would have stopped me.'

'All these years I spent protecting you and Letitia.'

'Protecting us? How can you say that? You *lied* to us.'

'What did you find out?' asked Gran. Did she hope it wasn't the full truth? Even now, did she hope to salvage something?

'I found out—' Pain wedged inside Joan's throat and her voice vanished. It was a moment before she could speak again. 'I found out that Estelle didn't run away.'

'She would have,' Gran shot back, 'if she'd had half a chance.'

'You don't know that. You can't know it. I read the newspaper reports of the trial and no one knew what she intended. They couldn't ask the lover because nobody knew who he was. He never came forward.'

'Are you defending her?' Gran demanded. 'What she did was despicable. Carrying on with her fancy man! Betraying her husband, betraying her wedding vows. I always told you she was a trollop and I was right.'

'You lied. You said she abandoned us.'

'She might as well have done. The moment she cast aside her wedding vows, she showed herself for the slut she was.'

'But she never ran away – and Daddy *didn't* die of a broken heart.'

Gran's eyes sharpened. 'Are you suggesting I should have told you the truth? Would that have been appropriate? Telling two small children their poor father, who adored them, had been hanged? Are you telling me that's what I should have done?'

'But you blackened Estelle's name.'

'Are you telling me that's what I should have done?' Gran repeated in a louder voice. 'Do you believe a responsible, loving adult and guardian should have burdened young children with that knowledge?'

'But—'

'Do you?' Gran demanded.

'Well—'

'So you admit I was right. Your mother was a faithless hussy. By telling you about her, I gave you and Letitia a strong sense of right and wrong. Her leaving you was an easy thing for you to understand. It was like she was the wicked stepmother in a fairy story. I did what any decent person would have done.'

Joan floundered. She hadn't thought of it that way. Or was Gran manipulating her? Had Gran really done it for their own good? Was it better to have grown up as the daughters of a runaway mother than of a murderer? Joan had come here expecting Gran to crumble, but instead she seemed to be stronger than ever.

'You wanted us to hate her,' said Joan.

Gran gave a bark of laughter. 'It was what she deserved. After what she did … ' Gran's mouth twisted and she looked away. 'After what she did to my Donald.' Her voice was a hoarse whisper.

'But he killed her. He strangled her. You make it sound like it was her fault.'

'It was her fault!' snapped Gran, all fire once more. 'You can't play fast and loose with your marriage and your

212

family life, you can't abandon decency and expect there not to be consequences. She pushed your father to the edge, the very edge of what anyone, any man, could be expected to cope with.'

Joan could hardly breathe. 'Are you defending him? Are you saying – are you saying she asked for it?'

'Actions have consequences. Bad actions have bad consequences.'

'I don't believe this. You blame Estelle for her own murder.'

'My Donald, my boy, was a good and decent man, a loving father, a good provider. He had morals and integrity. I couldn't have wished for a better son. And that woman – that woman—'

'Didn't deserve what happened to her,' finished Joan.

'He worshipped the ground beneath her feet. I always knew she wasn't good enough for him.'

Frustration and despair swelled inside Joan. 'Stop defending him!'

'I beg your pardon? Stop defending him? Stop defending my son? My poor, wronged boy. She drove him beyond what could be endured. As for defending my son, my flesh and blood, you wait until you're a mother and then you'll change your tune.' There was a sneer in Gran's voice as she added, 'You couldn't leave well alone, could you? You had to have your birth certificate. You had to ask questions. You had to go searching for the truth. Well, now that you've found it, I hope you've also found out that life isn't straightforward. Have you heard of the letter of the law and the spirit of the law? There's also the letter of the truth and the spirit of the truth. What I gave you and Letitia was the spirit of the truth and don't you ever dare suggest otherwise.'

Joan was stumped for what to say. Had she really believed Gran would back down and show remorse? Had she really thought that Gran would be overcome by guilt, that her eyes would fill and her shoulders would tremble with repressed sobs? Instead, Gran was brimming with self-righteousness. Estelle's murder wasn't Daddy's fault for putting his hands around her throat and squeezing the life out of her. It was Estelle's fault for provoking him, for 'deserving' it.

'I'm glad Letitia isn't here to listen to any of this,' said Gran, 'and those are words I never thought I'd hear myself say. She was a good girl. She was ... ' She worked her jaw and swallowed.

'She was what? Daddy's girl?' Joan swung about to look at the studio portrait of her handsome father. 'I spent years longing for him to be alive – years. You made us worship him. You made a favourite out of Letitia because she looked like him.'

'She was always special. So beautiful, so clever. A grand-daughter to be proud of.'

'Not like me, you mean.'

'Having Letitia gave me back some of what I lost when Donald was taken from me.'

'And having me didn't? Not that I can say I'm sorry.'

'Don't give me any of your lip. Do you want to know the truth about yourself? Then I'll tell you. You're right. Having you didn't give me back anything of Donald, because he wasn't your father.'

Joan's hand flew to her chest. Her skin prickled all over.

'Why look so shocked?' asked Gran. 'You should be pleased. You've come here to run him down. You don't deserve to be his daughter.'

'Are you saying that Estelle's lover ... ?'

'Yes.' But there was a flicker in Gran's eyes.

'Do you know for a fact that he was my father, that Estelle's man friend was my father? How can you?' Strength was returning to Joan. 'Estelle was known to have a lover, but no one ever knew who he was.'

Gran shrugged. 'It stands to reason. Of course you're not Donald's. Look at you: how can you be?'

Joan stood up. She had obeyed this woman all her life. She had backed away from confrontation. She had left it to Letitia to say what needed saying. Even today, when she had come here to have it out with her, Gran had ridden roughshod over her. Gran had told her twisted, self-righteous version of the truth and Joan had barely got a word in.

Now, at last, after a lifetime of obedience and good manners, Joan had had enough.

'That's an appalling thing to say. The truth is, you have no proof that I'm another man's child. It's just something you've made up because I have the temerity not to resemble Daddy and it gives you another reason to hate and despise my mother. Wait!' As Gran started to speak, Joan raised her hand. 'You claim you protected us and did your best for us. Oh yes, the mighty Beryl Foster – or should I say *Henshaw*? – never put a foot wrong, did she? If you're such a decent, upright person, why have you, without proof or justification, thrown doubt on who my father is? That wasn't the act of a loving grandparent. That wasn't the act of an honourable, respectable guardian. My mother deserves better than the treatment she has endured at your hands all these years – and I'll tell you something else: so do I.'

'Aren't you going to dress up to go out, Mabel?' Mrs Cooper asked. 'That's not like you.'

No, it wasn't like her. Mabel almost bit her lip, then turned it into a smile. She enjoyed getting dressed up, especially after wearing her work clobber on the permanent way. Last time she had gone out with Gil, she had worn

215

light green silk and high heels and even though she hadn't been interested in him romantically, she had enjoyed the admiration in his glance. But she didn't want to look special this time. Nor did she want him to escort her anywhere.

Not after what Alison had overheard.

Yes, Alison had made a huge blunder by fixing on the wrong Harry, and Mabel's first reaction should have been indignation – but it hadn't been. It had been guilt. She closed her eyes for a moment because even though she had never been unfaithful to Harry, the fact was that learning about Gil's war work had made her think of Gil in a different way.

Uniforms meant a lot to her. Harry's air-force blue was a source of great pride to her and his position as a bomb aimer meant far more to her than if he had been ground crew. She didn't want him to be in danger – she didn't know what she would do if anything happened to him – but his being a bomb aimer, which everybody knew was one of the most dangerous jobs in the RAF, if not *the* most dangerous, made her immensely proud. She only had to hear the RAF mentioned on the wireless or in a snatch of conversation and she felt tall and beautiful. Wasn't she the luckiest girl in the world to have Harry Knatchbull as her boyfriend?

When she had believed Gil to be having an easy war, it had made her even prouder of Harry. But then Pops had set her straight about the nature of Gil's work and she'd realised that far from having a cushy war, he was involved in secret work that called for specialist knowledge and skills, not to mention imagination. She had suddenly recalled all too vividly what she had seen in him when they'd first met. He was handsome and clever – she'd had no idea how clever, but it obviously required a sharp brain to do the kind of work he did, dreaming up ways to help POWs escape. The girl who ended up with Iain Gilchrist would definitely have a man to be proud of.

Which was why Alison's mistake had sent guilt rippling through her. It was like being found out, as if her secret thoughts had been laid out for all to see.

That was why she had chosen to wear a plain dress and cardigan with sandals this evening instead of something formal, and it was why she'd decided against letting Gil take her anywhere special.

She sat in the bay window, watching for him. The moment she saw him enter the cul-de-sac, she turned to Mrs Cooper and Mrs Grayson.

'He's here. I thought we'd go for a walk and then I'll bring him back here, if that's all right. We can play cards or just talk.'

'Of course it's all right, dear,' said Mrs Cooper.

Mabel left the house. Gil remained on the pavement, holding the gate open for her.

'Let's go to the rec,' said Mabel. 'It's mostly given over to allotments now, but there are still benches. We can sit and talk.'

'If that's what you'd like.'

The rec smelled of earth and greenery. Men with their shirtsleeves rolled up and women with their hair in turbans smoked or chatted as they worked their patches of ground, cabbages and carrots in evidence. Mabel and Gil had to walk halfway around the rec before they came to a bench where they could sit without being overheard. Mabel smoothed her skirt and tucked one ankle behind the other.

'How did you get on in Annerby?' Gil asked, turning towards her and resting his arm on the back of the bench. 'Did you visit Althea's parents?'

'Yes. Did you think I wouldn't?'

'I think you'll always do whatever you set your mind to.'

'It went far better than I had any right to hope for. I spent the whole morning with them, talking, remembering. Mrs Wilmore got out her photographs. It was sad and painful, but also rather uplifting. I've talked about my guilt, but I've never talked about Althea since she died. It made me realise what I've lost.'

'You'll be thinking about that your whole life,' said Gil. 'What you lost – and what Althea lost. All the experiences she has missed out on.'

'Don't. You'll make me cry.'

'Then there are the experiences you and I missed out on as well.'

Her heart thumped. 'What d'you mean?'

'I thought we were going to spend the rest of our lives together,' said Gil. 'So did you, back then.'

'I don't want to discuss that. Things happened the way they happened and ... '

'... and you and I lost our chance.'

Mabel thought she was going to say, 'You shouldn't say things like that. I'm happy with Harry now,' but instead honesty compelled her to say, 'Yes, we did. Althea's death changed everything. It even brought me here to Manchester to work on the railways, because I couldn't bear to remain at home.'

'And it sent me rushing to join up, once I realised that grief and shock had placed you beyond my reach.'

Gil's hand dropped from the back of the bench and took hers from her lap. She ought to pull away. Harry would expect her to. But there had once been such love and closeness between her and Gil. They had expected to get married, but circumstances had wrenched them apart. Besides, Gil had helped her. By talking about Althea, he had made her see it was time to do the right thing by the Wilmores.

He turned her hand over as if to read her palm. He didn't look at her face, didn't meet her eyes. His lowered gaze made him appear younger, uncertain. It made him look as if he could be hurt.

'Are you still within my reach?' he asked softly.

She finally said what she should have said in the first place.

'You shouldn't say things like that. I'm with Harry now and I'm happy.'

Gil nodded, still not looking at her face. 'I thought so, but I had to ask.' Now he did meet her gaze and the honesty and love in his eyes almost made her glance away. He dug in his pocket and brought out a pair of tickets. 'It's a Red Cross dance to raise funds. I've helped to organise it, as a matter of fact, and I'd hoped that you would be my partner, but I'm sure you'd far rather go with your Harry.'

'Please, Gil, you ought to find another girl. It won't be hard for a good-looking army man like you.'

'I don't feel like finding another girl just at the moment. Maybe I never will. You're a hard act to follow, Mabel Bradshaw. I won't be going to the dance now, so you can ask Knatchbull to escort you without worrying about seeing me. It'd be a shame to waste the tickets. Please take them. They're for a good cause.'

She wasn't sure whether she ought to, but she did.

'I hope it didn't upset you that I asked if you were within my reach,' said Gil. 'I won't ever embarrass you by trying again, not after this, but you do understand that I had to ask, don't you?'

Did she? Harry wouldn't. By crikey, Harry wouldn't. What had made her think that sitting in the rec would somehow make this a casual meeting? Was she playing with fire?

But she and Gil had meant the world to one another once upon a time. Nothing could take that away. And while Harry, if he knew, would be furious that another man had made a pass at his girl, Mabel knew there was nothing seedy or opportunistic about this. Gil wasn't a chancer. Above all, he was a man of integrity and she trusted him and always would. That was all there was to it.

Gently, she withdrew her hand.

'I understand,' she said.

Chapter Nineteen

Dot woke to find herself already rolling out of bed in response to the wailing of the air-raid siren. Some folk called it Moaning Minnie, but Dot didn't on account of having a sister called Minnie who was sick to death of being teased. Already the sounds of engines, ack-ack fire and explosions could be heard. Honest to God, it was a race sometimes as to which came first, the siren or the sounds of war. She threw on the warm clothes she left on the bedroom chair every night and opened the bedroom blackout curtains, front and back.

Downstairs, she put the kettle on, then fetched her coat from the peg in the hallway and tied a headscarf under her chin to cover her hairnetted rollers. Opening the front door, she put the buckets of sand and water beside the front step, then opened the downstairs curtains. You didn't want flames to be hidden behind the blackout. When Reg was here, putting the buckets out was his job, but he was on ARP duty tonight.

In the kitchen once more, she made a flask of tea, then switched off the gas and the water, locking the back door behind her as she headed for the Andy, sparing a moment as she always did to be grateful that the houses in Heath-side Lane, small as they were, had gardens at the back instead of yards, so they'd had somewhere to bury their air-raid shelter.

She placed the flask, the air-raid box and her bag on the ground before she opened the door. She liked to have her hands free to manoeuvre herself inside, as it was quite a step down. Then she turned to gather her belongings and close the door, using her torch to help her light the lamp. Lamp oil was becoming increasingly difficult to get hold of. What would she do if she couldn't get any more?

There was something darkly depressing about facing an air raid all alone. She much preferred having their Jimmy here to fuss over. Watching over him kept her mind off herself and helped her keep her pecker up. That was what you did when you had kiddies to care for. You kept them buoyed up. Not that their Jimmy required much of that. If anything, he was in need of a spot of squashing, but Dot still loved looking after him.

She'd had a go at Sheila after the business of Rosa putting on her finery and leaving Jimmy to fend for himself instead of waiting in with him for Dot to fetch him after work.

Sheila had defended Rosa. 'She knew you'd be along soon, Ma.'

'That's not the point,' Dot had said, 'and you know it. If Rosa isn't reliable, I'm happy to do more for Jimmy.'

'Says the grandma who got herself a full-time job and insisted on keeping it even though her grandchildren needed looking after during the summer holidays.'

That had stung. 'I'll have you know I agonised over what to do for the best.'

'And the best was you keeping your job.' Was Sheila taunting her? That was summat that would never have happened before this man-in-the-bedroom malarkey.

'Aye, that was the best thing.' Dot had made an effort not to snap. 'Where would the country be without women doing men's jobs? And I fixed up you and Pammy with a childminder for Jimmy and Jenny. Anyroad, the point is, I'm not happy with what Rosa did and you shouldn't be neither. The neighbours noticed an' all.

You're storing up trouble for yourself, getting on the wrong side of the neighbours.'

Would Sheila take heed? That remained to be seen.

Dot climbed into her bunk. It didn't matter how often you aired the bunks, it was never enough. The bedding didn't stay crisp. It wilted and even if it was dry, it felt as if it wanted to be damp. Should she have brought a hot-water bottle? But it was the end of May, for pity's sake. It would be June at the weekend.

It was no good trying to settle. She wouldn't sleep. She had too much on her mind. That made it sound like she had dozens of problems, but really it was just the two. Just? Ha! Two flamin' big problems. Sheila – and herself.

Herself. Imagine that. Her, Dot Green, causing a problem, and not just any problem but one concerning a man. Did that make her no better than Sheila? She had changed Sheila's name from Sheila the Slattern to Sheila the Slut in her head. Should she be calling herself Dot the ... the ... she couldn't think of a word for slut that started with D. Edie Thirkle-as-was already had her down as a man-eater.

But it wasn't like that. Her love for Mr Thirkle wasn't an impure, rampant feeling. It was honourable, because it had sprung from respect and companionship and a meeting of minds.

But if she acted on her feelings, that wouldn't be honourable. It would be mucky and deceitful. It would be proving Edie right. It would be showing that she was no better than Sheila. Dot Green – no better than she should be. Eh, the mere thought of those words had the power to turn her cold. How many times had she heard them spoken? How many times had she said them herself? 'She's no better than she should be.' It was the most damning thing that could be said about a woman from the backstreets.

Dot wasn't like that. She was above that kind of thing and so was Mr Thirkle. And so was their love. Was it so dreadfully wrong to long for more from their relationship? They were two good, decent folk and what had grown between them had developed from honest friendship. Their only physical contact had occurred that night at the railway shed when they had staggered to their feet after Rob Wadden had escaped. Far from being a passionate embrace, it had simply been a matter of helping one another to stand up.

But, oh, how she ached now for an embrace, for sweet, gentle kisses as his arms held her tenderly ... then the kisses would lengthen and deepen as his arms tightened around her ...

Enough! Dot sat bolt upright, cracking her head on the underside of the top bunk. She had no business thinking such things. She was a married woman. Aye, married to Ratty Reg, who took her for granted, and when he wasn't doing that, he was doing her down in front of the family. Some husband he was. Whatever had happened to love, honour and cherish?

She and Mr Thirkle would cherish one another. She knew it in her bones.

They didn't tell you about being cherished when you were a little lass. They told you fairy stories about falling in love and living happily ever after, so you grew up thinking that heady passion was what it was all about. But it wasn't. She'd rather be cherished any day.

Just imagine the depth of the passion that would grow out of being cherished. That was what she wanted, oh aye, that was what she wanted.

Dot unscrewed the top of the flask and poured herself a cup of tea. Would it douse her inappropriate thoughts?

The all-clear sounded. She gathered her stuff and returned to the house, which was still in one piece – thank you, God – though the stench in the night air proclaimed that an oil bomb had landed in the vicinity. She'd have to watch where she put her feet when she ventured out come the morning. That oil was a bugger to get off your shoes.

She switched the water and the gas back on and went upstairs to bed. No sooner had she lain down between the cold sheets than there was a loud knocking at the front door. Fear streamed through her. Were the children all right?

She went downstairs and answered the door. Mr Donoghue from up the road stood there with his ARP armband on his sleeve and his tin hat on his head.

'It's your husband, Mrs Green. He were trying to put out an incendiary.'

'What?' Dot clutched the door frame to keep herself upright.

'He's been took to Withington. I thought you should know at once.'

'Aye.' Her heart thumped. Her breathing was rapid and shallow. 'Aye,' she said again.

There was nowt to do but wait and the hospital staff didn't even want her to do that. They wanted her to shove off out of the way. Not that they put it like that, but that was what they meant and they were right, of course. But Dot couldn't go home, she just couldn't. It would be disloyal. Her marriage might be worn out, but Reg was still her husband and he was entitled to have her nearby, fretting. It wasn't as though there was anybody at home for her to comfort.

She didn't go far, only to Burton Road, where she propped her bottom against a low wall and hugged herself. Perhaps Burton Road wasn't the best place to choose. Back on New Year's Day, the public shelter there had taken a direct hit and everybody inside had bought it.

Would tonight be the night that Reg bought it?

No. Absolutely not. He didn't deserve that. But that was the whole point, wasn't it? Nobody deserved it.

Eventually, Dot trailed back to the hospital, where she threw herself on the mercy of the exhausted ladies staffing the front desk.

'No one by the name of Green has been added to the lists of last night's fatalities, so that's good news, but you'll appreciate everyone is very busy. You need to come back at visiting time.'

'I can't,' Dot exclaimed, 'not in the afternoon. I work on the railways. I'll be on the Southport train all day.'

'I'm sorry,' was the firm reply. 'If we made an exception for everyone with a special reason ... You understand.'

She did. It didn't help her at all, but she did understand. As Dot moved away disconsolately from the desk, a young nurse drew her aside. She wore a cloak over her uniform, meaning that she was either just coming on duty or else about to return to the nurses' home after a long night.

'I couldn't help overhearing. If you give me your husband's name, I'll see what I can find out. My dad and my uncles are all on the railways,' she added by way of explanation.

'Thank you so much.' Tears of gratitude sprang into Dot's eyes. 'His name's Reginald Green and he's an ARP warden. He were wounded putting out an incendiary – or trying to. It went off.'

'Stay here by the noticeboard. I'll send someone with information, but if you aren't standing exactly here, they won't come looking for you.'

Dot stayed put. At last, a middle-aged porter came down the stairs, clocked her and came over.

'Mrs Green?' His face was grey with tiredness. 'Nurse Johnson said to say your husband's injuries are slight and she's told him not to expect you until evening visiting.'

'Thank you,' said Dot, but she was speaking to thin air.

Her shoulders slumped as relief gushed through her. Slight injuries. Talk about luck. Reg had come off worst from a disagreement with an incendiary and all he had were slight injuries.

Strange as it felt, she had to treat this as any other morning and get off to work. She hurried home, stopping along Heathside Lane to knock at the Donoghues' to say Reg was going to be all right. Mrs Donoghue promised to tell her husband when he came off duty.

Dot flew about the house, getting herself ready, then dashed out early to call round at Sheila's and Pammy's on her way.

'I won't tell Jenny yet,' said Pammy, ever the protective mother, 'not until I know exactly what happened.'

'You'd better tell her, love,' Dot advised. 'You don't want her hearing it off our Jimmy at school. You can bet our Sheila won't keep it to herself. Besides, there'll be other neighbours that know.'

'Poor Jenny,' said Pammy.

'Don't take that tone with her or she'll think it's worse than it is.'

'There's so much death and destruction,' said Pammy. 'I don't want her to become hardened to it.'

'Course you don't,' said Dot. 'Just mind you don't upset her over this, eh?'

She raced round to Sheila's, using the key on its string to let herself in.

'Only me,' she called.

She bustled through to the kitchen, where Sheila, Rosa and Jimmy were sitting around the table. Honestly, there were two women in this house now. Couldn't they between them manage to pour milk into the jug instead of dumping the bottle on the table? Talk about slovenly.

'What brings you here?' Shelia blew smoke out of the side of her mouth, straight at Jimmy. 'Is everything all right?'

'Nowt to worry about,' Dot said cheerfully, looking at Jimmy. She would rather have talked to Sheila privately, but heigh-ho. At least this way she controlled what Jimmy heard. 'It's Grandpa, Jimmy. He had a bit of an accident last night and he's in hospital.'

'Is he hurt?' Sheila asked.

'He's fine,' said Dot, 'or he will be.'

'Was he on ARP duty?' asked Jimmy.

'Aye, love.'

'Did he do summat heroic? Cos if he did, then you'd both be heroes. There's what you did on that train when Jerry was firing at it, and now Grandpa.'

Rosa smiled at him. 'You'll have two heroes in your family.'

'Three,' said Jimmy. 'Don't forget Dad.'

'What happened?' Sheila asked Dot.

'Four,' said Jimmy. 'Uncle Archie.'

'Pipe down, Jimmy,' said Sheila.

'I don't know the exact details yet,' said Dot. 'I'll find out later. I just wanted to let you know. Now I must fly.'

'Are you going to the hospital?' asked Jimmy.

'I've got to go to work, chick.'

'I could go to the hospital.' Jimmy looked round brightly. 'I don't mind missing school.'

'You're going to school,' said Sheila.

'I don't mind—'

'Thanks a lot, Ma,' said Sheila.

*

Dot went through the motions, loading her flatbed trolley and weaving her way through the crowd on the concourse as she headed for the Southport platform. Her thoughts were all over the place. Was she really settling in for a day's work without having seen Reg in hospital? It wasn't right. Yet she couldn't miss a day's work. Folk were relying on her. You couldn't send a train on its way without its parcels porter. And after last night, there would undoubtedly be railway staff who wouldn't turn up for work today because they'd been injured or worse. She was able-bodied and her husband wasn't seriously injured, so it was only right and proper that she should do her bit.

'Morning, Mrs Green.' Mr Thirkle had opened the gate for her to bring her trolley through. 'Hold on a minute.'

'Can't stop.' Mustn't stop, more like. Emotion was threatening to get the better of her.

But Mr Thirkle stepped in front of her, obliging her to halt. She felt the tug inside her shoulders as she stopped the trolley.

'You don't look yourself, if I may say so,' said Mr Thirkle.

Dot had to swallow before she could speak. 'It's Reg – my husband.'

'Good heavens, he isn't—'

'He's in hospital. He was hurt last night. He's going to be all right, but ... '

'My dear Mrs Green.'

Mr Thirkle came closer. He was going to put his arms round her and she didn't care how it would look. She couldn't think of owt that would be more comforting.

But Mr Thirkle called out, 'Miss Trehearn-Hobbs, can you spare a moment?' and guided Dot a few steps until she found herself not in his arms, but in Persephone's.

'What's happened?' asked Persephone.

'Mr Green is in hospital,' said Mr Thirkle. 'He was injured in last night's raid.'

Persephone drew back slightly so she could look into Dot's face. 'And you're here to do your job? Oh, sweetheart, we can't have that. You have to go home. You have to be close to the hospital.'

'I can't.'

'Yes, you can. Shall I tell you something about posh girls such as myself? We're ever so good at getting things organised. Mabel says I do it through the sheer force of expectation.'

'Honest, I'm better at work,' said Dot. 'I can't see Reg until visiting time, so I might as well be here.'

'If you say so,' said Persephone. 'But I give you fair warning. You're not waiting for evening visiting. You'll be at Mr Green's bedside this afternoon. Now toddle off to Southport and leave everything to me.'

Dot looked round for her trolley, experiencing a thrill of panic when it wasn't there. Had someone pinched it? No, Mr Thirkle had trundled it along to the guard's van, where he and Mr Hill were loading up. How good folk were.

All through the journey to Southport and back, Mr Hill insisted on helping her with the parcels, even though Dot quickly pulled herself together and felt more than capable of managing on her own. She was embarrassed now to think of how it had all got too much for her at the station. Had she looked like one of those silly females who go to pieces in a crisis? What a clot.

Back at Victoria, when she was inside the wire cage, ready to start unloading the parcels that had been collected along the route, two women porters appeared.

'Off you go, love. We'll see to this.'

Turning their backs on her, they got stuck in, making her feel like a spare part. Climbing down onto the platform, she found Mr Hill in conversation with Mr Lamb, one of the parcels porters.

'Mr Lamb is taking over from you for the rest of your shift,' said Mr Hill. 'I hope you find Mr Green in good spirits.'

Dot went to clock off, boggling at what Persephone had achieved. Mabel was right. The power of upper-class expectation was indeed a wondrous thing.

She spotted Joan pushing her sack trolley and hurried over to her.

'You're going to the buffet this evening, aren't you, chick? Will you give my apologies?' She threw her arms around Joan. 'And that's a hug for Persephone. Pass it on for me, will you?'

Leaving Joan looking startled, Dot ran for the bus. She just had time to go home and change out of her uniform before going to the hospital.

She puffed up the stairs and arrived outside the ward just as the doors opened to admit visitors. She scanned the two long rows of beds, spotted Reg – then looked again. In that moment, he seemed to be wearing a black mask, like a highwayman. Walking down the ward, she realised he had two magnificent black eyes. The upper parts of his cheeks were black an' all. Dot winced. What bruises! Guilt tightened her chest. How could she have gone off to work when he had taken such a battering?

She arrived at his bedside. 'Reg, what happened? I'm so glad you're in one piece. Mr Donoghue said you tried to put out an incendiary.'

One eye was swollen shut. The other regarded her through a red-rimmed slit. 'Aye. I'd used up all the sand, so I had a go at stifling it with a dustbin lid.'

'Oh, Reg.'

'The damn thing went off, pardon my French, and everything blew straight into my face, including my hands and the dustbin lid. I gave myself these shiners with my own fists.'

'Still, the dustbin lid must have protected you.'

'Aye, you're not wrong. Albert Blunt were with me and the blast caught him in the side of the face. They operated on him this morning, poor bugger. He's lost half his jaw.'

'That could have been you, Reg. Our Jimmy says you're a hero and he's right.'

'Tackling an incendiary with a dustbin lid doesn't sound very heroic, does it?'

'I'm not so sure about that,' Dot said with a smile.

'I were thinking of telling our Jimmy that I got into a fist fight with a Jerry parachuter and he might have given me two black eyes, but I gave him two of the same *and* knocked his front teeth out.'

'What you did sounds pretty heroic to me,' said Dot. 'It's the kind of thing that goes down in family history, that is. The only problem will be stopping our Jimmy going everywhere with a dustbin lid in case of bombs. You know what he's like.'

Reg started to smile, then made a grunting sound. Smiling hurt, apparently.

'I'm that relieved you're all right,' said Dot.

'The eye doctor wants to have a look at my eyes when I can open them again.'

'They aren't worried that ... ' She couldn't finish saying it.

'They want to check, that's all. If what I can see through this slit is owt to go by, I'll be fine.' Reg reached out and brushed his fingers against Dot's temple. 'Touch wood.'

'You're supposed to touch your own head when you say that.'

'Ruddy heck, Dot. Can't you take a joke?'

'Of course I can,' said Dot. 'I'm just saying.'

'Blimey. Two minutes ago I were a hero and now you can't take a joke. God help us, you're a daft bat.'

Chapter Twenty

Mabel opened the door to the buffet and peeped in. Colette and Persephone were already there, but there was no sign of Alison yet. Good. Mabel loitered and the moment Alison appeared, she dragged her across to stand outside the grill room.

'I need a word before we join the others,' said Mabel. Was that a flash of guilt on Alison's face? 'I hear you've been talking about me behind my back.'

A rosy blush filled Alison's cheeks. 'I didn't mean any harm. I wanted to help.'

'Well, I don't know what you think you overheard,' said Mabel, 'but it was nothing to do with me. Kindly don't spread it around.'

'I haven't.'

'Then how come Joan knows?'

Alison looked away. 'I'm sorry.' Then she rallied. 'But you can't blame me for being worried about you.'

'You must have misheard,' said Mabel. 'It wasn't Harry's name. It must have been Larry or Barry.'

'I know what I heard and it was definitely Harry.'

'Well, it wasn't my Harry.'

'Then I wonder who—'

'Will you put a sock in it?' Mabel exclaimed. 'We'll never know who Dot and Cordelia were talking about – and that's just as it should be. It's none of our business. You've already upset me with your gossip.'

'I swear I wasn't gossiping. I'm ever so sorry.'

'The best way you can show it is by never referring to it again. Forget you ever overheard anything.'

There were tears in Alison's brown eyes and Mabel almost relented, but she knew she mustn't, for Dot's sake. She made sure she spoke kindly when she said, 'Let's say no more about it. Come on.' She linked Alison's arm and took her into the buffet. 'I'm glad we're seeing more of Colette these days,' she added and Alison seized the change of subject gratefully.

Not long after they had joined Persephone and Colette at the table, Joan walked in. She waved to them before going to the counter to get her tea. As she threaded her way between the tables, a smile tugged at her lips, making her look – well, mischievous was the only word. Mabel's heart lifted. Joan hadn't been quite herself since her trip down south. Poor girl, it must have been a huge disappointment not to have discovered anything about her family and the reason behind her grandmother's decision to change the family name. It did Mabel good to see her looking cheerful.

Joan set down her cup and saucer, but instead of drawing out a chair, she edged round the table towards Persephone.

'I've got something for you.' She bent to put her arms around Persephone and hugged her warmly. 'That's from Dot.'

Persephone looked surprised and then laughed, returning the embrace. 'How is Mr Green? Is there any news?'

Joan sat down. 'News of what? I don't know anything other than that Dot sent you a hug.'

'I don't know the details,' said Persephone, 'only that Mr Green was injured in last night's raid.'

'Poor Dot,' Colette and Alison exclaimed.

'According to Mr Thirkle, he'll be all right,' said Persephone.

'That's good,' said Mabel. 'I'm going to be nosy. Why did Dot send you a hug?'

'No reason,' said Persephone. 'I just happened to be in the right place at the right time.'

Cordelia came to the table and sat down, looking as elegant as ever and not at all as though she worked outdoors all day long, cleaning lamps.

'Cordelia, I assume you haven't heard about Dot's husband,' said Persephone.

'No. What's happened?' Cordelia looked alarmed, then her face settled into an expression of enforced calm. It was what happened to someone's face when they were about to be told what might be bad news.

'First of all, don't worry. He's going to be fine, but he was injured last night. That's as much as I know.'

'What a shock for Dot,' said Cordelia. 'I wonder if we can do anything to help.'

'I'm not sure about that,' said Persephone. 'You know Dot. She seemed determined to carry on as normal.'

'Which is entirely laudable,' said Cordelia, 'though perhaps not entirely practical.'

'It would help if we knew how long Mr Green is going to be in hospital,' said Colette.

'I know what we can do,' said Cordelia. 'I'll organise a few hours of Magic Mop for Dot's house. It'll be one less thing for her to worry about.'

'I'm sure Mrs Cooper would help out without being paid,' said Joan.

'I'm sure she would,' said Cordelia, 'but she's set up her little business and she needs the income.'

'Dot is very particular about her house,' said Mabel, 'but if she were prepared to let anyone else clean it for her, that person would be Mrs Cooper. They have a lot of time for one another.'

236

'How else can we help?' asked Colette.

'If Mr Green is kept in for a few days, and there's a night when Jimmy is meant to be staying with them,' said Joan, 'Bob and I could go round there and mind him while Dot is at the hospital – first aid permitting, of course.'

'That would be a kindness,' said Cordelia. 'Some people are happy to leave children unattended, but Dot isn't one of them.'

'Our cook sent me home with a bag full of ingredients from her store cupboard for Mrs Grayson,' said Mabel. 'I bet Mrs Grayson could make a pie or a pudding to pop in Dot's larder.'

'Good idea,' said Colette. 'I'll cook her something as well.'

Cordelia looked round at them all. 'Cooking, cleaning and child-minding. That should ease the pressure and give Dot the time to concentrate on her husband. Good show, all of you.'

'It's what friends are for,' said Mabel.

Joan left the buffet earlier than she had meant to. She was glad to have joined in with the plans to support Dot, but she knew that she wouldn't be able to hold on to her wonderful news if she stayed much longer. The temptation to tell her friends was overwhelming and she knew how thrilled they would be, but she needed to discuss it with Bob first. Until then, it wasn't news as such, just a hope. Her dearest hope.

She walked towards the ticket office with its long-panelled wall of polished wood inset with windows, each with a little shelf in front of it, and was about to turn the corner to pass the war memorial and leave the station when who should come round the corner but Margaret Darrell. Even before Joan could smile a greeting, Margaret dodged past her and kept on walking.

'Wait!' Joan caught her by the sleeve.

'What d'you want?' Margaret asked crisply.

Joan felt taken aback. 'Before I went away, we said we'd arrange to meet up.'

Margaret's hazel eyes were wary. 'Haven't you had second thoughts?'

'Of course not.'

'You can't deny you gave me the brush-off yesterday.'

'No, I didn't. I was in a tearing hurry, that's all.'

Margaret let out a breath. 'I thought you'd changed your mind. I wouldn't have blamed you.'

Joan's heart lurched. This girl had been made to feel as if she belonged in the gutter. Well, not any more, not if Joan could help it.

'I want us to be friends and I mean it. But at the risk of sounding like a broken gramophone record, I have to dash now – it's nothing personal against you, though. It's because I'm meeting my fiancé. Look, are you free around six tomorrow for a cuppa and a chat? We could meet here at this corner.'

'Thanks. I'd love to.'

Margaret's face, which had looked pale and tired, was transformed by a smile. She had been a pretty girl when she worked at Ingleby's, a bit of a looker, actually. The past year had ground her down, but maybe a new friendship would restore some of her self-esteem.

Joan watched Margaret go on her way, then raced back to the buffet. The others looked up in surprise.

'I've bumped into a girl I used to know at Ingleby's. She's a loco cleaner now.' Joan addressed Mabel, Alison and Persephone. 'Would it be all right to ask her along when we go to the flicks tomorrow evening? Assuming I'm not minding Jimmy Green, that is.'

'It doesn't matter if you are minding him,' said Persephone. 'Your friend can still come with us.'

'Thanks,' said Joan. 'Her name is Margaret Darrell.' She bent over and spoke to Alison. 'Do me a favour, will you? Tomorrow, can you quietly tell Margaret that my sister died. She never met Letitia, but she does know I had a sister.'

Alison nodded. Joan gave her shoulder a squeeze. Perhaps doing this important little job would make Alison feel trusted after the debacle of the Harry incident.

Joan scooted off. She and Bob both had first-aid duty tonight, so had agreed to meet in the Worker Bee café before going their separate ways. As she dodged her way between pedestrians, Joan's heart melted at the sight of him standing outside, waiting for her. She ran to him and he slipped an arm around her and kissed her cheek before opening the door for her to walk inside first.

The Worker Bee was a place where you ordered at the counter. They served your drinks immediately and you carried them to your table, then the food was brought to you when it was ready. Joan sat down and watched Bob fetch two teas. Her mouth went dry as her mind flooded with what she had to tell him. Even when she took a sip, her mouth remained as dry as a bone.

'Did you go and see your gran?' Bob asked.

She nodded. 'It was bizarre. I expected an apology at the very least, but she doesn't think she's done anything wrong. She even said it was better to be the daughter of a runaway mother than of a ... ' She glanced about to make sure she couldn't be overheard. Even though she was sure she couldn't be, she didn't complete the sentence.

Bob raised his eyebrows as he blew out a breath and shook his head. 'That doesn't make it right for her to have lied about your mother all these years. She could have made up something else about her, like dying in an accident.'

'That wouldn't have been good enough for Gran,' said Joan. 'She hates my mother even now. She said she brought it on herself.'

'That's a dreadful thing to say. Of course she didn't deserve what happened to her.'

Joan felt warm inside as gratitude washed through her. 'Thank you for saying that. Gran always made out that Daddy was in the right and Estelle was in the wrong, but it's far more complicated than that. I can hardly bear to think about it.'

Bob covered her hand with his. 'It's a tricky business and all the trickier for having to be kept secret. Promise me one thing. You must never feel you can't talk to me about it. It's hard for you and I want to share the burden.' He wiggled her engagement ring. 'It's my job now. It's official.'

Some of the weight she had been carrying fell away. Whatever had happened in the past, she refused to let it suck her into confusion and depression.

'What can I do to help?' Bob asked. 'There's one thing I can think of, but I'm not sure what you'll make of it.'

Joan's heart bumped. Could he possibly mean ... ? 'What is it?'

'I've already said I want us to get married as soon as we can. After what you've just told me, I want it even more.'

'You mean a special licence and a quick dash to the registry office?'

'No, not that. I want you to have a proper wedding with all the trimmings. How quickly can that be organised?' Bob now held both her hands and gazed into her eyes. 'I know you never wanted a long engagement, because if you had, Mrs Foster's permission would never have been an issue. Let's use her permission soon – not "quick dash" soon, but let's tie the knot in June. You'll make a beautiful June bride.'

Sheer delight made Joan laugh. June!

'Let's find out what leave we can both take,' Bob went on, 'and see if we can have a proper holiday for our honeymoon. Lots of couples don't get that these days, but maybe we can.' He leaned forward, his voice soft and caressing as he said, 'All I want is to be your husband, the man who takes care of you and loves you for ever. You've been through so much and I want you to start your new life with me as soon as we can organise it. Hey now, what's this?'

Tears spilled from Joan's eyes and Bob used the pad of his thumb to brush them away.

'Have I said the wrong thing?'

'No. You've said exactly the right thing. It's what I was thinking of myself. I was going to suggest it.'

And wasn't she glad now that she hadn't shared her hope with her friends in the buffet. Keeping her hope to herself had made Bob's suggestion all the more special. It was like being proposed to all over again.

'I want to marry you,' she said, 'and I don't want to wait. You are my present and my future.'

Eh, her railway friends were so kind. Their offers of cooking, cleaning and child-minding had made Dot go all emotional and she had felt herself welling up, which wasn't like her at all. She was normally too sensible, too practical, too busy for tears.

'Anyroad,' she told Cordelia when they bumped into one another on the concourse at the end of Dot's shift, 'there's no call for all that help, as it turns out. Reg will be home by the time I get back this evening. One of the neighbours offered to make sure he got home safe. Folk are good, that's what my dear old mam always said and she was right.'

'Especially in times like this,' agreed Cordelia. 'Have you time for a quick cup of tea? I don't wish to impose.'

Dot smiled to herself. What would Mam have said about her having a posh friend who used words like 'impose' just as if they were the kinds of words you might use down the butcher's?

About to refuse, she thought again. 'Why not? Our Pammy has arranged for her and Jenny to be there until I get home.'

Soon they were seated at a corner table, more or less hemmed in by knapsacks belonging to a crowd of soldiers.

'I'm that grateful to all of you for your offers of help,' said Dot. 'The neighbours have rallied round an' all.'

'How is Mr Green?'

'More shaken up by the injuries to his colleague than by what happened to himself. Poor Mr Blunt is badly disfigured and he's going to need a lot of attention. As for Reg, he's got the two biggest shiners I've ever seen. To start with, the hospital said they'd keep him in until the swelling went down enough for them to test his eyesight, but then they said he could come home and go back for his sight test later.'

'That's good,' said Cordelia. 'That suggests they expect his eyes to be undamaged.'

'The sight test is a precaution, really,' said Dot. She looked round at the crowded buffet. 'It's a good job we didn't choose today for one of our get-togethers. We'd have had to squeeze in behind the counter with Mrs Jessop.'

'The girls have gone to the pictures and they've taken a friend of Joan's with them, a girl called Margaret Darrell, whom Joan knew at Ingleby's. She works in the engine sheds now.'

'Did Colette go with them?' Dot asked.

'No. Her parents-in-law are coming round this evening.'

'I'm glad we're seeing more of her now.'

'And she and her husband visit Mrs Cooper once a week. I've met him a couple of times. He's an agreeable young man, even if he is overprotective. I'm glad he's come to his senses and has realised he was being—'

'A twit?' Dot suggested.

'I was going to say "a little unreasonable", but "twit" will do just as well,' said Cordelia. 'Speaking of unreasonable conduct, we never did finish talking about your daughter-in-law. Although do tell me to mind my own business, if you like.'

Dot experienced the dull, sinking feeling that thinking of Sheila brought on. She explained about Rosa moving in.

'Is she really such a bad influence?' Cordelia asked.

'Put it this way,' said Dot. 'I don't think you'd want her under your roof when your Emily comes home. She's one of them good-time girls you hear about, and never mind that she has a husband. Her and Sheila have been friends since school.'

'And you don't approve.'

'I don't, but if I'm honest, a lot of that is because I went to school with Rosa's mother and when I say she was the talk of the wash house, I'm not saying it as a turn of phrase, I mean it for real.' Dot sighed. 'If I'd known my plan to get someone billeted on Sheila would come back to haunt me like that, I'd have kept my big nose out.'

'No, you wouldn't. You had to do something.'

'Aye, that's true. I want to get our Sheila back on the straight and narrow and I want to do it without her knowing it's me. She's my Harry's lass and our Jimmy's mum. I can't have any bad feeling between us.'

'Especially as you know what you know because you were creeping around her house in secret.'

'If Reg's mother had come creeping round my house in the dead of night, I'd have called her a snoop and goodness knows what besides.'

'You weren't snooping, Dot. You had a good reason to be there.'

'Try telling Sheila that.' Dot glanced across at the clock and pushed back her chair. 'I'd better go.'

'Thank you for sparing the time,' said Cordelia.

That was the funny thing about Cordelia. She spoke all formal, but once you got to know her, you realised how likeable and caring she was.

On her way home, Dot decided to pop in at Sheila's to make sure she knew Reg had come home. If Sheila wasn't there, she would leave a message with a neighbour.

Giving a brief knock, she pulled the key through the letter box and let herself in, calling a greeting. The house smelled of stale tobacco, but there was the aroma of a fresh ciggy an' all. Dot headed for the kitchen, reminding herself to be bright and cheerful.

Oh. Rosa.

'Evening, Mrs Green.' Rosa glanced up. She was filing her nails at the table.

'Hello, Rosa. Sheila not here? Where's our Jimmy?'

'At work and out playing, in that order. Cup of tea?'

'No, thanks. I won't stop.' Something stirred inside Dot, something hot and spiky. 'I'm glad to see you here, anyroad. That time I came round when you were meant to hand over our Jimmy to me, you'd gone swanning off in your finery.'

Rosa blew on a fingernail. Were microscopic pieces of nail landing in the sugar bowl? 'I'm here today, aren't I? Mrs Whatsit over the road had a go at Sheila for that, and Sheila had a go at me, so here I am.'

With her fag dangling from her lips, Rosa held up her hands to examine her nails. There was a bottle of red nail varnish beside the ashtray.

'Getting ready to go out?' asked Dot.

'I shan't be going until later. Don't fret. Here – have a whiff of this.'

Rosa brushed aside the newspaper. Dot expected her to produce a bottle of scent, but instead it was a cake of soap. Not pure white, but creamy white. Rosa held it out.

Dot took it, lifting it to her face to inhale.

'Gardenia,' said Rosa.

'Where'd you get it?'

'It was a present.'

'Make it last,' Dot advised.

Did that smile on Rosa's lips mean there were more where this came from? Or was it Dot being bad-minded?

Rosa looked up hopefully. 'Have you come to take Jimmy to yours?'

'I've a message for Sheila, if you'd kindly pass it on. Tell her Harry's dad is home from hospital.'

'That's good news. You must be relieved.'

'I am.' Dot turned towards a loud knocking at the front door. 'I'll get it.'

There was a crowd at the door, or so it seemed in that first moment: Jimmy and three other lads, all with black eyes, and three mums, holding the boys by their collars.

'You're Jimmy's nan, aren't you?' demanded one of the mothers. 'Is his mum in?'

Dot was staring at the boys. All those black eyes. She pictured a terrible punch-up, but only for a moment.

'What's happened?' she asked, though she didn't really need to.

'Your Jimmy has only used a tin of shoe polish to black all their eyes.'

'We were playing at being heroes like Grandpa,' Jimmy began and received a clip round the ear from one of the mums.

'Look at our lads,' said another mum. 'I'm not using precious soap getting this off our Derek's face. That's your Sheila's job, that is.'

'My Gerald has got First Holy Communion class this evening,' chimed in another mum. 'He can't go looking like this.'

'Right.' Dot spoke decisively. 'You leave your lads with me. In you come, boys.' She marched them through to the kitchen. 'Do you know owt about this?' she demanded, giving Rosa a hard look.

Rosa's mouth dropped open. 'Jimmy asked for the Cherry Blossom.'

'Oh aye, and it never occurred to you to ask why? That's the first thing you do when our Jimmy wants summat, and if you bothered less about your hair and your nails, you'd have realised that. Where's that posh soap?'

'Hey! You can't have that!' Rosa leaped up, trying to snatch it back as Dot swooped on it.

'Hands off,' said Dot. 'Boys, get in that scullery and line up. You're going to go home lily-white and smelling of gardenia.'

Chapter Twenty-One

A June bride. Joan was filled with happiness, but at the same time she missed Letitia more than ever. They had always intended to be one another's bridesmaids. Today was Saturday, the last day of May – and Saturday of next week would be her wedding day. Bob hadn't wasted any time. They had decided on Wednesday to marry in June and on Thursday he had gone round to Gran's and waited while she wrote her letter of consent.

'There's no need for you to come,' he had told Joan. 'Let things cool between you.'

The church had been booked and the banns would be read tomorrow. Church was one of the places Mrs Grayson was able to get to, with company, though she declared herself so pleased that she'd walk there on her own if needs be, so as to hear Joan's banns. Mrs Cooper was going to attend as well, even though she was Roman Catholic and it was probably a mortal sin to set foot inside a Protestant church.

'You do realise it's because they're both so fond of you?' said Mabel. 'They won't be coming out of politeness. They care about you.'

'Really?' It hadn't occurred to Joan before. Was it because, as second-best granddaughter, she had never expected to matter that much to others?

'Yes, really.' Mabel laughed and gave her a hug. 'They love their Joan.'

With that, something fell into place in Joan's mind. It was wonderfully exciting to think of getting married so quickly, but there was a lot of organising to do. Yesterday she had gone to the Hubbles' for tea and the girls had been full of suggestions. Without Letitia to help her, and with things as they now stood with Gran, it had been tempting to put everything into the Hubbles' hands and let them sweep her along, but something held her back. She loved Bob's family dearly and couldn't wait to be one of them, but that was for afterwards, for when she was Mrs Robert Hubble. Was it silly of her to want people of her own to help organise her wedding day? She, who didn't have any family any more?

Except that she did, in a way. She had Mrs Cooper and Mrs Grayson, who had made her feel welcome and wanted after Gran had chucked her out. She had all her railway friends too. Their friendship meant the world to her and they would know how much she was missing Letitia at this important time. An idea unfolded in Joan's mind and warmth spread through her. It was perfect.

Bob came round late morning and took Joan out to a café, where they had fishcakes followed by apple pudding with ginger sauce. They went back to Wilton Close afterwards, but Bob couldn't stay long because he was due at work shortly. When he left, Joan walked with him down the front path to the gate and explained her idea.

'D'you mind?'

'Of course not. It's your special day and I want you to have whatever you want.'

'What I'm really asking is, will your mum mind? I got the feeling yesterday she was all set to start organising.'

'My mum is going to be the mother of the bride three times over. I think she can afford to take a back seat at our wedding.'

'I won't leave her out, but I want Mrs Cooper and the others to be involved.'

'So do I. I think it's a wizard idea.'

Closing the gate behind him, Bob leaned over to kiss her goodbye before she waved him off. Happiness bubbled up inside her. In one week's time they would be man and wife. After that, she would be seeing her husband off to work. Her husband!

As she watched Bob walk to the end of the road, Cordelia appeared round the corner and stopped to say hello to him. He then went on his way and Cordelia walked towards the gate.

'This is a flying visit,' she told Joan. 'I've come to do my monthly inspection.'

Joan opened the gate for her. As they went inside and Joan was about to close the door, a voice called from the pavement.

'Don't shut it, chick.'

'Dot,' called Joan, opening the door wide in welcome.

Dot came up the path. 'I've brought back Mrs Grayson's pie dish. It was kind of her to bake a pie to take the weight off my shoulders with everything that's been happening. Not that I really needed it in the end, with Reg coming home from hospital as quick as he did, but it was most welcome all the same.'

'Come in,' said Joan. She called to Mrs Cooper and Mrs Grayson. 'We've got visitors. Mrs Green and Mrs Masters are here.'

Mrs Cooper appeared. 'Come in, both of you. I'll put the kettle on.'

'I hate to impose on you,' Cordelia said to Mrs Cooper, 'but I'm here to do the monthly check.'

'It isn't an imposition,' said Mrs Cooper. 'It has to be done.'

'Even so, I never feel quite comfortable undertaking it.'

'Think of it this way,' said Mrs Cooper. 'If you hadn't said yes to doing it, Mr Morgan wouldn't have let me have the house. You have your look round and the tea will be ready when you're finished. You'll stop for a cuppa an' all, Mrs Green, won't you?'

'Aye, I will, thanks,' said Dot, 'but I can't hang about. I'm working later, so after this I've got to get back home in time to go out again.'

Joan helped Mrs Cooper make the tea and as they carried it through, Cordelia joined them in the front room.

'Everything in order?' asked Mrs Cooper.

'As always,' said Cordelia.

'No Mabel this afternoon?' asked Dot.

'She's meeting Harry in town,' said Joan. 'They're going to a matinee performance at the theatre, then staying out for dinner before going to a dance in aid of the Red Cross.'

'She's having a busy day,' said Dot with a laugh.

'She's taking a leaf out of Joan's book,' said Mrs Cooper. 'There's been no stopping Joan and Bob. They've booked the church and they've got the church hall for the reception.'

'And Gran's written her letter of consent,' Joan added. 'One thing I have to do is get a magistrate to write a letter confirming that even though I'm Henshaw on my birth certificate, I am legally known as Foster.'

'I'm sure my husband could organise that for you,' said Cordelia.

'What about getting a local solicitor to sort it out?' asked Dot. 'Mr Masters belongs to a posh firm in town and you know what they're like, they charge the earth. A local man wouldn't charge as much. I'm sure Joan and Bob aren't looking to have it done as a favour.'

'Of course not,' said Joan.

'Then take all your identification papers with you and go to a local chap,' Dot advised.

'And make sure he understands he has to do it quickly,' Mrs Cooper added. 'You haven't any time to waste.'

Joan smiled at Dot and Cordelia. 'We're getting married next Saturday.'

'Next Saturday?' Cordelia exclaimed.

'It doesn't sound very romantic, but it all came down to shift patterns. We wanted to get married in June, but if we'd waited the normal three weeks under an ordinary licence, we wouldn't have been able to have a honeymoon. By marrying next week on a special licence, we can.'

'Crikey,' said Dot. 'That doesn't leave a lot of time.'

'That's why I'm glad you're all here—' said Joan, excitement rising inside her as she started to make her announcement – only to be interrupted by the wail of the siren.

'Joan, fetch Mabel's flask from her knapsack,' said Mrs Cooper. 'We need as many flasks as we can muster.'

Soon they were all squeezed into the Anderson shelter. There were two chairs, which Dot and Cordelia insisted the two ladies of the house should have, and the other three sat perched on the edges of the lower bunks.

'I wonder when we'll get the all-clear,' said Dot. 'No offence, but I can't afford to get stuck here all afternoon. I've got a shift starting at three.'

'You'll be finishing late, then,' said Mrs Grayson.

'Midnight. I'm not on the trains today. I'll be sorting parcels.'

'If there isn't time for you to go home before work,' Joan offered, 'I can cycle over to Withington and tell your family for you.'

'Thanks, chick,' said Dot, 'but aren't we talking about the wrong thing? As I recall, you were in the middle of saying summat when the siren went off.'

Joan beamed. 'It's to do with my wedding. I need lots of help and I'd like all four of you to be my mothers of the bride.'

There was a moment of silence. Was her request inappropriate?

Mrs Cooper sucked in a breath, raising her fingers to cover her mouth. 'Really? You're asking us to do that?'

'It's a great honour,' said Mrs Grayson.

'It most certainly is.' Cordelia looked concerned. 'I'm sorry to throw a spanner in the works, but what about your grandmother?'

Joan tried to ignore an uncomfortable flutter deep inside. 'She may have given her consent, but it's clear she doesn't approve. I don't suppose she'll even attend. Things haven't been right between us since Letitia died.'

'Then I'm sure we're all honoured to agree,' said Dot, and there was a little eruption of pleasure and laughter.

'I want you all to sit at the front of the church,' said Joan.

'Eh, chick,' said Dot, reaching out to take her hand.

'If you're going to bring up Gran again, please don't. You're my family now. Mrs Grayson, please will you make the cake? I know that isn't an easy thing to manage these days.'

'Leave it to me.' Mrs Grayson's cheeks went pink with pleasure. 'I'll make one of those no-egg cakes and I'll get hold of some saccharine if there isn't enough sugar.'

'We'll give you whatever dried fruit we can,' said Dot. 'They do say you can used grated veg as a substitute.'

'There might be more dried fruit to be had now that food parcels are coming from America,' said Cordelia.

'I promise you one thing,' said Mrs Grayson. 'It'll be the moistest cake you've ever tasted.'

Mrs Cooper rolled her eyes. 'When she says moist, what she means is alcoholic.'

'We've got a bit of sherry,' said Mrs Grayson, 'and I can't think of a better purpose for it.'

'I can probably provide a little alcohol as well,' said Cordelia.

'Where will you go for your honeymoon?' asked Dot.

Joan smiled. 'Bob's organising it. A few days at the seaside.'

'Get him to bring his holiday clothes over here to put inside your suitcase,' said Mrs Cooper. 'Then we can take the case to the church hall next Saturday, ready for you to go away.'

Joan's cheeks felt warm. Was she blushing? Sharing a suitcase seemed a very married thing to do. One week from now ...

'I have some rather good writing paper in my desk that you are welcome to for your invitations,' Cordelia offered.

'Thank you,' said Joan.

'Now here's a thought,' said Mrs Cooper. 'Who will the invitations come from? Joan doesn't have parents and she can't ask her gran. Bob's parents?'

'No, that wouldn't feel right,' said Joan. 'From all the mothers of the bride? No, that's plain barmy. They'll have to be from Bob and me.'

'That's ... unusual,' said Mrs Grayson.

'It's wartime,' said Dot. 'Lots of things are unusual.'

Joan pictured it. 'It'll have to be "Miss Joan Angela Foster and Mr Robert Dennis Hubble request the pleasure ... " How does that sound?'

'Perfect,' said Mrs Cooper.

'A week is no time at all,' said Mrs Grayson. 'What about your dress?'

'I could just about make one in that time.'

'Only just,' said Cordelia, 'and it would leave no time for anything else.'

'It could take the whole week to find fabric of the right quality,' Mrs Cooper pointed out.

Cordelia started to speak, stopped and then said, 'You could try my wedding dress, if you like. I got married in nineteen-twenty, so it's rather a loose fit, no darts, no waist, but you could put some darts in if you wanted.'

'Or there's my dress,' said Mrs Grayson, 'but I got married early in the last war, so a young thing like you would think it very old-fashioned.'

'Plenty of girls are getting wed in smart jackets and skirts these days,' said Mrs Cooper.

'I definitely want to look like a bride,' said Joan.

'Then you shall,' Mrs Cooper promised. 'You're not to fret about anything. Between us, we'll make sure you have the perfect wedding day.'

Joan's heart drummed inside her chest. It was overwhelming to receive such kindness. How good these dear ladies were – her four wonderful mothers of the bride.

To start with, Mabel didn't think she would enjoy the performance because she was worried about going to the Red Cross dance later on. Had it been a mistake to accept the tickets from Gil? But he had given them to her after she'd made it clear he didn't stand a chance with her, so taking the tickets had been harmless – hadn't it? Or was she kidding herself?

Harry wasn't impressed, that was for certain. She wished now that she had told him about the dance in one of her letters, but that would have led to an awkward conversation when they had one of their telephone calls and she had thought it best to save the explanation behind the dance tickets until she saw him in person. She softened him up first by telling him he was invited to Joan and Bob's wedding next week, but when she explained about the Red Cross dance, his immediate response was that they shouldn't go.

'You're only saying that because the tickets came from Gil,' Mabel protested as they walked to the theatre. 'It's not as though he'll be there. He said he'd duck out so I could go with you.'

'Am I expected to be grateful?'

'We've got to go,' Mabel pressed. 'It's a fund-raiser. There'll be a raffle and other things. Persephone went to one the other night and for five bob you could choose what the band played, and Alison and Paul went to one where they had a dancing competition that you paid to enter.'

'You don't need to tell me how important it is to drum up money,' said Harry, still sounding grouchy. 'Yes, all right, we'll go, but I'll jolly well pay for the tickets before we go in. I won't have your old flame standing us a night out.'

'It's a good job we've got the theatre first,' said Mabel. 'It'll give you a chance to clear your head. I could almost wish I'd never met Gil again.'

'I'm glad to hear you say so.'

'Gil has helped me. I've found a peace of mind I never thought I'd achieve and I will always be grateful to him for that. I wish you could see that it's possible for me to have a deep regard and fondness for him without it posing a threat to our relationship.'

'I don't want you entertaining a deep regard for another chap. No man would be happy with that.'

'Well, I do and that's that,' Mabel said. 'Don't you trust me?'

Stopping, Harry turned her to him. 'Of course I trust you, darling – but I don't trust Lieutenant Iain Gilchrist.'

And before she could stop herself, dammit, Mabel glanced away. Oh, she should have carried on gazing into his eyes. Goodness knew what he was thinking now. Well, he undoubtedly thought that he was right to believe that Gil wanted more than a spot of auld lang syne with her, and he was right. Not only that, but by looking away, she had confirmed it.

'Come on,' said Harry. 'We don't want to miss curtain-up.'

Soon they were seated in their places in the stalls. The theatre wasn't packed to the rafters, but it was jolly full, probably with folk determined to make the most of the weekend, which was the start of the Whit-week holiday. The house lights dimmed and the performance began, but after twenty minutes the show paused and the curtains swished shut as a gentleman walked to the front of the stage. There was a soft rustling in the auditorium; everyone knew what was coming next.

'Good afternoon, ladies and gentlemen. I am the manager and it is my duty to inform you that the air-raid siren has sounded. If anyone would like to leave the theatre ... '

A few people did, but no more than that. It was the same as being at the cinema. The air-raid warning would flash up on the screen and the audience would stay put and carry on watching.

As the manager completed his announcement, an incendiary, which must have plunged straight through the roof, hit the top of the curtain and he leaped into the orchestra pit as one half of the vast curtain sagged, sending a quantity of heavy fabric pooling on the stage.

Even so, no one else left the theatre, as far as Mabel could tell, and the performance continued more or less as normal except for some impromptu community singing while pieces of burning backcloth were dealt with. The feeling that the Red Cross evening was hanging over her trickled away and Mabel started enjoying the afternoon. She sensed that Harry was getting into the swing of it too.

The show ended to a huge ovation and the manager walked onstage again to announce that the all-clear had sounded.

'Perfect timing,' said Harry as he escorted Mabel outside. 'Let's go and have something to eat. We've got plenty of time.'

He made no further reference to Gil, for which Mabel was grateful. Harry would enjoy himself once they reached the fund-raiser, she knew. He loved the fun and bustle of a night out.

Later, when they arrived at the dance, Mabel handed over her jacket to the cloakroom girl. Most of the ladies were in evening gowns and she felt momentarily self-conscious at being dressed in her velvet rayon in two shades of green. Tailor-made it might be, but it was all too obviously a day dress. But she didn't really mind. Harry made her feel beautiful, it was as simple as that.

Before they entered the ballroom, Harry rather ostentatiously paid for their tickets, then escorted her to the table where the raffle prizes were on display. In the centre, on a box covered with a piece of black velvet, was a large onion, the sight of which had people dipping into their wallets and purses with a will, onions having all but disappeared from the shops after the fall of the Channel Islands.

'Imagine being able to take that home to Mrs Grayson,' sighed Mabel, accepting the tickets Harry had bought and taking coins from her purse to purchase more.

'Put your money away,' said Harry. 'You don't pay for anything when you're with me. I'll buy you more tickets if you want them.'

He did so, but Mabel still bought more as well. They found places at a circular table seating a dozen, where those already seated made them welcome, and Harry went to fetch drinks.

They took to the floor for several dances and it was as they were returning to their table, Harry's hand gently on the back of Mabel's waist to guide her, that she saw Gil.

Looking smart in evening dress, he was chatting in a circle of people, a drink in his hand. He wasn't handsome in the dark-eyed, square-jawed way Harry was, but that smile of his lent warm appeal to his lean, serious face, and she could tell from the way he was looking at the person speaking that he really was paying attention – unlike the chap next to him, who was clearly waiting for the speaker to finish so he could jump in and say his piece. It was true that Harry made her feel beautiful, but with Gil, she had always felt listened to.

Was it crass of her to pretend to stumble in order to home Harry's attention on to her so that he wouldn't notice Gil? Harry tenderly directed her to her seat. Now if Gil would just clear off into the throng …

'What's Gilchrist doing here?' Harry demanded. 'You said he wasn't coming.'

'That's what I thought.'

'He told you he wouldn't be here,' said Harry. 'Good grief, don't say he's coming over.'

The group Gil was with had broken apart with polite smiles and dispersed. Gil looked at Mabel and walked across. Harry muttered something. Mabel's heart sank, then she felt annoyed. Why should she be made to feel uncomfortable? She had done nothing wrong. Harry was behaving like an oaf.

'Good evening, Mabel.' Gil smiled at her. 'Evening, Knatchbull.' He stuck out his right hand.

Harry rose to shake hands. 'Gilchrist.'

'It's a splendid do, Gil,' said Mabel. She spoke warmly, because that was what Gil, as one of the organisers, fully deserved. She just hoped Harry wouldn't accuse her of gushing. Well, so what if he did?

'It's not bad, is it? And people are being most generous. Have you bought your raffle tickets?'

'I've got my eye on that onion.'

Gil laughed. 'You and everyone else.'

'Why are you here?' Harry asked bluntly. 'I thought you weren't coming.'

Heat crept across Mabel's cheeks, but she kept her smile in position.

'I didn't intend to,' said Gil, 'but a couple of the other organisers have been taken ill and I was asked to step in.' He gave them a nod and a smile. 'Enjoy the evening.'

'We shall,' said Mabel, and watched him walk away before she turned to look at Harry. Frankly, she was ready to have words, but he gave her a beguiling smile and held up his hands in surrender.

'That's wasn't very gracious of me. I apologise.'

'I'm not the one you should apologise to.'

'Yes, you are.' Harry caught her hand and raised it to his lips. 'I'm jealous. I admit it. I don't like having your old flame hanging around – especially when he's on the spot in Manchester and I can only get across to see you when I have a pass.' He pulled her to her feet. 'Gilchrist has disappeared into the night and he can jolly well stay there for all I care. I've got the loveliest girl in the room to dance with and it's time to make all the other blokes jealous.'

She allowed him to sweep her onto the floor into a dreamy waltz beneath the glittering chandeliers. It was unfortunate that Gil was here, but now that they had exchanged a few words, she could relax.

'You truly have nothing to fear from Gil, you know,' she murmured.

'Anybody with eyes in their head can see he has feelings for you.'

'So what? I no longer have feelings for him. All that was over long ago. I've told you that before.' Did it sound like she was protesting too much?

'The thing is – I don't know whether I should say this.'

'You have to now,' said Mabel.

'Very well. It isn't just that I'm worried about Gilchrist chancing his luck. It's the thought of what *you* might do. I didn't exactly behave towards you like a gentleman to start with. Before I got to know you and fell head over heels in love, I was interested in your family's money.'

'And you think I might try to get my own back?' Mabel angled her head so as to look into his face.

'No one could blame you.'

'You don't know me very well if you think I'd do that.'

'I don't really think you would,' said Harry. 'It's just – well, I might deserve it.'

'Harry.'

'Yes?'

'You're an idiot.'

'I know.'

'But you're my idiot and that's what counts.'

'That's quite possibly the best and most reassuring thing anyone has ever said to me.'

'Harry.'

'Yes?'

'Shut up and dance.'

'Oh.' Harry pretended to be disappointed. 'I thought you might say "Shut up and kiss me."'

'Later,' said Mabel.

Chapter Twenty-Two

It was gone midnight when Dot clocked off – and what a night. What a shift. She had come on duty expecting to spend her time sorting parcels of all sizes and weights, making sure each was in the right place for the next leg of its journey, so that when the early trains were prepared, their parcels porters could gather their many parcels, confident that nothing had been misplaced. And she had done that, aye, and plenty of it. But when that train had come in ...

Mr Thirkle, bless him, had tried to warn her, but she hadn't stopped to listen because there were other porters about, including Mr Weaver, who a few weeks back had witnessed Edie Thirkle-as-was accusing her of chasing after Mr Thirkle. So instead of stopping to see what he wanted, Dot had gone straight through the barrier to where the train was coasting alongside the long platform. From the top of the engine came a prolonged hiss as the loco headed towards the buffers. The brakes shrieked and then there was a deep *clunk* as the mighty machine came to a halt.

Dot had opened a door and – 'shock' hardly described it. It was more than shock, worse, deeper. It was knowledge. That's what it was. Knowledge. One of those moments when you understood right to the core of your being the meaning of war.

Please, God, keep my boys safe. The prayer of every mother.

The train was filled with coffins – every door she opened. She could scarcely breathe. Each coffin had a flag draped over it, and that was summat, aye, that was summat. Showing respect for the fallen was important. But, oh …

Please, God, keep my lads safe. The heartfelt prayer of every mother.

How many mothers would receive a coffin into their homes tomorrow? Dear God, if one – or two – of those coffins should be destined for her house … but no, no, there would have been a telegram. Relief all but knocked her off her feet. Was it wrong to be grateful when so many other mothers were heartbroken?

Now, at last, her shift had ended and Mr Thirkle quietly offered to walk her to her bus stop. She should say no – shouldn't she? But if another male colleague had made the same offer at this time of night, she would have accepted, as long as she was sure she wasn't putting him out unduly. Mr Thirkle was only being gentlemanly. Even if he hoped to enjoy her company for a spell for personal reasons, he was still being gentlemanly.

'Thank you,' she said. 'That's kind of you.'

'It's no trouble,' he replied.

They left the station and picked their way across town towards Oxford Road. It was eerie walking through the darkness with only their dimmed torches to guide them between the burned-out ruins left by the Christmas Blitz. Why did it feel different to pass by a windowless shell or a building half eaten by a bomb than a place that had escaped unscathed?

They chatted as they walked. As he always did, Mr Thirkle enquired after her family. First off, he asked after Reg, which felt like having a bucket of cold water thrown over her, then he asked after the rest of the Greens. Dot wanted to confide in him about Sheila and seek his advice, but you couldn't tell a man summat like that. It wouldn't be decent. Besides, how could she say her daughter-in-law was possibly having it away with another man when … when she herself was entertaining inappropriate thoughts about Mr Thirkle?

Instead, she told him about Jimmy and the boot polish. Mr Thirkle always enjoyed hearing about the scrapes Jimmy got into. And she told him about Jenny coming top of the class for writing a poem. Then she gritted her teeth and asked after his Edie, knowing full well that Edie would want to scratch her eyes out for accepting Mr Thirkle's company on this walk through the blackout.

As they made their way around the curved wall of Central Library, the sound of the siren lifted into the night air. Dot reached out to touch Mr Thirkle's arm, an instinctive reaction born of the need to protect someone for whom she cared deeply.

'I'm not sure which is the closest public shelter from here,' said Mr Thirkle. 'Come on.'

As they ran, the onslaught commenced, the middle of Manchester once again the target. Hadn't Jerry done enough damage at Christmas? Across the road, a wall collapsed and a fire started. Mr Thirkle threw his arm around Dot's shoulder, bending over her as they hurried along, only to skid to a halt as an incendiary landed a few feet in front of them.

'Oh, my life,' gasped Dot.

They both shone their torches over the edge of the pavement beside the buildings, but why would there be buckets of water or sand outside damaged, deserted places? They could run for it, of course, but Dot had no intention of doing so and she knew Mr Thirkle wouldn't either. He ripped off his overcoat and, darting closer, chucked it over the incendiary, which was about the size and shape of a rounders bat. As he did so, the device detonated, the burst of flames lifting his coat into the air before it descended again. Mr Thirkle jumped forward and stamped up and down on his overcoat. Dot threw her own coat on top and joined the stamping, though they were all but jumping up and down before the fire was smothered.

'In here.' Mr Thirkle pulled her into the doorway of a bombed-out building. 'If we can get into the cellar, we'll be safer.'

Of all the ridiculous things, the big front door of this half-destroyed house was locked. Some windows were boarded up, but the one next to the door wasn't, possibly because its glass was intact.

'Stand back,' Mr Thirkle ordered.

He pulled off his uniform jacket, winding it around his hand and forearm. There was the sound of glass shattering, clear and oddly musical against the deep-throated throb of the aeroplane engines and the whistling of falling bombs.

'I'll give you a leg up,' said Mr Thirkle.

Dot lifted her foot and placed it in his clasped hands. As he gave her a boost, her sleeve caught on some glass still lodged in the window frame. When she wrenched herself free, her hat went flying. Wobbling on the window ledge, she aimed her torch downwards for the second it took to ascertain there was a floor in front of her, then she manoeuvred herself down as gently and quickly as she could. The floorboards held and she moved aside for Mr Thirkle to follow.

'The stairs down to the cellar must lead off the hallway,' said Dot.

'The floor might not be safe. Stay right at the edge.'

Hugging the wall, they made their way into the hall. Here, a wide staircase led up to nowhere. The building was open to skies criss-crossed with searchlights. Staying close to the wall, Dot hastened to the back of the hall, where, after opening a couple of doors, she found steps leading down in a curve.

'Down we go,' she said.

'I think we've ended up beneath the back of the room where we started,' said Mr Thirkle when they reached the bottom.

The cellar was enormous and felt filthy enough to smother an echo. Although there were wooden crates here and there, there was nothing to suggest it had ever been used as an air-raid shelter – no seats or tables, no bunks.

'We'd best go back and make ourselves comfortable on the steps,' said Dot.

'We should stay near the bottom,' said Mr Thirkle.

This they did. The air seemed thick and Dot was reluctant to inhale. She tried taking shallow breaths, but if that meant taking more breaths, wasn't that just as bad?

'We'd better switch off our torches,' said Mr Thirkle. 'Save the batteries.'

Dot's glance swept over him. He was beside her but on the step above. He had lost his coat to the incendiary and his jacket to the window. He gave her a nod before clicking off his torch, the image of his kindly eyes remaining with her as darkness pressed in on them. From far away came the sound and vibration of bomb blasts, but all within the cellar was still.

'Are you cold?' Mr Thirkle asked. 'We may be here for some time.'

'I'm fine. You're the one who'll get cold in your shirt-sleeves.'

She had read a romantic novel in which the heroine and the hero had been trapped in the snow and had snuggled together for bodily warmth. Was this the moment to suggest … ? What was she thinking? She wasn't a tart.

265

Or was she? Having feelings for a man other than your husband wasn't respectable. Oh, what a mess. What a ruddy mess.

'Penny for them,' said Mr Thirkle.

'Nowt, really. Just the usual things everyone thinks about during a raid. I hope the family's safe. I hope the house isn't hit. You know, all those things.'

'Aye, I do know.'

Dot shifted slightly. By, it was going to be uncomfortable if they ended up spending hours on these steps. Hadn't there been concern about 'shelter legs', caused by hours of pressure from the bar on the front of deckchair seats? Maybe she was about to discover a new phenomenon called 'stone-steps bottom'.

'Is your Edie at home tonight?' She felt obliged to ask.

'It's one of her WVS nights. She'll be out and about on the tea wagon or else staffing a rest centre.'

'There'll be plenty of folk needing the rest centres tonight, judging by the ... ' She was about to say 'the sound of it', but as a deep vibration passed through the cellar, she said, '... the feel of it.'

'It's a bad 'un,' said Mr Thirkle.

'It is that.' Were they going to discuss the raid until the all-clear freed them?

'Mrs Green,' said Mr Thirkle. He stopped, and it was a long moment before he said, 'I hope you won't take it amiss if I say how dearly I value our friendship?'

'So do I. We're natural friends, thee and me.'

'We see eye to eye. It's been a long time since – that is to say ... '

Dot's heart beat like a big bass drum. Her heart knew what he meant. She was terrified of him saying it, actually putting it into words, but at the same time she wanted him to, oh yes, she wanted him to.

266

All she had to do was say 'I know' and that would bring their feelings for one another into the open and seal things between them.

'I know,' she said.

A vast noise *whumped* all around them, above, every-where, accompanied by a dark cracking sound as if an ancient oak tree was being felled. All the dust and filth in the cellar was scooped up into the air. Instinctively, Dot drew her head into her shoulders, raising her arms. Mr Thirkle leaned over her, his chest against her back, shield-ing her, his arms coming round her.

Coughing and spluttering, they raised their heads as the moment passed.

'Are you all right?' Mr Thirkle asked.

Dot nodded. She couldn't speak. Her throat was full of dust. All she could do was cough.

'Stay here.'

Mr Thirkle switched on his torch and started up the steps. Dot had no intention of staying put. With a final, violent cough, she gained control of her breathing and followed, managing not to bump into him as she rounded the curve of the steps. It was like being in a pea-souper. The dirt swirled slowly in the air, showing no sign of falling to the floor. Dot blinked as grime hit her eyes, making them sting. Above them, the top of the steps had vanished beneath rubble and timber that filled the space all the way to the ceiling.

Mr Thirkle was holding his handkerchief to his mouth. He removed it for long enough to say matter-of-factly, 'It doesn't look like we'll be leaving that way.'

The hair lifted on the back of Dot's neck, but she matched Mr Thirkle's tone. 'We'd be better off in the cellar proper. We won't have to breathe in so much muck.'

She led the way down the steps, grit crunching beneath her shoes. They returned to the underneath of the front of the building. The air was clearer here, though that wasn't saying much.

Mr Thirkle used his sleeved forearm to brush the top of a crate. 'Your seat awaits, madam.'

Dot approached the crate from the other side, unwilling to pass beside him for fear of seeming to fling herself at him, though goodness knew, that was what her blood was urging her to do. They stood one on either side of the crate, facing each other. Dot took a step forward. Her toe struck the wood, but her gaze never faltered.

There was a sort of hissing sound. She was aware of it but paid it no mind. Then there was a creak and a sharp snap.

Mr Thirkle stepped away and headed across the cellar into the blackness, the pale light of his torch showing her where he was going. Dot could barely believe he had torn himself away from the moment, their moment, the moment when … when …

'Water,' said Mr Thirkle. 'A main must have burst. It's pouring in.'

Déjà vu. Less than six months ago, Mabel and Harry had reported for first-aid duty at the Town Hall when they had been at the end of a night out in town and a raid had started. That had been on the first night of the Christmas Blitz. Now it was the last night in May – no, actually it was June, because it was after midnight.

'Take a rucksack each from over there and join the first-aid parties that have gone to Peter Street.'

'Peter Street?' asked Mabel.

'Do you know the Theatre Royal and the Gaiety?'

'Yes. Is that Peter Street? I know how to get there.'

'They've both been hit. So has the Café Royal and the YMCA building.'

'Sounds bad,' said Harry, hefting a rucksack onto his shoulder.

'Aye. The upper floors of the police headquarters have been ruined and some Civil Defence messengers copped it. Reports are coming in from Cheetham, Strangeways and Salford. Jerry is dropping bombs, yes, but there are hundreds upon hundreds of canisters of incendiaries coming down. God knows how many fires there'll be. Fingers crossed it's not as bad as it was at Christmas. Anyroad – Peter Street. Get gone.'

Harry took Mabel's hand and together they hurried through the darkness. The blackout could be oddly disorienting even when you knew where you were going. Mabel focused her attention on their destination, pushing the noise of the aeroplanes and the AA fire to the back of her mind. Her feet got tangled in something and she would have come a cropper had Harry not hauled her sharply upright. She shone her torch down to see what had made her stumble. A coat? Bending over, meaning to sling it aside, she realised it was two coats – smelly, charred – and there was an incendiary beneath them.

She caught her breath. 'Harry! You don't suppose – I mean, you do hear of folk being too close to a bomb and – and afterwards there's nothing left of them.'

'That's bombs, not incendiaries. With an incendiary, you'd burn to death. There'd be a lot more left than coats – God almighty!'

An explosion behind them at the other end of the road shattered the flagstones, sending pieces flying. Harry grabbed Mabel, throwing her into a doorway and landing on top of her, protecting her with his body, his arms curling around her and holding her head down. Mabel felt something sharp beneath her. Glass? She was careful not to move. Not that she could have moved, with Harry's bulk squashing her.

When he helped her to her feet, she peered down the road, where a crater at least ten feet across now divided the street into two distinct sections, but at least flames weren't shooting out of it into the air, so presumably the gas main was untouched.

'Are you all right?' Harry asked, and when she nodded he strode over to pick up their rucksacks, which had been blown along the road.

Mabel dusted herself down, pulling her sleeve over her hand so as not to end up with splinters of glass in her fingers. Her foot struck something. Her torch. As she bent to retrieve it, her hand brushed against something – a hat. She clicked on her torch to test it was still working, automatically aiming the beam downwards. As its dim light swept over the hat, Mabel's heartbeat raced. It couldn't be – *could it?* It was preposterous to imagine that Dot was the only person with a hat like that. Even so ...

Mabel darted into the road and snatched at the burned coats. Oh yes, she'd know that coat anywhere. Dot called it her old faithful.

Harry took her arm, ready to urge her onwards, but she resisted.

'This coat ... and that hat over there ... they're Dot's – Mrs Green's. I know they are.' She cupped her hands round her mouth. 'Dot!' she yelled. 'Dot Green!'

Harry looked up and down the road. 'She's long gone. And she won't be alone. There are two coats.'

'If it was just the coats – but there's her hat among the broken glass.'

Mabel returned to the doorway, careful where she put her feet. It was stupid to keep looking at the glass. She lifted her eyes and was turning back to Harry when she realised where the glass had come from.

'Look. This window is broken. You don't suppose … ?'

'No, I don't,' said Harry, but he must have caught the expression on her face, because he added, 'But there's no harm in looking. Stand back.'

Placing his hands on the brickwork, he leaned a little way through the window and shouted, 'Is anyone in there? Mrs Green? Anybody?' He pushed himself clear and looked at Mabel over his shoulder. 'No one there.'

'Let's climb in and have a quick look. Please, Harry. I won't stop fretting if we don't.'

'I'll do it. You wait here. These buildings aren't safe.'

'Nonsense. I'm not playing the helpless damsel. Give me a bunk up.'

They clambered into a large, empty room and, skirting round the edge, made for the door. Mabel pushed it open, standing still, just in case. That was what they had been taught in first aid. The last thing an emergency called for was an impetuous first-aider falling down a hole. The door led into a hallway with half a staircase and no upstairs. The far end of the hall was blocked off by rubble. Harry coughed, flapping his hand in front of his face.

'That lot must have come down tonight. It hasn't settled. I told you this wasn't safe.'

Mabel's shoulders slumped in disappointment, but it was time to admit defeat. 'Let's go.'

They went back into the front room. As they headed for the window, Mabel looked over her shoulder.

'What was that? Did you hear something? Listen.'

A tapping? Or her imagination?

'Good grief!' Harry dropped to the floor, pressing his ear to the boards. 'There's someone down there – yes – voices.'

His face close to the floor, he shouted, 'We can hear you. Hang on!' He sat back on his heels and frowned at Mabel. 'The rubble at the end of the hall must have blocked their way out. We'll have to take up the floorboards. We need a crowbar and then rope, depending on how deep the cellar is.'

'I'll run back to the Town Hall. They'll have equipment there.'

'No, I'll go.' Harry stood up. 'It isn't safe out there.'

'It isn't safe anywhere.' Mabel was already at the window, preparing to scramble out. 'Stay here. See if any floorboards are loose.'

With help from Harry, she climbed the window and legged it down the road, slowing as she approached the crater. She stepped around the perimeter. As she reached the far side, a lorry swung round the corner and entered the road, the driver swiftly applying the brakes. The passenger door opened and a man jumped out. Oh great, just what she needed, another man telling her to get to safety. Then she saw who it was – Gil! She ran to him as the lorry began reversing in order to turn round.

'Mabel, what are you doing out here all alone? Where's Knatchbull?'

'He's in a building down there. We need help. There are people trapped in the cellar. I think one of them is a friend of mine. We need to get the floorboards up.'

'Righto.'

Gil ran back to the lorry, which was now facing the other way. He jogged back to Mabel, carrying a large cloth bag over one shoulder and a coiled rope over the other.

When they had circled the crater and were hurrying down the road, Mabel asked, 'Are you in a Heavy Rescue squad?'

'It's one way of whiling away the lonely nights.'

They arrived at the building and climbed through the window. Harry wasn't in the front room. Mabel led the way into the hall, where they found him part-way up the heap of rubble.

'I'm looking for anything I can use to prise up the floorboards.' Then he saw Gil and his mouth snapped shut.

'I should have what we need,' said Gil. 'In here, is it?'

He re-entered the front room, letting the rope slide down his arm to the floor while he lowered the bag, which clanked as it struck the wooden boards. Harry barrelled into the room behind him.

'Two crowbars and a sledgehammer,' said Gil. 'That plus muscle power will have to do.'

'Let's get to it,' said Harry.

'We must stay near the wall,' said Gil. 'The floorboards will be sounder.'

'Goes without saying,' said Harry. 'We'll be no use to man nor beast if we end up falling through the floor.'

Together, the two men made a start on hefting up some boards. Mabel almost danced with impatience. She spent her working day manoeuvring pickaxes and crowbars. Why couldn't Gil have brought three crowbars?

She peered into the long hole that was appearing. 'What's that?' She had expected to see anxious faces looking back at her.

'The cellar ceiling,' said Harry. 'Where's that sledgehammer?' Kneeling by the hole, he leaned down. 'Can you hear me? You need to move away.'

With Harry wielding the sledgehammer and Gil jabbing with his crowbar, plaster dust rose from the hole, setting both men coughing.

'Keep at it,' said Gil. 'We're nearly through.' After some more was done, he looked back at Mabel. 'If we hang on to you, could you lean inside and take a look?'

'I'll hold on to you,' said Harry. 'You needn't be afraid.'

Lying on her tummy, Mabel edged forwards, her stomach swooping as her top half went over the edge and down into the gap. She lifted her hand and one of the boys pressed a torch into it. She shone it downwards and her breath caught in her throat. Water!

'Are you there?' she called. 'Dot, is it you?'

'Mabel?'

There were slow swishing sounds, then Dot appeared. She was up to her waist in water.

Panic shot through Mabel, but only for a moment. She kept her voice steady and reassuring. 'We'll soon have you out. How many of you are there?'

'Two. Me and Mr Thirkle.'

'Are you injured?'

'Nothing that a warm blanket and dry feet wouldn't cure.'

'You'll soon be back on dry land.'

'Soon would be nice. Soon would be very nice. The water's rising.'

Good for Dot. She might be trapped in a cellar in rising water, but she was keeping her head and her sense of humour. She was the sort you needed in a crisis.

Mabel wriggled backwards and Harry lifted her to her feet.

'Did you hear that?' she asked.

'How deep is the water?' Gil asked.

'About waist-high.'

'Righto, let's get a move on. We need to make the hole bigger, then we can tie a loop in the rope and winch them out one at a time.' Gil looked at Harry for confirmation and Harry nodded. Gil turned to Mabel. 'I know you want to stick close to your friend, but I need you to find blankets. Towels as well, if you can. Those people will be freezing cold.'

It was a wrench to leave, but Mabel ran to Peter Street, where, in spite of the urgency, she couldn't help but come to a standstill at the sight of flames leaping from several buildings. A lone fireman at the top of a long ladder attached to the top of a fire engine was silhouetted against the blaze as he aimed a hosepipe. At ground level, rescue work was under way. Behind a second fire engine, a lorry was parked – Gil's Heavy Rescue team? ARP wardens in tin hats passed rubble backwards along a human chain.

Mabel peered around. The WVS was bound to be here. Spotting them, she ran across, taking care to jump over the hosepipes that snaked over the road, and quickly explained the situation.

'They'll need hot drinks inside them,' said one of the WVS ladies, 'and I'll bring blankets and towels.'

Mabel slung the linen over her shoulder and hurried back the way she had come, accompanied by the WVS worker, who carried a flask in one hand and two mugs in the other. She put the flask under her arm and took the blankets and towels from Mabel when Mabel climbed through the window, then she passed the things through.

'I'll wait here and run for an ambulance if one is needed,' she said. 'With luck, all they'll need is to go to a rest centre for a change of clothes.'

Mabel had arrived in time to see Dot emerge through the hole, hoisted out by Harry and Gil. Harry took the strain, allowing Gil to step forward and grasp Dot under her arms and pull her on to the floorboards. Mabel rushed forward to hug her friend before helping her shed the rope's loop, which Gil threw back down the hole.

Mabel wrapped a blanket around Dot's shoulders. 'Let's get your shoes off and I'll dry your legs.'

She rubbed vigorously, murmuring encouragement, while keeping an eye on Gil and Harry, who were now bracing themselves as the rope went taut and they took Mr Thirkle's weight, stepping backwards, steadying, then stepping back again, as if taking part in a tug of war. When Mr Thirkle's head bobbed into view, Gil called a 'Yes?' over his shoulder and Harry grunted a 'Yes' in reply, digging in his heels as Gil darted forwards, leaving him to take all the weight. Gil hauled Mr Thirkle clear of the hole and Mabel wrapped him in a blanket, pushing a towel into his hands.

'Thank you, miss,' he said. 'And to you boys, of course. I dread to think what would have happened if you hadn't come along. So much for finding safety in a cellar.'

'I'd better get back to my squad,' said Gil. 'Glad to see you're both all right.'

'Thanks, love,' said Dot.

'Good work,' Gil said to Harry.

'You too.' Harry grasped Gil's hand and shook it, clasping him by the shoulder. 'Couldn't have managed without you.'

Chapter Twenty-Three

It was meant to be exciting and romantic, going to church to hear your banns being read, and even more so in this case when there was going to be just the one set of banns instead of the usual three, but everybody was exhausted after last night's raid. It had lasted less than two and a half hours, but there was no doubting its severity. Mabel had been told by someone at the Town Hall that fourteen nurses had been killed at the Salford Royal. Fourteen! Perhaps some of them had been like Joan, engaged, looking forward to the future. And now they were gone. Just like Letitia.

Standing outside church in the Whit Sunday sunshine, Joan tried to close her ears to the talk around her, but it was difficult. Was it really only yesterday afternoon that she had sat in the Andy with Dot, Cordelia, Mrs Grayson and Mrs Cooper, making plans for her wedding and revelling in having four mothers of the bride?

A shiver passed through her. 'Thank goodness you and Harry were there to save Dot,' she said to Mabel. 'I'm proud of you.'

'I didn't do much. It was Harry and Gil who got them out.'

'But you were the one who insisted on checking the building. They might have drowned if you hadn't done that.'

'Don't,' said Mabel. 'I don't want to think about it.'

Joan looked around. Mrs Cooper and Mrs Grayson were already in church, it being easier for Mrs Grayson to be indoors rather than hovering outside. Where was Bob? He was supposed to meet them here. Was his family all right? It was impossible not to overhear people saying that Stretford had sustained damage. Someone had mentioned the Public Hall, someone else Longford Cinema.

'Here he is,' Mabel said as Bob arrived, flushed from hurrying but smiling all the same. 'You're cutting it a bit fine, Mr Bridegroom. I hope nothing bad has happened.'

'All's well at home,' said Bob, squeezing Joan's hand and giving her the boyish smile that made her heart turn over. 'I'm sorry to be a bit late.'

'Let's go in,' said Joan. 'Mrs Cooper is saving places for us.'

When her name and Bob's were read out, tears sprang into her eyes. She tried to blink them away but ended up having to fish out her hanky. The kindly but amused glances she received made her blush.

At the end of the service, when the congregation filed outside, Joan and Bob received congratulations from strangers, then Bob left Joan and Mabel and went off to join a conversation about last night's raid. But the congratulations weren't over.

'It does us all good to hear something happy,' said an elderly lady. 'I wish you the very best, my dear.'

'You aren't going to cry again, are you?' teased Mabel. 'You are lucky, you know, being able to see so much of Bob. I wish I could see more of Gil.'

'Gil?' said Joan in surprise. 'You mean Harry?'

'Harry – yes. What did I say? Did I say Gil?' Mabel's lips parted in a gasp and her brown eyes widened. 'I meant Harry. Slip of the tongue. God, how frightful. Please don't let it go any further.'

'I wouldn't dream of it.'

'Look, Mrs Cooper's signalling. I'll walk back with her and Mrs Grayson. You and Bob follow when you're ready.'

'We won't be long,' said Joan.

'Take your time, my little lovebirds. It isn't every day you have your banns read. The next time you're here, it'll be as a bride. Think of that.'

As Mabel went off to help escort Mrs Grayson home, a thrill of excitement made Joan bounce up and down on her toes. There was so much to do before next Saturday, but her friends would rally round and make her big day perfect.

Bob said goodbye to the folk he was chatting to and returned to her side. He was coming to Wilton Close for the rest of the day. When the Naylors came this afternoon, Bob would probably work alongside Tony in the garden. Joan released a gratified sigh. A husband and a husband-to-be doing their bit to dig for victory.

Sharing the bedroom at Wilton Close had brought Joan and Mabel close and Joan knew they would always be special friends, but once she and Bob were married, might she draw closer to Colette? She liked the idea of two young married couples spending time together.

'Ready to go?' Joan asked.

'I'm sorry,' said Bob, his face clouding, 'but I have to get home. I didn't say anything before the service because I didn't want to spoil the banns for you, but Auntie Florrie was bombed out last night.'

'Oh no. Is she hurt?'

'She's fine. Auntie Marie sent word. Auntie Florrie's house wasn't flattened and there is some furniture and what-have-you that's worth saving, so Dad and me are going over there to get shifting.'

'At least she's safe. That's the main thing.'

'Aye, it is.' Bob looked into her face. 'But you realise what this means, don't you? With Auntie Florrie's house gone, there's nowhere for us to live once we're married.'

*

Monday evening was one of those evenings when the women instinctively sought each other out. Even though a meeting hadn't been planned, they needed to be together. Joan wasn't going to be able to stay more than a few minutes, but she needed to see Dot. She had been reassured by Mabel that Dot was none the worse for her harrowing experience in the air raid, and in her head Joan knew it, but her heart wouldn't feel steady until she had seen Dot for herself.

As she entered the buffet, she saw Alison and Persephone hugging Dot. She hurried across to join them.

'My turn.' She slid her arms around her friend.

'It's not me you should be making a fuss of,' said Dot. 'It's Mabel. She's a heroine.'

'I only did what anyone else would have done,' said Mabel.

'Mmm.' Cordelia pretended to consider. 'Where have I heard that before? Isn't that what you said, Dot, after you saved the train when Jerry was peppering it with machine-gun fire?'

'Anyroad,' said Dot, 'I can't stop.' She picked up her shopping bag. 'I'm going home via Mrs Cooper's to drop off my dried fruit. Never mind me getting an unexpected bath in that air raid. It's our Joan's wedding you should be talking about.'

Finding everyone's gaze on her, Joan smiled. 'I'd love to stay and gossip, but I can't.'

'You have to,' said Persephone. 'We want to talk about wedding things.'

'I'm meeting my friend Margaret before I go home. She'll be waiting for me.'

The others glanced at one another.

'Persephone, Mabel and I met her when we went to the pictures,' said Alison. 'Why not ask her to join us?' She looked at Colette and Cordelia. 'That's all right, isn't it?'

Dot was ready to leave. Mabel stood up too.

'Sorry, all, but I have to skedaddle too. I promised to put a call through to Harry's base this evening.'

'Before you two go,' Joan said quickly, 'I'd like to ask something while we're all here together. Mabel, Alison and Persephone, will you please be my bridesmaids?' She waited for the exclamations of pleasure and acceptance to quieten before she added, 'And Colette, I'd like you to be my matron of honour.'

Colette glowed. 'Thank you. I'd be honoured.'

'The matron of honour is honoured,' Mabel murmured.

'Good.' Joan smiled. 'Now you're all involved, as bridesmaids, matron of honour and mothers of the bride.'

Mabel kissed her cheek. 'I'm honoured too. Now I must push off. Come on, Dot.'

Picking up her handbag, Joan followed them out and went to meet Margaret. Margaret wore a collarless, edge-to-edge jacket with flared sleeves that Joan recognised as having been sold by Ingleby's before the war. As well as her handbag, she carried a cloth bag, which presumably contained her work dungarees. She didn't have a gas-mask box. A lot of folk had given up carrying gas masks.

Margaret was pleased to be invited to join the others.

'Before that,' said Joan, 'let me tell you my news. I'm getting married on Saturday.'

Margaret's eyes widened. 'This coming Saturday?'

'We didn't want to wait any longer than we had to.' Joan delved inside her bag. 'And – here's your invitation.'

'You don't have to—' Margaret began.

'You're my friend and I'd like you to be there. Please say you'll come.'

Margaret laughed, a sound of pure pleasure. 'Thank you. I'd love to.'

'Good. That's settled.' Joan linked her arm through Margaret's and they headed for the buffet. 'I'm afraid you'll have to brace yourself for lots of wedding talk.'

In the buffet, Margaret was greeted with smiles by Alison and Persephone before Joan introduced her to Cordelia and Colette.

'Have you told Margaret your news?' Alison asked.

'The big news, yes. But I'm afraid there's bad news as well. We were all set to move in with Bob's Auntie Florrie, but she's been bombed out.'

'Where will you go instead?' asked Alison. 'I suppose if push comes to shove, you could stay put for now in Wilton Close and Bob can stay on with his family until you find somewhere.'

'We don't want to do that,' said Joan. 'I know there are times when newly-weds have to, but it isn't what anyone wants. Anyway, forget that for now. Let's talk about arrangements. The caretaker at the church hall let Mrs Cooper and me have a root around in the store cupboard yesterday afternoon and we found bunting from the Coronation, so we're going to hang that up.'

'That'll look festive,' said Persephone. 'There are masses of pinks in what's left of the flower gardens at Darley Court and Miss Brown says you're welcome to them for your bouquet and to decorate the tables.'

'How kind of her,' said Joan. 'I love pinks.'

'She says she's sorry she can't offer you the Bentley, but her store of petrol has almost run out, so she'll be relying on applying for coupons from now on. Between ourselves, she's been on the receiving end of some criticism for using the Bentley.'

'It's understandable,' said Cordelia. 'It's become such a large part of our thinking these days. My neighbour was called away unexpectedly and she asked me to look after her children for the evening. She said all I needed to do was read them a chapter from *The Wind in the Willows*. It turned out to be the part where Mr Toad drives around. Young Lucy asked where he'd got the petrol coupons and her brother said he must have got them off the black market.'

'They played "Bye Bye Blackbird" on the wireless the other day,' said Alison, 'and I was singing along, but when it got to the bit about "light the light", I found myself thinking: what about the blackout?'

Joan addressed Persephone. 'I quite understand about the Bentley. It hadn't occurred to me that Miss Brown might have lent it. I'm just delighted with the offer of the pinks.'

'These two with their patriotic responses to children's literature and harmless songs didn't let me finish,' said Persephone with a pretend glare for Alison and Cordelia. 'Miss Brown can't offer the Bentley, but how would you like the governess cart? Do you know what one is? It's a simple two-wheeled horse-drawn carriage with two seats facing one another. We've got one in the stables. It's in good nick and the seats are upholstered. Please say yes, because Mr Evans, who's a sweet old duck and as old as the hills, is busy getting it ready for you.'

'That sounds delightful,' said Cordelia. 'I think it will be a very smart way to travel on your wedding day, Joan.'

'Thank you,' Joan said to Persephone. 'I'll write Miss Brown a special thank-you letter when we return from our honeymoon. In fact, I've got invitations for her and Mrs Mitchell in my bag, if you wouldn't mind delivering them for me. And I've got a wedding present for you.'

'For me?' Persephone looked puzzled.

'Would you like to use my wedding as the basis for one of your articles? I don't mean for you to write about me personally, but if you'd like to write about friends putting a wedding together at short notice in these days when so many girls live far away from home, feel free to use examples from my wedding.'

'Such as Mrs Grayson's alcoholic cake,' said Cordelia.

'Thanks,' said Persephone. 'I'll do just that.'

'What shall your bridesmaids wear?' asked Cordelia.

'Pretty summer dresses,' said Joan. 'There isn't time to make special bridesmaids' dresses.'

'The main question is what are *you* going to wear?' asked Colette.

'I dashed to Ingleby's during my dinner hour, but there was no suitable material to be had.'

'That might be a good thing,' Cordelia suggested. 'Had you found some, you wouldn't have slept between now and Saturday.'

'Actually,' said Margaret, and they all looked at her, 'I know someone who might lend you her dress. If you've got time, we could go and see her now.'

'I couldn't,' was Joan's automatic response. 'Turn up on a stranger's doorstep and ask to borrow her wedding dress? You're joking.' But she couldn't help adding, 'Perhaps if you asked her first ... '

'May I remind you that you're getting married on Saturday,' said Alison. 'This is no time to be bashful.'

'You should go with Margaret this evening,' said Persephone.

'What's the worst that can happen?' asked Colette. 'She can say no.'

'Or she can say yes,' said Persephone, 'but the dress turns out to be hideous. Either way, you need to know.'

So, half excited and half appalled at herself for doing something Gran would have called the height of bad manners, Joan allowed herself to be carried off by Margaret on the bus to Longsight.

When they alighted, Margaret took her down a seedy-looking street of unkempt houses, the sight of which made Joan clasp her handbag tightly. Margaret's friend must be down on her luck to have ended up here. Margaret led the way to a tall house with soot-encrusted bricks and peeling paintwork, but instead of ringing the bell, she produced a key and let them in. The hall and stairs were bare – no carpet, not even lino. Music blared from behind a closed door and a man in a stained shirt with braces dangling from his ample waist was hammering on the door.

'Shut your noise!' he roared. 'How many times do I have to tell you?'

The door was wrenched open and a slanging match began. Margaret grabbed Joan's hand and pulled her up the stairs. Joan would far rather have run out of the front door and back to the bus stop. On the second floor, Margaret unlocked a door with a hole in its lower half, as if someone had had a go at kicking it down.

Inside, the wallpaper was faded, the woodwork scarred. There was a wicked draught at ankle level and Joan pretended not to notice a mousetrap in the corner. The sparse furniture was dilapidated and there were no curtains other than the blackouts.

Margaret shrugged her shoulders, though there was no concealing her embarrassment. 'I did tell you I live in a dump.'

Joan didn't know what to say. Margaret went to the wardrobe – and took out a wedding dress.

'It's yours if you want it – on condition you never tell another living soul that you got it from me.'

'You've got a wedding dress … ?'

'It's what you buy when you think you're getting married,' Margaret said flippantly, 'or in my case, it's what you buy when you're an absolute idiot who believes every word

285

that's said to you.' She hung the dress from the top of the wardrobe door.

'Oh, Margaret, you poor love. He really did lead you up the garden path, didn't he?'

For a moment, Margaret pressed a hand to her mouth, then she let it, or perhaps made it, drop away. 'It's my own stupid fault. I was a fool and there are plenty who'd say I deserved all I got.' Her voice sounded choked, but then she cleared her throat and went on, sounding stronger. 'I took one look at this dress and fell in love with it. I took it home secretly and sneaked it into my bedroom. Later, after he vanished and I realised he wasn't coming back, I stashed it in a trunk in the cellar, which meant it ended up being one of the few things that survived the air raid. I've thought about selling it, but I'm too embarrassed. Anyway, here it is. What do you think?'

A feeling of peace settled on Joan as she gazed at the dress that she knew would suit her to a T. It was of ivory rayon crepe, with a fitted panelled bodice and an ankle-length flared skirt. The short sleeves were puffed at the shoulder.

'There's this as well.' Opening a box, Margaret produced a tiara and veil. 'Do you like it?'

'May I try it on?' asked Joan.

Chapter Twenty-Four

Dot turned the corner into Wilton Close, thinking, as she always did when she came here, how lucky Mrs Cooper was to live in a smart house in such an attractive little road. She was grateful that this lovely lady, who had lost her husband and daughter, at least had a comfortable, spacious home to take care of – and it was a home an' all. Not a soulless house in which the lodgers kept to their rooms and had a timetable for using the kitchen, but an honest-to-goodness home where the residents lived together as a family, a state of affairs that was all down to Mrs Cooper's personality and her determination not to inflict her grief on those around her. Gentle and self-effacing she might be, but underneath that was a stout working-class heart.

When Mrs Cooper opened the front door, Dot lifted her chin and sniffed the air like one of the Bisto Kids, her mouth watering at the delicious mix of spicy-sweet and fruity.

'I brought my dried fruit round.' Dot offered her bag. 'Am I too late?'

'Not at all. Mrs Grayson is letting everything soak at the moment. Can you smell the orange zest?'

'She got hold of an orange?' Dot was impressed.

Mrs Cooper led her into the kitchen, where Mrs Grayson, a pinny covering her dress, was consulting a handwritten recipe.

'If this is how the raw ingredients smell,' said Dot, 'it's going to be a masterpiece of a cake. What are you using to soak the fruit?'

'Mrs Masters provided some alcohol,' said Mrs Cooper.

'She said she would,' said Dot, picturing dry sherry.

'There's brandy in there.' Mrs Grayson waved a hand towards the mixing bowl. 'And port.'

'Crikey,' said Dot. 'Everyone will be legless after one slice.'

'Well, it is a wedding,' said Mrs Grayson.

'I'll leave you to it,' said Dot, but as she headed for the front door, Mrs Cooper stopped her.

'I know you need to get home, but could you spare a minute? Come in the front room.'

'What is it?' Dot asked as they sat down.

'It's about Joan. I can't get out of my head what she said about her grandmother not attending her wedding. It breaks my heart to think of that dear child being apart from her only living relative. It's not right. I know they've had their problems, but this is Joan's wedding, for heaven's sake. You'd think Mrs Foster would unbend.'

Dot sighed. 'I think anyone else would unbend, but I'm not so sure about Mrs Foster.'

'Will you come with me to see her? I don't think it would do any harm and it might do some good.'

'Let's go now,' said Dot. 'She lives near the terminus and I have to go there anyroad to catch my bus.'

'Thank you,' said Mrs Cooper. 'It needn't take long.'

Aye, that was true enough. Dot couldn't imagine the formidable Mrs Foster putting up with being lectured to under her own roof, but she said nowt. It was important to give this a try, for Joan's sake.

It took only a few minutes to reach Torbay Road. It broke Dot's heart to think of the Fosters living so near to one another yet keeping apart, and it reinforced her feeling that

Mrs Cooper was in the right. She found herself walking more briskly as vexation swept through her at the thought of Mrs Foster choosing to separate herself from her one remaining grandchild. By heck, the woman deserved a good shake. Nothing on earth would induce Dot to turn her back on Jenny or Jimmy. They were the lights of her life.

When Mrs Foster opened the door to them, surprise appeared on her face, quickly replaced by suspicion, as if they were travelling salesmen and she was all set to declare 'I don't buy at the door' before shutting it in their faces.

'Mrs Foster,' said Mrs Cooper, 'we're sorry to disturb you, but may we come in? We'd like to speak to you.'

'Is Joan all right?'

'She's fine. Please ... '

With a nod, Mrs Foster stood aside to let them in. 'This way.'

Even though she knew what to expect, Dot felt her spirits sink as they entered the gloomy parlour. No wonder Mrs Foster was so stern and set in her ways. Anyone would be after years of not letting in the sunshine.

'What's this about?' Mrs Foster asked brusquely once they were all seated.

'It's Joan, of course,' said Mrs Cooper. 'She's getting married this Saturday.'

Mrs Foster raised her eyebrows. 'That was quick.'

'They got a special licence,' said Dot, 'but that's beside the point.'

'Indeed? What is the point?'

'I'd have thought that were obvious,' said Dot, then caught Mrs Cooper's glance and shut her trap. This woman got her back up, but it was no good letting it show.

'You're a remarkable woman, Mrs Foster,' Mrs Cooper began in her gentle way. 'You took in your two orphaned granddaughters and fetched them up on your own. It can't have been easy for a grandmother to have to be the parent.'

'Are you trying to soft-soap me?'

'I speak as I find.' There was a sharper note now in Mrs Cooper's voice that suggested that gentle she might be, but she was no pushover. 'Your Joan is a credit to you. She's kind and helpful and hard-working. I'm happy to have her under my roof, but I've never once forgotten that it's your roof she should be under.'

'I don't think that's any business of yours.'

'I know she was very silly about that young man – what was his name? Steven. But she's put that behind her and she's so happy now with Bob. They were made for each other. Wouldn't you like to see them make their vows?'

'There's a lot more to this situation than you are aware of,' said Mrs Foster, 'and it's got nothing to do with you, so don't waste your time asking.'

'We don't give a toss about your private affairs,' Dot retorted, 'and we're not here to dig for dirt. We're here because yon lass hasn't got a grandmother to do the decent thing at her wedding. D'you know what she's done? She's asked four of us to be her mothers of the bride, and unlike her holier-than-thou grandmother, we're proud to do the honours. But that doesn't make it right. Four mothers of the bride that aren't from her family don't make up for one grandmother that can't be bothered.'

The flash in Mrs Foster's eyes made Dot brace herself for an onslaught, but Mrs Foster's voice was cold and controlled. 'Can't be bothered? I've done nothing but bother ever since my granddaughters were babies. I brought them up decently; I gave them standards and morals; and I've done the right thing by them, always. You know nothing of our lives and what we've had to cope with – what I've had to cope with. Now it's time for you to leave.'

'Is that it?' Frustration rang in Mrs Cooper's voice. 'You're so wrapped up inside with I-don't-know-what, that you aren't prepared to think beyond it. Your Joan is getting wed on Saturday and thank goodness she has friends who are going to see to it that it's the happiest day of her life, because God forbid that her grandmother should make an effort.'

'Now see here—'

'No, you see here, Mrs Foster.' Mrs Cooper rose to her feet, the gentle little sparrow taking on the stern-faced dragon. 'I don't normally have a temper, but it fair makes my blood boil to think of you not appreciating that lovely girl. It isn't right. It isn't *fair*. Why should you ignore Joan when if my Lizzie was still here, I'd give her all the attention in the world? I adored my daughter. She meant everything to me, but I have to wake up each morning and she's not here, and I have to go to bed at night knowing she still won't be here tomorrow. And then there's you. You've still got your Joan and you can't be bothered. Don't you understand? It doesn't matter what happened or what went wrong. How *can* it matter? All that matters is that she's still here and you've still got her. I'll tell you this, Mrs Foster, and then we'll go away and leave you in peace. You don't deserve that girl, and that's God's honest truth. You don't deserve her.'

There was a queue outside the telephone box when Mabel pushed open the heavy door and came out. She held the door for the man at the head of the line.

'About time,' he muttered.

Mabel might have apologised, but he sounded so grumpy he didn't deserve it.

'Ringing your boyfriend, were you, love?' asked the plump, headscarfed woman who was now first in the queue.

'Yes. He's in the RAF.'

'Good for him. We need lots of his sort.'

'Thank you,' said Mabel. 'Yes, we do.'

She felt like hugging herself as she walked home. Talking on the telephone with Harry always left her with a dreamy feeling as she lived their conversation over again in her head. Every word mattered so much when all you had was a telephone call, each call ending with words of love and hope and Mabel trying desperately to sound cheery even though she knew that chaps who flew generally had a limited lifespan. But Harry would always come home safely. Her heart was sure of it.

He had asked after Dot and Mr Thirkle and she had assured him they were both none the worse for their experience, but mainly what she had wanted to hear was whether he would be able to attend Joan and Bob's wedding. She had told him about it on Saturday before he had got a bee in his bonnet about the Red Cross dance and he had been keen to come, of course, though whether he would be able to make it over to Manchester two weekends running was another matter.

'I've called in a favour,' he had told her on the telephone, sending her heart soaring. How wonderful to attend Joan's wedding on the arm of her handsome boyfriend. At a wedding, people always noticed which girls came alone and who was escorted.

She was deeply touched that Joan had chosen her railway friends to act as her bridesmaids. It was a sign of how close they had all become. It was lovely that she had her four mothers of the bride as well. The wedding was going to feel very special, which was just what Joan deserved. It was bound to be difficult for her not to have Letitia by her side on her big day, so it would be up to her friends to make the day run smoothly and be sensitive to her feelings.

When Mabel walked into the house, Mrs Cooper came out of the front room, pulling the door shut behind her.

'You've got a visitor.'

For a mad moment, she pictured Harry, but that really was mad because she had just spoken to him at his base.

'Who is it?' Mabel pushed the door open. 'Gil!'

He stood up politely. 'I'm sorry to drop in unexpectedly.'

'I've already told you,' said Mrs Cooper, 'that it's quite all right. We're always pleased to see the girls' friends, aren't we, Mrs Grayson?'

Gil looked at Mabel, clearly taking nothing for granted. She smiled warmly. She could afford to do that now. Performing the rescue together in the early hours of Whit Sunday had changed things between Gil and Harry. Harry had gone from grumbling jealousy to handshaking and backslapping. It was as if his jealousy had never existed. Working together, acting as a team, they had forged a mutual respect, for which Mabel was profoundly grateful. Harry's jealousy had been hard for her to cope with, but the events of that night seemed to have swept it aside in a way her own attempts at reassurance had never had a hope of doing. Perhaps she should feel miffed about that, but she was too relieved.

'I'll just be a minute,' she told Gil.

Removing her jacket and hat, she went upstairs to run a comb through her hair. She had already taken off her lengthman's clobber before she went to the telephone box, changing into her dress of light green silk with the button fastening and the inverted box pleats. Harry always asked her what she was wearing and she loved looking her best for him, even though they were miles apart.

Downstairs, she and Gil sat and chatted with Mrs Cooper and Mrs Grayson for a while.

'We've been hearing all about how brave you were that night, Mabel dear,' said Mrs Cooper. 'You were too modest when you described the rescue.'

'I didn't do much compared with what the boys did.'

'Running through the streets in search of blankets, with incendiaries raining down – I don't call that not much.'

'It said in the paper there were around nine hundred canisters of incendiaries,' said Mrs Grayson, 'and that's before you start counting the bombs. It was the worst night since the Christmas Blitz.'

'So don't tell us you weren't brave,' Mrs Cooper added, pretending to sound stern, 'because we know different. Now, I'm sure Lieutenant Gilchrist didn't come here to make small talk with a pair of old fogeys. Why don't you young ones go in the other room for a few minutes?'

Mabel took Gil into the dining room. The table and chairs were close to the window, leaving ample space for a pair of armchairs beside the hearth.

'Have a pew,' Mabel offered.

Gil hesitated. 'You might not want me to when you hear what I've got to say.'

Something shrivelled inside her. Oh no, he wasn't going to make advances, was he? That time in the rec, he'd promised he wouldn't try it again.

'That look on your face,' said Gil. 'Does it mean you know what I'm about to say?' He sat on the arm of the chair.

Mabel glanced away. Should she be vexed with him – or sorry for him? He knew perfectly well she was Harry's girlfriend. On top of that, he and Harry had ended up not liking one another, exactly, but more than tolerating each other. They had become what Mumsy would refer to as civil acquaintances. It was rotten of him to put her in this position. The word 'cad' sprang to mind and that wasn't a word she had ever imagined applying to Iain Gilchrist. Did he view this as a sort of last-ditch attempt? Even though he knew it was hopeless? Were his feelings for her so strong that he couldn't bring himself to let go?

'Go on,' she said softly.

'In my line of work, I'm in a position to find things out,' said Gil, causing surprise to flutter in Mabel's chest. 'I can dig pretty deeply.'

Good heavens, had he found out that Pops had told her about his secret work? Would Pops lose his chance to be involved in such important work, and all because of her own silly, misplaced scorn?

'The thing is, please don't be offended, but since you're so attached to Harry Knatchbull, and since I care about you deeply, I've taken the liberty of delving into his background.'

'You've what?' Mabel caught her breath. 'How dare you?'

'I dared because you mean so much to me and always will. I can tell you that his RAF record is exemplary.'

In spite of her indignation, Mabel couldn't help feeling proud to hear Harry being praised, but there was something in Gil's manner, in his eyes, that put her on her guard.

'Mabel, he does love you. I have no doubts on that score.'

'Thanks very much.' Bitter sarcasm chilled her words.

'I've agonised over whether to tell you this, but I need to give you a word of warning. In fairness, I need to tell you immediately that this doesn't come from any official record. It's ... well, let's say I heard a rumour.'

'A rumour?' Mabel's tone was scathing, but her nerves were rattled. Oh dear God, please don't let him have heard ... 'I'm ashamed of you. I never thought you'd stoop to listening to tittle-tattle.'

'It's more than that. I wish it weren't. Having heard it, I did some digging. This isn't an easy thing for me to say, and you'll probably hate me for ever, but I'm saying it as your friend and as someone who cares for you deeply – and also as someone who was a solicitor before the war. If you and Knatchbull – well, if you make a go of it, you should make sure that your father ties up the money such that—'

'What?'

'—such that it's all yours.' Gil made a hopeless movement with his hands. 'Just to be on the safe side.'

Chapter Twenty-Five

Mrs Cooper and Mrs Grayson oohed and aahed over the wedding dress. Joan had brought it straight home from Margaret's and now she stood in her bedroom, lapping up the admiration.

'You'll be a beautiful bride.' Mrs Cooper dabbed away a tear. 'And what a pretty veil.'

'I wish my bridesmaids could wear matching dresses,' Joan sighed. 'I know how selfish that sounds – even more so now that clothes rationing has been introduced.'

'All brides have to make compromises these days,' said Mrs Cooper.

'Especially ones that get married at a few days' notice.' Joan smiled. 'I'm having a silly moment, that's all.'

'Actually,' Mrs Grayson began, then hesitated. 'I wasn't going to say a word until I'd finished, but I'm knitting some white flowers for your wedding, one for each bridesmaid to pin on her hat so they all have something the same to wear.'

'What a lovely idea,' cried Joan. 'Thank you. That'll be perfect.'

'You're the one that will look perfect,' said Mrs Cooper. 'You couldn't have found a better dress if you'd made one yourself.'

'I need to alter the shoulder seams. The bodice is the tiniest bit loose on me, but if I alter the seams, it'll be a perfect fit. I'll prepare the seams before I go on first-aid duty this evening and I'll sew them tomorrow evening.' Anxiety bit her. 'I need to fit in looking for digs for me and Bob as well.'

'Leave the sewing to us,' said Mrs Grayson. 'We'll do it using the best of the daylight and that will free some time in the evening for you. Don't forget you've got first aid tomorrow night as well.'

'Do you think it's a mistake getting married at such short notice? There's so much to do.'

Mrs Cooper gave her a hug. She might be as thin as two penn'orth of copper, but a hug from Mrs Cooper was as comforting as a cosy blanket and a hot-water bottle. 'It's not a mistake. It's just the worry of where you're going to live.'

'If Bob's auntie hadn't been bombed out,' said Mrs Grayson, 'you'd be sailing through this week.'

Joan nodded. 'That's true. I don't want anything to spoil my wedding day.'

'Of course you don't,' said Mrs Cooper, 'so let me see if I can find lodgings for you. I'll have a look at the postcards in all the newsagents' windows and visit everywhere that looks suitable.'

'You'd do that for us?'

'With pleasure, chuck. It makes sense. Places for rent that are halfway decent are snapped up double quick because of the shortage. Going round them in the morning gives me a better chance than if you try in the evening.'

'Besides,' added Mrs Grayson, 'with first-aid duty tonight and tomorrow night, you want to spend your free time doing weddingy things, not trailing round searching for digs.'

And if Mrs Cooper could find her and Bob a home, it would be nearby, which would in itself be wonderful. The idea of moving all the way to Auntie Florrie's in Cheetham and not knowing anybody had been rather daunting. Was it silly of her to prefer staying where she knew? Immature? But that was how she felt.

'Mrs Cooper, there's something I want to ask you,' said Joan. 'I'd like you to be my witness at the wedding.'

Mrs Cooper caught her breath and her hand flew to her chest. 'Your witness? Oh, Joan! I'm – I'm overwhelmed. But wouldn't you rather have one of your friends? Mabel, perhaps?'

'To be honest, I don't want a young witness. It was always meant to be Letitia. You took me in when I left Gran's and you brought me here with you to this house. You didn't have to do either of those things. When I lost my home, you gave me a new home, and I don't just mean a place to live. I mean you made me welcome. You've always made me feel that I belong here and I'll never forget that, so, yes, I'm absolutely sure I want you to act as my witness.'

Mrs Cooper kissed her. 'I don't know what to say. It will be an honour. Oh, there's the front door.'

'Shall I answer it?' Mrs Grayson offered.

'I'll go,' said Mrs Cooper. 'It'll probably be the WVS collecting for their jumble sale. I've got a bag of things ready.' Wiping away a happy tear, she left the bedroom.

'Who's the girl who lent you the dress?' asked Mrs Grayson. 'You should invite her to tea so she can see you in it.'

'No can do, I'm afraid – she's joined the Wrens,' Joan improvised. 'She told Margaret, who is a mutual friend, to pass on the dress if someone needed it. Lucky me, Margaret passed it my way.'

'Then invite this Margaret to tea.'

'Thanks. I will. I'd like you to meet her, because I've invited her to the wedding. She's already seen me in the dress, but it'd be nice to have her here anyway.' Or would coming here make it harder for Margaret to return home afterwards to her grotty digs?

'Bring her home with you tomorrow, if she's free,' said Mrs Grayson.

The bedroom door opened and Mrs Cooper came in, looking flustered.

'Your gran's here.'

Joan stiffened. She couldn't bear it if Gran spoiled this for her. 'What does she want?'

'To speak to you.'

'We've said everything there is to say.'

'Joan, you must,' Mrs Cooper urged her. 'She's your grandmother, your only family.'

'You're my family now. I told you. I want my mothers of the bride all sitting at the front.'

Mrs Grayson laid a hand on Joan's shoulder. 'She's still your grandmother.'

Joan gave in. 'Very well, but she isn't seeing me in my dress.' And if that sounded childish, she didn't care. Gran didn't deserve to see her in this beautiful dress. She turned her back to Mrs Grayson. 'Will you undo me?'

'I'll go down and say you're on your way,' said Mrs Cooper.

'While you're down there, could you give her her wedding invitation? Please do,' she added quickly, forestalling Mrs Cooper, who looked uncertain. 'It's in a sealed envelope. There's no need to say what it is.'

Joan bit the inside of her cheek. What did Gran want?

'Auntie Mrs Walters has gone,' said Jimmy, and Dot's ears pricked up. Rosa, gone? Talk about ending the day on good news. There had been a run of good things lately: Reg's eyesight was all right, Joan and Bob's wedding, herself being asked to be a mother of the bride, which was like a dream come true for a mother of sons. And now Rosa had slung her hook. Dot's muscles relaxed as the tension she had carried inside her ever since Rosa's arrival finally faded away. Oh, Harry, her darling boy. Sheila would still need to be kept on the straight and narrow, but at least Rosa was no longer under Harry's roof, contaminating the good name of his house.

'Auntie Mrs Walters?' Sheila raised her eyebrows.

'Auntie Rosa,' said Jimmy.

'I told him he should call her Mrs Walters,' said Dot. 'It's respectful.'

'And I told him he could call her Auntie Rosa.' Putting her ciggy to her lips, Sheila inhaled deeply, then blew out smoke across her kitchen table. 'Anyroad, she's gone now, so it makes no odds.'

'She packed her case and everything,' said Jimmy.

'Go out and play, Jimmy.' Sheila put on the tired voice she employed when she wanted her audience to know what a handful she had to cope with.

Jimmy didn't need telling twice. He left in a scramble of flying limbs and scabby knees.

'Rosa's gone, then?' Dot might feel like doing a quickstep round Sheila's kitchen, but she contented herself with taking a sip of tea.

'Aye.' Not a stream of smoke this time but a couple of smoke rings. Sheila tipped her head back, made a goldfish mouth, then another, and out floated the rings. Dot wasn't sure how ladylike smoke rings were. On the other hand, they were infinitely preferable to that ludicrous cigarette-holder that Posh Pammy had affected for a year or so until Archie had trodden on it accidentally on purpose.

'Go on,' Sheila said drily. 'I know you're dying to ask. You want to know if the neighbours ganged up and chucked her in the canal, don't you? I know they had words with you. I know they told you to do summat about her.'

'If you know that, then you'll also know I never said a word against her.'

Sheila shrugged. 'Maybe, but you never stood up for her neither, did you?'

'I'm sorry, love, but – actually, no, I'm not sorry. I've never been happy about her living here.'

'Just because you don't like her mum.'

'I'll have you know that in her day, Donna Bardsley-as-was must have had lead lining in her drawers, cos they were that heavy she couldn't keep 'em up.'

'And you're taking it out on Rosa.' Sheila's expression was somewhere between a sulk and a sneer. 'Just like the neighbours.'

'Anyroad, she's gone,' said Dot. 'Let's you and me not fall out, love, please.'

Sheila's reply was another shrug. By, but she could be an obstinate devil when she wanted. Childish an' all. Dot reined in her thoughts. Don't go down that road. Having bad thoughts about someone was a sure step towards trouble and she had sworn to herself that her lads' wives would never have owt but love and support from her even if they weren't the daughters-in-law she would have chosen. It was a wise woman who loved her son's choice of wife. Aye, a wise woman and a flamin' frustrated one.

'What happened?' Dot asked. If the neighbours hadn't stormed the house and frogmarched Rosa as far as the parish boundary, had she run off with a fella? The ghost who turned out to be a baker sprang to mind. Floury handprints on Rosa's coat sprang to mind.

'Her Rodney's been shipped home injured. He's going to be all right, but it'll take time.'

'Eh, I'm sorry to hear that.' And she was. It could so easily have been Harry or Archie. 'Poor lass. Has she gone to be with him?'

'He's ended up in a hospital in Hampshire and there's a munitions in Farnborough, so she's going to get a job there.'

'Poor lass. Poor Rodney an' all. I remember him kicking a ball through our window way back when, and Reg chasing him up Heathside Lane.'

For the first time, Sheila's expression softened. 'Thanks for not saying he's copped a Blighty.'

'I'd never say that. Folk say that as if the soldier's lucky to have his injury and I'd never say that. If he's been hurt bad enough that they've shipped him home, likely it'll be with him for the rest of his days. He doesn't deserve that.' Dot smiled sadly. 'Not for kicking a ball through our window, he doesn't.'

Sheila blew out more smoke, blinking hard, but it wasn't the smoke that was interfering with her eyes.

Time to get down to business. 'Listen, love. Was Rosa here on an official billet?'

'Yes, she was. I told you. I got her to move in after I had the billeting officer round. The billeting office made it official and gave me the allowance.'

'Then you need to get down there quick smart and say she's left. If they pay you the allowance after she's gone, you'll be fined. You can even be sent to prison.'

'I bet they billet someone on me. I don't want any old stranger moving in.'

Dot felt a rare moment of sympathy for her wayward daughter-in-law. She wouldn't want strangers moving in with her either. It was all very well saying this was war-time and everybody had to muck in, but it was hard on those folk who'd had to open up their homes to strangers. You'd have to be a saint not to mind that.

'I've an idea,' said Dot. 'Tell them Rosa's gone, but say you might have new lodgers to take her place. A girl I work with – and she is a girl, she's only twenty – is getting wed this Saturday and she and her intended urgently need somewhere to call home. The place they were due to move into got bombed. Why not offer them your spare room?'

'I don't know.'

'At least meet them. They're a nice couple. You'd never find anyone nicer. You can always say no.'

But if Sheila said yes, and Joan and Bob said yes, it would get the soon-to-be newly-weds out of a fix – and it would get Dot out of a fix an' all, because what better way could there be of protecting Sheila's virtue?

As Joan entered the front room, Mrs Cooper rose from her seat, giving Joan a sympathetic glance before she left. Gran was seated on the sofa, back straight, her handbag beside her feet, her brown hat with its turned-down brim locked in position by her mother-of-pearl-tipped hatpin.

Was she supposed to give Gran a kiss? Joan sat in Mrs Grayson's usual armchair, folding her hands in her lap because she didn't know what to do with them.

'I hear you're getting married on Saturday,' said Gran.

'Yes.' Who had told her?

Gran nodded. Her gaze shifted around the room before returning to Joan. 'We didn't part on good terms.'

'That's hardly surprising, given the circumstances.'

Gran's eyes glinted. 'Don't get snippy with me, miss. I didn't bring you up to cheek your elders.'

'No, you brought me up to worship my father and despise my mother. Funny how things change, isn't it?'

'I did what I did for the best of reasons.'

'You did it to protect your beloved son's memory.'

'And for the sake of Letitia and you. I told you. It's better to be the daughters of a runaway mother than the daughters of ... '

'Of a wife-killer.'

Gran's mouth twisted, making her face ugly with anger. Then the emotion vanished, leaving her careworn and frustrated. She shook her head. 'Believe what you want. I acted for the best.'

'That's a good excuse, isn't it? "I acted for the best." You can get away with anything if you claim that.'

'Get away with it?' Gran's voice dropped. 'I'll tell you what I got away with. I was closer to fifty than forty and I was left with two babies to bring up. We couldn't carry on living down there – we'd have been outcasts. I lost my home – my name – my son. Oh yes, I got away with it all right.' She gave a bark of laughter, then her mouth tightened. 'I had to give up being a grandmother and become a parent instead. Dear God, starting all over again at that age. That was hard. And it would never have happened if—' Her lips snapped shut, pressed together so hard they turned white.

Joan held up her hands, palms outwards. 'I don't want to hear it. I especially don't want to hear it when I'm preparing to get married. I want to put it behind me.'

Gran nodded. 'I hope you can, I really do. That's a luxury I've never had. But you're young and this can be a fresh start for you.'

'Yes, it is.'

'I always pictured you walking up the aisle with Letitia as your matron of honour.'

'So did I. I've got four dear friends following me up the aisle – in fact, five, because there's another girl I haven't asked yet, but I could have two dozen bridesmaids and it would never make up for not having Letitia.'

'I'm surprised at you getting married so soon after her death. It's hard for me to think of you doing that.'

'It's hard for me too. It's hard knowing I have to live the rest of my life without her, but right now I have the chance of a good life with Bob and I'm going to grab that chance with both hands, regardless of what you think.'

'I didn't come here to fight,' said Gran.

Tiredness swamped Joan. 'All you do is fight. You have to be right all the time. You have to put everyone in their place.'

'I'd better go.' Gran picked up her handbag and stood up. 'My life has been one long fight ever since – ever since your mother died.' She walked to the door, where she turned back – not just turned, but swung round. 'I took the nets down this morning.'

'The nets?'

'The net curtains in the parlour. I took them down. The sun comes through the windows now. I wish – I wish I'd done it when Letitia was here to see it.'

Chapter Twenty-Six

At the end of her first-aid shift, Joan cycled home shortly after six on Tuesday morning. She had one more shift to go and then she would have ten whole nights off. When she had gone through her mad phase and had been seeing Steven on the side, she had got herself into such a state that she had tried for a time to avoid both Steven and Bob, something she had achieved in part by doing extra shifts when colleagues were in need of a night off. Now she had called in those favours, thereby earning herself a run of free nights.

Wednesday, Thursday, Friday, Saturday. In four mornings' time, it would be her wedding day. Eagerness expanded inside her chest. Today, Mrs Cooper and Mrs Grayson were going to alter her dress and Mrs Cooper would try to find lodgings for her and Bob. It was so kind of her to offer to traipse round, searching for digs, but that was Mrs Cooper all over. Maybe when Joan came home from work this evening, it would be to the news that her first married home had been sorted out.

After a hasty breakfast, she went to work early, wanting to catch Margaret before she started in the engine sheds. She found her having a mug of tea and a slice of toast in the mess. Lord, did the poor girl eat all her meals at work?

'Morning, Margaret,' she said cheerfully. 'I wanted to say thank you again for the dress.'

'You're welcome.'

'And to invite you round to my digs this evening to see it in all its glory once it's been altered. Please say you'll come. My landlady and the other lady who lives there love it when friends come round and Mrs Grayson is a wizard cook. It was her idea to ask you.'

'If you're sure, thank you.'

'We're all sure, me, Mrs Cooper, Mrs Grayson – and Mabel.' Come to think of it, Mabel hadn't been as enthusiastic as she might have been, or was that Joan's imagination?

Leaving Margaret, she hurried to clock on.

'There you are.' Dot appeared by her side. 'I need a quick word. I might have found you and Bob a home.'

'Oh, Dot, where?'

'With my daughter-in-law, Sheila. You know, Jimmy's mum. You can come round and see it this evening, if you like.'

'I've just invited Margaret round for tea. Besides, Mrs Cooper is looking for digs for us today, so she might find something.'

'And if she does, she'll snap it up,' said Dot. 'But if she doesn't, there's our Sheila's. Or even if she does, there's still our Sheila's. Then you could have a choice. I hope you don't think I've took a liberty, but I saw Mabel a few minutes ago and I've asked her to get Mrs Hubble to send Bob round to yours after work, so you can bring him over to Withington. You don't think I'm being pushy, do you?'

'I think you're being an attentive mother of the bride and I'm grateful, but I know Bob won't be able to come. He's got gas-attack training this evening.'

Imagine if, by the end of today, she and Bob had a home to move into. That would be perfect and it would mean she could concentrate on her wedding without this worry hanging over her.

That evening, Margaret went home with Joan and Mabel.

'What a beautiful house.' Margaret stopped at the gate to look.

'Make sure you say that to Mrs Cooper,' Joan said lightly. 'She's ever so proud to be the housekeeper.'

Inside, Cordelia was in the front room with Mrs Cooper and Mrs Grayson. Joan introduced Margaret to the two resident ladies, then Cordelia stood up.

'It's high time I made a move.'

'What brought you here on your day off?' asked Joan.

'Wedding matters, but nothing for you to know about quite yet.' Did the usually serious Cordelia have a twinkle in her eye?

Joan was intrigued, but Mrs Cooper, having seen Cordelia out, diverted her with news.

'I'm sorry, Joan, I didn't find anywhere for you and Bob, but I did try.'

'I know you did. Thank you.'

'I went to the billeting office as well, but all they could do was put you on a waiting list. You haven't been bombed out, so you don't get priority, especially after last weekend.'

Before Joan could explain about Sheila Green, Mrs Cooper reached for a sizeable parcel wrapped in brown paper whose creases showed it had been used many times.

'Your grandmother brought this round.'

'What is it?' Joan asked.

'Open it.'

It wasn't sealed. Joan simply had to fold back the paper. Should she believe her eyes?

'Are these ... ?'

'They're your gran's net curtains,' said Mrs Cooper.

Joan was too bewildered to speak.

'She told me she's given them a good soak before washing them by hand. This afternoon, she pressed them and brought them round here.'

'Why?' Please don't let Mrs Cooper put them up at the windows. The thought of such gloom eating away at this house …

'Yesterday you told her about your bridesmaids and she thought there might be time to run up some simple bolero jackets for them.'

'Bolero jackets?' She had gone from not believing her eyes to not believing her ears. 'From net curtains?'

'Lace curtains,' said Mrs Cooper. 'Thick lace an' all.'

Oh aye, thick lace, thick enough to smother the brightness out of the daylight, thick enough to turn Gran's parlour into a sepia world. Joan had lived most of her life in that world.

And yet her dressmaker's eye couldn't help but envision …

'I hate those curtains,' she said.

'Good,' said Mrs Grayson. 'Then you won't mind chopping them up. We can't make those jackets without your help. You'll have to work out the pattern pieces.'

'You don't need to decide this minute,' said Mrs Cooper, handing her an envelope. 'Your gran brought this round an' all. I think it's her reply to the invitation.'

The hairs stood up on Joan's arms as a shiver ran through her. She opened the envelope, which was her own envelope – or rather, Cordelia's – that Gran had reused in accordance with instructions to use paper as many times as possible.

Mrs Beryl Foster thanks Miss Joan Foster and Mr Robert Hubble for their invitation …

'It's a refusal,' said Joan, folding it again. How was she supposed to feel? Relieved? Disappointed? Affronted?

'Never mind,' said Mrs Cooper in a bright voice. 'Go upstairs and try your dress on for Margaret.'

The three girls went upstairs. Joan expected Mabel to assist her with her dress, but she disappeared into the bathroom. Margaret helped her into it and stood back to admire her, but not before Joan glimpsed the sheen of tears in her eyes. Perhaps it was a good thing Mabel wasn't here.

'It can't be easy, seeing me in your dress,' said Joan.

'It's not my dress any more.' Margaret lifted her chin. 'It never was my dress, really. I paid for it, but that's all. I never had a wedding day. I never had a man who loved me. It's your dress and I'm happy for you to wear it – truly. You look lovely.'

'Thank you. I've got something to ask you. Would you like to be one of my bridesmaids?'

'It's kind of you to offer, but you really don't have to.'

'I shouldn't have said "Would you like to?" I should have said "Please will you", because I'd very much like you to. It wouldn't be enough to have you there simply as a guest.'

'But you and the others are such close friends.'

'Exactly.' Joan smiled. 'I think you're going to fit in perfectly.'

Margaret uttered a small gasp. 'You mean it?'

'Is that a yes?'

'Yes, please,' Margaret exclaimed and they hugged one another. 'Thank you. I'd be delighted – oh, but I haven't got anything good enough to wear.'

'Borrow something of mine,' Joan said as Mabel returned from the bathroom. 'Mabel, Margaret is going to be a bridesmaid, but she needs something to wear. If I haven't got anything suitable, would you mind if she borrowed off you?'

'Of course not,' said Mabel. To Margaret, she added, 'Joan knows what I'll be wearing. Other than that, help yourself.'

Throwing a smile over her shoulder, she left the room and ran downstairs. Joan was taken aback. Mabel might have sounded bright and breezy, but there had been something distinctly offhand in her offer. Joan knew Margaret wouldn't dream of taking one of Mabel's dresses now.

'I have just the dress for you,' said Joan. 'It's one I made for my sister.'

Margaret came to stand beside her in front of the open wardrobe. 'I was sorry to hear what happened to her. I hope you don't mind, but Alison took me aside and told me when we went to the pictures.'

Joan nodded. 'I wanted you to know, but I didn't want to be the one to tell you. I've got used to responding when people know and offer their sympathy, but I find it dreadfully hard telling someone who doesn't know. Here, this is the dress I mean, the lilac. I made it for her to go dancing in. Try it on.'

'Thank you,' said Margaret as Joan helped her into it. 'It's a long time since I've worn anything as lovely as this. I lost all my things in that air raid and afterwards it never felt right to have pretty clothes.'

Taking her hand, Joan looked into her face. 'It's time to stop thinking that way. You made a mistake, but you can't keep on punishing yourself. You have a new life now. You deserve a second chance.'

'I'm not sure my father or our old neighbours would agree with you,' said Margaret, 'but they aren't part of my life any more, are they? I should try to see things differently ... see myself differently.'

There was a tap at the door and Mrs Cooper popped her head inside. 'Tea will be on the table in ten minutes. Oh, look at our Joan. Doesn't she look beautiful? And you've changed since you came upstairs an' all, Margaret. Are you girls having a dressing-up session?'

'Margaret has agreed to be one of my bridesmaids,' said Joan. 'This is what she's going to wear.'

'It suits you, chuck.' Then Mrs Cooper eyed Joan. 'The question is, will she be wearing it with or without a lace bolero jacket?'

Joan laughed. 'With. They'll all wear their dresses with.'

'I'm pleased to hear it. Get changed and come down.'

Soon they were all seated round the dining table. Margaret admired the china, which was in the same sort of blue and white as Willow Pattern, but painted with blue flowers and dainty sprays of leaves.

'It all belongs to the Morgans,' Mrs Cooper told Margaret. 'They've gone to North Wales for the duration and I'm taking care of the house for them. I'm allowed to have lodgers, though not men.' She looked at Joan. 'Otherwise we might have been able to turn this dining room into a bedsit for you and Bob. I'm sorry I couldn't find you somewhere to live. I'll try again tomorrow.'

'You might not have to,' said Joan, and she explained about the possibility of moving in with Sheila Green. 'I'm going to go round there before first-aid duty.' She turned to Margaret. 'I'm sorry. It's not exactly hospitable to invite you here and then announce I'm going out later, but Bob and I are in rather a fix.'

'I understand,' said Margaret. 'I'll go home straight after tea.'

'You most certainly will not,' said Mrs Grayson. 'You can stop here with me and Mrs Cooper and help us make a start on the lace jackets. No arguments. Mrs Cooper and I are two of Joan's mothers of the bride and if you're a bridesmaid, we want to be acquainted with you.'

Joan smiled across at Mabel. She was pleased at Margaret's being accepted and she wanted Mabel to be pleased too, but Mabel didn't seem to be paying attention. What

was the matter with her today? Normally, she was politeness itself.

After tea, Joan got ready for a night on duty and set off on
her bicycle. She went to Dot's and then, pushing her bike,
walked with Dot round to Sheila's. Sheila's house was bigger than Dot's. That was good. More room for three adults.

Dot performed the introductions and Joan shook hands
with Sheila. They hadn't met properly before, but Joan
remembered all too clearly that night in the Christmas
Blitz when Jimmy Green had been trapped beneath a pan-
caked house and Sheila had been gaunt with worry,
smoking cigarette after cigarette. A woman smoking outdoors – Gran would have had something to say about that,
no matter what the circumstances. Joan had had to adjust a
lot of her ideas since wriggling out from under Gran's rule.

'I'll leave you to it,' said Dot. 'If you want to talk it over
with Bob, you can give me your answer tomorrow. I'll see
you in the buffet after work.'

'Come in,' said Sheila. 'The spare room is a double.' She
threw open a door off the hallway. 'We have this front parlour, which I never use, so you can have this as your sitting
room.'

Joan walked in. Her first impression was of green and
cream wallpaper and a rug on the stained-wood floor. A
sideboard stood against the wall at right angles to the
brown-tiled fireplace and there were a couple of chairs and
a small table. The room smelled of polish, fresh polish,
which was fair enough. Sheila had evidently made an effort
with the parlour. Hang on a minute. Was that ... ? Yes,
there was a cobweb up there in a corner. Joan turned away,
not wanting to be caught looking.

They went upstairs to see the spare bedroom, then came
down to the kitchen, where a faint sense of dampness in
the air suggested the floor had been washed in her honour.

The cupboard tops were tidy and there was a table with chairs. Gran would have sneered at eating in the kitchen, but Joan found it cosy.

Jimmy, who hadn't been allowed to accompany them round the house, now bounced into the kitchen, asking, 'D'you like it? Are you going to come and live with us? Does Mr Hubble like football? Does he like cricket?'

'Hush up, Jimmy,' said Sheila, 'and stop racketing about. Stand over there out of the way.'

Jimmy did so, balancing on one leg. He wobbled and knocked against a cupboard, the door of which swung open and a variety of bits and bobs fell out so freely it was obvious they had been stuffed inside in haste.

'Jimmy!' hissed Sheila.

'Have I discovered your big tidy-up operation, Jimmy?' Joan tried to make light of it.

'Aye, that's what it was,' chirped Jimmy. 'Like spies doing a secret operation, only ours was tidying and Nan did the polishing.'

'I wonder how quickly you can pick all those things up,' said Joan.

'What do you think of the place?' asked Sheila. 'Are you interested?'

'Yes,' said Joan carefully, 'but can I let you know? I have to talk to my fiancé.' Oh, wasn't that the best word in the world! There was only one downside to getting married so fast, which was that in a few days she wouldn't be able to say 'fiancé' any more.

When the front door shut behind her, she walked away with her bicycle, heading for St Cuthbert's, her mind full of what she'd seen. She and Bob were desperate, that was the truth, and this might be their only chance of finding somewhere before the wedding. And they would have their own sitting room. But those things that had come clattering out of the cupboard said that the kitchen wasn't normally tidy, and apparently Dot had done the polishing. Joan had no intention of being stuck with doing more than her share of the housework, but on the other hand, she and Bob were desperate ...

And then there was the matter of the secret she and Mabel knew about Sheila Green.

Chapter Twenty-Seven

After the severe air raid in the early hours of Whit Sunday, there had been short raids in the small hours of Monday and Tuesday, and now here it was happening again, just after three o'clock on Wednesday morning.

'Let's hope it doesn't happen in the early hours of Saturday morning,' Mabel heard another girl say to Joan, 'or you won't get your beauty sleep before the wedding.'

Mabel felt a twinge of guilt. She should have been the one to say that; she was Joan's friend. But she had been so preoccupied since Monday evening that her stomach felt as if it was tied in knots. Not that that was any excuse. This was Joan's special week and she deserved all the care and attention her friends could lavish on her.

The raid was mercifully short and the St Cuthbert's depot had no call-outs. When the all-clear sounded, Mabel went to sit with Joan. So far tonight she had kept to herself, but it hadn't done her any good. All it had achieved was to make her even more wound up.

'I'm sorry if I've been moody,' she told Joan. 'I shouldn't say "if". I know perfectly well I have been.'

'You were a bit off with Margaret.'

'The poor girl, on her first visit to our house as well. I'll apologise.' She gave Joan a nudge. 'We can't have your bridesmaids falling out, can we?'

'What are you upset about?' Joan asked. 'And don't say you're not. Come on, this is me you're talking to. We've been room-mates for the past few weeks and we've shared

317

a lot. I told you I wanted to get back together with Bob before I even told Bob, and I'm one of only two people you told about Harry originally being after your father's money.'

Mabel let out a soft groan. 'You've hit the nail on the head.'

'Your father's money? Mabel, you don't mean—'

'No, absolutely not. Harry isn't after the money. I love him and I trust him and I've put all that behind us – or I thought I had.'

'What's happened?'

'It's Gil. I'm so angry with him. Honestly, my pulse is racing just thinking about it. He came back into my life and Harry was madly jealous until last weekend, when the two of them rescued Dot and Mr Thirkle. That changed things and they seemed to end up liking one another, or at least getting along.'

'That's a good thing, surely?'

'You'd think so. Then I saw Gil on Monday evening.'

'Yes. He came round before Gran did.'

'I really thought he was about to throw his heart at my feet and beg me to go back to him, but instead ... instead, he said he's looked into Harry's background—'

'He's done what?' Joan exclaimed.

'You heard me. And – and he gave me a warning. He said that if Harry and I make a go of it, meaning if we get married, I should make sure Pops ties up the money in such a way that Harry can't get his mitts on it.'

'Oh, Mabel.'

'I know Harry started out intending to marry for money, but I also know he fell in love with me for real. Gil has stirred everything up and I'm furious with him. I've been humiliated again and that makes me angry with Harry too, which is unfair when he's changed and I've forgiven him.

It's stupid to be upset all over again. How could Gil do this to me? I wish he'd kept his nose out.'

'I'm sure he had your best interests at heart. He wasn't to know Harry's a reformed character.'

'I hate thinking that Gil knows what Harry was after to begin with.'

'If you're happy with Harry, it shouldn't matter what Gil or anyone else thinks.'

'But it does. It matters what Gil thinks because I respect him. I always have and now he thinks me a chump for being taken in by a fortune-hunter.'

'Didn't you set him straight?'

'Of course not. For a start, I was too shocked, and then I was too proud. I could see how sordid it must appear to him and I was ashamed. I don't want anyone to know why Harry first took an interest in me.'

'You've nothing to be ashamed of. If you and Harry love one another and everything is straight and above board between you, that's all that matters.'

'I know you're right, but I still feel all churned up. It's funny. Harry's the one who's been rattled by Gil all this time. Now the two of them are fine and I'm the one who's rattled.' Mabel leaned closer. 'The fact is, it's rather beastly knowing that Harry used to be a fortune-hunter. When people ask "How did you meet?" it makes an amusing story to say he was visiting someone else in hospital and found me a lot more appealing, but underneath all that is this grubby little secret. Most of the time I don't think about it, but Gil has dumped it front and centre.'

'You'll feel better when you see Harry again.'

'I don't know how I'm to wait that long feeling like this.'

'Then telephone the base first thing in the morning and speak to him.'

'I can't tell him what Gil said. He'll explode.'

'Have a normal conversation.'

'But I only telephone at agreed times.'

'Tell him you wanted to hear his voice and let him work his charm on you.'

Would that calm the serpents writhing in her belly? Drat Harry and his old fortune-hunting ambitions, and drat Gil for finding out. This felt like her punishment for being so arrogant as to think Gil had been going to declare his undying love for her.

She and Joan were given a job checking supplies, then they were asked to make tea for everyone, which also meant washing up afterwards.

'I have no objection to making tea and clearing up,' said Mabel, as Joan took the last mug out of the bowl, placed it on the draining board and picked up a tea towel to help with the drying, 'but I don't see why the men should always be waited on. We're all here to do the same first-aid work, but it's always the girls who have to do the housewifely things.' She laughed. 'I shouldn't say that to you, should I? You'll soon have your own home and a husband to run around after. What was Sheila Green's house like?'

'She offered us the parlour as well as the spare bedroom.'

'That's good. I take it you snatched her hand off.'

'No, I didn't, actually. I got the impression Sheila's not the world's most finicky housewife.'

'Was it bad?'

'Difficult to say for certain. The spare room and the parlour had been polished, but then it turned out Dot had done it, and there'd obviously been a big tidy-up before I arrived. Obviously, I'm happy to look after our rooms, but what about sharing the kitchen? What about the hall, stairs and landing? I don't want to end up doing the lion's share.'

'You'd have to set rules,' said Mabel.

'I can't make rules in someone else's house. Besides, it isn't just the housework. It's ... *you know*.' Joan dropped her voice. 'Is she flighty? I wouldn't be comfortable with that.'

'If you and Bob move in, it would cut down her chances to be flighty – assuming she is that way inclined. Remember, we don't know for certain it was Sheila's Harry that Dot was talking about. We can't even be sure Alison overheard accurately.'

Joan gave her a look. 'Now you're snatching at straws.'

'What it comes down to is this,' said Mabel. 'Mrs Cooper hasn't found you a billet. I take it Bob's folks have been looking as well?'

'Yes, with no luck.'

'Then either you accept Sheila's offer or else when you come back from your honeymoon, you go back to Wilton Close and Bob goes home to Mother. You wouldn't be the first couple who've had to do it.'

'We definitely don't want to do that.'

'Then Sheila's it is.'

'I know. I'll tell Dot tomorrow.' Joan's face broke into a radiant smile. 'We've got our first married home. Who cares if it isn't perfect?'

Mabel hugged her. 'It will be perfect, because you'll be together.'

'Yes, that's all that really matters, isn't it? Now all we have to do is get you and Harry back on an even keel and everything will be fine for the wedding.'

That was all it took to set Mabel's stomach rolling with dread once again. She felt peeled and vulnerable. She didn't even know what she wanted to say to Harry. Part of her very much wanted to give him what for. It was bad enough his having once been a fortune-hunter, but had he really had to tell his friends?

But when her telephone call was put through to RAF Burtonwood at breakfast-time, all her rage and humiliation evaporated when Harry's friend came on the line and told her that there had been a mission last night and all the planes had returned safely – except one.

'We aren't meeting up today, are we?'

Dot looked round. She had been about to enter the buffet, but now, finding Cordelia close by, she stood aside with a smile to let the couple behind her go through the door. She joined Cordelia.

'No. I'm seeing Joan for a few minutes, that's all. She looked round our Sheila's house yesterday and she's going to tell me if she wants to lodge there.'

'Has Sheila's friend left, then?'

'Aye, and good riddance, though I should be kinder. The lass's husband has been shipped home injured. Anyroad, I offered digs to Joan and Bob.'

Cordelia raised her eyebrows. 'Do they realise they'll be acting as guard dogs, keeping undesirable males at bay?'

Dot clicked her tongue. 'Of course not. And before you say owt else, yes, I am uncomfortable about it. I don't like to think of using my friends. But think of it this way. If it hadn't been Joan and Bob, it'd have been a stranger – or more than one stranger – because believe you me, now that Rosa has gone, I'm going to make sure Sheila lives in a respectable way.'

Cordelia glanced round. 'There's no sign of Joan yet. Shall you and I find somewhere to sit?'

'Aye, let's.'

A minute or two later, armed with cups and saucers, they settled at a table.

'Do you think it's wrong of me to ask Joan and Bob to move in?' asked Dot.

'Not wrong, no. They're lucky to have the chance of a home. It's just unfortunate, shall we say, that you have an ulterior motive.'

'Ulterior motive? I'm a crafty so-and-so, you mean.'

'It's bound to take a bit of the sparkle off it.'

Dot felt deflated. 'That's exactly it. It's good to offer Joan a home, but Sheila's carryings-on will always be at the back of my mind.'

'Chin up,' said Cordelia. 'Your way is better than leaving it to the billeting officer. And I'll tell you another advantage. It'll do young Jimmy good to have a man about the house.'

'Aye, it will. Bob's a good sort. He'll pay Jimmy a bit of attention and that'll do the lad good.' She drew a sharp breath and released it before she said, 'Eh, Cordelia, what am I saying? It isn't Bob that Jimmy needs. It's his dad. It's his dad who should be at home, fetching him up and setting him an example and taking him to the park for a kickabout. I don't mean no offence to Bob, but it should be Harry. It should be Harry.' All at once her eyes were packed with tears. 'I'm sorry. This isn't like me. I'm not one to feel sorry for myself.'

'My dear Dot, I can't imagine you ever feeling sorry for yourself. For one thing, you haven't got the time. You're far too busy rushing around getting everything done. For another thing, it isn't self-pity to wish for your family to be together again. It's what every mother wants.'

'Aye, the trains are packed solid this week with parents heading off to visit their children.'

'I wish I could say that maybe everyone will be reunited in time for next year's Whit week, but we all know that won't happen. We still have a long struggle ahead.'

'We do, but you'll have your Emily home with you soon – well, I hope so, anyroad.'

'As do I, Dot. My husband is still talking about her staying away to keep her safe. If she does come home, I fear I'll be in a similar position to you: wanting her with me, then feeling guilty for bringing her into danger every time there's an air raid.'

'It's a constant worry,' agreed Dot. 'Look, here's Joan. I wonder what she's decided about Sheila's house.'

Joan came from the door straight to their table and slid into a seat.

'I've only got a minute. I need to be with Mabel. Harry flew on a mission last night and his plane didn't come back.'

'*No.*' Dot and Cordelia spoke together.

'That was the situation this morning when Mabel telephoned. All she wanted, of course, was to hang about and keep telephoning, but she had to come to work and spend all day out on the permanent way.'

'The poor girl,' said Cordelia. 'She must be in turmoil.'

'She's on her way to Hunts Bank now,' said Joan. 'I went to see Miss Emery earlier and arranged for Mabel to telephone from her office.'

'That were kind of you.' Dot's heart reached out to Mabel – and to Joan an' all. Living together had brought those two closer and Joan must be in agony for her friend.

'Anyway, Dot, I'm here to say yes please to the digs.'

'That's grand,' said Dot. 'Sheila will be pleased and I am an' all.'

'There's just one thing.' Joan glanced away for a moment. 'It isn't an easy thing to say, but, well, I got the impression that Sheila isn't the most house-proud person and – and I don't want to get lumbered with doing more than my share. I'm sorry.'

Oh, cripes. 'Nay, lass, don't apologise. You're right. I'll have words with our Sheila—'

'If I might interrupt,' said Cordelia and they both looked at her. 'This might be the moment to tell you about the wedding present I've organised for you, Joan. It's why I went to see Mrs Cooper yesterday.' She smiled. 'I'd like you to accept two hours a week of Magic Mop for eighteen weeks.'

Joan breathed in audibly, her mouth dropping open. 'That's so generous. Are you sure?'

'Naturally.'

Dot squirmed inwardly. 'I feel that wretched.'

'There's no need to be embarrassed, Dot,' Cordelia said firmly. 'The state of your daughter-in-law's house is her responsibility, not yours. Besides, this was to be Joan's gift regardless of where she lives.' She looked at Joan. 'It's a big thing to look after a home on top of working full-time, even if the home is only a room or two. This present will help you along as you adjust to married life.'

'Thank you,' breathed Joan.

'Now go and find Mabel,' said Cordelia. 'She needs you.'

'And give her a big hug from us,' Dot added. When Joan had left Dot said to Cordelia, 'That's a splendid present.'

'A sensible present, I'd have said.'

'Aye, that an' all. And generous. Two hours a week for eighteen weeks? Why eighteen?'

'Two guineas,' said Cordelia. 'My husband's secretary is getting married this summer and he asked me to find a suitable gift to the value of two guineas. At the time, I thought it excessively generous, but now I'm glad because it has enabled me to insist upon spending that amount on Joan and Bob.'

'It's taken a load off Joan's mind, anyroad. After Magic Mop finishes, she and Bob can look for another home if they feel they need to, but let's hope it won't come to that.

I'll be having sharp words with our Sheila, you can bank on it.'

'We aren't so very different, you and I,' said Cordelia. 'You needed to clip Sheila's wings and in doing so, you've done Joan and Bob a good turn. I wanted to give them a useful wedding present and in doing so, I've also put some work Mrs Cooper's way.'

'Oh aye?' A smile spread across Dot's face. 'Now who's got the ulterior motive?'

'I can't imagine what you mean.' Cordelia pretended to put her nose in the air. 'But if you're suggesting I'm a crafty so-and-so, I wonder where I could possibly have learned it from?'

Chapter Twenty-Eight

Mabel followed Miss Emery up a flight of stairs and along a corridor. She was still in her lengthman's clothes and must look a sight compared to the assistant welfare supervisor for women and girls, who looked as smart as always in a brown jacket and skirt with a cream blouse. Her short string of graduated pearls would have been equally suitable for a woman twice her age.

'It's very good of you to let me telephone from your office,' said Mabel.

'I couldn't possibly leave you to make a call of that nature from a telephone box, having to fiddle about inserting coins and pressing button A and button B,' said Miss Emery. 'You won't actually be telephoning from my office. I've arranged for you to use someone else's. You'll see why in a moment,' she added in a dry voice that caught Mabel's attention in spite of the dread burning a hole in her stomach.

They turned a corner and passed a staircase, after which there was a large alcove. It took Mabel a moment to realise that part of the alcove was sectioned off. Inside, there was a desk and a small table with a typewriter on it. Between the two was a chair that, if turned round, would do for either the desk or the typewriter. There was another chair against the wall and a cupboard at the back.

'Behold my domain,' said Miss Emery.

'I always imagined you in a proper office.'

'Four walls and a window onto the outside world, you mean?' Miss Emery's tone had changed from dry to tart.

'That's what I used to have, but then it was needed for someone else and I was presented with this.'

'You ought to have proper accommodation,' said Mabel. 'Your job is important.'

'I couldn't agree more.' The tartness vanished and Miss Emery looked upset, but only for a moment. 'Women come to see me about all sorts of matters and it's difficult to speak freely in this glorified alcove. Still, that's not why we're here. This way, please.'

She escorted Mabel to a door further along, knocked and opened it to reveal a small outer office in which a middle-aged woman with salt-and-pepper hair sat behind a desk at right angles to the closed door to the inner office.

Miss Emery waved Mabel into the room. 'Mrs Cartwright, this is Miss Bradshaw, who has come to use your telephone.'

The secretary gave Mabel a sympathetic look. 'I've finished for the day. I'll be out of your hair in a minute.' Glancing at the inner door, she added, 'Mr Ridley won't be back today.'

Mrs Cartwright popped something into her desk drawer and locked it before putting the cover over her typewriter. Taking her jacket and hat from the coat stand, and her handbag from a cupboard, she nodded to Miss Emery and Mabel and left the room.

Miss Emery gave Mabel a kind smile, though her voice was matter-of-fact. 'Lift the receiver and the switchboard will answer. I'll wait for you in my office.'

Mabel nodded, a thickness deep in her throat preventing her from speaking. Miss Emery quietly closed the door behind her. In her mind's eye, Mabel saw herself leaping across the room to snatch up the receiver and give the number to the switchboard. She had been yearning for this moment all day. She had even broken down in tears on the permanent way because of the strain of waiting and not knowing and hoping. Now, here she was at last, with the telephone in front of her, and her feet were glued to the floor.

What if Harry's plane still hadn't returned? As terrible as it was not to know, not knowing meant there was hope. Not knowing meant she still had Harry, her handsome, brave, cheeky blighter. Not knowing had cleared her mind and heart of all the worries and reservations of last night and brought her feelings into painfully sharp focus.

How could she have been so upset about Gil's warning? It hadn't exactly made her doubt Harry, but it had unsettled her deeply because – because it was Gil who had given her the warning. If anyone else had dared to cast aspersions on Harry, she would have been outraged and dismissive. But Gil mattered more to her than that. His reappearance in her life had brought back so much that she had kept hidden from herself. Those memories, plus the revelation from Pops about the important nature of Gil's secret work, had opened her up to feelings of fondness and admiration that had been hard to ignore. She had told Harry repeatedly that he had nothing to be jealous of, but hadn't she needed to convince herself as much as him?

Not any more, though. That telephone call this morning before work, that moment when she had been told that Harry's plane had not yet returned, had dashed everything else aside and shown her precisely what she wanted – what she needed – and that was Harry. Her one and only, her cheeky blighter – yes, her fortune-hunter turned hero.

He had to be all right. He had to be. She had spent all day telling herself that. Bernice, Bette and Louise had emphasised it as well. The thought – the hope – of Harry having safely returned was the one thing that had kept her upright and on her feet all day instead of crumpling to the ground and curling up between the railway tracks.

She had to make the telephone call. It was preposterous to hang back. Yet the thought terrified her.

'You can do it, Mabs,' Grandad's voice whispered in her head. 'You can do it, my brave lass.'

Mabel picked up the receiver.

Joan sat on the wooden chair in Miss Emery's new office. She had been in here once before, on the day she had been given her porter's job – Lizzie's old job – but Miss Emery had had a real office back then. Look what she had now. A pretend office that was open to the corridor and anyone passing by could see inside. Miss Emery must feel like she was on show the whole time. Joan was too polite to make a comment, but she felt indignant on Miss Emery's behalf.

Besides, it didn't feel right to be bothered about a pretend office, however crummy, not when Mabel was making her all-important telephone call. A tingling sensation crossed Joan's skin and she huffed out a breath, feeling cold and tense on her friend's behalf. Please let Harry be safe. It would break Mabel's heart clean in two if she lost him.

Each time she heard footsteps, Joan looked up anxiously, only for a stranger to walk past. Then at last came the sound of hurrying steps and she knew it was Mabel – hastening to share her happiness or rushing to fling herself into a pair of comforting arms? Joan stood up, aware of Miss Emery doing likewise.

Mabel appeared in the centre of the opening and stood there, just stood there, eyes wide. For a moment, all three of them seemed frozen where they were, then Joan understood that Mabel's eyes were wide with joy, not despair, even before Mabel exclaimed, 'He's safe. He's *safe*,' and they launched themselves into one another's arms and hugged each other, laughing and crying at the same time.

Loosening her hold, Mabel went to Miss Emery, who was also wiping away a tear. 'Thank you for arranging for me to telephone in private.'

'It was a pleasure. I'm delighted you have had a happy outcome.'

'Now we must go home and reassure Mrs Cooper and Mrs Grayson,' said Joan.

'Yes, they'll be worried sick, poor dears,' said Mabel.

'And we ought to go via the buffet in case Dot and Cordelia are still there,' Joan added.

It wasn't long before they were on their way home. They burst in with their good news, creating a storm of tears and relief amidst a great deal of hugging.

'This is what a family should be like,' Joan remarked when things had calmed down, 'not afraid to share their feelings. We *are* a family, aren't we, the four of us?'

'I think we are,' said Mrs Grayson, 'don't you, Mrs Cooper?'

Mrs Cooper touched Joan's cheek. 'And our little one is going to fly the nest in a day or two.'

'Speaking of which,' said Mrs Grayson, 'we must get those bolero jackets finished.'

'All hands on deck,' called Mabel. 'We'll get them done tonight.'

'Would you mind if I left you all to it for a while?' asked Joan. 'I'd like to see Gran. I haven't thanked her for sending the curtains.'

'Yes, you go, chuck,' said Mrs Cooper, 'and tell her the jackets are going to look proper bonny. No one will ever guess how they started life.'

After tea, Joan combed her hair. On impulse, she put on her snood, gently scooping her hair inside it. Gran used to insist she and Letitia wore snoods nearly all the time. After leaving home, Joan had vowed never to wear hers again, except for work and first aid. But this evening she wanted to wear it, because Gran had done a good thing by providing the net curtains and she wanted to do a good thing in return. Would Gran notice? If she did, would there be a barbed remark? It didn't matter. It felt like the right thing to do, just this once.

Arriving at Gran's, Joan opened the gate, her gaze immediately drawn to the front windows, bare of nets, the evening sun catching the glass. It was then that it really struck her that the nets were gone. She had known they were, but seeing the windows, seeing *through* the windows, made it real.

She touched her snood self-consciously as she waited for Gran to answer the door, dropping her hand to her side before the door opened.

'Hello, Gran. May I come in?'

Gran nodded and stepped aside. Joan went into the parlour – and stopped dead. The room was so bright. All her life it had felt dingy and dark and just look at it now. How big the windows were. The furniture, which had always looked old and heavy, now seemed aged and handsome. If only Letitia could have seen her home this way.

Gran came in behind her and Joan moved aside.

'Oh, Gran.' She wanted to say how lovely the parlour looked, but didn't quite dare in case Gran hated it. Instead she said, 'What a difference.'

'Yes, it is. Have a seat.'

Even after leaving home – after being thrown out, to be accurate – back in February, it was still disconcerting to be treated as a visitor. Gran sat in the armchair where she always sat, where she had sat for as long as Joan could remember, and Joan sat opposite.

332

'I've come to say thank you for the nets. We're making bolero jackets out of them for the bridesmaids, just like you suggested.'

Gran nodded, but all she said was 'Good' in rather a clipped voice.

'I'd like to talk about you not coming to my wedding,' said Joan.

'What is there to say? After everything that's happened, I'm sure you don't want me there. You invited me as a matter of form and I appreciate your good manners, but I've no desire to be the spectre at the feast.'

'If you want to come, you'd be welcome. You're the only family I have.'

'You've made up for your lack of family, though, haven't you? All those mothers of the bride. Ridiculous.'

'No, not ridiculous,' said Joan. 'Necessary. I want my wedding to be happy. I want to be surrounded by people who care about me and Bob. Having four mothers of the bride is exciting and fun and memorable. When you haven't got any family of your own, you have to find your family where you can.'

Gran was silent for a minute before she said, 'It's hard having no family. It was hard for me, bringing up the two of you on my own. Not that I wanted anybody else. It wouldn't have been safe. Our secret wouldn't have been safe. But it was lonely. Every day I felt how alone I was.'

'Gran,' Joan whispered.

Gran's head jerked up. 'Don't feel sorry for me. After – after your father died, I was at a crossroads and I had to decide what to do. That sometimes happens in life. I made the choice to move away from everyone I'd ever known and revert to my maiden name. I did what I had to do. Whatever you choose to think, I acted for the best. There's only one thing I shouldn't have done.'

Instinct prodded Joan to sit up straighter to listen. She had to force herself not to move in case it put Gran off.

Without looking at her, Gran said, 'It was wrong of me to say that Donald wasn't your father. It was my opinion of your mother, my dislike of her, that created the doubt in my mind and led me to speculate. But it was only speculation and I should never have said anything to you. It was not a grandmotherly thing to do.' Now, at last, she looked at Joan. 'I do regard you as my granddaughter and I always will. Whatever your mother did or didn't do, you are my granddaughter.'

It seemed like an olive branch, but before Joan could say anything, Gran stood up.

'I'm sorry, but you have to leave now. I'm going out shortly. The WVS has organised an evening of clothes sorting at MacFadyen's. Thank you for coming round. I hope the wedding goes well on Saturday.'

'Thank you,' said Joan, 'and thank you again for the nets.'

Gran shrugged. 'It was another crossroads. I had kept the secret for so long and lived in darkness and then you went in search of the truth. It isn't easy to live with, is it? As for losing Letitia ... I wish I had let the light into the house when she was still here. I did it for her. I let the light in for her. Giving you the nets to make jackets, well, the idea just came to me. I thought it would have made Letitia laugh.'

Joan smiled. 'Yes, it would.' Oh, how she missed her sister.

Gran saw her to the front door. 'There was another reason I gave you the nets.' She opened the door and as Joan stepped outside and looked back, Gran said, 'I thought, that is I hoped, it would make you happy.'

Chapter Twenty-Nine

Dot sat in Sheila's kitchen, watching as her daughter-in-law lit the gas and put the kettle on. The kitchen was tidier than normal, thanks to yesterday's big tidy-up, but already Sheila's lackadaisical ways were reasserting themselves and it wouldn't be long before things were back to their haphazard normal. Dot smothered a sigh. The milk bottle was on the table. Dot had asked Jimmy to keep an eye open for the milk jug during the grand tidy, after which Dot had put it on the shelf, saying as casually as possible, 'There. In easy reach.' But here was the ruddy milk bottle back on the table and the jug was still on the shelf.

She got up and fetched it and poured in some milk, then placed the milk bottle on the marble slab in the pantry. She glanced at Sheila, but Sheila wasn't bothered. The girl who was happy for her mother-in-law to tackle the bulk of her spring-cleaning wasn't going to care about a milk bottle.

When they had their tea in front of them, Sheila lit up and inhaled.

'That Miss Foster you brought round seemed an all right sort of girl. Is she going to take the rooms?'

'Aye, love, she is – they are. That's good, isn't it? And another friend is giving them some hours of cleaning as a wedding present, but you need to know that Magic Mop will only—'

'Magic Mop?'

'That's the name of the cleaning company.'

'A cleaning company? Not a cleaner, but a cleaning company. Very posh, I don't think.' Sheila blew out smoke. It was funny how expressive a stream of smoke could be. This one had a distinct sneer about it.

It was vexing to hear Mrs Cooper's business having fun poked at it. 'Aye, Magic Mop, and a jolly good service it is an' all. But mind, Sheila, it's for Joan's benefit, not yours, so Mrs Cooper will do Joan and Bob's bedroom, but not yours or Jimmy's, and she'll do their sitting room. There'll need to be an arrangement about the kitchen. She'll do Joan's cupboards and I suppose she'll do the cooker, but that doesn't mean you can skimp on your share.'

'I don't need a lecture,' said Sheila.

Dot had spent the past dozen years not lecturing Sheila, practically having to tie her tongue in knots so as not to let it all come spilling out. She said in the moderate tone she was frequently obliged to adopt when speaking to one or other of her daughters-in-law, 'Magic Mop won't be around for ever and Joan won't stop here if you don't pull your weight. Joan and Bob are a lovely couple. You don't want to lose them.'

'A lovely couple?' Sheila rolled her eyes. 'I'm not stupid, Ma. I know you wanted to pick who lodged here next. You never wanted Rosa here. It's not easy having a friend that everyone disapproves of.'

'You can't deny she's a flighty piece.'

'That's just what I mean,' Sheila exclaimed in exasperation. 'I say it's not easy being friends with a girl no one has a good word for, and you immediately criticise her. You're the same as everybody else. It's always been that way. And the more everyone takes against her, the more I feel I need to stand by her.'

'Aye,' said Dot. 'Obstinate.'

'There you are, you see. What you call obstinate, I call loyal.'

Dot had never thought of it that way. Obstinacy. Loyalty. Where did one end and the other begin? For years she had been sniffy about Rosa, wanting to put Sheila off her, but had she instead contributed to Sheila's need to stand up for her friend? Was Sheila's . . . loyalty something to be admired?

'Rosa's fun,' said Sheila. 'Goodness knows, there's little enough fun to be had these days. All I do is work long hours down the munitions and when I'm not there, I'm trying to keep the tin lid on our Jimmy's antics. When I think how proud I was to have a boy when Pammy only had a girl . . . ' Another stream of smoke. 'If I'd known then what I know now, I'd have swapped 'em at birth.'

'You don't mean that.'

'Don't I?'

'No.' After the initial shock, Dot felt herself to be on firmer ground. 'You don't. You're fed up and feeling overwhelmed, that's what it is. You're missing Harry, you're working long shifts, you're coping on your own with our Jimmy, and I'll be the first to admit that he's more trouble than a bagful of weasels.'

'A bagful of what?'

'Weasels. It's summat my dad used to say. Eh, love, I know it isn't easy, but it's the same for everyone. We've all got a lot to put up with.'

'Aye, and having you as a mother-in-law doesn't help.'

Dot's mouth dropped open so far it almost hit the table. 'I've done nowt but help since the day our Harry told me and his dad that him and you were courting strong.'

'Oh aye, you're just perfect, aren't you? There's nowt you can't cope with. Have you any idea how galling it is to have a mother-in-law who is the ideal housewife, mother and

337

grandmother? And now you're doing all that and holding down a full-time job on top.'

Dot went cold inside and out. 'Is that how you see me? Don't be daft. I'm just an ordinary body getting everything done.'

'An ordinary body being a ruddy marvel, more like. I know you don't think I'm good enough for your Harry.'

'Oh, Sheila.'

'Well, it's true, isn't it?'

'Let me tell you summat.' Dot's heart was pounding. 'My lad chose you. He fell in love and you were all he wanted. As far as I'm concerned, if Harry wants you, then so do I. I would never jeopardise my relationship with my son by taking against his wife. Never.'

'For Harry's benefit, not for mine.'

Dot sat up straight. Did Sheila dislike her? Resent her? She had only ever tried her best to do the right thing by her sons and their wives. 'You want to know if I care about you? Well, I'll tell you. I care enough that on the night I slipped round here to fetch our Jimmy's PT kit and I heard voices upstairs, one of them a man's, I didn't go pounding up them stairs to play merry ruddy heck.'

Sheila's face drained of colour and her eyes widened, but smoke got in them and set her blinking rapidly. She crushed her ciggy into the ashtray.

'You – you know about that?' Her breath came in a series of short gasps.

'Aye. I've known all along. Who d'you think gave your address to the billeting office?'

'That were you? You thought you'd fill my house with strangers to stop me playing away, did you? And now you've got your little friend and her husband moving in. And you dare to say you're doing it for my benefit?'

'I am,' Dot said fiercely. 'I'll not lie to you. First and foremost, I'm doing it for Harry, but I'm doing it for you an'' all – and for our Jimmy. I'm doing it to keep your family in one piece – to keep my family together. I know you love Harry and I know that if not for this damn war, you'd never have strayed. I wanted to stop you doing summat stupid, summat you'd end up regretting for the rest of your life, and I wanted to do it without Harry knowing, without anyone knowing – including you.' A strange tiredness washed over her. Had she alienated Sheila for ever? Dot's voice went quiet. 'I wanted you to hang on to your marriage. God knows, there'll be enough broken marriages by the time this war is over and I don't want yours to be one of them. Times have moved on since the last war. There'll be divorces this time round, thousands of 'em, just you wait and see.' Her eyes, her throat, her chest filled with tears. 'I just wanted to stop you.'

Sheila looked away. Raising a hand, she swiped it across her cheek, dashing away a tear.

'There were no need,' she said at last. 'I stopped myself. I admit I was lonely and fed up and – and I got pally with a bloke from the munitions. I liked him and he liked me and it seemed it were the answer, but when it came to it ... ' Sheila let go a brief laugh and made another swipe at her cheek. 'There we were upstairs and I couldn't go through with it. I love Harry and I couldn't go through with it.'

'Oh, love.'

'And you've known all along.' Sheila's lips twisted. 'You flaming well would, wouldn't you? I suppose you hate me now.'

'Well, I haven't been best pleased with you.' Dot laid her hand over Sheila's. 'You came close to making a terrible mistake, but you didn't make it and that's what counts. I'll tell you summat else an' all. You're the lass my son chose and that's all that matters to me. And you've given me the best grandson in the world and I'll be grateful to you for that, for our Jimmy, until the day I die. It's family what matters, Sheila, first, foremost and for ever. And you and me are family.'

She had her answer right there in front of her, didn't she? Ever since the night when the thief was trapped in the railway shed and Dot had fully realised that her friendship with Mr Thirkle had blossomed into true love, she had agonised over what to do, longing to be close to him and never daring to make a move ... until that dreadful air raid last weekend when the two of them had hidden in that cellar, only to find water gushing in and threatening their lives.

'I know,' she had said in the cellar.

'It's been a long time since ... ' he had said before she had uttered her words. 'That is to say ... ' And then he had stopped.

It had been up to her. She could have kept her trap shut and said nowt. She could have held her feelings in. She could have pretended. But she hadn't.

'I know,' she had said.

I know what you're thinking. I know what you're feeling, because it's exactly the same for me. I know your feelings of friendship have grown into love, because that's what has happened to mine for you. I know you are an honourable man and you would never have gone looking for this, any more than I would. I know what you feel and I know how deep it runs.

'I know,' she had said.

I know, I know with all my heart.

What might have happened if that bomb hadn't fallen just then, blocking their exit? What if that water main hadn't burst?

I know with all my heart.

340

But listening to Sheila's confession had struck deep inside Dot, right to her immortal soul. Sheila hadn't transgressed after all. She had been tempted, more than tempted, but at the last moment she had seen sense, had seen into her own heart and had pulled back. Sheila had remained faithful. She had been true to her husband, true to her family.

And that had shown Dot what she had to do. Family 'first, foremost and for ever', she had said to Sheila. That was what it came down to. Yes, she had fallen out of love with Reg long since – if, indeed, she had truly been in love with him in the first place.

True love had come to her late in life and it would take all her strength to turn away from it. But she had another true love to sustain her, a love more powerful than anything.

Her love for her boys and their children.

Family first, foremost and for ever. Family was everything. She had learned that from her dear old mam and it was true. It had long been the guiding principle of her life. Dot had fallen head over heels in love with Archie when he was first placed in her arms and later she had fallen in love all over again at her first sight of Harry. If anyone had told her back then it would be possible for her to experience such overwhelming love for anybody else, she would have laughed … until each day her two grandchildren came into the world and her heart had almost shattered with love once more.

She had spent the greater part of her life living for her sons and then also for her grandchildren. That was true love for you, the truest of all, the love of a mother. That was who and what she was and she mustn't, couldn't, wouldn't put it at risk, not for anything, not even for another true love.

Family first, foremost and for ever.

Dot Green, mum and nan, first, foremost and for ever.

*

'Thank you for coming, Mr Thirkle.' Dot gave him a tight smile as he came to her table in the Worker Bee café. It had seemed the only place for this conversation. It wasn't summat she could say at the station, sitting on the bench where they had enjoyed so many chats. And there did have to be a conversation. She couldn't just let it hang. Mr Thirkle was a gentleman, her friend, her soulmate, and he deserved to be told.

'Allow me to fetch our drinks.' Mr Thirkle headed for the counter.

What was in his mind? Did he imagine she had asked him here to arrange an assignation? That was what it was called when two people who weren't supposed to, met up in secret. She knew that from a novel.

Mr Thirkle returned with two cups of tea. He placed hers in front of her. Reg would never have done that. Reg would have sent her to the counter.

Mr Thirkle smiled at her, his eyes gentle. 'I hope you haven't suffered any ill-effects from that soaking last weekend.'

'Nay, I'm fine, thank you. The only after-effects are those that come from the raids we've had each night since.'

'We could all do with a night of unbroken sleep.'

Dot picked up her cup, bending her head to meet it half-way to her lips because her hand was trembling. She replaced the cup and there was a little clinking sound as it touched the saucer.

'Mrs Green ... '

'Mr Thirkle ... '

They both stopped.

'After you,' said Mr Thirkle.

Now. Say it now.

'Mr Thirkle, we've known one another a fair while now and we've become good friends. I value your friendship more than I can say and – and ... '

342

Was he about to reach across and touch her hand? She didn't want him to. Yes, she did. No, she didn't – mustn't. No, she mustn't.

He leaned forward, but his hand didn't move. 'Your friendship means a great deal to me as well. We're in tune with one another. That hasn't happened to me since I lost my dear wife.'

Tears thickened Dot's voice and she could only whisper, 'I know, but it can't go on. In a different world, where we met when we were young, I would have spent my life taking care of you and being cherished by you and lapping up every moment of being cherished.' She managed a small laugh and even though tears shone in Mr Thirkle's eyes, he smiled too. 'But we aren't in that world. We're in this one and in this one, I have a family. I have my sons and my grandchildren and they are all the world to me.' Her throat closed, trapping the rest of the words inside.

Mr Thirkle bowed his head and she couldn't see his face. He cleared his throat and looked up. He nodded.

'I understand. You will not put your family at risk. I respect that. I welcome it in a way, because it shows what a good person you are. But at the same time … well, it was foolish of me to have my dreams.'

'I had dreams an' all, but they were only dreams. I have to do what's right. My lads are away fighting and it's up to me to hold the family together. I can't do that if I'm playing away, not if I'm going to look my sons in the eye when all this is over. Family first, foremost and for ever.'

'Family first and foremost,' said Mr Thirkle. 'I would have cherished you in that other world, Mrs Green. I would indeed.'

343

Chapter Thirty

'Wake up, sleepyhead.' Mabel reached across from her bed to Joan's and administered a gentle shake. 'It's wedding eve.'

Joan pushed herself up on one elbow. 'Don't tell me we've got through an entire night without an air raid.' She flopped back. 'What bliss.'

Mabel had never been one for leaping out of bed, but she had felt energised ever since she had learned that Harry was safe and now she threw back the covers and swung her feet onto the rug between the beds. It was as if her spirit was welcoming this new day because it was a day that contained Harry, even if they couldn't be together.

But tomorrow they would be.

Over breakfast, Mrs Cooper and Mrs Grayson detailed everything they were going to do today to prepare for the wedding.

'... and we'll go to the church hall and set out the tables and hang the bunting.'

'You can't do all that,' Joan protested. 'There'll be a whole team of us to do it this evening.'

'We can and we shall,' said Mrs Grayson. 'Isn't that right, Mrs Cooper?'

'It most certainly is. You and your bridesmaids are going to spend this evening doing one another's hair and creaming your hands and your elbows.'

'While these two mothers of the bride drink tea and try not to feel their age,' added Mrs Grayson. 'If we don't feel our age this evening, I'm sure we will tomorrow morning after a night with all those girls in the house, no doubt stopping up until all hours.'

Mabel grinned. 'It'll be like boarding school. Can we have a midnight feast?'

She loved to think of Joan being surrounded by so much attention. She finished her toast and drank the last of her tea before tucking her flask into her knapsack along with the packet of meat-paste barm cakes that Mrs Grayson had provided for her midday meal out on the permanent way.

It was like the day preceding a holiday. Mabel had that jolly feeling and not even her strenuous job could shake her out of it. Bernice was the same.

'My Bob couldn't have picked a nicer girl.'

'Do you mind that your lasses aren't going to be bridesmaids?' asked Bette.

'No. Joan's asked her friends and that's fine by me. If Bob had just the one sister, that'd be different, but he's got three. Besides, my Den is giving Joan away and that's a big honour.'

At the end of the day, the four of them parted company, Lou and Bette offering their best wishes for the wedding. Mabel made her way to the buffet, where the friends were meeting up, including Margaret. Was Margaret becoming a member of their group? It seemed so. After all, she wouldn't be their first new member. Persephone hadn't become a railway girl until just before Dunkirk.

Remembering how offhand she had been towards Margaret when she had come round to see Joan in her wedding dress, Mabel made a point of sitting next to her.

'Hello again. Look, I know I was a bit off the other evening. I want to say I'm sorry. I know it's no excuse, but I had a lot on my mind.'

'Don't mention it,' said Margaret. With her brown hair and hazel eyes, she was a pretty girl, or she would be if she widened her smile and let it reach up into her eyes. But she was likeable, besides which it couldn't be easy joining a group of such established friends. Joan obviously thought well of her and that was all Mabel needed to know.

'It'll be grand having all the bridesmaids staying overnight,' Mabel said, 'though I can't answer for how comfortable everyone will be.'

'That won't matter,' Alison chimed in. 'What matters is that Joan has all her bridesmaids with her.'

'And her matron of honour,' said Dot, smiling at Colette. 'I'm glad your Tony has agreed to you staying the night, love.'

'He couldn't really say no, with all the others doing it,' said Colette.

'Here she comes,' exclaimed Mabel as Joan walked in and headed for the counter to get herself a cup of tea.

When she came towards their table, Alison started singing 'Da, da, di, dah' and they all joined in with the 'Here Comes the Bride' tune, leaving Joan both blushing and laughing.

'Stop it,' she begged, subsiding onto a chair.

'That's your last buffet cuppa as a single girl,' said Persephone.

Getting up to leave, the middle-aged couple at the next table caught Joan's eye and said, 'Good luck.' They weren't the only ones either. A few other nearby patrons kindly wished her all the best. Joan looked radiant.

'I'll miss you,' said Mabel. 'I've enjoyed sharing a room.'

Joan smiled. 'It won't be long before Mrs Cooper finds you another room-mate.'

Mabel shook her head. 'I expect she'll want to move back into the big bedroom. She only moved into the single so we could share the double.'

'Talk of the devil,' said Dot and they all looked round.

Mrs Cooper stood in the doorway. She saw them and came over. Was her smile a little forced? There wasn't a spare chair. Mabel gave up her seat for her, asking the folk at a table nearby if she could pinch an empty chair.

'What brings you to town?' Cordelia asked Mrs Cooper.

'One or two errands,' said Mrs Cooper, adjusting her headscarf. 'I hate to be a spoilsport, but we do need to make sure all the lacy jackets fit properly. Mabel's does and Miss Persephone popped round yesterday to try on hers, but that still leaves three. Joan, dear, why don't you take Alison, Margaret and Colette home with you now? Then if any alterations are needed, they can be done quickly.'

The four of them got up. Margaret, Alison and Colette picked up their bags containing their overnight things and their dresses for tomorrow.

'Aren't you coming too?' Joan asked Mrs Cooper.

'Since I'm here, I'll stop and have a chat, but you run along.' Mrs Cooper smiled brightly and waggled her fingers in farewell, but as soon as the four girls had gone, her shoulders slumped.

'What's the matter?' Dot asked.

Mrs Cooper's eyes were bright with unshed tears. 'Me and Mrs Grayson went to the church hall this afternoon to do the tables and put up the bunting and we found that a pipe had burst in the kitchen.'

'Can it be cleaned up in time for tomorrow?' asked Cordelia.

Mrs Cooper shook her head. 'No one had been in there since yesterday and the water had been pouring in all that time.'

'But Joan's wedding reception … ' said Persephone.

'I know,' said Mrs Cooper. 'That's why I'm here. Me and Mrs Grayson decided the best thing was not to upset Joan with it, just let her go home and not tell her. What we've all got to do now, ladies,' and Mrs Cooper lifted her chin and looked at them one at a time, 'is work out what we can do to save Joan and Bob's wedding reception.'

Chapter Thirty-One

Joan couldn't remember whether it had been Mrs Cooper's idea or Mrs Grayson's, but there was no doubt that having her bridesmaids to stay the night before her wedding had been exactly the right thing to do. The house was alive with excitement and who cared about the queue for the bathroom? After breakfast, everyone piled into the kitchen to help Mrs Grayson make the final items for the buffet meal.

As they were finishing, Dot and Cordelia appeared.

'Make way for the mothers of the bride,' Dot called, marching in. 'Have you got a pinny I can wear, Mrs Cooper? Give it here and I'll pop the kettle on while the girls get dressed.'

'Joan, dear,' said Mrs Cooper, 'do you want to get dressed first or last?'

Joan looked at her bridesmaids. 'Why don't you all go and get started? I'd like to have a word with my mothers of the bride.'

As the girls bustled out of the room and up the stairs, Joan looked round at these four special ladies with whom she had formed a warm and lasting bond. Dot was wearing the bluey-grey skirt and soft pink blouse with elbow-length sleeves that she had worn on the afternoon in early April when the railway girls had held a tea party in her honour to celebrate her courage. Cordelia, in dove grey with discreet jewellery, was elegant in an understated way. Mrs

Cooper and Mrs Grayson were still in their dressing gowns and curlers.

'I want to thank all four of you from the bottom of my heart. I could never have got this wedding organised without you. You baked and sewed and got the church hall ready.'

The four women exchanged glances. It was Cordelia who said, 'It's been a pleasure.'

'When I asked you to be my mothers of the bride, I never imagined you doing so much for me.'

'We just want you to have the best day possible,' said Mrs Grayson.

'Now shoo,' Cordelia said to Joan. 'There won't be a wedding at all if the bride isn't dressed.'

Laughing, Joan went upstairs. The coat hangers that had dangled from the picture rails all night were now empty of the pretty dresses they had held. Colette's dress was the colour of bluebells, the hazy blue perfect for her fair skin, blonde hair and blue eyes. Alison's dress was pale yellow and Margaret was in the dress Joan had provided, and if anyone recognised it as having been Letitia's, no one said so. Mabel and Persephone were both in simple summer dresses, and you didn't have to have worked in Ingleby's sewing room to see they were superbly tailored. Mabel's was apple-green and Persephone's a bronzy shade that complemented her honey-blonde hair and violet eyes.

They all fussed around Joan, helping her into her dress, the feel of the rayon crepe against her skin sending tiny shivers of joy cascading through her. She stood still while Mabel fastened the tiny fabric-covered buttons up the back. Margaret was joining in and apparently enjoying the moment as much as the others, but what was she thinking? Was she remembering the man who had let her down so badly and had come close to ruining her life?

'That is such a lovely dress,' said Persephone. 'It couldn't look better on you if it had been made especially for you.'

'I have Margaret to thank for it.' Joan caught Margaret's hand and squeezed it, hoping to convey her support should Margaret be in need of it. 'She's the one who arranged for me to borrow it from her friend.'

Once the dresses were on, it was time for hair and make-up, then Joan sat down and let the others arrange her veil, settling the diamanté tiara in position and fluffing the dainty fabric.

'Stand up,' Alison ordered. 'Turn round.'

Joan bit her lip as she turned to face her friends. Did she make a pretty bride? Their expressions, soft and warm, said she did. With a call of 'Knock knock' from Dot, the door opened and the four mothers of the bride walked in, stopping at the sight of her.

'You're beautiful,' breathed Mrs Cooper.

'Bob's a lucky young man,' said Cordelia.

Emotion welled up and Joan's eyes filled.

'None of that,' cried Dot. 'We can't deliver the bride to the church with a blotchy face. Who's got a hanky?'

Several were pulled out and everyone laughed as they realised Joan wasn't alone in being a bit tearful.

There was a knock at the front door.

'That'll be Bob's dad,' said Mrs Cooper. 'Mrs Masters, will you let him in? Me and Mrs Grayson still have to get ready and these girls need helping into their lace boleros.'

When everyone was ready, they made their way downstairs.

'It's time to see what your future father-in-law thinks,' said Mrs Cooper.

Breathless with nerves and excitement, Joan descended the stairs and entered the front room, where Mr Hubble turned round from the window and let out a sigh.

'My son is a lucky man, and so am I to be gaining such a lovely daughter-in-law.'

'It's a great honour to give away the bride,' said Cordelia.

'I shan't be giving her away,' said Mr Hubble. 'I'll give my daughters away when the time comes, but when I walk Joan up the aisle, it'll be to welcome her into my family.'

Mrs Cooper fluttered a hanky. 'Don't or you'll set me off again.'

'Girls, put your hats on,' said Mrs Grayson, picking up the white flowers she had knitted. 'Have you got the pins, Mrs Green?'

A flower was carefully attached to the side of each hat. This detail, added to the matching boleros, created a unifying look, even though the five girls were all in different dresses.

'It's amazing what you can do with a bit of wool and some old net curtains,' said Mabel.

Persephone was at the window. 'Transport's here.'

There was a rush for the windows. The others stepped aside to let Joan through. The governess cart was a sturdy but elegant little vehicle with a single large wheel on each side. It was decorated with rosettes and streamers made from white ribbon. Even the horse had rosettes on its harness. The driver was a paunchy, red-faced old boy in a tweed suit and a bowler hat. There wasn't a separate seat for the driver at the front; he sat sideways on an inside seat.

'That's Mr Evans,' said Persephone. 'He's been a gardener at Darley Court since he was a lad way back in the mists of time.'

Mr Evans opened a little gate set into the rear of the cart and climbed down onto the road. Then he turned back to remove a box filled with flowers from the floor of the cart. This he carried into the house, bringing with it a glorious scent. Joan's bouquet and the bridesmaids' posies were made of pinks with greenery mixed in. For Mr Hubble there was a buttonhole and the mothers of the bride had pretty corsages.

'I never expected this,' said Mrs Cooper.

'We don't do things by halves at Darley Court,' said Persephone. 'Let me pin that on for you.'

She did so, then helped Dot with hers. Mrs Cooper moved to stand beside Joan.

'Don't they all look beautiful, your bridesmaids and your matron of honour?'

'They do,' Joan replied quietly, her words for Mrs Cooper alone, 'but there should be more of them, shouldn't there? And I don't just mean Letitia.'

Mrs Cooper's chin trembled but she pulled it under control by pressing her lips together. 'Bless you for thinking of my Lizzie.'

'Time to go, ladies,' said Mr Hubble.

'Mr Evans can take one person sitting opposite him,' said Persephone, 'or two if you breathe in. Who's going first? There's plenty of time for several journeys.'

Two at a time, the mothers of the bride and then the bridesmaids left the house to be ferried to the church. After all the excitement, the house felt strangely quiet when it was just Joan and Mr Hubble left. Presently, the cart returned. Mr Evans drove it past the house so he could use the wide part at the top of the cul-de-sac in which to turn around.

As if she was in a dream, Joan took Mr Hubble's arm. Mr Evans pulled down the step at the back of the cart and Mr Hubble held Joan's hand to steady her as she climbed aboard, taking a moment to arrange her dress before she sat down. The cart swayed as Mr Hubble joined her, then swayed again as Mr Evans climbed up.

Then they were on their way, travelling through the morning sunshine. Passers-by waved and Joan waved back. Some of them clapped and called their good wishes.

Outside the church, Mr Hubble helped Joan down and she joined her bridesmaids in the porch, her heart thumping as they fussed with her dress and drew her veil over her face. Then they all got into position, with Colette behind Joan, then Mabel and Alison behind her, and Persephone and Margaret behind them.

Mr Hubble offered his arm to Joan. She leaned forward to look into the church and caught her breath. Was that …? Yes – Gran was seated near the back.

She let go of Mr Hubble's arm and turned to speak to her friends.

'Gran's there. She said she wasn't coming.' She lifted her veil from her face and tried to flick it over her head. 'Please will you fetch her?' she asked Mr Hubble.

'Are you sure you want to speak to her?' asked Mabel. 'You don't want to cast a cloud over your wedding day by having words.'

'I can't explain it. I just know it's the right thing to do.' Joan turned to Mr Hubble. 'She's on the left-hand side, over there.'

Mr Hubble went in, returning with Gran, who looked white-faced.

'If you want me to leave, I'll go,' she said to Joan, 'but I fail to see the harm in my sitting at the back.'

'I don't want you to leave.' Joan addressed Mr Hubble and her attendants. 'Would you all mind slipping into the back of the church for a minute, please? And could you ask the organist to keep playing?' When they had gone, she turned back to Gran. 'You've come to my wedding.'

'It'd be a rum do if I didn't want to see my only remaining granddaughter get married.'

354

'I'm glad you're here. Thank you.'

'I'll go back inside. You don't want to keep everyone waiting. I've never held with brides being late.'

'You ought to sit at the front,' said Joan.

Gran snorted. 'It looks to me as if you've got enough women in the front row.'

'I may have four mothers of the bride,' said Joan, 'but there's only one grandmother of the bride. I'd like you to take your rightful place.'

'Well ... '

'Please, Gran.'

'I suppose it wouldn't do any harm.'

'That's not the most gracious way of accepting.'

'You're right. I should have said thank you. But I think your mothers of the bride,' and there was a sharp edge to Gran's voice, 'would be most surprised if I inserted myself into their pew.'

'Only if you walk up the aisle on your own. If you walk up the aisle with me, it'll be perfectly natural for you to sit at the front.'

'What are you talking about?'

'I'm asking you to give me away.'

'Don't be absurd. Is this some sort of modern wartime nonsense?'

'No. I think it's Foster family nonsense, except that it isn't nonsense. It's about being at a crossroads. You had to make choices that affected the rest of your life – and my life and Letitia's. I'm at my own crossroads now. I'm about to move from the past into the future and it feels right that you should be the person to walk with me from one to the other. Will you do that for me?'

Chapter Thirty-Two

Dot nudged Mrs Cooper and nodded across the aisle to where Mr Hubble was joining his wife and daughters in the pew behind Bob and his best man. What was going on? Bob turned round, leaning over the back of the pew, and his dad spoke to him, which made Bob look down the aisle. Dot wanted to peer down the aisle an' all, but she didn't have the brass neck to do summat so blatant.

The organ music paused and when it started up again, the opening notes of 'Here Comes the Bride' brought everyone to their feet. Dear Joan was about to get her happy ending at last. Not only that, but she, Dot Green, had a front-row seat in her capacity as a mother of the bride. That was what every mother wanted to be, wasn't it? Even mums of sons had the occasional secret yearning.

Across the aisle, Bob turned to watch his beloved coming towards him. Dot smiled indulgently. Joan had picked a good 'un there. But if Bob's dad wasn't walking Joan up the aisle, who was? Others were turning now to see the bride, so Dot did an' all. Good heavens, that old witch Mrs Foster was doing the honours. Crikey, talk about a turn-up for the books – but a good turn-up, because it must mean she and Joan were reconciled.

When they reached the top of the aisle, Mrs Foster stepped into the front pew and the mothers of the bride shuffled up to make room. Joan turned round for Colette to lift her veil while Mabel held Colette's flowers. Then Joan turned to face her future husband.

The ceremony began. Vows and rings were exchanged and there was a collective sigh of contentment when Bob and Joan were pronounced man and wife.

'You may now kiss the bride.'

Bob placed one hand at Joan's waist and with the fingertips of his other hand lifted her chin. His kiss was tender. Beside Dot, Mrs Cooper sniffed into her hanky. Dot didn't cry, but she couldn't deny feeling all sentimental. Young love: there was nowt like it. Lasting love an' all. That was what Joan and Bob had: lasting love. If Dot experienced a moment's regret for the staleness of her own marriage, she quickly thrust it aside. This wasn't a day for regrets. Today was for Joan and Bob, for their happiness and their future together.

It was time to sign the register. Instead of leaving the pew, Mrs Cooper leaned forward and Joan came to her.

'Shouldn't you ask your gran?' Mrs Cooper whispered.

'I want you to do it,' Joan whispered back.

Dot and Mrs Foster turned sideways in the pew so Mrs Cooper could shuffle past and accompany Joan and Bob into the vestry, along with the best man. A few minutes later, Mrs Cooper emerged on the best man's arm as he accompanied her back to her pew before resuming his seat.

Then Joan and Bob appeared, arm in arm, and took their places at the top of the aisle, smiling their heads off as they paused for the organist to play the opening notes of the 'Wedding March', which brought everyone to their feet to watch the newly-weds start walking down the aisle. Once they were halfway down, Mr Hubble stepped across and politely offered his arm to Mrs Foster. The mothers of the bride followed her out of the pew.

'I know it's not the done thing to barge the family out of the way,' Cordelia murmured, 'but we do need to get outside quickly.'

Should they let Mrs Hubble precede them? After all, she was real family. But there was the matter of explaining things to the happy couple.

'Here, Mrs Hubble.' Dot stuck out her elbow invitingly. 'Let's you and me follow on.'

It was the best she could manage. The bridesmaids were in the pew behind the mothers of the bride. Exchanging glances with Persephone, Dot knew that her young friend understood the need to get outside pronto, though Mabel was busy leaning over the back of the pew to make eyes at her Harry, who was seated a couple of rows behind her with Tony Naylor and Alison's Paul. Mr Masters was here as well, as was Reg in his Sunday-best suit. Dot flung him a brief smile, but her thoughts were on the job she had to do.

The moment they reached the church porch, Dot let go of Mrs Hubble and darted over to Bob and Joan, who were staring at the carts lined up along the road. In front of the gates was Mr Evans with the governess cart, behind which were two farm carts, both decked out with rosettes and streamers made from what looked like hessian. Two fresh-faced young women sat on each of the bench seats.

As Joan looked round in consternation, Dot and her fellow mothers of the bride hurried forward.

'Now then, chick,' said Dot, 'there's nowt to fret over, but there was a little mishap at the church hall.'

'What kind of mishap?' Joan asked.

'A very wet kind,' said Cordelia.

'But you're not to worry,' said Mrs Cooper, 'because we've arranged to hold the reception elsewhere.'

'It happened yesterday,' Dot explained. 'We never said owt, because we didn't want you to be upset.'

'Those are Miss Brown's land girls driving the farm carts,' Persephone chimed in. 'After the photographs, you and Bob will go in the governess cart, everyone else will pile into the two big carts, and off we'll all go to your new venue.'

'Which is where?' Bob looked bemused.

'The buffet at Victoria Station, of course,' said Dot. 'Where better for a porter lass and her signalman husband to hold their wedding reception?'

Dot almost burst with pride when she saw the station buffet. Yesterday evening, they had pinned up the coronation bunting in loops across the ceiling from corner to corner and Mrs Jessop had promised to twist the arms of the staff in the first-class restaurant into lending them table linen for the occasion, but Dot hadn't realised the room was going to look this smart. As well as a starched tablecloth, each table had a centrepiece of pinks from Darley Court, which must be where all those vases had come from an' all. A notice in the window proclaimed *Closed for Wedding Reception*.

Joan and Bob stood holding hands in the middle of the room, surrounded by family and friends all exclaiming over the improvised arrangements.

Joan's blue eyes were full of happy tears. 'It's wonderful. No one would ever imagine it had been done at the last minute. Thank you all. The church hall would have been lovely, of course, but this is perfect. How on earth did you manage it?'

'The pixies came and did it in the night,' said Persephone.

'Mrs Cooper rescued the bunting yesterday when she found the church-hall kitchen sopping wet,' said Dot, 'and she had it with her when she came here to tell us, so we put it up before we went home. I say "we", but the other customers helped once they knew what was happening.'

'The food will be here in a minute,' added Mrs Cooper. 'It's in boxes in the other farm cart. Mrs Jessop is letting us do any heating up that's needed.'

'So all you two have to do is greet your guests and enjoy yourselves,' said Cordelia. 'Your suitcase is coming in the cart as well.'

'And a carpet bag with your going-away dress,' added Mrs Cooper. 'When you get changed, your wedding dress can go in the carpet bag and I'll take it home for you to collect after you come back from honeymoon.'

'Don't worry about where you're going to get changed,' said Cordelia. 'Miss Emery has arranged for you to use one of the offices in Hunts Bank.'

'Just so long as it isn't her office,' quipped Dot.

'What's wrong with her office?' asked Bob.

'Never you mind,' said Dot, 'but you wouldn't want your wife getting undressed in there.'

Joan pretended to cover her ears. 'I don't want to think about taking off my lovely wedding dress.'

'Every bride feels that way,' said Mrs Cooper, going all misty-eyed.

'I hope you don't mind that we invited Miss Emery to your reception by way of a thank you,' said Cordelia. 'It seemed only right.'

'The more the merrier,' said Bob.

Joan looked round. 'You've done all this for us. You've thought of everything.'

'It's a good thing you decided to have a team of mothers of the bride, chick,' said Dot. 'It might have proved a bit much for one mother to cope with, but the four of us put together – we're unstoppable.'

Joan hugged and kissed them in turn. 'You're wonderful, all of you.'

Then Bob hugged and kissed them an' all.

'Much as we'd like to hog all the glory,' said Dot, 'it wasn't just us. Mabel and Persephone were involved. Persephone went scooting off to Darley Court to make arrangements with Miss Brown and Mrs Mitchell.'

'And of course we wouldn't be here in the buffet at all without Mrs Jessop's consent,' added Cordelia.

'I can see I've got a lot more kisses to dispense,' said Bob. 'I'd better get started.'

'Oy, you.' Dot gave him a nudge. 'Shouldn't you be saving up your kisses for your bride?'

Bob winked at her. 'A chap has to put in some practice.'

The boxes of food arrived. Dot busied herself helping get everything ready. It was all laid out along the counter and the closest table for guests to help themselves. Sardine pancakes, stewed mushrooms in puff pastry, slices of bean and tomato pie, and a mixture of cucumber sandwiches and meat-paste sandwiches, cut into triangles. For pud, Mrs Grayson had made apples in rice.

'It's a jolly good spread,' said Reg, coming to stand beside Dot. 'You've done your young friend proud.'

'Mrs Grayson is the cook, not me.'

'I don't mean just the food.' Reg waved an all-compassing hand. 'I mean all this. When you said you were going to be a mother of the bride, I thought, there she goes, sticking her nose into other folk's business. But it's a good job you did, you and your mates. Otherwise, that young couple wouldn't have had a wedding reception at all.'

If you ignored the bit about sticking her nose in, it was a compliment of sorts and, in honour of the day, Dot elected to take it as such. 'Thank you, Reg. It's nice to be appreciated.' Especially when it only happened once every Preston Guild. 'Let me introduce you to the other mothers of the bride.'

Reg said how do and shook hands all round, but as soon as they started talking about the details of the reception, he skedaddled.

On a table of its own stood the cake, complete with a Dinky Toy locomotive on the top, courtesy of Jimmy. Ruddy typical: while the women discussed the agonies of producing a cake in these days of rationing, all the blokes were interested in was the toy train. The cake was a single tier, with no icing. Was icing now illegal or had that person in the butcher's queue who had told Dot been exaggerating?

'I wouldn't have minded if Joan had wanted one of those fancy cardboard pretend cakes to put over hers to make it look like a proper wedding cake,' said Mrs Grayson, 'but she said the cake is just right the way it is, because I made it.' The dear lady stood tall with pride.

'I'm glad everyone will see it, love,' said Dot.

'Just don't let them get too close,' laughed Mrs Cooper, 'or they'll pass out from the alcohol fumes.'

From beside the counter, Mrs Jessop called Mrs Grayson away, leaving Dot with Mrs Cooper and Cordelia.

'She's coping very well, isn't she?' said Mrs Cooper. 'I sat beside her in the cart and she shook like a leaf all the way here, but she was determined not to be left behind.'

'She seems fine,' said Cordelia. 'I imagine that being busy with the food is a help.'

'Though how we're going to get her home again afterwards is anyone's guess,' said Mrs Cooper, looking concerned.

'There's no need to worry about that,' said Cordelia. 'Kenneth and I will travel home by taxi and we'll take her and you with us. Please don't try to say no, because I won't listen.'

'If it was just me you were making the offer to, I would say no,' said Mrs Cooper, 'but on behalf of Mrs Grayson, I say thank you for your kind consideration. That will make things much easier.'

'We can't have today being spoiled,' said Cordelia.

'No, we can't,' Dot agreed, 'and I suppose that applies to everyone, doesn't it?' She nodded across the room in Mrs Foster's direction. 'I can't say I care for her, not after the way she's treated Joan, but if Joan wants her here, then the least we can do is make the effort. Let's go and speak to her, make her feel welcome like.'

'I've a better idea,' said Mrs Cooper. 'Let's do it one at a time and spread it out a bit.'

Dot went over to her first. Mrs Foster was looking across at Mr and Mrs Hubble – the parents, not the newly-weds. Something about the way they stood close together said how dear they were to one another.

'Let's hope that'll be Joan and Bob one day,' Dot remarked.

Mrs Foster glanced at her and nodded. 'I was widowed young.'

'You get wed with such hopes, but you don't know what lies ahead, do you?'

Dot certainly hadn't. She had got married in good faith. Pregnant, aye, and therefore with no choice in the matter, but that had been fine by her. All she had wanted back in those days was Reg and she had married him gladly and in the expectation of a long and happy marriage. She would never have made so free with her favours if she had had even the tiniest doubt about him. She wasn't to know he would turn into Ratty Reg. She wasn't to know that the love of her life wouldn't appear until she was a grandmother. A grandmother, for pity's sake. You just assumed that it would happen to you when you were young.

By, this wasn't the time or the place for all that. She chatted to Mrs Foster for a few minutes, then introduced her to Miss Brown before going to have a word with Colette and Tony.

'I remember you buying that dress fabric last year,' said Dot. 'You've said since you're not best pleased with how the dress turned out, but I think you look lovely and I'm not just saying that.'

'Don't you like your dress?' Tony turned to his wife. 'I think you look beautiful.'

All the bridesmaids looked beautiful in Dot's opinion, but the loveliest of all was the bride, who was radiant with joy.

Dot saw Mabel across the room. Now there was another radiantly happy girl. She was talking with Alison and Paul. Give Alison her due, she had taken Joan's engagement and swift wedding on the chin, but surely she was wondering when it would be her turn. If ever a lad needed a good kick up the whatsit, it was that Paul. If he and Alison were right for one another, they should get on with it and make the most of their lives. Dot's heart ached. Oh, Mr Thirkle ... She was in no doubt that she had made the right decision, but even so, Mr Thirkle ...

Persephone nudged Mabel and tilted her chin towards the clock that hung above the fireplace. 'Time for Joan to get changed,' said Persephone. 'You fetch her and I'll gather the bridesmaids. Miss Emery has given me the key to the room we're going to use.'

'Do you think we should take the mothers of the bride as well?' Mabel suggested.

Persephone laughed. 'If we do, there'll be hardly a soul left in here. I think it should be just the bridesmaids. We helped her get dressed and now it's our job to help her change into her going-away dress.'

They separated. Mabel joined Joan, who was talking to a pair of middle-aged ladies wearing what Mumsy would have called 'competing hats'. One was green straw with a circlet of plump yellow roses around the crown. It was difficult to say exactly what style the other one was, because it was largely invisible beneath masses of feathers. Mabel smiled to herself. To her eyes, nothing could compete with the knitted flower each bridesmaid wore attached to her hat.

Joan turned to her, impulsively reaching for Mabel's hand to draw her into the group. 'This is Mabel Bradshaw. She's my friend and, until now, my room-mate.'

'You'll have a different room-mate from now on,' said the woman with the roses.

The other woman nudged her none too gently. 'Don't be vulgar, our Marie.'

'Mabel, these ladies are Mrs Towler and Mrs Leonard, Bob's Auntie Marie and Auntie Florrie.'

'Your aunties as well now, love,' said Auntie Marie.

'Auntie Florrie is the one we were going to live with,' Joan added.

Mabel shook hands. 'I'm pleased to meet you.' She smiled at Auntie Florrie. 'I was sorry to hear about you being bombed out. I hope you've found somewhere to live.'

'Aye, I've moved in with our Marie, for my sins.'

'And there have been many sins, believe you me,' added Auntie Marie.

'You should know,' retorted Auntie Florrie, 'since I were just the innocent little sister tagging along behind you.'

'Ladies, would you excuse us?' asked Mabel. 'Joan needs to get changed.'

She drew Joan to the door, where Persephone, Colette, Margaret and Alison were waiting. Harry was there too, holding the carpet bag that contained Joan's going-away things. Mabel's heart swelled. Typical Harry. He understood how important small attentions were. Oh, she was so lucky to have him.

The group walked onto the concourse, which was humming with Saturday-afternoon activity. Some folk were standing around waiting, others heading purposefully in the direction of the platforms, but one and all, they turned to look at the young bride and her attendants hurrying for the exit. Some onlookers clapped and others called their good wishes.

At Hunts Bank, Persephone produced the key, which had a label dangling from it. 'Here.' She gave it to Alison. 'You know your way round.'

In high spirits, they went upstairs and along a couple of corridors until Alison, pausing to check the label, unlocked a door. As she entered, Mabel turned round in the doorway and placed a hand on Harry's broad chest.

'Men not allowed.'

He dropped a kiss on her nose. 'Spoilsport.'

She took the bag from him, her skin tingling as their hands brushed together, and closed the door. The others were grouped around Joan, who was gazing down at her dress.

Now she raised her eyes to look at Margaret and her voice was soft and sincere as she said, 'Thank you.'

'And thank you to Margaret's friend as well,' Alison added.

'Yes,' said Margaret, returning Joan's smile. 'That was a stroke of luck.'

'It's going to be difficult for brides in future – even more so than it is already,' said Colette, 'now that we've got clothing coupons. Mind you, I'm not saying coupons are a bad thing. The cost of clothing has gone up so steeply since the war started.'

'My mother says that when it comes to getting married,' said Alison, 'girls will largely have to choose between a good wedding dress and a good going-away dress.'

'There'll be a lot of passing on of wedding dresses,' Persephone predicted.

Mabel opened the carpet bag and drew out Joan's going-away dress, which Persephone had rolled inside a length of tissue paper to keep creases at bay. Mabel removed the paper and gently shook the dress before holding it up. It was a pretty dress with a flattering boat neck and a gently flared skirt.

'I made it for Letitia,' said Joan.

'Which makes it perfect for you to wear today,' said Colette.

They helped her out of her wedding dress and into her going-away dress. The soft violet hue would have looked special against Letitia's fair colouring, but it also suited Joan's brown hair and blue eyes. She had trimmed a straw hat with a violet band to which one of Mrs Grayson's knitted flowers had been pinned. Margaret helped her put it on.

They returned to the station and nipped into the ladies' waiting room, where there was a large mirror. Joan had only a few moments to admire her appearance before the others clustered round, all laughingly trying to insert themselves into the reflection. How happy they all looked. Never mind the photographs that had been taken outside the church – this would have made the best picture of all. Joan had had a wonderful wedding day and Mabel couldn't have been more delighted for her.

Back in the buffet, Joan received lots of compliments on her dress. The bridal bouquet of pinks had been standing in a vase all through the reception and now she lifted it out. Mrs Jessop wiped the stems with a cloth to dry them.

The newly-weds started a circuit of the buffet, saying their thank-yous and goodbyes.

'At least they won't have a mad dash for the train,' said Alison. 'Perhaps this will start a new fashion for holding wedding receptions in station buffets.'

'Mrs Jessop has enjoyed it,' said Persephone. 'She hasn't stopped smiling.'

Harry materialised at Mabel's side. 'Come with me.'

'Where to?'

'You'll see.'

Taking her hand, he led her out onto the concourse and over to the machine that dispensed platform tickets. Digging in his pocket, he produced a heap of pennies.

'Here, you start getting tickets. I'll get some change from the bookstall. Better to wave them off from the platform than from the barrier, don't you think?'

Mabel felt as if she was glowing. It was another example of Harry's ability to make things special. Yes, it would be much better for everyone to go onto the platform, and how typical of Harry to make it possible without any fuss. Shortly, they returned to the buffet, laughing, their hands full of tickets.

'You don't escape from your guests that easily, you two,' Harry said to the happy couple. He held up the tickets. 'We're all coming on holiday with you.'

Everyone laughed and cheered. Mabel and Harry handed out the tickets, then the wedding party surged across the concourse, darting around the other passengers.

On the platform, the maroon-liveried coaches stretched in a long line towards the gleaming loco at the front. The carriage doors were open and passengers were climbing aboard.

There were final hugs and kisses, then Joan held her bouquet aloft. Laughing, the single girls got into position as she walked away and turned her back to them – Alison, Persephone, Mabel and Bob's three sisters. They larked around, pretending to jockey for position. Joan held her bouquet in front of her, swinging it down, then up a couple of times, practising for the over-the-head throw.

Then the flowers spun an arc as they sailed through the air beneath the station canopy. Mabel instinctively lifted her hands, dimly aware of other hands being raised around hers. She stretched her arms – and sweet fragrance showered her as the bouquet landed in her hands.

All around her, there was laughter and applause, together with cries of 'You next, Mabel!' She saw that Harry was on the receiving end of a few nudges and joking remarks. For half a second, she hovered on the verge of hideous embarrassment, but it was swept aside when Harry looked at her with a knowing smile that suggested – no, not just suggested, it told her – promised her, that her turn, *their* turn, would come.

Joan was in the middle of another round of hugs and kisses and it gladdened Dot's heart to see her putting her arms around her grandmother. Mrs Foster didn't exactly hug her back, but she raised her hands to Joan's shoulders and placed them there. It wasn't the warm embrace Dot would have given one of her own sons or grandchildren, but it was probably the most emotion the strait-laced Mrs Foster had shown in public in many a long year.

When Joan and her grandmother separated, the bridesmaids clustered around her.

After a minute, Bob gently disentangled them. 'Time to go.'

The newly-weds climbed aboard the train, waving before they disappeared through the doorway. Along with the other guests, Dot moved towards the carriage and a few moments later, Joan and Bob appeared again, waving through the open window. Bob hoisted their suitcase into the net luggage rack and they sat down side by side just as the guard commenced his walk along the platform, slamming shut all the doors. Mrs Cooper firmly linked arms with Dot, waving madly with her free hand. Dot waved an' all. Oh, she wished these two young 'uns the very best, she really did. The wedding party shifted out of the way to let the guard past, then moved forwards again in a cluster outside Joan and Bob's window.

The guard blew his whistle and Dot glanced round to see him stepping up into the guard's van, from where he leaned out to wave his green flag. The first loud hiss heralded the appearance of the steam; then came the huge pulse of sound as steam burst forth from the funnel as the mighty locomotive moved on its way, the couplings between the coaches protesting at first. The wedding group waved frantically, calling their goodbyes. Joan and Bob were laughing as they waved back, Joan breaking off for a moment to wipe away a tear. The train pulled out, the wedding group moving as one to keep up, but it was only a moment or two before the train outpaced them. With final waves and calls, they stopped and watched as the train chuffed away out of the station.

They all watched until the train vanished and it felt as if every single one of them sighed when it was gone. Then they all glanced at one another, sharing smiles.

Mrs Cooper smiled at Dot. 'You know what we should do? I think the mothers of the bride should have a cup of tea together before the clearing up starts.'

'Good idea,' agreed Dot.

Mrs Cooper hesitated. 'I beg your pardon. That was presumptuous of me. You probably want to be with Mr Green now.'

Dot linked arms with her. 'No, not just now. This is mothers-of-the-bride time. We have to make the most of it, because it'll soon be over.'

They collected Cordelia and Mrs Grayson and returned to the buffet to get cups of tea and take the weight off their feet.

'I think that was rather a good wedding reception,' said Cordelia, 'given that it was put together so quickly.'

'Rather good?' said Mrs Grayson. 'It was splendid.'

'Aye, it was,' said Dot. 'It couldn't have been better if we'd put weeks of preparation into it.'

'It's what comes of having four mothers of the bride,' said Mrs Cooper, 'not to mention helpful friends.'

'Joan's a lucky girl,' said Cordelia, 'when you consider that out of everyone who put this reception together for her at the last minute, not a single one was her family.'

'You're wrong there, Mrs Masters, if you don't mind me saying so,' said Mrs Cooper. 'Strictly speaking, I don't have any family left, except for my sister and her husband, but I choose to look at it in a different way. To me, Joan and Mabel, living in my house and being looked after by me, have become my family – and so have you, of course, Mrs Grayson. Family isn't just who you're related to. It's who you care about, who you'll put yourself out for. And a lot of people put themselves out to make today go smoothly for Joan, so I reckon she can count herself one of a loving family of special friends. Don't you agree, Mrs Green?'

'Aye,' said Dot. 'I do. Family has always meant everything to me, but I'll tell you summat I've learned from working on the railway: I've learned that friendship can run deeper than I ever thought possible. It's to do with all of us working together and working hard, doing our bit. Dear heaven, it's to do with being at war. I never thought there'd be owt to be grateful for about the war, but I'll say this for it: it builds strong friendships. And you're right, Mrs Cooper. Friends like that can become a sort of family.'

'I should like to propose a toast.' Cordelia lifted her teacup, holding it poised in mid-air as the others looked at her expectantly, ready to raise their own cups. 'To family and friendship.'

'Aye,' said Dot. 'That'll do. Family and friendship.'

Family and friendship. What could matter more?

She raised her cup and clinked it against the others.

Welcome to

Penny Street

where your favourite authors and stories live.

Meet casts of characters you'll never forget,
create memories you'll treasure forever,
and discover places that will stay with
you long after the last page.

Turn the page to step into the home of

MAISIE THOMAS

and discover more about

The
Railway Girls
in Love

Dear Readers

A question writers are often asked is 'Where do you get your ideas?' The answer is that they come from all over the place – a snippet of overheard conversation, something on the news, a picture, a song … I once got a terrific plot idea from listening to a talk given on a training day at work! If you have read the acknowledgements at the front of the book, you'll have seen that I am indebted to two unknown people who each took a photograph of a wartime wedding. These two photos provided me with inspiration for the wedding in *The Railway Girls in Love*.

One photo is a close-up of three women – the bride and two bridesmaids. The bride is wearing a suit and hat, as many wartime brides did. As the war wore on, it became harder to find new wedding dresses and many dresses were passed from bride to bride. So what was it about this photo that made it special for me? Well, it was the hats worn by the bride and one of her friends. Each hat had a frothy decoration attached to it, a cross between a flower and a pompom, to make the hats more suitable for a special occasion. The moment I saw these, I knew that knitting-mad Mrs Grayson would love to add the coordinating touch of knitted flowers to the wedding hats in my story.

The second picture is a group photo showing the bride and groom, an adult bridesmaid, two men and three child bridesmaids. It was the way the three little girls were dressed that gave me my second idea. I'm not going to say here what it was in case you haven't read the book yet, but you may well work it out when you get to that part in the story.

However, when a writer gets an idea, it doesn't just mean using that exact snatch of conversation or that particular detail from a photo. What happens is that the original thing, whatever it was – in this case, these two photographs – blossoms and expands into something bigger inside the writer's mind. Looking at the two wartime wedding pictures (which you can see for yourself in *Bombers and Mash* by Raynes Minns, published by Virago Press – they appear on page 177 in my paperback copy) didn't just provide me with ideas for wedding clothes. Suddenly I was able to see the whole of the wedding day happening in detail from start to finish inside my imagination, complete with everything that would make it into the very special occasion that I loved putting on paper for you. I hope you enjoy the wedding too – consider yourself invited!

Much love,

Maisie xx

Mrs Cooper

Would you like to know the truth about Mrs Cooper? She was only ever supposed to have a brief walk-on part in *The Railway Girls*, but I liked her so much that I wanted to see more of her and get to know her better.

Mrs Cooper is typical of many people in wartime who experienced shattering bereavements but had no time to grieve before they were back at work, back in the long shopping queues, and back in the air-raid shelters when the sirens sounded. Mrs Cooper lost her husband early in the war when he was run over in the blackout. The blackout itself was nothing new to people old enough to remember the Great War, but the major difference second time round was that there were now many more motor vehicles on the roads. Mr Cooper died in October 1939 and when Joan first met Lizzie in February 1940, Lizzie and her mum were just getting to grips with life without him.

Then, less than a year after losing her husband, Mrs Cooper's darling Lizzie lost her life in an air raid – which was the point where Mrs Cooper entered the pages of the story in person. Before that, she was a background character, who was spoken about frequently by Lizzie and it was obvious that the two of them were close and that Mrs Cooper was a devoted mother. Losing Lizzie made Mrs Cooper feel that the light had gone out in her life, but she plodded on, the same way that everyone in that situation had to.

So what was it about her that made me like her so much that I wanted her to be a regular character in the series? I suppose it was her courage – her simple, unassuming courage in the face of this appalling bereavement – a courage that so many people must have shown in those dark days of wartime. Her common sense, too, is very appealing, as is her awareness that, as difficult as things may be for her, others face the same personal difficulties, and the best way, the only way to cope is to knuckle down and get on with life and do the best you can.

No matter how bad she feels inside, Mrs Cooper always keeps a caring eye on others and she would be the first to tell you that this is how she keeps her sanity as she faces life without Lizzie. Knowing this, Dot came up with the ingenious idea of asking her to offer a home to Mrs Grayson when Mr Grayson and Floozy were all set to take Mrs Grayson's home from her. A little later in the story, Mrs Cooper offered the same warm hospitality to Joan, accepting Joan into her little household with a caring heart and an open mind that was the complete opposite of the rigid, judgemental atmosphere in which Joan had grown up with Gran.

After that, thanks to the Luftwaffe and Cordelia's splendid idea, came the move to Wilton Close and I can't begin to tell you how happy that made me. To have some of my characters living together is perfect – and what could be better than having dear Mrs Cooper to take care of them and watch over them?

Further Reading

In writing *The Railway Girls in Love*, I have consulted various books, many of which have already been acknowledged in the two previous Railway Girls novels. Here, in keeping with the subject of my letter to you, I'd like to mention a few books that provided both inspiration and information for particular scenes in the story.

A couple of lines in *Our Longest Days: A People's History of the Second World War, by the Writers of Mass Observation*, edited by Sandra Koa Wing (Profile Books Ltd, 2008) grew into the chapter that starts with Dot waking up when the air raid siren sounds and ends with her visiting Reg in hospital. Dot also benefited from the guidance provided in a Ministry of Home Security leaflet about what to do in the house before leaving it to go into the shelter. This leaflet was reproduced in *Blitz Britain: Manchester and Salford* by Graham Phythian (The History Press, 2015). Mabel and Harry's disrupted afternoon at the theatre is also due to this book.

Bombers and Mash: the Domestic Front 1939-45 by Raynes Minns (Virago Press, 1999), as well as containing the photographs mentioned in my letter, also helped Mrs Grayson to cater for the wedding.

Female Railway Workers in World War II by Susan Major (Pen & Sword Transport, 2018) and *Railwaywomen: Exploitation, Betrayal and Triumph in the Workplace* by Helena Wojtczak (The Hastings Press, 2005) helped Margaret in her job as an engine cleaner.

Lastly, I'd like to mention two books which are constantly by my side as I write this series: *Luftwaffe Over Manchester: The Blitz Years 1940-1944* By Peter J C Smith (Neil Richardson, 2003) and Norman Longmate's *How We Lived Then: a History of Everyday Life During the Second World*

War (Hutchinson, 1971). The former title, with its details of every air raid, is an essential resource for anyone interested in the war years in Manchester; and the latter is the most comprehensive and detailed book I have found about the Home Front. It is also immensely readable and entertaining. This book provided numerous small details throughout the story, including sharing Joan's train journey and helping Dot write to Harry and Archie.

Any mistakes are, of course, my own.

Turn the page for an exclusive
extract from my new novel

Christmas with the Railway Girls

Coming September 2021
Available to pre-order now

CHAPTER ONE

Late June, 1941

Cordelia stood at the foot of the tall pole, looking up at the pair of railway signals jutting out high above her. It used to be scary to climb a ladder that was vertical rather than one propped up at an angle, but she was used to it now and didn't think twice about settling her knapsack on her back, grasping the sides of the ladder and placing her foot on the bottom rung. Some signals weren't all that high off the ground. It was all a matter of their being visible to the train driver. These two signals were at least twenty feet up, because of the water tank beside the permanent way that would have obscured the train driver's view if the signals were lower.

She climbed to the top. If there was more than one signal, she always began at the top and worked down. As she stepped from the ladder onto the wooden platform, she felt the usual little swirling sensation in the pit of her stomach, but after all these months of experience in her job as a lampwoman, it lasted only a moment. It was another cool day. Last week had been gloriously hot, but the end of June looked set to be significantly less warm. Beneath overcast skies, Cordelia removed the lamp from the signal arrangement, cleaned it and put it back in position before swinging herself back onto the ladder to climb down to the platform beneath.

The upper signal was for the main line, the lower for the branch line. How proud she had been when she had learned that. The feeling of becoming good at her job above and beyond simply going through the motions of the endless cleaning and putting back of lamps, the feeling of actually understanding the workings of the railway, had made her rock on her heels with satisfaction. But who was there to share her small triumph? Not Kenneth. He didn't like her working on the railway. He would have infinitely preferred her to join the Women's Voluntary Service or take on a role in the Citizens' Advice Bureau, like her friends had.

She couldn't tell her friends either – not *those* friends, her old, long-established friends, with whom she had for years played bridge, learned flower-arranging and attended matinée performances at the theatre. Those ladies were similar to herself, married to well-to-do professional men and living in smart houses, with at the very least a daily help, not a live-in maid. These friends did their bit for the war effort dressed in the green of the WVS – the whole uniform, mark you, not just the hat or the jacket with which less well-off women had to make do – while for her war work, Cordelia wore sturdy dungarees and a headscarf – though, she acknowledged with a smile, her headscarves were pure silk.

She had new friends now. My goodness, what an eye-opener that had been. Whoever would have imagined before the war that Mrs Kenneth Masters, Mrs thoroughly middle-class Kenneth Masters, would make friends with women from lower down the social scale? They weren't superficial friendships either. She truly valued, even loved, her circle of railway friends, especially Dot, dear, working-class Dot, whose big heart and common sense Cordelia treasured.

It was thanks to Miss Emery that the group had got together in the first place. She was the assistant supervisor with responsibility for women and girls of all grades. On Cordelia's first day on the railways, Miss Emery had given the newcomers a piece of advice that had – well, Cordelia couldn't speak for the others, but from her own point of view, it had changed her life, if that didn't sound too dramatic. It all came down to class distinctions. Take her and Dot. As Dot had rightly pointed out, in normal circumstances, she would have been Cordelia's charwoman, beating her rugs and scrubbing her kitchen floor. But Miss Emery's advice had been to set aside disparities in class and become friends. Cordelia had hidden her initial shock at the very idea. Fortunately for her, she had had the good sense to appreciate that Miss Emery wouldn't suggest such an extraordinary thing without a solid reason and she had soon found that the assistant welfare supervisor was right.

Cordelia had grown fond of the younger girls who made up the bulk of their group, Mabel, Joan, Alison, Colette and Persephone, who were all in their twenties; and she had developed a real rapport with Dot, who, like herself, was in her forties, married and a mother, though had two grandchildren as well. In recent weeks, their group had opened its arms to welcome newcomer Margaret, whom Joan used to know when the two of them had worked at Ingleby's before the war.

If anybody (namely Kenneth) had ever doubted the sincerity and depth of the railway girls' friendship, Cordelia believed that a certain event at the beginning of the month had proved it beyond doubt. This was when she and Dot had had the honour of being mothers of the bride to Joan. There had been four mothers of the bride altogether, the other two being Joan's then landlady, Mrs Cooper, whose daughter Lizzie had herself been a railway girl until her tragic death in an air raid, and Joan's fellow-lodger, Mrs

Grayson, who had an unhappy past involving a dead baby and an errant husband.

Joan and Bob's wedding had been a touching and emotional occasion, but the reception that followed had been even more special because, following a water leak in the church hall where the reception had been due to take place, Joan's friends had mucked in and put together a fresh reception with all the trimmings in the station buffet, to the delight and astonishment of the happy couple, from whom the disaster of the water leak had been kept a secret. Cordelia had been proud to be involved. It was one of the best days she had had, if not the very best day, since war had been declared.

She was due to meet up with her friends in the buffet after work this evening and it was going to be one of those special times when they were all present, something that didn't happen often because of shift patterns and compulsory overtime. Warmth radiated through her as she thought of the tickets she was going to hand out.

She climbed down the ladder to the ground and set off at a brisk pace for her next set of lamps. Sometimes she worked in the yards outside Victoria Station, removing, cleaning and replacing the side-lights and tail-lights on the wagons. Other times, like this week, she walked the line, cleaning the lamps along an allocated stretch of the permanent way. That brought another smile to Cordelia's lips. To the rest of the population, it was the railway track, but she, being in the know, called it the permanent way. Just another tiny piece of knowledge that, added to all the others, made her feel professional, a feeling she very much enjoyed. She had married in 1920, and since then her life had revolved entirely around the home, which was only to be expected of a family such as hers – but how wonderful it was now to have a life and a purpose outside the home.

Her job was menial, according to Kenneth.

'People of our sort don't work with our hands.'

If she was honest, Cordelia had felt somewhat taken aback when she discovered what her war work on the railways was going to involve, but she had hidden that response, just as she had hidden her initial response to Miss Emery's advice, and afterwards she was grateful that she had, on both counts.

'It's a novelty for now,' Kenneth had told their friends, speaking with the confidence of the gentleman whose well-bred wife would never contradict him in public. 'When Cordelia gets tired of it, there are plenty of more suitable roles where she can be far more useful.'

Cordelia felt extremely useful where she was, thank you very much. Her job might involve working with her hands and it might not be the most intellectually stimulating task, but, by crikey, one thing you could never say about it was that it wasn't useful. Keeping the lamps clean so they could shine clearly helped to keep the trains running and helped keep the railways safe. Her job as a lampwoman might not seem like much on the face of it, but the contribution she was making to the war effort was, in her own small way, to help keep the country's essential transport system moving. Britain couldn't manage without its railways. How else could they have sent hundreds of thousands of children to safety at the outbreak of war? How else could thousands upon thousands of soldiers rescued from Dunkirk have been dispersed speedily throughout the country? How else were food, fuel, munitions and troops to be moved around efficiently? The way Cordelia saw it, the railways were every bit as important as the army, the navy and the air force.

She realised she had thrown back her shoulders as she walked to the next set of signals. Quite right too. She was proud of her job and proud too of the work done by each of her friends. Dot was a parcels porter, working on the trains, Joan a station porter, assisting passengers in Victoria Station itself. Persephone was also based at Victoria Station for her work as a ticket collector, though her chums sometimes joked that she had the additional job of giving men's spirits a bit of a boost by being so beautiful. Margaret worked in the engine sheds cleaning the locomotives, while Alison and Cordelia both had clerical positions in nearby Hunts Bank. The only other member of their group who worked outdoors on the permanent way was Mabel, who belonged to a gang of lengthmen, whose job was to shore up the ballast beneath the railway sleepers, the eight-foot long wooden planks on which the tracks lay. The difference between Mabel and Cordelia was that whereas Cordelia sometimes worked in the yards and sidings belonging to Victoria Station, Mabel was out on the permanent way every single day come rain or shine.

Cordelia gradually made her way down the line, covering today's portion of this week's section. A week's work was around a hundred and fifty lamps, including those on level crossings. When she finished for the day, she walked up the slope onto a station platform. While she waited to catch the next train into Manchester Victoria, she nipped into the ladies' to spend a penny – though she didn't actually put a penny in the slot to unlock the lavatory door. One distinctly annoying aspect of working on the railways was the shocking scarcity of facilities for female employees, most notably the lack of lavatories. Women railway workers were obliged to use the same facilities as the women passengers, which was fine up to a point, but many of them drew the line at paying for the privilege. Not to worry, though, as a cleverly bent nail could undo the lock if you knew precisely how to manoeuvre it. Although it irked her that the London Midland and Scottish railway hadn't seen fit to make proper provision for its many women workers, it didn't sit well with Cordelia, maybe because she was married to a solicitor, to cheat LMS out of its pennies and she made up for it by putting half a crown a week into the Red Cross Box. She was the local collector round where she lived, and also in the lamp-sheds, for the Red Cross's successful Penny A Week Fund, which bought comforts for the troops.

Standing in front of the mirror over the pair of basins, Cordelia removed her green silk headscarf and checked her clip-on earrings were still in place: she wasn't dressed without her earrings. Then she delved in her knapsack for her comb, powder compact and lipstick. Wearing dungarees was no reason not to look her best. Shaking out her scarf, she folded it in half into a triangle, laid it over her head and tied it at the back of her neck, beneath her hair, careful not to disturb the stuffed stocking around which her hair was rolled, making it sit just above shoulder-length.

She used to wear her hair shorter and fashionably shingled while she was in her thirties; but as she, oh horror, had drawn ever closer to her fortieth birthday, she had grown her hair longer because it was her last chance to have a bit of length. Then the dreaded age had hit her and she had discovered that being forty didn't feel any different to any age starting with a thirty and she had ended up keeping the additional length.

She went onto the platform just as the train came into view, white clouds puffing from the funnel. As the train ran alongside the platform, the white clouds stopped appearing and there was a hissing noise, then the brakes shrieked and some of the doors were thrown open even before a deep clunking sound signalled that the mighty vehicle had come to a halt.

The train was packed, which was par for the course at this time of day. Cordelia squeezed aboard, holding her knapsack close to her body so as not to bash anyone with it. She edged into a corner, giving a general smile to the passengers who had somehow made room for her, and pretended not to notice the glances that came her way. She was well aware of the disparity between her workmanlike dungarees and her air of well-bred elegance. She liked the contrast. She was proud of it. It showed what she was made of.

Cordelia Masters – lampwoman.

Hear more from

MAISIE THOMAS